Praise for Karen Kay's
She Steals My Breath

"I was so extremely touched by this story...there are parts of this story that...(will make) you cry so much your heart will hurt, and other parts that will fill you with joy.

Amazon Review by Cinderella 7

"...this is a superior story to most western stories or any stories for that matter."

Amazon Review by Janalyn

"No one writes Indian romance better than Karen Kay."

Amazon Review by Kathy

Look for these titles by
Karen Kay

Lakota Series
Lakota Surrender
Lakota Princess
Proud Wolf's Woman

Blackfoot Warriors
Gray Hawk's Lady
White Eagle's Touch
Night Thunder's Bride

Legendary Warriors
War Cloud's Passion
Lone Arrow's Pride
Soaring Eagle's Embrace
Wolf Shadow's Promise

The Warriors of the Iroquois
Black Eagle
Seneca Surrender

The Lost Clan
The Angel and the Warrior
The Spirit of the Wolf
Red Hawk's Woman
The Last Warrior

The Clan of the Wolf
The Princess and the Wolf
Brave Wolf and the Lady

The Wild West
The Eagle and the Flame
Iron Wolf's Bride
Blue Thunder and the Flower

She Steals My Breath

By

Karen Kay

The Medicine Man Series

Book One

PK&J Publishing

1 Lakeview Trail

Danbury, CT 06811

She Steals My Breath

Copyright © March 2022 by Karen Kay

Print ISBN: 979 8 44798 1 518

Cover by Darleen Dixon

Blurb created by BlurbWriter.com and Karen Kay

DEDICATION

This book is dedicated to my good friend, Steve Reevis, and his wife, Macile Reevis. I will always treasure your friendship.

Also, to the Girl-with-pretty-hair, my granddaughter, Lila.

And, to my husband, Paul, whom I love with all my heart.

ACKNOWLEDGEMENTS

It would be rare, indeed, if an author didn't find inspiration from others. And so, here at the start of the book, I would like to acknowledge the following writers, artists and presenters:

John Trudell
Poet, songwriter, actor, activist and writer, your insights into life and the world around you opened my eyes to many things.

Tom Brown, Jr.
Scout, writer and teacher, his book, *THE WAY OF THE SCOUT*, is filled with thrilling stories of scouting. His depiction of the Indian scout's spiritual kind of warfare gave this author many hours of pleasurable reading.

Mr. Brown also teaches a survival school in New Jersey, Tom Brown Tracker, Inc., which one can find online at https://www.trackerschool.com.

James Willard Schultz
Author of the books:

MY LIFE AS AN INDIAN;

BLACKFEET AND BUFFALO;

THE SUN GOD'S CHILDREN;

and *BLACKFEET TALES OF GLACIER NATIONAL PARK.*

Jeffrey Prather

Author of *INITIATION, Boys are Born, Men are Trained.*

Walter McClintock

Author of *THE OLD NORTH TRAIL.*

Charles Alexander Eastman, Dakota Tribe

Mr. Eastman's stories have kept me riveted to the pages of his works. In particular, the book *OLD INDIAN DAYS* and the story "The Love of Antelope" were exciting and beautiful.

"The Pikuni Bigfoot Storytelling Project"

"The Facts by Howtohunt.com"

SPECIAL ACKNOWLEGEMENT TO THE MUSIC OF THE FOLLOWING ARTISTS:

The Left Banke

"Just Walk Away Renee"

Roy Orbison and his beautiful works, specifically

"A Love So Beautiful" and

"I Drove All Night"

Frank Waln

Lakota-born hip-hop artist and American Indian activist, his

songs, his words and his struggles touched my heart.

John Trudell, activist, poet and philosopher

"My Heart Doesn't Hurt Anymore"

"Takes-My-Breath"

"After All These Years"

Spirit of the Glen
The Royal Scots Dragoon Guards

A NOTE ABOUT THE WORD "INDIAN"

At this time in history, the term "Native American" did not exist. The Indians were called simply "Indians," although within their own culture they were more usually known by their tribal name. Also, even in the present day, depending upon the tribe, American Indians often call themselves "Indians" and are proud of it (as an example, the Blackfeet "Indian Days Pow-wow"). This is true of the Blackfeet, the Lakota and several other of the northern tribes. There are, however, several tribes that I know of who prefer to be called "Native American" or, in some cases, "First Americans." But, once again, these are modern terms and simply did not exist at the time period of this novel.

Additionally, there are those within the Native American community who say the commonly held history of this word "Indian" is not accurate and that the word, as it was originally used, was the Spanish word "*Indio*," meaning "to walk with God" or "God's children." If one does a thorough search of history, one can find Christopher Columbus using the word "*Indio*" to describe the people he met, and he explicitly notes them as "God's Children."

ADDITIONAL NOTE TO THE READER

At the time when this story takes place, there were three different tribes of Indians that, together, comprised the Blackfeet, or Blackfoot, Nation: the Piegan, or Pikuni—their name in the Blackfoot language; the Blood, or Kainah; and the Blackfoot proper, or Siksika.

The Piegan, which is pronounced "pay-gan," were also divided into the northern and southern bands.

All three of these tribes were independent and were known to the early trappers by their own individual tribal names. But, because the three shared the same language, intermarried and went to war with the same enemies, it became more common to call these people Blackfoot, or Siksiká.

When this story takes place, the names "Blackfoot" and "Blackfeet" were used interchangeably, meaning one and the same group of people.

However, during reservation days, the story goes (as I was told it) that the US government utilized a misnomer, calling the tribe of the southern Piegan, or Pikuni, the "Blackfeet." The designation stuck, and to this day this tribe resides in northern Montana on the Blackfeet Reservation and is referred to by the government as the "Blackfeet" (although they are really the southern Piegan, or Pikuni).

Consequently, when we speak today of the Blackfoot tribes, or the Siksiká Nation as a whole, we talk of four different tribes: the Blackfoot; the Blood and Piegan bands in Canada; and the Blackfeet band in Montana.

.

Thus, when referring to the "Blackfeet," one is speaking of the band of Indians in Montana, whereas the name "Blackfoot" refers to the band of Indians in Alberta, Canada.

If this seems confusing to you, I can assure you, it baffled me at first.

Thus, in this story, because the Blackfeet and the Blackfoot names were interchangeable at this point in history, I have used "Blackfeet" as a noun (I went to visit the Blackfeet) and "Blackfoot" as an adjective (I went to Blackfoot country). I did this for no other reason than consistency.

However, because the prologue of this story takes place in a more recent time, I refer to the reservation of the Pikuni Tribe in Montana as it is known to us today — the Blackfeet Reservation.

In addition, I am defining some words used often in this story to assist further understanding.

The Crow — A tribe of Indians who inhabited the Montana Territory around the upper Yellowstone River. They were at war with the Blackfeet.

Medicine — Described by George Catlin in his book, *Letters and Notes on the Manners, Customs, and Conditions of North American Indians:*

"'Medicine' is a great word in this country; …

"The word medicine, in its common acceptance here, means *mystery,* and nothing else; and in that sense I *shall* use it very frequently in my Notes on Indian Manners and Customs.

"The Fur Traders in this country, are nearly all French; and in their language, a doctor or physician, is called '*Medecin.*' The Indian country is full of doctors; and as they are all magicians, and skilled, or profess to be skilled, in many mysteries, the word 'medecin' has become habitually applied to every thing mysterious or unaccountable..."

Sits-beside-him-woman or **wife** — In Indian tribes which practiced polygamy, this referred to the favorite wife — usually the first wife — or wife of a man's heart. She directed all the other wives and had the right to sit next to her husband at important meetings.

THE GAME OF *COS-SOÓ*

In one of my stories, *THE SPIRIT OF THE WOLF* (Book Two in The Lost Clan Series), I introduced the game *Cos-soó*, a game played by the men of the plains tribes. Because the game is revisited in this story, I would like to say a word about it.

Cos-soó, sometimes called "the game of the bowl," was a common game known to the Indians on the plains—all tribes. A game of chance, it was played only by men, and the stakes were often desperate.

Because this book delineates the rules for this game within its text, I won't repeat them here. However, I would like to bring notice to an observation made by Edwin Thompson Denig in his book, *The Assiniboine:* "It has been observed in these pages in reference to their gambling that it is much fairer in its nature than the same as carried on by the whites and this is worthy of attention..." Mr. Denig was a trader in the early 1800's who was married to an Assiniboine woman.

The game was often kept up for forty-eight to seventy-two hours without a break except for meals. And it was usually played until one or the other of the players was ruined totally.

Horses, guns, weapons, clothing and women were all stakes in these games. Again, Edwin Thompson Denig observed, "We have known Indians to lose everything—horses, dogs, cooking utensils, lodge, wife, even to his wearing apparel..."

PROLOGUE

The Blackfeet Reservation
The Early Twentieth Century

Although the old man wore the reservation clothes representative of a new and modern people, his pipe was centuries old, had belonged to his family for hundreds of years, and had been passed down from one generation to another. His gray hair was plaited in the older, traditional style, with two braids at the side of his face and one braid in back. A single eagle's feather was attached by a clip behind his head and stood up straight.

His hands were gnarled, were littered with brown spots and blue veins, and his fingers shook when he held up his pipe toward the sky. As he sat on his trade blanket within his canvas tepee, he watched as the many children from the Blackfeet reservation stepped over the bottom fold of the tepee's entrance flap, and, finding a seat upon his fur-lined buffalo robe, sat down in a semicircle around him.

The time of the year was the Moon of Home Days (July and August), and the stars in the night sky reminded him that, on this night, his duty was toward the young who might beg him to tell them the centuries-old stories of their ancestors. Although he was well aware that these tales were often thrilling to the young people, sometimes it was important — perhaps more important — to relive the legends of old, those which had been passed down through the ages from father and mother to son and daughter. In this way these stories might always be preserved.

On this warm summer's night, the stars shone brightly outside, and, from the smoke hole at the top of his lodge, the old man could see the moon, aware that its full shape was slowly waning and becoming smaller each night. At present, it was shining down directly into his tepee, encircling him in a large moonbeam, as though it were alive and the circle around him was a gift from the Creator, sent here to remind him of another time, another place and a quest his people might never forget.

For this reason, he felt it right to pass along this tale of his ancestors — a story of romance, of adventure and of a way of life to be kept alive. Also, its accompanying legend must be told, since the tale involved the compassion of the Creator toward a race of people He loved dearly. Perhaps in the retelling of it, the young people of today might be reminded of the bravery and honor that was once held to be amongst the highest of Blackfoot virtues.

The old ways were slowly passing into history, perhaps never to be experienced again. Indeed, it was true: different values than those of their common ancestors were sought by the youth of today, for the lure of the incoming civilization, along with its gadgets and its promise of ease, seemed to fit more prominently into their lives. But, now and again, the young gathered around oldsters like him.

In a low, shaky voice, he began by welcoming these adolescents to his lodge and said, "*Nitsikobtaahsí kikáó'toohsi,* I am glad you have arrived."

No one spoke back to him, for the Blackfoot language was disappearing amongst these youthful people. It seemed none of the children had understood what he'd said. However, there was one young lady — perhaps a child of seven — who smiled back at him and said in Blackfeet, "*Soka'pii.*"

This greatly pleased him, and he answered her, saying, "You speak our language well, child. It gladdens my heart to hear the words of your forebears come from your lips. May your parents and others within our circle continue to encourage you along this path."

She smiled at him, and he returned the gesture before beginning his story. With his right hand sweeping outward to indicate the group in general, he began, "This is the legend of the Creator's love for a people who were on the brink of extinction. But, I go before myself. Let me begin at the beginning."

Settling himself into a more comfortable position, he said, "This is the saga of a people we know as *Ómahk ótapi'sin*, the Big People. It has been told to me, as I now tell it to you, that the Creator, or Sun as we once addressed the Creator, was greatly troubled because there lived a people in His land who were dying. These were the Big People, who stood perhaps seven to nine feet tall. Their bodies were covered with hair, which was the reason they were a dying race, for the land of Sun is fiery and hot.

"Behold, there was a reason why the Creator loved these people so dearly. Listen, and I will tell you what happened. It began in a time so long ago, we can barely conceive of the passage of so many years. Now, it happened at this time that a she-wolf and a woman from the tribe of the Big People saved the life of the Creator's daughter, *Ap-ai-kai-kon,* Little Skunk. Ap-ai-kai-kon was so young she didn't understand the ways of the land of the Sun in which she lived, and this became a problem.

"One day Ap-ai-kai-kon could not bear the heat of the day, and so she traveled to a distant land where lived wolves who possessed the magical power of creating the water used to cool the land. There, she met a she-wolf.

"Ap-ai-kai-kon begged the wolf to make a watering hole for her. There, she might drink and cool herself.

"Now, because Ap-ai-kai-kon was the daughter of Sun, the wolf did as His daughter asked and caused the skies to rain down upon a certain valley, but only upon that valley because the Sun must always be blazing and hot. In her enthusiasm, the she-wolf had not taken into account how deeply the valley cut into the surrounding land. Soon, the watering hole became a lake.

"But, Ap-ai-kai-kon rejoiced, for the water looked refreshing. In very little time, she had splashed into the stream and had set out toward the middle of the lake. Suddenly, she dropped into a hole. She couldn't swim, for she possessed no knowledge of water and its dangers.

"The she-wolf, seeing Ap-ai-kai-kon's distress, swam toward her and dove down, down, down, all the way to the bottom of the lake. There she found Ap-ai-kai-kon and brought her up to the surface of the water, but, being too fatigued from her exertion, the she-wolf was unable to swim back to the distant shore. She, too, began to struggle.

"It so happened that a young girl named *Natáyo,* Lynx, from the tribe of the Big People, had watched these two, keeping herself hidden and at a safe distance from them. But, seeing the danger to Ap-ai-kai-kon and the she-wolf, the kindhearted girl left the safety of concealment and waded through the water toward them. It is well known the strength of the Big People, and, because Lynx was a large girl, she grabbed hold of both the wolf and Ap-ai-kai-kon, gathering them into her arms. And, striding back to shore, she set the two of them delicately onto the lake's grassy beach.

"She didn't wait for their praise, if there were to be any forthcoming. Instead, she ran away and disappeared back into the safety of the woods.

"Now, the Creator beheld these acts of bravery in defense of His only daughter, and, in His wisdom, knew he must help the wolves as well as the Big People. To honor the wolves, He gave them an intelligence that far outshone any other animal, except perhaps man. To show His esteem for the Big People, the Creator, in His wisdom, gave them a new home more suited to their needs: it was a land of snow, ice and deep forests, a place much better suited for these dearly beloved people.

"But, the Creator had caused a different problem by bestowing this land to the Big People: how could He bring them to this new terrain? Because the distance between His realm in the sky and this other environment was so great, there was no bridge to get there. It was the she-wolf who wisely whispered to Sun that a pathway formed from sunbeams or even the silvery light of the moon could be made into a trail, and it could connect His realm of great heat and light to the land of snow and ice.

"And so, it was done. This is how the Big People came to live in our land all those thousands or perhaps millions or even billions of years ago. It is said by the wisest of our men that the Big People can visit the Creator whenever they wish, for the path remains always open to them.

"But, this road connecting our lands is not for any other creature; it is only to be used by the Big People. In truth, if any other being should venture onto this bridge of sun or moonbeams, that life form is trapped there, perhaps forever.

"It is said this passageway still exists in the land of the Blackfeet. It is also believed the corridor is located somewhere in the mountains of

Montana. But we, as human beings, cannot see the path between our worlds. Instead, all we can perceive of is a circle of light.

To this day, we know of no human being who has ever come upon this place...that is, except once...."

CHAPTER ONE

Fort Union Trading Post

The Eastern Montana Territory

October 1834

"*I* tell you true, there is such a creature as a white woman. I have seen her here this very day."

Eagle Heart cast a doubtful glance at Gray Falcon, his *napí,* friend. "A white woman here?" he asked. "What you say cannot be so. All the tribes are speaking the same words about the white man: he has no women. In all these years we have known this man, we have never seen his women."

"*Ha'!* I do not lie, my friend. I saw her here. Today. Come with me to the trading room. You will see her, too."

"I am not interested," replied Eagle Heart. "But, tell me, does she have long hair on her upper lip and chin, as well as all over her body, like the white man? Does she smell as bad as all white men do? And, is her hair dirty and greasy from failing to bathe? *Saa,* I do not wish to see this creature. I might lose the contents of my stomach."

"I will not tell you any detail about her, my friend. Come and look at her and decide for yourself if she has all these features you speak of."

Eagle Heart shook his head. "I do not wish to witness the ugliness of this white woman. It might spoil the image of a woman's beauty for me. Besides, I must make inquiries about my brother since, as you know, this is the only reason I have made the long journey to the white man's fort."

"*Napi*, my friend, it will take but a moment to come and look at the woman. Then go your own way."

Eagle Heart sighed. Truly, he was not interested. However, if taking a glimpse at this being would appease his young friend, he would do it. And so, he found himself saying, "*Okí*, let us go so I might look at this ugly and smelly creature."

"*Áa*, yes…this is a good plan." Gray Falcon smiled.

"*Okí*. Shall I hold my breath so I do not have to smell her stench?"

"Perhaps, my friend. Perhaps."

****

The trading room was busy this day in early October, the season when the leaves turn yellow. With a quick glance around the room, Eagle Heart memorized the details of this place. These included a long counter for trading where a large buffalo hide had been spread upon it; there were several beaver pelts, mink and even raccoon furs which had been shoved to the side. A large book, with many of the white man's papers, lay open on the counter.

On wooden shelves behind the trader were stacks of many more furs and neatly folded woolen blankets. Off to the side of the counter were mounted moose horns, and these were holding up pots, pans and various items of clothing: belts and hats, moccasins and a few fur-lined jackets. Kegs of liquor stood upright on the highest shelves in the room, out of easy reach.

Robes and furs could be traded here for guns, but no guns of any description were on display. Perhaps they had been put out of sight purposely.

At present, there were three Blackfoot men standing at the counter, quietly bargaining with the trader, Larpenteur, over the price of their furs, while seven Indians from an enemy tribe, the Crows, and ten Indian men from another foe, the Assiniboines, lounged against the cottonwood logs that were used for the walls of the room.

Because all the Indians, himself included, had been divested of their weapons upon entering the fort, not a man in this room could be seen who carried his quiver strapped to his back; there were no bows, no lances, not even the usual gun on display, that usually being carried in a man's arms. It was an odd sight for Eagle Heart to behold his enemies without their customary means of defense.

The owner of this place, McKenzie, insisted upon stripping a man's weapons from him before entering the fort. The white traders stated this was a common practice within these trading centers and was done for the Indians' and the company's safety. And yet, the white men and trappers who frequented this place were always armed. So deaths occurred here anyway.

It was why Blackfoot men did not allow their women to accompany them inside the white man's gates. Simply put, it was too dangerous.

Eagle Heart took a deep breath at the same moment he realized the room did not stink. Instead, it was scented with the aroma of trees, logs and the distinctive fragrances of autumn leaves. Certainly, he didn't notice there was much unusual this day, and there was no white woman he could bear witness to. But, giving his friend his due, he decided to wait.

Looking around the room, he noticed Gray Falcon had positioned himself so he was leaning against a far wall, directly across from the table used for trading. Eagle Heart joined him there, and, leaning back, crossed his arms in front of his chest, prepared to wait.

Unexpectedly, the delightful sound of a feminine laugh filled the air. He frowned, surprised, for the voice was pretty.

And, then he saw her: she had slipped into the trading center from a room in back and was standing behind the trader, Larpenteur. When she moved slightly, Eagle Heart caught a glance of bouncing brown curls with a hint of gold within them. And, those locks were shimmering against a very pretty face. She laughed again and took a few steps around the clerk, a smile still affixed to her lovely countenance. She was glancing up at Larpenteur, and Eagle Heart experienced a startling reaction: he forgot to breathe. She was that beautiful.

Her figure was slim and small, her profile showing off a perfect nose that turned up slightly at the end. Her eyelashes were long and brown, and her eyes were a brilliant color of green. Her cheeks were rosy, and her full lips were still smiling. The brown color of her hair, with gold intertwined, was of a shade he had never before seen on a woman until this moment, and the length of it fell down her back in luscious curls. And, he saw not a single hair on her face.

Eagle Heart tried to breathe in. He couldn't. She had literally stolen his breath away.

At this moment, he couldn't force himself to look elsewhere, and he felt as awkward as a young boy who was besotted by a girl. It was, however, impolite to stare, so Eagle Heart at last glanced away from her, only to return his gaze upon her when he heard her say, "Mr. Larpenteur, how good of you to write down all of your transactions. It is to be regretted, however, that I cannot read your handwriting." She grinned up at the man.

And, Eagle Heart experienced the sensation of his stomach dropping, as though there lived both moths and small butterflies within it. Of course, he had no idea what she'd said, for she didn't speak the same language as he. All he knew was her voice sounded as engaging as the song of the meadowlark.

"*Ohpo'kiiyoo!* Follow!" Gray Falcon nudged him in the ribs. "I am leaving here. *Okí!* Come on, let us go."

"*Saa*, I do not wish to leave from here yet." From his peripheral vision, he saw Gray Falcon frown at him.

"I admit she is pretty," said Gray Falcon. "Still, I do not understand how a white man's seed can make a woman to be so comely. But, it is so, is it not?"

"*Áa*, it is so."

Within a moment, another man, a tall, dark-haired fellow with a mustache that curled at its ends, stepped out from the adjacent room behind the counter. He put his arms around the woman's waist, and she didn't admonish him, as Eagle Heart thought she should since this was a public place. Instead, she laughed softly and turned into the man's embrace.

She must be married to the man.

Eagle Heart couldn't fully understand the feeling that swept over him, for his spirits plummeted. It was odd, because whether she was

24

married to the curly-mustached man or not, it was nothing to him. She was beautiful, yes, but she was also married, as any fine-looking woman should be.

"It is told to me that she is not yet this man's wife," said Gray Falcon as though reading his friend's thoughts. "Although it is also said they are soon to be married. I think the man uses her, for he should not be keeping her so closely to him if they are not married...and before all eyes to see."

"It is so, my friend," Eagle Heart responded. "Yet, the whites are a strange people, and we do not know all of their ways. Perhaps a white man is permitted to hold her, even if they be not married. But still, he should not do this in front of others in case her reputation will be soiled. *Okí,* come, let us leave. I must ask the white men in this fort if they have any knowledge about where my brother might have gone, for I would be on my way."

Gray Falcon simply nodded, and the two friends quietly left the trading room.

****

Laylah McIntosh watched as two young Indian gentleman stood away from the wall in front of her and, turning, left the room. She wasn't certain what it was about them that caught her eye, for there were many Indian men here. Perhaps it was the elegant manner in which the two of them were attired, for their buckskin clothing was bleached a startling white, and, set off as it was with the contrast of their black hair, their dress alone looked as elegant as any man's might, white or Indian.

Or perhaps it was the muffled sound of their footfalls that brought her attention to them, for they made little sound as they crossed the room. With no boots to announce their departure, their footfalls were almost silent. They were both tall, also; their shoulders were squared back and their steps seemed oddly graceful.

"Mr. Larpenteur," asked Laylah softly. "What tribe of Indians are those two men? The ones wearing white." She nodded toward them.

"Dey be *Pieds Noirs*, Mademoiselle."

"*Pieds Noirs*? Do you know the English name for the tribe?"

"De Blackfeet, Mademoiselle."

"The Blackfeet? The Tigers of the Plains?"

"*Oui,* Mademoiselle."

"How strange they should be so well dressed," she said. "I have heard the Blackfeet guard their land well and will kill any white man they find in their territory. It seems rather savage, and yet, to look at them...they seem almost stately."

"*Oui,* Mademoiselle. De Blackfeet look so, but rob...I am rob by the *Pieds Noirs* too much! De *Pieds Noirs* wild. Eet has been so since Monsieur Lewis and Monsieur Clark kilt a man of de *Pieds Noirs,* de Blackfoot Injin."

"It is good you have told me about them. I shall do all I can to keep them distant from me, and shall make a mental note to never go into their country."

"Indeed, you shall not," agreed Thomas Sutter, who was Laylah's fiancé. He placed his arm around her waist and drew her in close to his chest. "Instead," he continued, "we shall return to St. Louis as soon as your visit to this land is finished. And, once there, we shall marry. Where would you like to live, m'dear. Here? Or in St. Louie?"

"I am uncertain, yet, as you know. I love my home in St. Louis, but there is some undefined aspect about this land that causes me to feel peaceful, as though this is my home." She sighed. "But, we don't have to decide now, do we? After all, we have yet to explore the woods and plains in the country. Indeed, if the intriguing scent of the autumn leaves and the atmosphere in this country is a sample of the beauty to be found here, I admit to being captivated by it." Stepping out of his embrace, she chanced to give Thomas a flirty smile from over her shoulder as she laughed up at him. "Excuse me, Thomas, for I must put my attention on business. My father has asked me to look over the transactions we've had today. As you know, I have an affinity for numbers and often help him with his accounting."

"Shall I assist you with it?"

"Only if you please. This will take me but a moment." She scanned down the dealings that had occurred so far for the day, committing each sale to memory so she might recount them later to her father.

As the daughter of Robert McIntosh—one of Fort Union's partners—she had unconsciously made herself into a business asset when her father had discovered she could memorize a page of numbers quickly and remember them again at will. And so, according to her father, her talents were to be kept within the family of traders, thus her upcoming marriage to Thomas, who, though a young man, was already a junior partner in this business. Of course, his family had helped obtain his status, for they had financed this fort in part, as well as the trading post, Fort William.

Although one could argue her upcoming marriage was one of convenience, she believed this was not entirely true. She had fallen under Thomas' spell almost from the first moment she'd met him. His fine manners and his tall, good looks had combined to urge her to say "yes" to his proposal of marriage. That her father had encouraged her to wed Thomas had also swayed her decision, for the marriage would tie their families financially.

Her mother had been silent concerning her daughter's upcoming marriage. True, she had shown no negative emotions, though there had been no positive encouragement, either.

Her younger sister, Amelia, was, of course, excited about the upcoming marriage. But, Amelia was young and her nature tended to be naïve at best, and, in truth, she was prone to question very little in life.

Laylah sighed, thinking back to the two young Blackfoot men. Untamed they might be, but it had been a crowning feather in her father's cap that he had convinced the Blackfeet to come to Fort Union to trade; especially since the Blackfeet held the reputation for being the most feared tribe of Indians on the plains. Of course, the Blackfoot men had objected at first, for they hadn't wished to make the long journey to Fort Union. Yet, here they were.

She frowned. It was hard not to notice the two Blackfoot men, since both were young and handsome in an exotic and uncultivated way. But, she put thoughts about them from her mind. Good-looking though they might be, they were still Indian, and, therefore, dangerous.

Besides, she would never see them again. On this thought, she put her speculations to rest and, having committed the page of numbers to memory, turned around to hug her fiancé.

****

Eagle Heart despaired of ever coming to know what had happened to his brother. No one at the fort seemed to remember seeing a man who looked much like Eagle Heart, himself. Yet, he couldn't be certain what these people said, since it was almost impossible to communicate to the whites. Why no one at this fort had learned the language used everywhere on the plains—the language of gestures—was a mystery.

He wished he could make inquiries of the other Indians at the fort, for they were familiar with the gesture language. But, he couldn't. These other Indians—the Crows and Assiniboines—were his traditional enemies. Not that he was afraid of them. It was simply that, being enemies, they were honor-bound to lie to him.

Somehow he would have to make himself understood by these white men. There was no other way.

So, it was to this end, he stepped into the room used for trade. It was a sunshiny day in this month of "the leaves falling," and, while a part of him hoped She-steals-my-breath, the beautiful white woman, might be present, another part of him dismissed her from his thoughts. She could mean nothing to him. With a force of will, he put her out of his mind.

Yet, as he stepped up to the trading counter, he saw that she stood on the white man's side of the table. Looking up, she stared straight at him, and, though it was forbidden for a Blackfoot woman to face him so boldly, he was yet reminded how beautiful a pair of green eyes could be....

****

"Mr. Larpenteur, I believe he is asking you for information about either his friend or his brother. I'm not certain which it is."

The trader frowned down at her. However, she didn't flinch. "How do you know dees, Mademoiselle?"

"My father," she said, glancing downward, "hired an older Indian gentleman from one of the Eastern tribes to instruct both me and my younger sister on this language of gestures. He insisted on our learning it before we were allowed to make this trip into the North Country. He said if anything bad ever happened to us, we would at least be able to make ourselves understood. Shall I ask this man what it is he is seeking?"

"*Oui*, Mademoiselle."

She nodded and, inhaling deeply, brought her right hand up to ask the Indian, "Question, who is it you are seeking?"

"Halt!" he said in gestures, bringing his right hand up, instead of down, for emphasis. "I do not speak to women." He added a frown and looked so sternly at her, she felt faint in reaction.

28

But, she didn't faint. Instead, she gulped and, looking down and away from him, signed, "No one here speaks the language of gestures. If you wish to be understood you will have to communicate to either me or my younger sister. If you prefer to talk to my sister, I will fetch her."

She chanced a quick glance up at this man who towered over her. *Why, he must be over six feet tall.* He was also outrageously handsome in a wild sort of way: black, straight hair, which was decorated with a single feather hung from a braid on the right side of his face; it was his only hair ornament. He had pulled a portion of his bangs forward and had cut them so a part of them fell down over the center of his forehead, as seemed to be the custom in this untamed land.

He still wore the handsome, white clothing she had seen him wear a few days previously, and up close she could see and admire the blue, white and yellow circle sewn onto his shirt. It was placed in the middle of the buckskin clothing, was level with his chest and looked to be made of porcupine quills, as well as beads. Rows of colorfully sewn porcupine quills of the same colors decorated the outer portion of his sleeves, while white fringe, situated next to the porcupine quills, draped from those same sleeves. She noted that some of the fringe was also composed of black hair. She shivered to think of the reason why this kind of hair ornamented his shirt.

Fierce though he might be, there was an unknown quality about him that drew her to him. His eyes were black, his nose straight and slightly aquiline, but not overly so. His lips were full, and the color of his skin was tan, not red, though there might have been a slight tint of red running beneath the outer layer of his skin. He wore no paint as did most of the Indians here at the post. This observation eased her nerves a little, for she had heard it said that the Indians painted themselves only when going to war.

Still, she shivered at the thought of any man having to go to war with an Indian like this.

But, he was answering her question, and she gave his hand gestures her full attention. He said, "I see I have startled you. There is no threat or insult meant to you; rather, a man should not speak to a woman who is not his wife. To do so abuses her standing with her people and can cause a man's woman to be jealous, also."

"You are married, then?" Laylah signed, then gulped and looked away from him. Why had she asked him this?

But, he seemed unoffended and was responding to the question. "I am not," he stated by means of the gestures. "But, I believe you are."

She shook her head and signed, "I am not yet married, but am soon to be."

He nodded, then signed, "If you do not object to the possible harm speaking to me might bring to your reputation, I do have questions no one has been able to answer. Do you object?"

She shook her head, "No."

"This is good. I am seeking my brother," he signed. "He looks much as I do, but is older than I. He came here a few months ago with a party seeking trade. The others returned home, but my brother was not with them, and none of them knew what had happened to him. My family worries about him. Besides trade, it is why I am here. He was last seen at this post."

"What is his name?" she signed.

"Chases-the-enemy."

She nodded, then asked Larpenteur, "Sir, do you know a Blackfoot man called Chases-the-enemy?"

" *Oui*, Mademoiselle. He ees Blackfoot chief."

"Chases-the-enemy is this gentleman's brother, and he is trying to discover what has happened to his kin. People from his tribe say he was last seen here. Do you know any stories concerning him that might indicate where he could have gone or why he didn't return home with the rest of his party?"

"*Oui*, Mademoiselle. Der be here a Crow girl from de West called Little Dove. He stole her. He is to be gone…with Crow girl. Her family very much…angry. Go after."

"You're certain of this?"

"*Oui,* Mademoiselle."

Laylah nodded. Then, turning toward the Blackfoot gentleman, said aloud, "Mr. Larpenteur"—she pointed to the clerk then continued in sign—"says your brother stole Little Dove, a Crow girl, and left. Her family went after him."

He nodded. "When?" he signed.

Laylah turned to Larpenteur. "When did this take place?"

"I am to tell you, Mademoiselle, eet be five month. Maybe he captured."

"This happened about five months ago," she signed. "Mr. Larpenteur"—she pointed again to the clerk—"says your brother and the girl might have been captured."

With his hands flat and extended outward, he sent them forward and toward her in a sweeping motion, effectively saying, "Thank you."

She nodded, then signed, "What are you called? My name is Laylah." She spoke her name aloud.

But, he didn't answer. Instead, he reached upward to the feather in his hair, loosened it, put it in his palm and extended it toward her. When she reached out to take it from him, he closed his other hand over hers, and, when she gazed up at him, he nodded and gave her the understanding the feather was now hers.

Then he smiled at her and said, "*Nitsíniiyi'taki, Aakíí-ikamo'si-niistówa-siitámssin,*" and Laylah thought the earth might have moved beneath her feet. She didn't know what to do.

The timbre of his voice was low, baritone, pleasant, and it, added to his touch, affected her oddly. Her entire body was shivering, but whether from fear or a reaction to his words, his touch or his voice, she didn't know.

She did, however, accept the feather. Moreover, she thought she might come to treasure it. Always, it might remind her of a handsome Blackfoot warrior who had once shown her kindness.

****

She is beautiful in both body and spirit.

She hadn't wanted to speak to him. Everything about her had told him she was afraid of him. And yet, despite her reluctance, she had talked to him in the language of gestures.

He had been impressed with her beauty from the first, and now he was captivated by her courage as well as her knowledge of the gesture language. It was to be regretted that soon she was to be married. But, at least he had been able to give her a part of him by extending the feather to her. And, she had taken it from him. He could hope that maybe she would not forget him.

31

He thought back to what he now knew: his brother had found himself a Crow woman and had stolen her. Had his enemies found him? Not likely, since his brother was a scout, as well as a chief, and could hide in a way that would not allow another to discover him…unless he wished it to be.

But, if his brother were well, the silent and distant communication between them would not be so irregular. Because of this, he knew something was wrong. But, what?

He was going to have to talk to She-steals-my-breath once again and ask if she might inquire about who the Crow girl was. He did not wish the white woman to speak to the Crow people about this, however—there could be danger for her in doing so. But, there would be no harm in asking her to make inquiries of other white people. Someone might know who the girl was and might even have more information.

Perhaps tomorrow, he would seek her out again. He was surprised by the instant pleasure that washed over him at the thought. And, even reminding himself that she was soon to be married didn't cause the pleasure to dim.

****

She was surprisingly taken by the manners of the Indian gentleman. He had been firm in his questions to her, yet had also been kind, being considerate about her reluctance to speak with him. He had shown her respect, as well as sensitivity to her situation by giving her the option to withdraw from speaking to him. Further, once he had obtained the information he had sought, he'd given her an eagle's feather. She knew enough about the tribes to realize the gift was bestowed in appreciation. But, there was more: it had come from his heart. His hand over hers had symbolized this. And, the gift had, indeed, touched her.

Oddly, her hand still remembered the feel of his touch. She placed her fingers to her face, imagining her fingers were his and were smoothing over her skin.

No! She dropped both of her hands.

What was wrong with her? Perhaps he was simply too handsome and too…charismatic. Never had she ever imagined she would react to an Indian man in such a way.

Instead, she had expected the natives to be dressed in cavemen-like fashion: in repulsive skins and furs, with gaudy feathers, tattoos and ornaments covering every inch of their bodies. Never had she thought to admire an American Indian's dress nor his manners. Moreover, besides the obvious beauty of his people's clothing, she had never expected to see a gleam of intelligence behind the Indian man's dark eyes.

She sighed, realizing she was thinking about this Blackfoot Indian much too greatly. It was a useless mental exercise, for it was unlikely she would ever see him again, which was as it should be. She reminded herself she was soon to be married.

But, her encounter with the Blackfoot man did cause her to ask questions of herself: was it wise to marry Thomas when his touch did not affect her in an emotional, passionate way? A man who did not make her tremble in anticipation?

The thought was troubling because she *had* felt a spark between herself and this Blackfoot man. But, surely her reaction was not a flicker of pleasure; probably, it was fear.

He will be gone tomorrow, and I will never see him again. And, this is very good!

33

CHAPTER TWO

"*C*areful where you step, m'dear," cautioned Thomas as he and Laylah led their horses toward the outer gate of the fort. "I fear no one has been about yet this morning to clean up the grounds, and you might step into something that will require you to change your boots."

Laylah laughed. "I thank you for your warning, for this could very well be so. I will be careful where I place my feet."

"Good. Are you excited to begin the day?"

"I am, Thomas. It seems we have talked about an excursion like this for weeks, and at last we are doing it. I cannot wait to put our plans into action. Indeed, I have longed to leave the fort and travel the paths of the prairie to see what it looks like in the autumn. Yes, there are many trees we can see from the fort, but it's not the same as being out there. And, now, with the scent of autumn within my breath, I can hardly wait to experience the beauty of it all." She smiled at Thomas. "Are we also looking at the grounds for other reasons?"

He chuckled. "We might be, m'dear. We might be."

Laylah returned his grin as they slowly stepped toward the gate. She drew in a deep breath of the dry, refreshing air, filling her lungs with the abundant supply of sweet oxygen. Taking a moment, she looked around the fort.

It was a bright and beautiful morning. There was plenty of sunshine to caress the growth of trees hugging the hills around the fort, and, looking up, she espied many fluffy clouds sailing by overhead. Truly, they did appear to be sailing through the sky, for the incessant wind in this place was giving speed to those white puffs. The atmosphere felt warm on this day in early October, and she had to admit to being excited about leaving the fort, if only for half a day.

She and Thomas had diligently set their plans this past week, having put aside this day to ride out upon the prairie, there to admire the landscape which was generally brown at this time of year. It was an odd sort of beauty: the prairie itself was flat and brown, yet high cliffs—tinted brown, tan or white—rose up majestically from the prairie floor.

She had already explored the woods housing many different kinds of hardwood trees that grew on the hills close to the fort. Even now, their leaves brightened the brown plains with their yellow and gold colors.

Laylah's enthusiasm was fueled by the traders, the clerks and the trappers who had spoken about the many coulees which cut into the prairie, and she had heard stories from Thomas of the beauty to be found within these gorges. Additionally, several of the trappers had described these in more detail to her, their descriptions painting pictures within her mind of the short grasses and rivulets that ran through them. She could imagine the cedar and juniper trees that clung to the cliff walls; she could envision the look of the cottonwood, the willow and the ash trees that hugged the shores of the creeks that flowed within these coulees.

Imagine the beauty Thomas and I shall discover today.

She could barely keep the feeling of excitement from bursting out from within her. But, it seemed silly to be so excited about leaving the fort to merely peep at the colored leaves, since there were many and varied deciduous trees within easy range of it. Indeed, the fort was graced by patches of cottonwood, elm, ash and weeping willow trees that grew up strong on the north, south and eastern slopes surrounding it. Even to the west, across the coffee-and-cream-colored waters of the Missouri River, were groves of these same kinds of trees. Yet, the idea of being free upon the plains, with the wind in her hair and upon her face, had taken hold of her as though either it or she were enchanted.

However, in the back of Laylah's mind was an additional plan which gave her an even more distinct feeling of pleasure: today she and Thomas might find a piece of ground they both liked enough to build a home upon it. Perhaps there they would settle down at last and begin the adventure of raising a family.

But, there was a slight negative about this, though she tried not to consider it. At the back of her mind was always the question as to the safety of the northern prairie. Perhaps this was why she was here: to determine whether their eventual home would be here or in St. Louis.

This past week, she and Thomas had spoken about their plans for this day and had decided that, in addition to viewing the prairie, they would pack a picnic dinner to enjoy around midday. To this end, they had secured several blankets to set out over the ground and had also filled many baskets with the kind of food that was in abundance in this land: dried meat of all kinds, fresh berries and bread.

Thomas had piled all of these onto the back of their packhorse. And, although it was still early in the morning, a stable boy had already saddled their three horses—her gray quarter horse included—and had secured their baskets and blankets.

They had already come to stand at the main gate of the fort and were awaiting the men on watch to open it, when the good-looking Blackfoot Indian approached them. She frowned at him, for she was slightly annoyed at him. It had been a week or so since they had first shared their thoughts by way of the language of gestures, and, although she had seen him standing about the trading room several times this past week, he had paid her no attention, not even giving her a passing glance.

He was called Eagle Heart, she'd learned, but this knowledge had been hard to come by. She'd waited for the man, himself, to seek her out and tell her his name personally since, upon their first acquaintance, she had asked him for this information.

But, he hadn't acted as she had expected. Instead, she'd been required to make discreet inquires of Larpenteur. And, it irritated her that the information had not come forth from the man, himself.

Eagle Heart was his name—she'd been told it was a good Indian name and an honorable one.

But, what good did this knowledge do now when the man ignored her? He had taken no notice of her despite the custom from her part of the world that required him to introduce himself to her. Perhaps this particular etiquette was not a Blackfoot custom, however it was her understanding that simple introductions were considered good manners everywhere, even in this wild land.

Perhaps it was this which caused her to feel some displeasure when Eagle Heart stopped Thomas at the fort's gate. He looked at Thomas and said by way of a frown and the language of sign, "You must not go out onto the plains today."

"What did the Injun say, Laylah?"

"He tells us not to go out riding on the plains today," she said simply.

Thomas laughed and stared hard at Eagle Heart. "Ask him why not." Thomas didn't glance at Laylah, but glared instead at the Blackfoot man.

Obediently, Laylah made the inquiry using hand gestures. "Why should we not go out onto the prairie this morning?"

"*Ipahka'pii,* storm coming," Eagle Heart said aloud in his own language, but he used sign language at the same time. "*Máakai'piiyi,* blizzard."

"A blizzard?" she asked in sign. "But, it's a beautiful day."

"It is so...now," he replied in gestures. "But, many forewarnings have I seen here today. Also, there was a warning in my dreams about the blizzard coming this day."

"I don't understand how this can be so," she said aloud. "Do you know something I don't know?" She didn't, however, translate her words into the language of sign.

"What is it, m'dear?" asked Thomas.

She turned toward Thomas and answered, "He says a blizzard will come to the plains today."

Thomas laughed. "A blizzard? Snow? Today? With the sun and blue sky overhead? And, it's warm today. I say, these Indians who frequent the fort are nothing but fools. Stupid is what your father and I call them."

Laylah was careful not to translate Thomas' words into the gesture language. Probably, Thomas' voice alone communicated what he thought of Eagle Heart and his suggestion. She was glad, however, when Eagle Heart didn't ask what Thomas had said. Nor did he speak or sign anything else.

"Tell him to stand aside," snapped Thomas. "We are leaving, and we're leaving now. I will not stay inside these walls on this beautiful day because of what a dirty, stupid Injun says."

"I will tell him what you plan, Thomas, but, before I do, let me ask him why he thinks there is a storm coming, for I have heard from several trappers that the Indians can tell the approaching weather from signs in nature. Perhaps he has noticed something that causes him to warn us. It's the only reason I can envision as to why he might be cautioning us to stay inside the fort."

"Do you think this Injun knows better than I do, then?"

"No, of course not, Thomas, I—"

Thomas reached out and shoved Eagle Heart aside, continuing to walk the three horses toward the gate. "Come along, Laylah," he called over his shoulder.

"All right," Laylah responded, though she realized she no longer felt irritable toward Eagle Heart. She smiled at him, as if in apology for her own and Thomas' rudeness, and signed, "My future husband wishes to go for a ride anyway."

Eagle Heart nodded and signed, "You must do as he says, then, if he is to be your husband. But, I tell you no lie. There are many signs that urge a man to beware, for a bad snowstorm is to come upon the plains this day."

"What signs did you see?"

"Geese are flying high in the sky and are traveling south in a hurry," he signed. "Was also a ring around the moon several nights ago. Rings mean very bad weather coming. This morning, when I awakened, I saw two sun dogs along with the sunrise. There is more: the songbirds have left the prairie to gather themselves into flocks, and there is a quiet feeling of dread in the air. Also, as I already mentioned, my dreams have shown me a terrible snowstorm is coming."

She nodded. "I will tell him," she signed, ignoring his comment on his dreams. She'd heard about the Indians' superstitions in this part of the country, of course. And, while she didn't share their beliefs, she also realized it was fruitless to discredit what he held to be so.

His acknowledgement was no more than a slight nod of his head before he turned aside.

Meanwhile, Thomas had spun around and, letting go of the reins on all three of their animals, had stepped back toward her. He said, "Come, Laylah, let us not delay."

"Yes, yes, I will follow you. But, I should tell you what he has said."

"I am not interested."

Still, she was determined, and, facing Thomas, she relayed the message in English, saying, "He says there are many warnings to indicate there will be a blizzard today. Geese are flying high and going south. Songbirds are retreating into groups, and there is a feeling of doom in the atmosphere."

Thomas shook his head. "And you believe him because he watches birds?"

"But, there is more. There were rings around the moon several nights ago, and sun dogs accompanied the sunrise this morning. He believes these alone indicate a blizzard is coming here today. Maybe tomorrow. But, he says his dreams tell him the storm will come today."

"Nonsense," Thomas spit out. "A dream? He expects us to stay here because he saw something in his dreams? The Injun is dimwitted."

"I'm not sure I agree with you, Thomas. While I also don't give credit to the superstitions of these Indians, I wouldn't completely discount what he says."

"Then, stay here. Maybe you'll enjoy his company better than mine."

"Thomas, no! You know that's not true."

"Then, come with me." He turned on his heel and retraced his steps toward the horses.

"Yes, very well. I will."

She smiled at Eagle Heart, then stepped past him, following Thomas through the fort's gate and out onto the open prairie.

****

There was not a cloud in the sky when they stopped to picnic on a bluff overlooking the wide prairie. The day was so beautiful and warm that Laylah was beginning to agree with Thomas about Eagle Heart's prediction of snow and danger. Perhaps he had wrongly read the signs of the weather.

"Come on," encouraged Thomas as he came up to his feet and extended a hand to her to help her up. "Let us go and investigate the prairie. Perhaps there is a place where we might find some privacy."

He smiled at her, and she giggled a little, even though a wave of embarrassment swept over her instead of the thrill of anticipation. She frowned a little. What was wrong with her?

After announcing their engagement almost a year ago, she and Thomas had often kissed and hugged one other, and she had always felt their embraces were enjoyable. Not until now had she experienced embarrassment.

She sighed. Perhaps she should give in to her father's demands and marry Thomas with all possible speed. Her thoughts were too often concerned with the Blackfoot Indian of late, and this was wrong, so very, very wrong.

Yes, she would speak to her father. Certainly marriage would solve the difficulty she was facing and would put thoughts of the Indian man to rest.

Her determination to marry might also cause her father a fair amount of relief, because she'd encountered one problem after another since the announcement of their engagement, especially since Thomas' visits to St. Louis were rare. Too many times she'd had to postpone their marriage due to conflicts. Indeed, her father was more than a little frustrated with her.

But, perhaps he was right. Maybe she had been sitting on the fence about her upcoming marriage for far too long.

In truth, this was another reason for the trip into the northern territory of the wild Indians: to spend more time with Thomas and allow him to court her properly. Yes, now that she was finally here in this beautiful country, she would do her best to please her father and become a more obedient daughter.

****

The land was a contradiction in heights. Brown, flat prairies extended in all directions, while in the distance were high bluffs and buttes rising up majestically from the prairie floor. In some places, the prairie extended endlessly toward the horizon, blending in with it. Yet, in other locations, the prairie ended abruptly, giving way to the towering buttes and hills.

As was told to her by the French traders, this land was also scattered with lush coulees and ravines, where streams were flanked with flowers and grasses and where groves of cottonwood and willow trees took root. The coulees were not easily seen from the fort, however, and she was barely able to contain her excitement, for she and Thomas had discovered one today.

She had become accustomed to looking out upon the woods that hugged the shores of both sides of the Missouri River. She had discovered it was from these woods where most of the timber was gathered and used for constructing and repairing the fort. When she had first arrived at Fort Union, she had wondered how long these groves of trees would last before surrendering to civilization's push. Hopefully, the men here wouldn't cut them all down. Or, if they did, perhaps they might plant new ones.

At present, she and Thomas were riding at the bottom of a wide coulee that cut an extensive tear into the land. Earlier, they had spread their blankets beneath a large willow tree and had waded in the stream that flowed through the bottom of the gully. There they had splashed and teased one another.

But, recently it had started to rain, and, looking skyward, Laylah espied a large black cloud moving swiftly toward them. A heavy wind blew in suddenly with that cloud, and the temperature dropped within what seemed a matter of seconds.

She shivered and wondered: was Eagle Heart right? Was there some danger in being out on the prairie today?

"Do you think we should be getting back to the fort?" she asked Thomas. "It's starting to rain a little, and the wind is slightly stronger and is suddenly cold."

"No, I think it will soon pass," he answered. "It's only a little rain and nothing to worry about."

"But, have you noticed how cold it has become...and suddenly?" she questioned as she waded toward the shoreline. "Maybe we should stay safe, as Eagle Heart suggested, and leave here to go back to the fort as quickly as possible."

"You mean that Injun from the fort? You're taking your knowledge of weather from him? Not me?"

"No. It's simply that there is a black cloud overhead now, and it's raining. It might get worse." She bent to dry her feet and pull on her boots.

Suddenly the rain became stronger and, without warning, water poured down out of the heavens upon them, causing Laylah to feel as though she stood beneath a waterfall. The strength of the rain even caused Thomas to rush up beside her, and, gathering his boots together, he quickly pushed his feet into them. As soon as it was done, he turned away from her to step toward their horses. Climbing up onto his mount, he led Laylah's horse to her and, dismounting, helped her up into her seat.

"Perhaps," he said, "you are right, and we should heed the warning signs of a rainstorm. I agree with you that it is now wise to return to the fort. Let's climb up out of this coulee before the way out becomes too slippery due to the rain."

She nodded.

"Follow me. I'll set our path."

"Yes, I will."

They were on the northern side of the gully because it was an easier way to ascend to the top of the chasm. Several cottonwood trees, as well as many juniper and cedar trees, took residence up close to the cliffs. And, there were large rocks as well as the roots from the trees which allowed better footholds for the horses.

A tiny spark of fear rushed over Laylah, but she dared not consider the danger of climbing out of the ravine. She tried to tell herself there was nothing to fear; they had made their way down into the gorge. They could climb out. But, she found she didn't quite believe it, though she didn't know why.

The rain was coming down much harder and faster now, and she felt as though the power of the rain had gone from being likened to a waterfall to that of tidal waves washing over her. The ominous black cloud had blown in with the wind and was now directly overhead. And, with the cloud came another temperature drop.

Suddenly, the furious gale caught at her skirt and whipped it into her face, as though it were trying to unseat her. Within moments, her fingers felt cold, too cold, as though they were slowly freezing. This affected her handhold on the reins, and her grip tightened.

"Careful, Laylah," cautioned Thomas as he led his own mount and the packhorse to the top of the coulee. "The dirt is a little slippery because the rain is beginning to freeze. Ease up on the reins and let your horse lead you to the top."

"Yes. All right," shouted Laylah. Thomas' warning rang true. She was holding the reins so tightly, she was pulling back on her pony and not allowing the mare to make her way back to the side of the ravine.

As soon as she changed her grip, Honey Sugar, her pony, responded favorably and picked her way over the rocks and roots. Indeed, Laylah was halfway to the top of the coulee when suddenly a flash of lightning struck one of the trees clinging to the side of the gully, blowing it apart. And, although the hit must have been a mile away, the noise of the strike and the blast of the explosion spooked her horse.

Honey Sugar reared, throwing Laylah from the saddle. So unexpected was her fall, she screamed all the way to the ground.

Worse, her pony lost its footing and slipped down the coulee, falling onto its flanks. She watched as Honey Sugar struggled and couldn't seem to right herself. Perhaps, thought Laylah, it was a lucky break that she had fallen free of her pony, for her injuries might have been worse had she kept her seat. Instead of being trapped by the weight of her pony, she had landed on a soft, wet spot of mud, and had done so without hitting her head. But, she had fallen onto her right arm and leg, both of them taking the brunt of her fall.

At first she seemed to be all right. However, as she tried to get up to her feet, pain suddenly streaked through her right leg, causing her to lay back. There was pain in her right arm also, and, worse, it wouldn't work properly. Indeed, when she tried to use it, spasms of agony streaked up and down it, as well as over her entire body.

"Are you hurt?" called Thomas.

She looked up and saw that Thomas had blazed his way to the top of the coulee and was looking down at her. She didn't answer right away as the breath seemed to have been knocked from her. But then, gathering her wits together, she answered in as loud a voice as possible, "I think so. I can't move my leg and can't put any weight on it. My right arm isn't working, either. I can't even raise myself up."

"I'll be right down."

"Yes, please."

The rain now contained ice and was coming down in sheets upon her. So furious was the icy rain, it was plastering her hair to her scalp and her dress to her body, causing her clothing to stick to her. Even worse, her fingers felt as though they were freezing. She tried to move them; it was difficult to do.

At last Thomas made his way to her and came down onto his knees beside her. He tried to pick her up by her right arm, but when she cried out, he let her go.

"I fell on my right leg and arm, and neither are working properly," she explained.

"I know. I saw it. Let me pick you up."

She nodded. He reached under her, but she screamed out in terror when a sudden pain streaked through her and swept down her spine, creating more pain than she'd ever experienced. As he continued to try to pick her up, she screamed again and again. She couldn't help it.

"Oh, Thomas, what am I to do? I can't move. It's too painful!"

"I'm sorry," he said, "but I have to do this. I have to gather you into my arms. There is no other way to get you back to the fort. And, I must take you back to the fort at once."

"Yes, of course you do. But, please be gentle. I think your attempt to make me sit up did some damage to my spine."

"You're blaming me for this, aren't you? I can't help it if my attempts to aid you are hurting you. I must pick you up."

"Thomas, I'm not blaming you."

"Yes, you are. You're probably thinking this is my fault because of what that stupid Indian said, aren't you? But, it's not my fault."

"Truly, I do not believe you are to blame for this," she countered, biting down on her lower lip. "It is only when you tried to raise me up just now, it created more pain than I have ever known."

"What do you want me to do, then?"

"I honestly don't know. But, I'm afraid something bad might happen to me if you try to move me again. Perhaps I broke a bone in my back when I fell, and moving me will create more harm."

Thomas looked away from her. "If it hurts you to be picked up, and you think you might have broken a bone in your spine, then I will have to get help, Laylah. Otherwise, I could harm you if I try to move you. Do you understand? I don't wish to leave you. Rather, I would like to stay here with you, but I have no option now but to return to the fort and get others to help me. It's not my fault."

"I know this, Thomas. I see the dilemma facing you. But, I agree with you. You must go. Please be quick. The storm is getting worse. "

"Of course I will go there as quickly as I can. Do you think I will not?"

"No, I do not think this at all. But, please do all you can to get back here as soon as you can. Perhaps, before you go, you would leave me all the blankets you brought so I have some protection against the cold and the rain?"

"Yes, I will," he said simply. Standing up, Thomas picked his way out of the coulee and, grabbing the blankets off the packhorse, returned to her. "I'll hurry."

"Yes, please do."

He turned then to retrace his steps to the top of the coulee, and it wasn't until he'd left when she took notice of a fact that bothered her: he had gone away from her without kissing her or even saying goodbye.

He is concerned. That's all. It doesn't mean he does not love me.

She shut her eyes, breathed in deeply and began to pray.

****

"*Tsimá náápiáaii?* Where is white woman?" Eagle Heart repeated the question in sign.

He had been waiting for the white man and She-steals-my-breath to arrive back from their adventures on the prairie; he had waited through the early morning and into the afternoon, watching for their return. He was concerned about her well-being and, being concerned, had equipped himself with emergency supplies, fearing the coming blizzard would catch her and her man on the prairie where they might be difficult to find. Even young and healthy men, accustomed to this weather and its sudden storms, sometimes died when unprepared for them.

Yet, what did he see here? Before him was the white man riding into the fort with his packhorse behind him. But, where was the beautiful woman with golden sun in her hair?

Had this man come here without his woman?

What was the meaning of this? No man, white or red, ever left his woman alone on the prairie...and in the beginning stages of a blizzard. Never.

The white man didn't understand his question, and, desperate to make himself understood, Eagle Heart at last used his hands to create an image of a curvy woman in the air, adding a question with body motions and raised eyebrows, questioning where she was. The rain had turned to sleet, then snow, and it was accumulating more quickly than he liked to consider. Worse, the temperature had dropped again. Didn't the white man realize his woman was in real danger if she were still out on the prairie?

But, perhaps She-steals-my-breath was simply lagging too far behind. Was this the reason Eagle Heart didn't see her?

"*Tsimá náápiáaii?* Where is the white woman?" he asked once again, repeating all the gestures.

The white man finally appeared to understand what was being asked of him and said, "She's still out there. Hurt. Couldn't move her. Not my fault. Have to get help and go back to her."

Eagle Heart nodded. Despite language barriers, he had understood the man's intonation and gestures. "*Tsimá?* Where?" He repeated the word in gestures.

Somehow, Curly-mustached-man understood what he was being asked and pointed in a general direction. "She's in a coulee." And, he added his own attempts at communicating with signs. "She's hurt bad. Couldn't move her."

Eagle Heart nodded. He understood. He knew the general direction of where she was, for he had seen into Curly-mustached-man's mind.

Luckily, Eagle Heart had already tied emergency supplies onto his packhorse, including robes and food enough for three; he had anticipated problems, knowing Curly-mustached-man had no knowledge or experience with how sudden prairie storms could be. The temperature changes alone could kill a man.

Preparing to leave the fort, he retrieved his weapons from the man on duty. Quickly, he drew on his quiver full of arrows, pulled his bow over his shoulder and grabbed his lance and shield, as well as his gun. Only then did he jump up to seat himself on his own steed, a spirited Appaloosa. Lastly, he reached out to take hold of his packhorse's reins, and, to the rhythm of the wind and the swirling of the snow around him, he set his course out of the fort, moving as fast as he dared over a ground that was amassing snow so quickly, even the horses' hooves were disappearing beneath a layer of white.

Eagle Heart was honestly worried, and, to counter this, he reached out into the environment, looking for She-steals-my-breath in the age-old manner of communication known and practiced by and between medicine men, as well as the Indian scout. Was she still alive?

He could no longer check his path for accuracy. The snow was too thick and spinning about the ground, and he could not see even a few hand lengths in front of him. There was now danger of losing his direction, as well. But, he wouldn't be turned away. No woman as beautiful as she should be made to die because her man did not understand the dangers of this land.

He reached out to her with his mind until he thought he'd found her, then said to her in the ancient way of medicine men, "I am coming for you. You must talk back to me with your mind so I can locate where you are. The snow is too dense, and I could lose my way. Can you speak to me with your mind so I can find you?"

"Yes," came her response.

With relief, he let out a deep breath. She had heard him and had even spoken back. He reached out again with his mind and said, "It is I, Eagle Heart, from the Pikuni tribe. Are you cold?"

"Yes. My fingers are frozen, I fear."

"Are you hurt?"

"Yes," she answered with her mind. "I can't move my right leg and my right arm. I fell upon them. My spine is hurt, too, I think. Maybe it's broken, for the agony in my spine when I try to move is very painful."

"I understand. You must remain warm, for the blizzard is coming upon us fast. I am going to see if there are wolves close to you who might come and surround you to keep you warm until I can get to you."

"Wolves? I'm afraid of wolves."

"You will not be afraid of these. I will try to find them and speak to them so they can come to you. If I locate them, they will help you and keep you from freezing. Do not be afraid of them."

"But, how can you do this?" she asked. "Talk to wolves?"

"I am speaking to you this way. I can also speak thusly to the wolves. I will send them to you. Do not be afraid of them."

47

The communication between them stopped, and, quickly, he reached out to her again and said, using the same ancient manner of communication, "You must keep talking to me with your mind even if I do not answer, for I am also seeking to find the wolves. Wait! I have found them. They are close and will come to help you. Let them keep you warm."

"I will try," she silently spoke back to him. "If I am to continue talking to you, as you say, what shall I tell you? I know not how to help you find me, and I am afraid for my life because I am so cold. Is there something else I could talk to you about to keep my mind off my fear?"

"Tell me about yourself. Why are you here? Are you in love with the man you are to marry?"

He sensed she might have found a little humor in his question. This was good. If she could laugh—even a little—perhaps she wouldn't center all her attention on her fear.

She silently spoke again in the mind-to-mind speak and said, "My name is Laylah McIntosh, and I have come here to help my father and also to marry the man I am engaged to."

"Do you love him?"

"Why do you ask?"

"It matters."

"Then I will tell you honestly," she told him, "that I don't know if I love him or not. I have believed I am in love with him, but recently I am beginning to experience doubts."

"How old are you?"

"I am eighteen years old. How old are you?"

"I am twenty and four snows."

"Snows? Do you mean years?"

"Yes."

"Mr. Eagle Heart, the wolves are here. I am afraid of them."

"Do not be. Let them lie next to you. They have answered my plea and are there to help you. You are close to me now. I have found the coulee, for I almost fell into it when I dismounted from my horse."

"Are you certain it is the coulee I am in?"

"Yes. The snow here is already deep. I do not wish my horses to lose their footing, so they and I must climb down to you slowly, one step after another."

"I understand. Should I keep talking to you with my mind?"

"Yes."

It was a slow, tortuous climb down the incline. But, at last, he and his ponies managed to step onto a more level ground and he found her lying there before him. Indeed, he almost stepped on one of the wolves who had come to surround her. He then said to her with his mind only, "I am here, but you must continue to speak to me silently and with your mind, for I must construct a shelter for us. Do not let yourself sleep. Stay awake."

"Very well. Should I continue to talk, then?"

"Yes. Can you see me?"

"No. The swirling of the snow is too thick."

"I am going to bend down toward you. Do not fear me. I am going to feel your body for injury. I shall try to touch your arm, your leg and your spine."

So saying, he bent toward her while the wind blew the snow around them. Reaching out to her, he felt underneath the blankets placed over her and ran his hands along her right arm and right leg. He said in Blackfeet, "I believe both your arm and your leg might be broken. I cannot feel your spine at this moment. I will need to move you carefully into a shelter, where I can determine if you have broken bones or if your muscles are merely strained."

"I don't understand you," she said in English, but he was aware of the concept of what she said anyway.

He nodded, then realized the snow was so thick, she couldn't see the movement. He repeated his words, but with the mind-to-mind talk only. Then he told her, "I must make us a shelter and a travois so I can move you without further injury. Do you understand?"

"I do."

"I have a warm buffalo robe to place over you to keep you as warm as possible. Stay close to the wolves and allow them to share the robe while I make a shelter and a travois to carry you. You have only to reach out to me with your mind if you need me. Thank you, my friends. My family. Please stay with her a little while longer. And, even when the storm passes, please stay close to me if you can. I might need your help again."

Only then did he rise to his feet, and he soon left to build a shelter that might keep them warm against the storm. And, it had to be quickly done.

CHAPTER THREE

$\mathcal{L}$aylah felt a little warmer, but she was still very cold. It seemed as if the temperature had dipped even further, causing her to wonder if the air in the canyon was well below freezing. She couldn't feel her fingers anymore and her toes were now following the same pattern as her fingers.

With her mind, she reached out to Eagle Heart and said, "I believe I am freezing to death."

He didn't answer. Was he still there? She panicked. "Eagle Heart, are you still here?" she yelled out in English.

"I have not left you," he answered without words. "I must secure a shelter. Keep awake. Do not freeze. It will be ready soon. Instead of the cold and snow, think of a fire and how warm you are as you sit beside it."

"I will try."

The communication dropped then between them, and she felt so sleepy of a sudden, she could barely keep her eyes open. But, she tried to envision a fire and its warmth.

She wasn't aware how long it was before she felt him beside her again. Carefully, and yet with manly strength, she could feel him lifting her onto some contraption that she thought must be made out of wood, for she could feel some of its branches beneath her. Then, she was aware they were moving through the spinning, heavily-falling snow.

But soon, a particular kind of tiredness closed in upon her.

"Do not sleep," he said, using his mind only.

"I must."

"No, do not do it. We are almost at the shelter. Keep awake. Speak to me, either with your mind or words."

"I can't."

"Yes, you can."

"I tried thinking of the fire. But, I was so cold, I couldn't do it any longer."

"Then, tell me of things you find joy in."

"Christmas, new clothes. Fashion. Strips of cloth I use to curl my hair. And you. I am suddenly thinking you bring me joy."

"You flatter me. We are here at the shelter at last. Do not leave me."

"It's so hard to keep from sleeping."

Suddenly, his arms were around her, and she was so cold she didn't feel the pain when he picked her up. Soon, he was carrying her into a place of warmth.

He deposited her onto something soft, and, without pausing a moment, he began to rub her hands and then her feet. It went on and on. She felt his hands all over her.

Suddenly he was speaking to her in concepts only again. "Do not be alarmed. I must remove your clothing, for it is wet and frozen. I have a warm robe that is not wet, and I will wrap you in it. I will have to move you a little to remove the clothing from you. I might have to cut some of your clothing from you."

She didn't answer. It was beyond her.

Again, with his mind alone, he said, "Talk to me." When she didn't answer, she heard him speak to her in his own language. She tried to communicate back to him, but found she couldn't and so remained silent.

However, she held on to the sound of his voice, afraid to sleep for fear she might not wake up. There was a quality about his words she found beautiful, and she responded to his voice and to him, refusing to give in to the darkness. Indeed, it was as though with his touch and his voice alone, he were keeping her alive and conscious.

She felt him pick her up and wrap her in something very warm, and, as she settled back into its heat and against her bed, sleep claimed her at last.

****

There was not a moment to spare to even build a fire, not if he were to save her from death. He knew if he were to leave her, even to collect wood for a fire, he might lose her. Besides, the falling snow and its blanketing effect over his robes and the branches, which had become their roof and walls, was keeping warmth within the little hut. All else could wait, since he had already loosed his Nokota pony, Goes Far, who had pulled the travois. Had he not done this, the pony would not have been able to move about and find shelter.

No, he couldn't leave this beautiful woman until he was satisfied she was warm and breathing normally.

Removing her icy, wet clothing had proved to be more difficult than he might have ever imagined. She wore layer upon layer of clothing, and it had all been wet, frozen and cold. He'd had to cut away some of the garments under her dress, for their removal had proved to be difficult and troublesome. Some of her clothing had also baffled him as to how it was removed.

And, even as he'd cut away the clothing, he had paused to rub her body so as to keep warmth within her. His tools were his hands and his voice, and, as he'd rubbed her legs and feet, her arms and hands, her torso and neck — even her face and head — he had known he would have to keep her alive with no more than the warmth of his touch.

He began talking to her in Blackfeet, then, telling her of his life, explaining why he was able to communicate to the wolves and why they were all brothers or sisters to him. Even though he knew she didn't understand his words, he believed his voice might keep her with him a little longer, giving him the opportunity to save her life.

At last he removed the final piece of her wet, icy clothing, leaving the loveliness of her body before his eyes, and he did look, if only for a moment. Quickly, he wrapped her in his own inner robe which was still warm from his body's heat and the fur of the buffalo which lined it. Then, he set to rubbing her everywhere, encouraging heat to warm her face, her chest and side, her arms, legs and feet — keeping away from her right side which was injured — yet admiring the beauty of her as he did all he could to bring warmth to her.

Darkness came and still he was stroking her up and down, drawing as much heat back into her body as he could. At least she was still breathing, though she was no longer conscious.

Hours crept by as he kneaded every part of her body, avoiding only those private and feminine places, for it was not his right to contact her there. It was well into the late hours of the night when she felt warm to his touch and her breathing became even, not difficult or constricted.

Because of these positive responses, it was only then when Eagle Heart felt safe enough to leave her for a little while to collect enough dry wood to build up a small fire—and a very small fire it must be because their shelter was composed mostly of pine boughs and logs.

There would be no sleep for him tonight. For one thing, the fire would require more fuel; for another, she still needed him to rub warmth into her. The friction kept her warm, as well as him.

He didn't go far from their hut in his search of wood because visibility was near zero. Still, there were enough dry branches close by which would keep the fire alive, and, quickly collecting them, he crawled back into their small hut and started the fire. Then, he glanced at her.

Sighing deeply, he knelt beside her and began to rub warmth into her once more, his hands moving up and down her body. Once the night had fallen completely, he began to recite ancient legends to her and said in the Blackfoot tongue, "Let me tell you the legend of how *Napi,* or old man, came to fall in love with a woman. Perhaps," he continued, "it is to be my fate, also, for I greatly admire you."

****

Laylah had a problem, a bad problem. Her bladder was overly full, but she couldn't relieve herself. In dreams, she tried to let it all go, only to realize the dream was not allowing her to correct the problem.

She tried to sit up, but became painfully sensitive to the fact she could not. Then, she cried. It was hurtful enough to try to get up considering her injuries, but with an overly full bladder, it was impossible. How was she to relieve herself?

She tried again to simply let it all go, but it was not to be. Alas, she was well aware she wasn't alone. *He* was here with her. She peeped her eyes open a little and, slightly turning her head, glanced at him.

He had gone to sleep sitting up beside her, his head bent down over his chest. How long had he been sleeping? She recalled being on the verge of consciousness sometime during the night and recalled listening intently to his voice. Sometimes he had spoken to her; sometimes he had sung strange melodies while beating on an object that sounded like a drum. Although she hadn't recognized his words, it had seemed to her that she might never forget the sound of his voice, for it had appeared to her that he was entreating her to stay alive.

And, so she had remained alive, as though in doing so she were only appeasing him. Yet, here she was...alive. But, with a full bladder and nowhere to empty it.

She tried to go back to sleep, but the problem was becoming so painful there in her nether region, she realized she had to try to communicate her problem. Taking a breath for courage, she said aloud, "I must relieve myself, and soon."

Her voice was not over a whisper, but it still awakened him. Opening his eyes, he bent down close to her face, putting his ear close to her lips. She repeated, "I have to...urinate...bad."

She was never certain how he came to understand what she'd said, but it appeared he did.

Squatting beside her, he used the language of sign and gestured, "I have made a place outside our shelter for this. I will carry you there."

"Yes, please," she said in English, finding she was too weak to even bring her hands up in the language of sign.

"I must put your boots back on your feet, for there is still a great snowstorm blowing outside this shelter. You will have to stand a little."

"Yes," she said in English. "But, do hurry."

At last it was done: her shoes were on her feet, and he picked her up in his arms. And, then it came to her: what was she wearing? Certainly, these weren't her clothes. Indeed, she was dressed in nothing more than a soft, yet furry leather robe. Where were her own clothes?

An even worse thought came to her as she realized he'd had to undress her.

Could she be more self-conscious?

He kept hold of her even when he had to come down onto his knees to exit their tiny shelter, and she clutched the robe around her with her free arm, keeping it into its proper position and covering her nakedness. The place he had constructed for this purpose was close to the shelter, for he took only a few steps to get to it. But, she couldn't see it, so intense was the fury of the snow and the storm's wind.

All of a sudden, the snow was less, and, looking up, she saw the reason why. This place was set beneath the boughs of a pine tree. Even here, however, the wind sounded like many howling ghosts, and she shivered to think how close she had been to never awakening again.

Soon, Eagle Heart was setting her down and, when done, turned his back on her, giving her a small degree of privacy. She bent over, preparing to squat, but found she couldn't do it and remain on her feet. She paused.

The snow was not deep in this space, and there was a natural shield of bushes on one side of it. Eagle Heart had scraped out the snow and the dirt below it, making a narrow trench so that any waste would stream downhill. In front of her was the trunk of a tree that she could reach out and take hold of in order to keep her balance. But, she couldn't put her weight on more than one foot and could only keep hold of the tree with merely one of her arms. It was inevitable: she fell.

He turned toward her at once and lifted her up. She cried. She couldn't do this on her own, for she couldn't stand on her feet. But, she also couldn't do it with him hovering over her, either.

Never had she felt so embarrassed. But, as he held her up, she raised her uninjured hand to sign, "I am so sorry, but I cannot do this when you are here, and I cannot do this alone because I can't stand on my own. What am I to do? I am so embarrassed."

"I will hold you," he gestured back.

"I think you will have to, but still I cannot do it when you are here," she managed to sign using only the one hand.

"I will look the other way." Again, he spoke in sign language.

"But, I am embarrassed," she spoke in the same manner. "What am I to do about this? Don't you understand? I am too self-conscious to do this so long as you are here."

"I understand," he signed, sweeping his hand outward, thumb up and index finger extended. "I think my sisters would feel the same. But, nature has created us all with the need to eat and to relieve ourselves. All life must do this. Also, until you are well enough, I may have to help you to do this again."

She gasped and said in English, "But, it is demeaning." She paused. "Yet," she continued, "it seems there is no other way." She sighed. There was more, and, gaining his attention—for he was not looking at her—she used her free hand in the language of sign, "I will require something to clean myself."

He responded, again using sign, "There are many leaves from the surrounding trees. They are soft and are at your feet, or use the snow."

She sighed and said in sign, "Please, can you give me some of those leaves, for I cannot bend down?"

Although he did as she asked, she could not remember a time when she had ever felt so mortified. Yet, her need was great, and when she had at last accomplished what she had to do, she cried.

She couldn't even stand on her own; she was dependent on him to hold her upright. And, the tears wouldn't stop falling down her cheeks, though they froze almost as soon as they were shed.

"I am finished," she said in English.

He nodded, as though he understood her words. Then, turning so he faced her, he pulled her up and put the robe back into place around her. Then, he hugged her, whispering in his own strange language as though to give her courage. And, though she couldn't understand him, the sound of his voice was so comforting that, for a moment, she relaxed.

And, then it happened. A part of who she was reached out to him instinctively, and she felt as though she were becoming a part of who he was. It was as though, for a moment, she became him and he, her. Indeed, in the space of an instant, she had never felt closer to any other human being.

No! It couldn't be. She couldn't feel this way about a man so alien to her. She cried because, emotionally, this was simply out of her experience.

This man was a stranger to her—a man from an unknown culture. Yet, suddenly and without her willing it, she felt so close to him that she was certain she not only knew him well, she also understood who he was.

Was this what it felt like to be attached to someone to the depth of one's soul? It was sometimes called "love"? Yet, it wasn't love; she didn't love him, nor did he love her.

Despite this, he had come to her rescue at the risk of his own life. He had stayed with her the night through, and she was certain if he hadn't been with her, rubbing warmth into her body, she would not have survived.

She fought her feelings about this now, realizing there could be no love between them…ever. She cried new tears, recognizing the dual nature of her feelings: she was tied to him, but she didn't want to be.

She tried to hold back the sob rising up from within her, but it escaped her lips anyway. A thought went round and round in her mind: was he, then, to be a part of her for the rest of her life?

She gasped as fresh tears fell down her cheeks, but this only caused him to pull her more deeply into his embrace. He spoke to her in his own language then, as though she were a child in need of comforting.

His sympathy for her plight seemed to aid her state of mind, however, and a calmness of spirit settled in over her. Perhaps it wasn't so bad. Maybe such a feeling of closeness between them was natural and would go away, given time. After all, one didn't save another person's life, and then return to the way they had each one been before, with no thought of the other. The truth was, whether she wished it or not, she realized she was here and alive now only because of this man's help and quick thinking. Of course she would feel a pull of affection toward him. It was unavoidable.

Yet, she was well aware she was engaged to Thomas, and she loved him, not this man who was holding her in his arms and speaking softly to her as though she were a babe in need of protection. But, might his kindness be a ruse? After all, he was a Blackfoot Indian…from the tribe of Indians known by the trappers and traders as the Tigers of the Plains, the same tribe who hated all whites.

She was white. Did this mean he hated her? If this were so, however, why had he rescued her, with no thought of the danger to his own well-being? And, not only had he come to save her, he had also kept her alive through the night.

As she stood in this place within his arms, she was more than aware that, from this point forward, her life would change even if she didn't want it to. But, would the change be good or bad?

Ugh! She was certain it would not be good. She knew very well that no one in her family would understand what she was going through, for, in her society, this feeling of closeness with Eagle Heart was not only forbidden, his presence in her life would be considered degrading to both her and her family. She closed her eyes as the tears continued to fall down over her face.

****

She was crying. She had every right to cry, and yet her tears cut into him like the stab of a knife. He was well aware of the moment when she had come into the knowledge she would have perished without him. But, he didn't want her praise, if this were the emotion she might be experiencing.

He was here simply because no woman should die because of her man's lack of wisdom. What he was doing he did freely and without any intent of being repaid by her in any way.

Yesterday, when he'd realized her man had come back without her, there had been no thought that could have entered his mind that would have prevented him from leaving the fort to find her and save her life, if he could. After all, he was accustomed to the storms in his country, and, though treacherous even to a man who understood them, her need was greater than the danger to himself.

The previous evening had been turbulent for him, not knowing if she would come through this alive. But, here she was, standing before him, even if she were shaky on her feet. Didn't she know how happy he was to see she was still alive and was with him in this place and at this time?

Still, he understood her embarrassment. After all, he was well aware that his sisters would probably experience a similar discomfiture.

Perhaps speaking to her might lessen her unease, so he said in Blackfeet, "I do not understand why most females feel embarrassment because of the needs of their bodies. Are not the requirements of their flesh the same as any other person's? Is this not also a part of living?"

She didn't respond, except perhaps her crying became less.

Still holding her in his arms, he sighed. But, he continued speaking and uttered softly, "I have not yet determined the extent of your injuries. There was not a moment last night to examine what happened to your body that kept you in the coulee and unable to return to the fort with your man."

It was true. It had been all he could do to keep rubbing warmth back into her throughout most of the night. There had not been time to examine her injuries.

He continued, "As soon as we return to the shelter, I will try to find out what kind of damage your fall caused you."

"I do not understand your words," she responded in a whisper. "But, I like the sound of your voice. It's as though I dreamed all night of your speaking to me, singing to me and sometimes even accompanying your song with steady drumbeats. Forever, the tone of your voice will live within me, as will the beat of your drum."

She didn't use the language of gestures to indicate what she'd said. And he didn't press her to, for, as she stood in his arms, he felt the essence of her reach out to him, and he answered her in kind, drawing close to her in spirit. It was not a new experience for him to touch another in the spiritual world. Indeed, sometimes matters not of the flesh seemed more real to him than those of the physical.

But, what was being forged between them was more than a soul-to-soul communication. There was a bond forming between them that even he hadn't expected. He could feel it; indeed, he welcomed it. Standing as he was so closely to her and with her wrapped within his arms, it happened: she became a part of him and he a part of her, and, so attuned was he to her, he understood her thoughts.

He knew then: she didn't want this closeness between them. She was fearful of its power over her. Yet, there was nothing she could do to change it. It simply was.

Hoping to ease her mind, he murmured in his own language, "I know you are afraid of me. I also understand you are already in love with a man and now find yourself alone with another man…a man who is from a different culture than your own." He didn't add another thought which was that they would be together for several more days as the Wind Maker spent his fury upon the prairie.

But, he felt her relax, and so he continued, "I realize you don't know what to expect from me. Will I help you, or will I demand more from you than you are willing to give?" He set her slightly away from him so he could use sign to communicate these last words.

She nodded and looked away from him.

When she gazed back at him, he signed, "I promise you now, before Sun, my Creator, and also before your Creator, I will not demand anything from you except perhaps your healing."

Indeed, he meant it. It would be his lot to ensure that upon the day when he returned her to her people, she would be as physically whole then as she was now.

But, he continued to explain in sign, "Perhaps what I should talk about is my absolute duty to my people and what this has to do with keeping the promise I have now given you. For, though I am too young to have been given this honor, I am one of my tribe's men of mystery. Your people call them 'medicine men.' If I were to do more than simply help you, I might lose my power to bring health to my people."

"Why?" she returned in sign. "Why might you lose your power?"

"Because I am attracted to you, and this might cause me to want to experience more with you than to simply give you aid. This would not be good, for I cannot marry you. My duty to my tribe forbids this."

She frowned and shook her head.

"If I were to surrender to the desires of my body," he explained further, "I could ruin you so you might not be able to marry another. This ill act toward you could cause me to lose my power. Therefore, my responsibility to you and to myself is to help you heal. Nothing more."

"Did you say your tribe would forbid a marriage between us? I don't understand. I thought you were a free people, and, because you are a free people, you could decide for yourself what kind of woman you would take as a wife."

"Possibly 'forbids' is too strong a concept," he responded in sign. "Rather I should say my elders might regard me as having no honor, and this might keep me from being able to help my people."

"And yet," she signed, "I have not spoken to you of marriage, and I certainly have not asked this of you. Indeed, I am set to marry another, as I have already told you."

"I know this," he responded in sign, "but I have empathy for you, and, because I have come to help you, this might cause you to feel more kindly toward me than is good for you. And, like the wild rose, I fear my affection for you could blossom into a fondness that might end in a bad way for us both. I believe you know this, too, and you fear it."

"Yes," she said, nodding. Then she paused. He felt her gulp before she asked, "You feel affection for me?"

He smiled. Her response was all sweetness and femininity, and he couldn't help noticing she was very much like his own sisters. They, like she, would most likely center their attention on this fact and would ask him about it. He answered in sign, "It is true. I feel affection for you. Also, no woman should die because her man does not understand this land. Especially a woman who looks as you do. But nothing more can happen between us."

"Yes, I understand," she signed. Then, she paused. "But," she continued, "what if you had thought me ugly and so did not care to risk your life to find me? Would I now be lying dead?"

He laughed. "Do you make a joke?"

"A little. But, my question is also a bit serious. What if we hadn't spoken to one another?"

"But, we did share a conversation. Perhaps Sun knew you would soon need me and sent me to you so I would help you."

"Sun?"

"The Creator of this world."

She nodded.

"Áa, but there is more I must say to you. I sense you fear the interactions between a man and a woman, and this uncertainty causes you grief. I remind you I have promised I will not do more than keep you alive and permit you to heal. I will keep my word."

She didn't respond. Instead, she looked away from him and seemed distracted. At last, however, she signed, "I understand, and I thank you for taking the time to enlighten me about your thoughts and feelings."

He sighed. He had left another consideration on this unsaid: until he knew more about her and about himself in relation to her, he would keep a part of him distant from her, as he had now sworn to do. But, there would come a time when their eventual parting would present them with another, more serious, problem: they had touched one another in spirit, soul to soul, and a strong bond between them was already in place.

This was rare, he knew, and usually happened only between two people, long married. What he and she were experiencing was unusual for persons who barely knew one another.

He frowned. Although his intentions were to keep her pure, having now met this beautiful woman in spirit, how, then, would he ever be able to fall in love with another? Marry another? How could she?

And yet, they must.

With the fury of the storm still raging upon the land and the wind frantically whistling through the trees above them, he realized, however, this was not the time to think about this too greatly. She was probably cold and was also too shy to tell him of her discomfort.

So, without another moment passing between them, he picked her up in his arms, ensured the robe he'd given her hid the temptation of her body from him and carried her though the raging blizzard back to their refuge, which he hoped would keep them both sufficiently warm and sheltered from the storm.

CHAPTER FOUR

$\mathcal{E}$agle Heart laid Laylah down on the buckskin robe positioned atop the pine boughs he'd placed over the dirt and snow which gave her bed an extra cushion and barrier against the cold. Ensuring his robe covered her completely, he knelt on one knee at her injured ankle, feeling it this way and that, though, at his touch, she drew in her breath and jumped as a spasm shook her.

He couldn't be certain yet, but it appeared she had not broken her leg or ankle bone. Perhaps a muscle had pulled away from the bone, which could be as painful as a full break. But, it might heal a little quicker. Rising up, he shifted positions and squatted next to her right arm. Again, she squirmed and jumped at his touch. The major bone in her forearm was definitely broken, though the break seemed to be a clean one.

Glancing up toward her face, he signed, "I believe your ankle bone is not broken, but the big bone in your arm is. Both will heal with time, but I will need to wrap them so you do not move them while they heal. I must now look at your back. It may hurt."

She nodded.

He asked, by way of gestures, "If I help to turn you, can you shift onto your left side?"

Again, she nodded and tried to move as he'd asked, but it appeared she couldn't do it. He aided her to move until they had accomplished it, then repositioned her so her back was facing him.

He felt the bones in her spine, from the top of it to the bottom. When done, he sighed with relief. It was not broken. However, several muscles attached to the bones were stiff, which possibly aided the bones in moving out slightly from the spine. No wonder it was so painful.

He would leave her spine untreated for now. Sometimes those muscles healed without interference and, with rest, allowed the bones to go back into position. Not so her ankle and arm. As he'd told her, these would require him to wrap them.

He touched her gently before helping her to again lie on her back. As she turned over, her green eyes—so stunningly pretty—seemed large as she gazed up at him. Raising her free hand, she asked in sign, "What do you think the damage is?"

He responded in the same manner, "I do not believe your spine is broken, but there are bones there that have moved out from where they should be. This could be why there is much pain there. I will need to put the bone in your arm back in place again, and then wrap both your ankle and arm. To do this, I will have to take out my knife so I can cut up one of my robes into strips. Do not be alarmed because of the knife. I mean you no harm."

She nodded. "I know," she said in English, but he didn't understand, and she didn't use sign to communicate her words.

He sat back on his haunches and told her in sign, "My other robe and another buckskin blanket is tied to my pack animal. Also, there are several days of food on my packhorse. I will have to go out into the blizzard to find my animals and get my robes and other supplies. I will also need to lead my horses to safety, see to your pony and guide them all to the grove of cottonwood trees close to the water. Horses love the bark of the cottonwood tree to eat, and this will keep them from starving. But, I could get lost because the wind, blowing the snow in all directions, does not allow me to see or keep my sense of direction. Will you talk to me with your mind?"

"Yes."

"It is good, but I will also leave you a rock and some wood so you can beat them together if you feel I may have lost my way in the blizzard," he signed. "The sound can lead me back here. Can you do this?"

"Yes," she said, nodding.

Using the gesture language again, he signed, "I will look for a good stick that might help you to walk so you can attend to personal matters without my having to stand over you. There is no reason to keep embarrassing you when I can make a cane for you."

"I would like that," she signed.

"But, you must know," he went on to communicate, "that I can never allow you to be alone outside the shelter without me there to guard you. I will turn my back to give you privacy, but I will always have to accompany you."

"But, why?"

"There are dangers on the plains from enemies or animals, even in a snowstorm. Would you have me leave you to danger?"

"No, but I don't want you there, either."

He sighed. "Yet, it must be. Even when my tribe is camped together, the men always guard the women when they are alone at their bath. There can be hidden enemies about, and none of our men dare to take a chance of possible harm coming to our women. So it will be with you, too. I will guard you."

"But—"

"You should know," he signed," that it is considered an act of cowardice, as lowly an act as a dirty dog, to look at women at their bath."

"And so, no man ever looks?" She added a frown along with her signs.

He laughed, but said nothing.

"Are you leaving now?"

"I am. I may be gone for much of the afternoon because I will need to ensure we have a fresh supply of water that is not cold from the snow, for you might wish to bathe. Perhaps I might find a piece of wood wide enough to catch the snow so you might accomplish this. We will need ample wood supplies for fires and for warmth, also. Do not be alarmed if I am long in returning here."

He glanced at her face and saw she was crying again. But, why? He asked, using gestures, "Are you hungry? Is this why you cry?"

"I am hungry," she said aloud, then signed the meaning of her words. "But," she continued, "this is not why I am crying. Do you think I am unaware of the danger you have put yourself in because of me? And, what would I have done if you hadn't come to look for me? I would have perished. I know this is true. In many ways, I don't understand why you have rescued me and why you are taking such good care of me and expecting nothing in return. It causes the words of my grandmother to haunt me."

"Your grandmother?"

She nodded, but she didn't elaborate further. She was continuing to speak to him in sign, however, and said, "I know you have told me you are attracted to me, and I am glad of this, but we had only spoken to one another that once. And, within my memory are several times when I saw you in the trading room and you never spoke to me nor even looked at me."

He felt like grinning, but he didn't. Of course he had looked at her, though discreetly. Seeing and admiring her was the only reason he had come to the trading room, for he'd had no business there. He wondered, did she not know how beautiful she was and that a man might do most anything to simply have her smile favorably at him?

In sign, he asked, "How could I let you die when I knew I might find you and keep you safe?"

"But, why would you risk it simply because of an attraction?" she asked. "When you set out to find me, you did not even know me."

He had no inclination to try to explain why a man might do most anything to gain a pretty woman's attention. Instead, he said in sign, "A man must give something back to a woman who has shown him compassion; especially when the kindness she gave him was unnecessary and required courage from her."

"You are, of course, speaking of that one time in the trading room when I tried to help you, though you believed I might be disgraced for doing so?"

He nodded.

"Well, I disagree with what you say about this. What I did required little courage. Besides, did you not give me an eagle's feather in return for the favor?"

"The feather is not enough. When a beautiful woman shows bravery to a man, and she does it with understanding, a man must be ready to defend her, regardless of the danger to him. It is his duty."

She hesitated, but after a moment signed, "Did you just now call me 'beautiful'?"

He grinned. He couldn't help himself; he was strangely moved by her question. And, though he would like to tell her there were some things a man might do for a woman simply because he had to do them, he would keep the knowledge to himself.

And so, he didn't answer her inquiry, for to do so might cause her to feel uncomfortable. Instead, he signed, "I will get you food and water, but, as I have said, I must leave you for a time to care for the horses and ensure our shelter will be strong enough against the Cold Maker. Do not think I have left you on your own."

"But, what if I fall asleep? Don't you need me to pound the rock on the wood to give you direction back here?"

"Do not fear I will lose my way. It is simply easier if you can help me with this. But, most likely I will not become lost. Sleep is good, so do it without worry."

Arising, he grabbed one of his buckskin blankets and wrapped it around him for warmth against the snow and wind. Putting a fur cap on his head, he glanced at her quickly before he bent over to exit their shelter.

Once outside, his view of the horses was blocked by the immense cover of sleet and snow that fell and blew around him in the wind's fury. Except for the wind, however, the world around him was silent and its stillness was spiritually comforting.

Looking back at the place where he'd built the shelter — up close to the coulee's wall — he was glad to see the snow was slightly less there and so was protected a little from the storm. Looking forward again, he took his bearings from here before he stepped out into the storm.

He'd not had time last night to bring the horses to a shelter next to the small grove of cottonwood trees. He would do so now. Besides the bark of the trees which would feed the animals, the little glade would allow the ponies to huddle together to keep each other warm.

He also had to find Steals-my-breath's quarter horse. Hopefully, it had survived its injuries and had found the other two horses.

Fighting against the snow, sleet and wind, he yet came in sight of the ponies and saw there were three, not two, beneath the cottonwood trees: his own two horses and her one.

This was good.

Treading forward, he stepped toward Steals-my-breath's horse. Squatting down, he examined the pony's legs, feeling all four of them up and down. It was good; only one leg was injured, but not broken.

Quickly, he stepped toward his own animals and spoke to them gently, asking, "*Tsá kaanistáópííhpa?* How are you? *Istto't opii,* stay together." Then he rubbed his hands all over the three of them, petting them and encouraging them to stay close to one another until the storm was gone from this land. His Appaloosa, *Sisákkiikayi,* Spotted Pony, answered him with a quiet neighing.

He smiled and said aloud, "You are a good friend."

Then, he untied the food he had packed—enough for three people, since he had thought he would have to rescue both Steals-my-breath and her man. There were a few tools he'd packed, also, since he'd known he would be required to cut up wood for the fire.

"*Istto't opii,* stay together," he reminded each horse before he stepped back toward the shelter, gathering as much wood as he could find without having to cut up any. He would need to make a large pile of wood next to the shelter for the fire. It was required not only for warmth, but for water hot enough for her to bathe.

He sighed. Snowstorm or not, he had a great deal of chores yet before him.

***

She couldn't sleep, though she tried. But, soon she came to understand it was pointless. She felt helpless…helpless and guilty. Indeed, she couldn't stop remembering that if she had taken Eagle Heart's warning into account, she would now be safe and warm at the fort, as he would be, also. But, she hadn't given his advice the attention it deserved, nor had Thomas.

So, how could she nap when she was well aware she would have died had this man not come to her aid? She was uncomfortable in the knowledge that, not only was she beholden to him, there was a strange closeness between them now. It was as though their minds were connected by some invisible force. And, though she wished she could ignore it, she couldn't.

She wondered, by the simple act of drawing close to Eagle Heart, had she committed an act against her moral character? Against Thomas?

69

Her status as an engaged woman hadn't changed. And yet, she trembled at Eagle Heart's touch.

What did this mean about her? About him?

She was reluctant to answer these questions, however, even if they were only asked silently and to herself. Only a short time ago, she'd inquired of him why he had come to her aid, and her query had been a serious one. She wondered again, why had he really come to assist her?

He'd told her about his attraction to her. But, he'd also said it was his duty. Could she believe this?

She wasn't certain, but it did cause her to wonder about the duty of her father and Thomas to find her and give her aid. Were they even now looking for her? She assumed they were. But, they did not have the same skills in this country as Eagle Heart. Indeed, they might never have found her in time to prevent her passing away from this earthly realm.

Regardless of her feeling of guilt, she whispered a prayer of thanks to the Lord for sending Eagle Heart to her.

At least she could rest assured that once the storm abated her family would find her. But, an odd thought struck her: did she wish to be found?

It was a dangerous consideration, and, unfortunately for her, she wavered back and forth between wanting to like Eagle Heart, for it was good and natural to do so. Yet, she knew she must not like him too greatly.

This worried her. He had gone out of his way to explain why he would not attempt to draw her into lovemaking. Yet, if he did ask her, she knew she would feel obligated to do it.

Also, was he really so honorable? She'd heard so many bad things about the Indians' character, from her father, from Thomas and from other traders, how could she trust Eagle Heart to his word?

Without warning, she recalled that he'd had to undress her. She understood this, for her dress had most likely been wet and frozen to her skin. But, as she lay here beneath the warmth of buckskin and fur, her nudity caused her a certain amount of panic.

The problem was, she didn't have any experience in these matters. And, there was another factor to be considered: because he had saved her from death, wasn't it true in both their cultures that she now belonged to him?

He hadn't mentioned this, although she had thought of it. Wasn't this another one of those natural laws? Again, she heard her grandmother's warning to her so many years ago:

> *"When a person saves another's life, it is the duty of the one saved to return the deed. Unless this comes to pass, the one saved is forever bound to his or her rescuer. If this ever happens to you, my child, remember this: do not be like me. Return the favor, if you can."*

Her grandmother had been forced to marry her husband only because he had once saved her life. It had been done in a time long passed, when a father considered it his right to press his daughter into such a marriage, even though his daughter had objected.

Laylah sighed. Not only was she tired, her thoughts were becoming burdensome. So much was this true, she wanted to go to sleep and simply forget her worries. Yet, she couldn't. She couldn't stop thinking and worrying about the future...her future. Worse, now that she was awake, she was becoming more and more aware of another concern: she was very hungry.

Eagle Heart had said he would bring her food and water, but even in this, she fretted over another very real problem. Food and water would surely cause her the need to relieve herself again, and Eagle Heart had already informed her he would have to accompany her.

She cried aloud. How she wished she had not ridden out onto the prairie yesterday.

It was upon this unpleasant thought when Eagle Heart reentered their tiny earthen shelter. Briefly, a cold wind accompanied him, and she pulled the leather coverlet closer around her. Looking up at him as he squatted by the entrance — their abode was too small to allow a man to stand upright — she saw the several inches of snow covering the cap on his head; his leather cape was coated with snow, also, and his moccasins appeared to be white instead of tan. He caught her looking at him and smiled. But, she glanced away.

He seemed unaffected by her attempt at indifference, however. She listened to the sounds of him throwing off his cape and hat, and, when he

71

approached her with the dried meat and cold water, she found she was quite willing to accept the gifts.

He came to squat at her left side and asked by way of gestures, "If I help you, do you think you can sit up?"

"I will try," she answered.

It was accomplished with some difficulty, considering her lack of dress and the necessity to keep herself covered. Yet, it was worth the effort for she was now in a position to feed herself. He'd set her up against what felt like the trunk of a tree at her back, and she wondered how he had constructed this shelter and what, besides the boughs of trees, he had used to stabilize this tiny refuge, for it was keeping the snow, as well as the wind, at bay.

He sat next to her, his legs crossed American Indian style, and began to offer her one piece after another of the dried meat, then he presented her with water from a pouch he carried. Oh, the water was cold.

She found she didn't wish to consume too much of the food, however, even though she was hungry. After all, she didn't know how much of the fare he had packed nor how long the storm would last.

These worries plagued her further, yet, strangely, when she glanced up at him and he smiled at her, her fears seemed to lessen. She ate one more piece of the dried meat and washed it down with the cold water. Only then did she return his grin.

"Thank you," she said aloud, then translated the words into sign.

He nodded, the movement slight. "Are you finished eating so soon?"

"I am," she signed.

"But, you have not consumed very much. I packed plenty of supplies on *Ipii oo*, Goes Far, my Nokota pony, for I thought I might be called upon to rescue two people, not one. Also, I did not, and still do not, know how many days the storm might last. I have plenty. Eat. Drink. You need your strength."

"It is enough for now," she signed.

He frowned at her, and she smiled at him in return, though her grin was probably a little bleak. Then, deciding honesty might ease the tension between them, she said, using signs, "I fear that if I eat too much, I will have to visit the outside again, and, knowing now that you will have to accompany me, I am not longing to do it."

He chuckled, the sound gentle rather than loud. Then he signed, "Would you rather I make some place in this tiny hut for this?"

She gasped. "Oh, no! Not that. How embarrassing." She'd spoken aloud in English, but he seemed to have understood.

They fell into silence then. After a while, he signed, "The ponies have fared well in the storm. Your own horse injured her leg, but it is not broken. She will recover."

"As will I," she said aloud, "thanks to you."

He frowned at her, but she didn't translate the words. One moment of silence followed upon another until at last he asked, "Do you wish to sleep?"

She shook her head.

"Tonight I can tell you some Blackfoot stories. But, not now. My people do not relate these tales of our ancestors' adventures during the day."

She nodded, and again they fell into silence.

"Perhaps we might spend the afternoon gambling. There is not too much else to do while the storm blows outside."

"Gamble? You mean like playing cards? Or perhaps poker?" She spoke the word "poker" aloud.

"I do not know what these games are," he said to her with the gesture language. "We could play the stick game or, as we often call it, the hand game. It is a good one."

"The hand game? You would have to teach it to me, for I have never heard of it. But, if we are to gamble, what would we gamble with?" She paused for a moment before saying, "And, don't tell me our clothes, for I have but this one robe at present, and I would surely lose this covering in your game, since I have never played it."

His grin at her was so charming, she found she could barely look away from him. But, he didn't say a word back to her, nor did he sign a thing.

She signed, "I am afraid to place a bet with you."

"Come, you don't have to gamble with the robe. There are many other prizes we could use as the stakes."

"I am afraid to play games with you. I know you will win, and then I will be even more indebted to you...and perhaps naked, too, for this robe is all I have right now."

"Naked? This is a pretty picture you cause me to think about."

"I didn't mean it that way."

He winked at her. "I know," he signed. "But, come, what does this 'indebted' mean?"

She swallowed. She shouldn't have signed the word "naked." But, she decided to ignore the feeling of uneasiness and said in gestures, "Indebted means I must return the favors or the kindness you have shown to me. You see, I am already beholden to you, and I don't wish to become further obliged."

"You are still afraid I will ask too much from you? That I would require something you are unwilling to give?"

She nodded and looked away from him. She stared into a corner of the small hut; she couldn't look at him, but she signed, "I don't know you well enough to judge this correctly."

"*Nitáaitasaa,* I will not. I have given you my promise." He tapped her on the shoulder, and, when she looked back at him, he signed the meaning of the words. "But," he continued, "if we do play and if you win, then perhaps your stakes in the gamble shall be that you will win your freedom from what you think is your 'obligation' to me."

"Really?" she asked aloud, then switched to sign. "I would like this. But, I fear I will lose, and so I must know, if you win, what is it you would like from me?"

He frowned, the two furrows between his eyes deepening, but the expression lasted for only a moment. His silence, however, continued for some time. At last, he signed, "If I win, what you must do for me is to get well."

"I intend to get well anyway, whether I win or lose. Choose something else. Something you really want that you think might cause me to be a little concerned."

He grinned at her and looked so handsome, she found herself grimacing. At last, however, he signed, "If I win, I choose that you shall not marry the man who brought you here and then deserted you. I think he is a coward."

"You have chosen a thing I cannot bet with, for I have promised to marry him, and I can't break my promise. And, he is no coward; he didn't really desert me. He had to leave me to get help to bring me home."

"Yet, he did not gather together this help you speak of. Or if he did, he and those men are lost. We are here. He is not."

"Please," she signed, "do not speak of him in an ill manner. Besides, how do we know he isn't out there right this minute, trying to find me? And, then there is my father. I know he will not rest until I am found."

"And yet," he signed, "I say again, they are not here. However, if you wish it, I shall speak no more bad words about this man you have said you will marry. But, I have a question about him and about you."

"Yes?" she signed.

He paused for a long moment before he signed, "In my society a woman and a man who are not married are not permitted to touch each other, and rarely are they allowed to speak to each other without supervision. Yet, I once saw you permit this man to touch you and even to hug you. You have also gone out riding alone with him. In my society, this kind of conduct would look very bad against you. Not against him, but against you. I tell you true that I have seen a man do this to a woman, and it is he who brings shame to her. Because of him, she will have a difficult task to marry a good man.

"You are a good woman, and I do not understand this. Tell me, are you secretly married to him?"

She didn't answer his question. Instead, she asked, signing, "If this is what is thought about a man and a woman merely touching and speaking to each other, is it your intention, then, to bring shame to me because we are talking to one another and by chance have had to touch each other? Further, do you believe I am shameful because I have permitted you to hug me and to speak to me?"

"I do not intend to bring shame to you," he answered, signing his reply. "I tell you true, I do not think this about you. Further, it is not my plan to take from you what is yours. Again, I have given you my promise, and I do not break my promises once given. However, I see what I have asked has created worry for you. It is not my wish to cause you more concern. Instead, I would like to make peace with you about this, and I wish now to withdraw the question. From this point and into the future, you do not need to answer me about whether or not you are secretly married to him."

"And yet, I will answer your question," she responded in sign. "In my society, it is thought to be a good idea for a man and a woman to get to know each other before they become married. This is all. Thus, we who are preparing to marry are permitted to talk, to touch and even to kiss. We are also permitted to be alone with each other. There is no shame in it."

"When you say 'get to know each other,' do you mean the physical act that causes a man and a woman to become married?"

"No." She signed the word, then looked away from him. Oddly, she was not embarrassed by his question. The real problem was that she was finding the conversation more stimulating than it should be.

She bit her lip. It wasn't wrong of him to ask these questions. The difficulty was her reaction to *him*.

But, he was continuing and signed, "So, if I insist that if I win, and the stakes are that you are not to marry this man, it will not bring harm to you?"

"No, it won't. My father might be upset with me if I were to break off my engagement. But, it will not harm my reputation. However, I find that I have a question for you. You say that, if you win, I must not marry Thomas. How will this benefit you, the winner?"

"I cannot explain. All I can tell you is this has value to me."

"Why?" she asked.

He shrugged. Again, he became silent. At length, however, he signed, "There are some matters a man does not speak of to a woman who is not his own."

"'His own?' What do you mean by this? Are you referring to a wife?"

He nodded. "Áa," he said aloud, then signed, "We, you and I, are not married. I may not speak to you of this which you ask me."

"I understand, I think," she said, using gestures. "Does '*áa*' mean 'yes'?"

"It does," he signed.

"Huh." She uttered the word aloud and sat for a few moments, actually considering betting with him. If she won, her debt to him would be forgiven and forgotten. If she lost…was she willing to call off her engagement? Most likely Eagle Heart would be the kind of man who would ensure she kept her end of the bargain.

Interrupting her thoughts, he signed, "A good wager must be about a thing the person who is betting is unwilling to gift to another."

"By telling me this, are you really saying you would like me to be indebted to you?"

He laughed, and she was at once fascinated by how this man looked when humor shone within his dark eyes. She mentioned this, signing, "You appear much like a young boy when you laugh."

"Do not be fooled," he signed in return. "It has been a long time since I set aside a boy's dreams and his ways. I am a man full grown with manly likes, desires and duties."

"Is this a warning?"

Again, he grinned at her. "It is. It is, indeed, a warning."

"Good," she signed. "I will play the game with you, but without having any stakes or betting. Teach me the game so I may play it well. Only then will I decide if we should bet or not. But, I think not. Somehow I think you will win it all. But, as you say, we are here with little to do but play games and tell stories in the evening. What are the rules for this game?"

"Usually," he answered in sign, "we play with a stick, and the song of the hand game is sung by both of us while the one with the stick makes many motions of his hands until he hides the stick in one of his hands, which he then places before him for all to see. The opposite side now has to guess which hand the stick is in. If this person is right, he wins the bet. If he is wrong, the other person with the stick wins, giving him the opportunity to keep the stick.

"But, because you cannot use but the one hand, we might use large shells to hide the small stick beneath one of them. The first one to win twenty games wins all the stakes. There are other more complicated games, but many of those are for men only, others for women only. In the stick game, both men and women play. It is a simple game and has simple rules, but when one adds prizes, it becomes more interesting. Shall we play?"

"Yes," she signed. "We have a game similar to this at home that I have engaged in with my sister. We call it 'hide the button.' You say we must sing a song? What song, then, shall we sing?"

"We will sing the hand game song. There are many of them. Shall I teach one of them to you?"

"Yes."

"It goes like this:

"Nitáa' waiai'taki,
Nitáa' waiai'taki,
Aakíí waaníí vai saa,
Aakíí waaníí vai saa.
Nitáa' waiai'taki,
Nitáa' waiai'taki,
Aakíí waaníí vai aa,
Aakíí waaníí vai aa."

He signed, "Can you repeat those words to me?"

"I am not certain I can."

"Let me teach them to you," he signed, then said, "Nit-aa-wai-ai-ta-ki."

She repeated them.

Then he said the next line aloud, "Aa-kii-waa-nii-vai-saa," which she again repeated.

The lesson continued for several moments until it was all said.

"What do those words mean?" she asked.

He looked away from her and shook his head as he signed, "I cannot say it."

"But, how can I repeat these words if I don't know what they mean? I should know what I am saying."

He sighed, yet answered her question and said aloud, *"Nitáa' waiai'taki"*—then continued in sign—"means 'I ask for a wife.'"

"And the rest?"

"Aakíí waaníí vai saa"—he spoke the words aloud before signing—"means 'she said no.'"

"Aakíí waaníí vai aa." He said the words, then signed, "This is the last part of the song, and it means 'she said yes.' What the song is about is the woman's suitor keeps asking her to marry him until she says 'yes.'"

Laylah grinned and caught him looking quickly at her lips before he lowered his eyes and glanced away.

A few uncomfortable moments passed by between them before he asked by way of gestures, "Shall we play?"

"Yes."

"*Soka'pii.*"

"What does that word mean?" she asked.

"Good," he signed. "It means 'good.'" He paused a moment and frowned, then said, "As you learn the game, we should wager a thing that would benefit us both and would not cause either of us much trouble with the betting. It will make the game more interesting."

"Oh?" she asked.

"I suggest that if you win the hand game," he signed, "I will be required to learn to speak your language as well as I can. But if I win, you must learn mine. This would be good because we could have many days of leisure to spend here while the storm rages outside. Perhaps we might use this time to gain more knowledge of each other's culture."

She nodded and smiled. "This is a good idea," she agreed, then signed the meaning of her words. But, when she looked up at him, she saw him staring at her lips again. Hurriedly, she gazed away.

"Do you have the shells and a small stick so we might play?" she asked with sign, but did not look at him.

"I do," he responded. "I will come and sit on your left side so you might play the game more easily."

She nodded and watched as he arose and came to sit next to her. His position was in the usual cross-legged position. However, having him sit so closely to her was playing havoc with the waywardness of her body, and, when she gazed up at him and saw his look of admiration staring back at her, she almost forgot to breathe.

CHAPTER FIVE

"*Ha'ayaa,*

Ha'ayaa,
Ánistsska'si,
Ánistsska'si,
Nitáa' waiai'taki,
Nitáa' waiai'taki,
Aakíí waaníí vai saa,
Aakíí waaníí vai saa.
Nitáa' waiai'taki,
Nitáa' waiai'taki,
Aakíí waaníí vai aa,
Aakíí waaníí vai aa."

Eagle Heart waved his hands in the air, showing the small stick now and again as he and Steals-my-breath played the hand game. She had learned the words to the song easily enough, and her higher-pitched voice added a sensual quality to the melody he'd never heard in the song before.

He sighed and, at the same time, suppressed his feeling of rising affinity for her. The trouble was, she was so beautiful, both in body and spirit, that sometimes when she smiled at him he still found it difficult to swallow, let alone breathe. He wondered if she noticed his tongue was often tied when he spoke aloud.

He put his hands behind his back, placed the stick under the shell in his right hand and brought his hands—both of them holding shells—out and around to the front, letting her guess which hand the stick was in. She tapped his right hand, and, as he looked up into the loveliness of her face, it happened again. He couldn't find his breath.

He smiled at her, glossing over his inability, and was glad when she signed, "Since I am keeping your score, I believe you have won fifteen times. As you are keeping my score, I am wondering if this last win of mine makes my score twenty? Weren't we playing so that the first one of us who accomplished twenty wins is the winner of the entire game?"

He nodded. It was all he could do, for words seemed to clog his throat.

"That does it, then," she signed and spoke the words aloud. "You must learn my language. Do you agree?"

He nodded.

"But, where to start?"

"Perhaps with simple words," he suggested, using signs, not words.

"All right. This word is simple. 'You.'" She spoke the word and pointed at him.

He grinned at her, pointed at himself and said, "You."

"No, no." She shook her head. She pointed at him again and said, "You." Then, pointing at herself, she said, "Me."

He smiled, and, directing his index finger at her, said, "Me."

"No, no." She frowned. "I'm me and you're you."

He chuckled a little and repeated, "'I'm me and you're you,'" using all the wrong signs quite purposely.

"Oh, you!" she said. "You're teasing me. You know very well what I'm saying." This last she signed.

He grinned at her and was pleasantly surprised when her green eyes, so beautiful, lingered on his face. But, she looked quickly away.

"How do you say it in your language?" She both asked and signed the question.

He pointed at her and said, "*Kiistó.*"

"And this means 'you'?"

He nodded, but when he pointed toward her again, he deliberately said in English, "Me."

She shook her head, but laughed nonetheless. "Let us take a break from the language lessons for a little while." She spoke the words and

81

signed their meaning, also. "I am wondering, Mr. Eagle Heart, how you came to be able to talk to wolves and also to speak to me without words. I remember your saying you would tell me about this one day. Since we are not repeating legends, which you have said must only be told in the evening, and since this is not a legend, would this be a good time to share your story about how you came to be able to talk this way?"

"Áa, it is a good time," he said in sign. "And, I will tell you with words and also with signs so you might come to know my language as I say it."

"Yes, good. We should do this with each other whenever we are using the language of gestures."

"Áa, this we can do. And, now I will start my story. When I was still a baby," he began, "our people were engaged in moving our village. When we, the tribes, move, all our possessions are carried on strong lodge poles attached to our ponies. It is a sight to see, for a village on the move makes a line that stretches out for long distances across the prairie.

"It was summer, and I have been told the weather was warm and the day was beautiful. Now, my mother had three other children besides myself who were taking her attention. I was the youngest. I was tied onto one of our faithful dogs during our move. But, as sometimes happens, the dog saw many rabbits in the distance and ran to chase them. Down he went into many coulees and across the countless streams that line the prairie. By the time my mother noticed I was gone, she didn't know how far back it was when our dog had left us for the chase. She placed my brother and my sisters in the care of our grandmother and came back to try to find me.

"I am told she searched for me for the rest of the day, and when our father finally learned what had happened, he accompanied many scouts to go out and see if any one of them could find the dog's trail. They discovered the dog, but the buckskin ties had been bitten off. They never found me. Indeed, I came to learn they believed I was no longer alive, yet for several months my father and mother searched for me. However, they could not find me.

"As the story goes, many moons later, a hunter discovered a pack of wolves while out on the hunt and noticed one of them had detached herself from the others and came within shooting distance of him. She looked at him with her slanted, yellow eyes. She didn't move away. But, when he raised his bow to shoot at her, she moved and placed herself out of his range. He followed. This went on many times until, in the distance, he heard a human baby's cry. I am told this was me.

"He found me, left food for the wolf who had brought him to me and took me back to his village, which was also the village of my parents. You can be assured they were surprised and overjoyed to see I was alive and was at last returned to them.

"But, something happened while I was in the care of the wolves for all those months. As I grew up, it came to the notice of several of the men of mystery in our village that I could talk to animals without speaking to them, and this was especially true of wolves and dogs. Others began to call me Strange Boy, for I was different from the other boys. I played their games, but I rarely became friends with any of them, preferring to be with the dogs. Mostly, other children avoided me and called me odd.

"As I grew older, it was observed that this thing which came naturally to me might be used to help our people. This was because I could speak to and understand even the language of many of the plants and trees growing on the prairie. Seeing this, one of the mystery men in my tribe sought me out and asked me to talk to many different plants, so I might determine what use they could have for our people. After I had done this, he asked me if I would like him to teach me how to use the mystery of what I could do to aid my people. This was how I came to be chosen to become a man of mystery, or, as the white men call us, the 'medicine men.'

"It is unusual that I should walk this path, for a man of mystery often comes from a family who has birthed many of these kinds of men. But, this is not true for me; there have been no men of mystery in my family until me. Perhaps it is because of my unusual childhood."

"Yes, perhaps," she agreed. Then she signed, "I think I may know what a 'man of mystery,' or a 'medicine man,' is, but could you tell me a little about these men and why they are especially chosen?"

"Áa, to my people, the men of mystery are those men who have learned how to aid those who are ill or injured. Many of these men have become learned enough to drive out the evil spirits from the body of a sick person and thus allow him to return to health. Sometimes a man, or even a woman, might use roots and plants to bring about the recovery of a person. A boy has to show an inclination to aid his people in this way to be chosen."

83

"So, it is rather special, isn't it?" she asked, using sign.

"It is."

"Tell me, can these men, like you, speak to others at a distance?"

"Yes. Our men of mystery can speak to people without words, and distance has nothing to do with the mind-to-mind talk. Our scouts also use this form of communication, but often the scout must learn it. For me, I have never known a time when I wasn't able to talk using only one's mind to speak. Sometimes people hear me and talk back to me. Sometimes they do not.

"This, now, is how I came to be a brother to the wolves of the prairie and how I was able to speak to you at a distance."

She was quiet for some time, and, after several moments, he raised his eyes and looked at her. She gazed back at him, saying and signing, "This is a fascinating story. Did you ever feel, yourself, that you were 'strange'?"

"*Saa*, I did not. Many times what I am able to do has been useful to my people. But, come, now that I have shared a bit of myself with you, won't you tell me a little about you?"

"I will if you want, but it's not as interesting a story as yours."

"I disagree." He both signed and spoke the words in Blackfeet. "How were you able to hear me and speak back to me?"

She frowned. "I…I don't know. At first I thought I was dying and you might be an angel."

"What is this 'angel'?"

"An angel is a messenger from God."

"God?" he asked in sign.

"God is the Creator of our world. Now, it took me several moments to realize I was speaking to you, and I only knew it was you and not an angel because you told me who you were and that you were coming to help me. Aren't you glad I knew your name? Do you remember you did not tell it to me when we first spoke to one another?" She looked away from him as though she were upset with him about this. "Even though I had asked you?"

He said and signed, "It is wrong for a man to speak his name to a woman who is not his wife. It is thought to be bragging. How did you learn what I am called?"

"From the trader."

84

"Did you ask him?" He grinned at her shamelessly. "Did I impress you enough to be curious about me?"

Again, she glanced away from him and looked down. "I don't know what you're talking about."

He laughed aloud, but said nothing. He was impressed; she had asked another about him. Perhaps, she had liked him a little.

His attraction to her suddenly felt full and warm within him. But, he suppressed the lure of her, because, much as he might like to know her more intimately, he did not believe it wise to marry her, and a man of mystery did not have "relations" with a woman who was not his wife.

And so, instead of letting his eyes linger upon the beauty of her face, he asked her a question verbally, and, when she looked around to read his signs, he used his hands to say, "Have you ever been able to use the mind-to-mind talk with anyone else?"

"I don't remember doing so. Why I could hear you and talk back to you, I don't know. Perhaps it was an act of God. This could be because I was praying to God to help me. And, I now believe your talking to me and me speaking back to you saved my life."

"*Áa.*"

"Do you think I will always be able to talk to you in this way?"

"*Áa.* I believe," he signed, speaking also in Blackfeet, "this way of talking to one another might never leave you. Once I had learned to speak to others with thoughts, I found I could listen and hear all of life chattering to   me."

"All of life… What a beautiful and poetic observation you make." She spoke the words and gestured their meaning. "There was a time," she continued, "when I might have thought you strange for this ability you have. But, you are not strange. You are a man of honor and a man any woman would be proud to call her own."

He swallowed hard and was silent for many moments, his tongue feeling large within his mouth. At length, however, he asked in sign, "Are you offering to be this to me?"

She retreated into silence, and he waited. At last, she shook her head and said, "No." And, in response, his spirits plummeted.

But, she was continuing and said with signs, "I am already engaged to marry another man. When I said you are a man any woman would be proud to call her own, I was speaking to you as a mother might talk to her son in order to give him courage."

He frowned at her. "I do not look upon you as my mother."

She laughed a little. "I am glad to hear this." She used both words and signs to speak. "I am, after all, younger than you."

He responded to her words with another question, asking with signs, "If you had not already given your word to marry this other man, would you consider me?"

He caught her eye. There it was. He knew he did not intend to marry her—he had even told her this—yet, he had this moment asked her to do so. True, he had said it in an indirect way, but still he had asked.

Briefly, he scolded himself. Why had he done this? Could he not exert control over himself?

Hánnia! What might she assume about his character? Would she think him weak, since he was acting like an *ohko nínaa,* a contrary man, perhaps even an *asóótokiaa nínaa,* a foolish man?

He would not blame her if she did. After all, it had taken him a great amount of skill to convince her that she was safe with him, for he could never marry her; yet, he had this moment asked her to be his woman.

Also, if she said "yes," he would be obligated to marry her whether or not his action might be looked upon as a betrayal to his people. Suddenly, he frowned as a thought occurred to him: was it right he should be bound by the unknown opinions of others? Indeed, when it concerned his personal life, was it a mistake to care too greatly about others' ideas of how he should best live his life? After all, no man could tell another man what to do or how to do it.

But, she hadn't yet answered—not yes or no. Instead, she glanced up at him and, catching his eye, stared at him for several long minutes. At last, she said softly, "I will, if you want me to. After all, you own me now."

He frowned and he signed, "I don't understand your words."

She looked away from him and seemed to focus sadly on a corner of their little abode. But, she didn't translate her words into gestures.

In response, he groaned, the sound deep in his throat. He didn't move, nor did he speak. Why was his question followed by a look of such despair? Because of his proposal?

He hoped this was not so, but there was little he could do except wait for the translation of her words.

"It is complicated," she signed at last. "I admire you," she said with signs and the white man's words. "In many ways, a person might say I have great feelings for you because I feel closer to you than I have ever felt to another person. Indeed, I feel nearer to you than even my own mother. And, certainly, I have more of a connection with you than I do with the man I have agreed to marry."

She paused. And, he waited.

"But," she signed after a while, "I believe you are right when you said we would not easily fit into each other's lives. If I were to marry you, where would we live? A woman needs to have a home, not only for her, but for her husband's needs and for the children she will bear. I cannot live with you in your village for long periods because I would miss my mother, my sister and all my relatives. And, I don't even know if your people would accept me. Let me ask you this: could you live in my world?" As her hands finished asking the question, she looked directly into his eyes.

"I…" he began, but dropped his hands as he considered the many aspects of his life he would be required to change were they to marry. At last he signed, speaking also in Blackfeet, "I feel I am long to admit this to you, but I have admired you since the first time I ever saw you. I was at first fascinated with your beauty. Then, when I witnessed your courage as you spoke to me, my admiration for you grew. It is why I am here with you now. And, I do not understand why this man you are to marry left you behind and is not here in my place. I would rather die than let you remain in a blizzard alone. If the blizzard were to take you, then it would take me, also.

"But, you ask if I could live in your world? Become a white man? And, to do this despite my duty to use my talents for the good of my people? If I were to do this, I fear that forever I would not be able to live in peace with myself, having deserted my people. Could I be a white man? Live a white man's life? Leave my people? If this be what you are asking me, my answer is that I cannot."

She sat silently for many moments, until at last she spoke and signed, "I understand, for I feel the same about this as you. Perhaps I should give you my answer about marriage in this way: if I lived in your world, I would not hesitate to be your wife. After all, you own my life now, and if we lived in the same village becoming yours would be easier."

He frowned. "Own your life?" he asked with sign. "What do you mean 'own'?"

She hesitated before speaking, until at last she raised her hands to sign, "Had you not found me, I would have died. But, you did find me, and I am alive now only because of you. And, it's not simply that you came to me and found me; there was something in your voice when you spoke to me during the first night when I was between the dead and the living...it was as though you were begging me to live. And so, I did live, perhaps only to please you. Therefore, it follows that you own me now, which means I am a slave to you, or perhaps you could say I must now spend my life serving you instead being the master of my own life. This is because without you and your actions, I would not be alive."

He was stunned. Indeed, he was speechless, for her words and hands conveyed a concept he did not understand. He hesitated, not knowing what to say. However, after taking a moment to collect his thoughts, he signed, "It is true. I was begging you to live, but I did only as any other would do. By 'owning' and living only to serve me, do you mean as I might own a horse? Is this what you are telling me?"

"Yes, I suppose you could say it in this way."

"But, you are not a horse. Why would you think I would do this to you?"

She shrugged. "I don't know. Maybe because there are some in my society who do believe they own their wives and their families, their children...sometimes they feel they own others who aren't even related to them. My grandfather saved my grandmother's life, and my grandmother was required to marry this man. Her own father insisted upon this. Theirs was not a happy marriage.

"Before my grandmother died, she confided to me that she had been in love with another man who had asked her father for her hand in marriage. But, it was not granted. And, upon my grandmother's marriage to my grandfather, the man she truly loved took his life. She never forgave herself."

He closed his eyes and sighed before he signed, "Such strange customs these are, to cause these young people so great an unhappiness. And, you wish to stay with these people who believe this way?"

"I have grown up in this society. It is all I have known. Were I to leave it, I think I would be lost. But, because I owe you my life, I will agree to marry you if you want me to. It will be difficult, but if I must, then, like my grandmother, I must."

"Must?" he signed. "Owned? Serving only me? To be unhappy like your grandmother? This is not right. You do not *have* to marry me simply because I have saved your life. I asked you when perhaps I should not have mentioned this at all. You are not 'mine,' and I will step out of your life if you want me to as soon as I return you to the fort."

She was crying, and his tongue seemed to fail him yet again. What could he say to her to bring about a change in her viewpoint?

He began to speak again, his hands translating his words. "It is not in my heart to cause you grief. Indeed, a marriage between us would be very hard on us both. Let us speak of this more. Surely, you know that no man can own another man, and this includes women. Sun, the Creator, which gives life to us all, does not choose one man over another. I do not 'own' you. I do not now, nor would I ever, require you to serve only me. Indeed, all men in my tribe are expected, even required, to come to the aid of a woman in need. Do you understand? It is expected. It is required of a man." He said it and signed it twice to give it emphasis.

She paused before signing, "Perhaps it is required in your society, but not mine; just as it is true that no man ought to own another. But, still, it happens. Understand, please, when I tell you because you saved my life, I believe I now owe you my life. And so, if you wish me to marry you, I have no choice but to do so."

"No choice?" he asked in sign, shaking his head and frowning. "This cannot be right. Every man and woman has a choice. Are you telling me that if you came to live in my village, you would always be unhappy in your life because you were unwilling to, yet had to become my woman?"

"I...I do not know how to answer that. If I say 'yes,' then I am saying I would be unhappy living with you. If I say 'no,' I am speaking about a life I do not have any experience with. How could I truthfully say 'no'? But, also, how could I truthfully say 'yes'?"

He sighed, then paused for a moment in thought. "I now have no choice," he said in sign.

"What do you mean?"

"I must free you from the belief that I own you. *Áa,* you must become free of my actions and of me."

"I don't know how that's possible unless there might come a time when I could save your life. Then I would no longer be in your debt. But, this seems unlikely, doesn't it?" she asked, using both words and signs. "And so, I suppose if you want me to marry you, then I must. If you do not wish me to marry you, however, because, as you say, you do not know if I might cause you to lose your power to help your people, then if you agree, I will return to the fort and marry Thomas. Either way, I do not believe I will be happy with my choice."

"This cannot be," he responded, feeling as though he were out of his depth in attempting to understand this woman. What she said was completely alien to him. He repeated, "You owe me nothing. And, it is my wish you should be happy, not unhappy about the choices you must make."

"I no longer see happiness as being part of my future."

He didn't respond to her right away. His viewpoint about the same incident was so different from hers. Perhaps he should tell her his own thoughts. Yes, this might ease the trouble between them.

And so, he signed, "While I understand how you feel, have you thought about the many people who come into a person's life to aid him? One does not owe one's life to these people."

She frowned. "You are right, but one's life does not necessarily depend on those people. But you…you risked your life, everything you are, to come to me and save me. And, ever since I have awakened, you have been kind to me, not even mentioning your sacrifice. I remember being in pain during the night and sleeping mostly, but I also recall awakening occasionally to hear your voice talking to me, and your hands were rubbing warmth into my body…all night. It's true, I didn't understand your words, and yet I know you were asking me to live, to breathe and to stay alive. And, so I did. But, I think I did it only for you. How can I ever repay you for what you have done and risked on my behalf? Do you understand now the debt I must bear? It is one I can never repay. And so, this is why I am telling you that if you wish me to marry you, I will."

"But, you don't want to?"

She didn't answer. Instead, she looked down and away from him.

He waited until her gaze came back to him, and he signed, "When you don't speak to me of this and do not answer my question, I think your silence is your answer. Know this: I would never take you for my woman unless you desired it. Come now, it is not so bad that I have come here to ensure you live. Let me tell you why. A Pikuni boy is trained by his father and his uncles to go to war and to defend his people. To be a good warrior and save lives brings great honor to his family. It is the duty of a man. Do you understand? You owe me nothing."

"But, I am not of your tribe. Your duty did not extend to me when you came to save me."

"Come, we have talked of this before. You showed me kindness and understanding at the trading post, though you risked your reputation to do it. It is I who was then in your debt. Now this is finished. Neither of us owe the other anything."

"I disagree. What I did required little courage and so you were never in my debt. Simply speaking to you did not include risking my life to save yours."

"This is not true. You risked your reputation. For a woman it is the same."

"It is not at all the same," she signed.

"It is to me. Try to see it my way. I believe that even if you think you owe me something for coming to your aid, to feel you must give yourself to me in marriage—and especially when you do not wish to—is not necessary or even good."

"But, did you not ask me if I would consider you as a husband?"

He frowned. "Áa, I did."

"And so, I have told you my answer. I will if you want me to."

"I should not have asked this of you. I asked the question when, perhaps, I shouldn't have. This is my problem, not yours. I have been trained all my life to think before I speak, and I did not do this. Had I better self-control, we would not now be having this conversation."

"It doesn't matter whose fault it is or whether you should have asked me or not. The point is you did ask. If you wish this, then I will leave

Thomas and my family to follow you." She looked away as tears escaped her eyes to rush down her cheek.

He was stumped. Did he wish to marry this woman? Perhaps, if their lives were more alike. He did admire her and would welcome spending much time with her. If this were love—and he thought it could be—it had happened with them each one knowing little of the other. From this might spring everlasting love. But, conversely, if he did take her in marriage, their way would be filled with trouble and problems for them both...within his tribe and within hers. And, importantly, he especially did not wish to tie her to him when the thought of doing so made her cry.

How then was he to aid this beautiful woman? If only *she* could save *his* life.

Suddenly, he sat up straight. There might be a way, for he had brought with him a game that...

A little excited now, he brightly said in Blackfeet as well as signed, "You must save my life. Then you will be free of me and your decisions, once more, will be your own."

He then took a good look at her and was disconcerted to see more tears streaming down her cheeks. Also, she still stared away from him.

To get her attention, he said in English, "A way...is...there." And, when she glanced over her shoulder at him, he signed, "There is a way you might be able to save my life."

Her lips trembled as she turned toward him and signed, "I don't wish you to risk your life that I might save it."

"Yet, there is a means to do this. It might be difficult for you, it is true, but it could be done without either of us having to leave this tiny shelter."

She frowned. "I don't understand."

"*Cos-soó*," he said aloud. Then he signed, "*Cos-soó* is a game of chance and is a game of war played only by Indian men of all the tribes. But, I will play it with you and give you a chance to save my life."

"I'm sorry. I still don't understand."

"This is a game of war and is often played by enemies. Deaths have sometimes occurred because of this game."

"But, why?"

"It is because the rules of the game are thus: it is played until one or the other of the players is ruined utterly. This is the main rule of the game. One of the players must completely devastate the other. It is a game where one of the men might lose all he owns; it is a game where a man could become so ruined, it is as though he has died, and, in some instances, he does."

She continued to frown at him. "It sounds like a terrible thing to do to another. I don't wish to ruin you. And, I certainly don't wish you to ruin me."

"But, this is what you must do, don't you see? You could ruin me and then save me by returning all of my possessions to me. *Cos-soó* is a game of war, but instead of killing a man, one wrecks him completely by taking from him everything he owns. If a man plays this game with another man, one of them stands to lose everything, even to the man's clothes, his lodge, his ponies and even his wife. Think of what could happen. If you win against me, you would become free of me." He paused as he glanced at her. "And, then you would again be the one to decide what you wish to do and what you don't wish to do with your life."

She sat silently before him and stared at him as though he had lost all sense. At last she signed, "Perhaps this is possible, if, by losing everything, it is considered a person has lost his life."

"*Áa*, it is so. Such men who lose this game have to start their lives over again."

"Truly?"

"*Áa*." He nodded.

She frowned before she glanced at him again, then said with gestures, "Please permit me to ensure I understand this: if I were to win and have in my possession everything you own and then give it all back to you, it would be as though I have saved your life?"

"It is so. It is considered to be the same."

"But, I don't know how to play this game. Surely, not knowing it, I would lose."

"I will teach you so you will win," he signed. "After all, I would not have 'saved' you only to see you become sad because you feel you must change the direction of your life. I will tell you what we will do. We must play together many times. At first, there will be no betting so you can learn how the game is best played. Then, when you feel you have mastered its rules, we will play with all we have. I will not hold back so you might win. And, I will play the game with all the cunning I have."

She hesitated, then signed, "By stating this, that you would play using all of your 'cunning,' are you telling me you let me win the hand game we played earlier?"

He grinned at her. He couldn't help himself. But, he didn't say a word.

CHAPTER SIX

"*This* is the game of *Cos-soó*," spoke Eagle Heart, utilizing both signs and the Blackfoot language. "Some call it the 'game of the bowl', but we will call it by its Indian name, *Cos-soó*."

Laylah watched as Eagle Heart reached into one of his bags and dragged out an odd-looking circular wooden bowl with a flat bottom. The bowl looked to be about a foot in diameter, and its sides were glued in place by some means and were about two inches in height.

"You travel with a bowl like this?"

"I had thought," he signed, "I might gamble with your 'to be husband.' *Áa*, because of this, I brought this deadly game with me into the storm. Blizzards are for storytelling and gambling."

"Oh," she said simply. "You were plotting to gamble with my fiancé? Was part of your plan to win me?"

He didn't answer the question. Instead, he gazed away from her and became suddenly serious. At length, he signed, "These are the objects we play with."

She watched as he held up a single large claw which was red on one side and black on the other.

He signed, "There is only one large claw. If it stands up on the throw, it counts as 25 and only for 5 if on its side. And these four smaller crow claws"—he held them up for her inspection—"are painted red on one side, as you can see, and black on the other. If the black side is up on the throw, it counts for nothing. If the red side is up, it counts as four each."

She nodded. "I understand so far," she signed. "I must warn you, I am good at counting and have an excellent memory."

He grinned at her. "I am also good at counting and have a fine memory, as well," he signed, saying his words in Blackfeet, also. "I shall continue," he signed and set out five plum stones. Both sides had been smoothed out and one side was black, the other side was white. "Black side up is four points," he signed. "White side up is nothing."

She nodded.

Next, he set out five pieces of blue china, chiseled until they were round. He continued his instructions and signed, "As you can see there is a blue side and a white side of these small circles of china. Blue side up on the throw counts for three; white side up counts nothing."

He next set out five trade buttons. "The button's eye side up is two points; smooth side up counts nothing. And, here is the last: five brass tacks we Indians obtain in trade. When the side is up that curves inward, this counts one. If the side is up that pushes outward, it counts nothing. In this game, I keep your score and you keep mine."

"Is there also a song we sing?"

"Only if you wish there to be one," he answered using both words and signs. "Usually there is none, for this game is played only between men, with you being the exception. It is a serious and a desperate game because it is played until one of the players is brought down utterly. This man loses everything, even his wife, unless the players agree beforehand not to let the game go so far. But usually, because this is a game of war, it does go this far and a man can lose everything: his clothes, his horses, his wife. Sometimes the game goes on for days, the players breaking only to eat, for there is no sleep when one is playing *Cos-soó* .

"However, we will take breaks to sleep whenever you need to rest because you are recovering your strength. But, we will play until you win everything I own."

"What?... 'Until I win everything'? What do you mean?"

"We will keep playing the game until you win everything from me," he repeated.

"But," she objected, "what if you win this game instead of me?"

"This will not happen. We will play this game until I lose everything. The game of *Cos-soó* is war, only no one needs to die."

Laylah blinked. "But," she signed, "what if I keep losing to you? Will I not have to give you everything I own? Aren't those the rules?"

"We shall not play by those rules," he signed and spoke the words in Blackfeet. "We will agree beforehand to continue to play until you win everything from me. Yet, it will not be easily done."

She shook her head before staring at him, feeling as though her eyes were wide open and owl-like. She signed, "But, if we play until only I can win, it's not really a game with real stakes, is it?"

"It is if we agree it is. You are to win your freedom from me, and we will not stop the game until you do. Do you agree?"

"I don't know. It seems unfair to you."

"*Saa*," he said the word and signed it. "The idea that I somehow own you is what is unfair. But, since you believe this, we will play and you will win your freedom from me." Suddenly, he grinned at her. "Then, you can choose between the two of us: the man who left you here to die or me…if you wish to choose at all."

"But, wait!" She raised her voice a little. "I am confused," she signed. "I understand you asked me to marry you a little while ago. However, before that you had said you might lose your power and not be of any use to your people if we were to ever marry. And then, while we were talking, you told me you should not have asked me to marry you and that you should have exercised better control. Is this not true?"

He sighed. "It is."

"Well, it seems to me, Mr. Eagle Heart, that you don't really wish to marry me, and you spoke when you shouldn't have. Nonetheless, you are now telling me if I win I could choose between you or Thomas. So in a way, aren't you asking me to marry you again? Even when you say you shouldn't?"

"*Áa*, you make a good argument, and I admit it seems I have done this. Also, it appears I do not know my own mind and I may even seem to be weak-willed."

"Weak-willed?" she asked with signs. "I do not think this of you. However, what could be happening is you might like me a little, and, were there not such great barriers between us, we might become friends."

"We are already friends."

"Yes, we are. But, I meant a little more than friends."

He laughed. Then, with a twinkle in his eye, he signed, "Say what you mean." His smile, however, made him look a little too much like a well-fed and satisfied cat.

And so, in response, she signed, "I will not." Her hand movements were firm and exact. "You know very well what I am talking about."

He was still grinning when he signed, "I did ask you to be my woman, it is true, when perhaps I should not have. Or"—he laughed—"maybe my 'tongue' knows better than I do what is good for me."

She giggled a little. She couldn't help herself.

"I will not take back my question to you, whether I should have asked you to be my woman or not. But, come now, you do not have to choose anyone."

She sighed. "Eventually, I will have to choose. I cannot forever remain unmarried."

"Not when you look as you do."

She shook her head, but smiled nonetheless.

"As I understand it," he signed, "I need to free you from being my slave, especially since my people have no slaves. Therefore, you must win. We should agree about this before we play."

She sat staring at him for several moments, feeling as if her head were spinning. On one hand, this man teased her with suggestions of marriage, yet, on the other, he insisted he did not wish to take her for a wife.

And she? What did she think about the possibility of marriage to him...if she were free to choose? This was an easy question for her to answer: she could never marry an Indian or live an Indian life. Never.

After a while, she said in the language of sign, "I do not understand you, but let us set this aside and return our attention to the business of this game. Please, let me ensure I understand these rules you wish to impose upon us both. What you are saying is that we continue the game until I win. Is this right?"

"Áa."

"Then, it's not a game of chance," she protested, speaking in both signs and words. "This is not fair to you. As I see it, I am not really playing. If I win, I get all you own?"

"Áa."

"But, if you win, you are not taking anything from me?"

"*Áa.*"

"This is not fair," she signed. "If you are to play this way and lose everything, then the same rules must apply to me."

She watched him closely as his lips thinned. He sighed, then grunted deeply in his throat.

"I cannot play this game with you," she continued, "unless it really is fair. This means that I play with the same penalties as you."

He frowned, then said, "The penalties and wins will be the same as when two men play this game. It is only that we should agree to continue to play until you win. If at first you lose, we will simply start the game again and will do it over and over until you win it."

"No." She spoke the word and shook her head. "I don't want to play a game where you lose everything while only I can win. Then, I'm not really saving your life, am I? For, unlike you, I have risked nothing."

"And, *I* do not wish to have you as my woman when you are agreeing to it only because you feel you are my slave. I wish to free you of this."

"Then just give me my freedom."

"And, this would be enough for you? I say you are free and you no longer feel any obligation toward me?"

"Yes." She signed and spoke the word. Yet, it was a lie, and she knew it. Indeed, she couldn't look at him.

It appeared her thoughts on the matter were known to him anyway, for he signed, "Look at me when you say this, for I would see the truth or lies within your eyes."

She drew in a deep breath and slowly released it. Then, she paused while she tried to understand this man. But, it was useless, and at last she said by words and signs, "No, we will not play this as you say it. We must play only in this way: if I lose, you will gain all I own including me, even if you don't want me. It is the only way I will play with you. To rig the game so that only I can win is not right. No, I won't do this."

"What does this mean to 'rig' the game."

"It means 'to cheat.'"

"We will not cheat. We will play until you win."

"No, it's not fair, and I won't have any part of it. And, it is, too, cheating. You are condoning and allowing me to cheat. No, I will not play by these rules."

He fell into silence and was quiet for so long, it felt like hours had passed. Indeed, she started to go to sleep awaiting his reply. As it was, he had to awaken her by touching her shoulder.

Once she opened her eyes, he signed, "I have this to say to you: it is my wish to return you to your home in the same condition I found you before the storm, if you feel you must go back there. But, if you come with me, you must do so because you wish it, and not because you feel you owe it to me. This is why I feel we must play the game in the manner I have said. I wish you to be happy."

"That's impossible now." She signed her words.

"Why is this impossible? If you wish to return to Fort Union, I will take you there in the same physical condition you were in before I found you."

"I know, but what you fail to understand is that I am not the same as I was before you came to rescue me," she signed. "I have changed, perhaps forever."

"And, how have you changed?"

Again, she paused, and when she glanced up at him she saw him watching her intently. However, she looked away from him as she gathered enough courage to say and sign, "Because I love you. This is how I've changed. After all, how could I not love you? You saved my life. Does this mean I love you as I might love a husband? I can't say 'yes, I do,' but, then again, I can't say 'no,' either. It is confusing to me. However, this I do know: I can't live the life of an Indian, so I shall never willingly come with you."

When she glanced back at him, she saw his look at her was so sober, she wanted to shake some emotion into him. But then, she didn't wish to shake him, either. All she knew was she was tied to this man in a way that seemed impossible to break.

Why didn't he take the decision from her?

After all, she had heard from her father and other traders that an Indian man could steal a wife, only to discard her if she did not please him. Why didn't he simply take her as his wife and be done with it? If she brought trouble into his life, he could bring her back to the fort and that would be that. At least, in this way, she would have repaid her debt to him.

As she awaited his reply, her attention went to the howling of the wind outside and the shaking of their little hut as the buckskin ropes that held it in place whistled against the gale. Only the sparks from the fire added to the roaring sound of the blizzard outside. Once again, she was reminded that if not for this man she would still be out in the storm and dead.

At last, he raised his hands to sign, "You say you love me, though not as a man you might marry. I admire your courage in speaking to me in this manner.

"And, now I say this to you: I, too, have loved you almost from the moment I first saw you, but have not felt it my place to make you aware of my feelings, for you have already given your promise to marry another. Unlike you, however, I know I would desire you to be my wife if our ways of living were more alike. It would be difficult, as you say. But, I am willing to try. What I cannot do is take you to be my woman when you do not wish it. It is wrong."

"But," she signed, "if marriage to me has been in your thoughts, don't Indian men sometimes steal the woman they want to marry?"

"Yes, they do," he responded in sign.

"Wouldn't this be a better way to settle this? You take me. You are unhappy with me. You bring me back. My debt to you is repaid."

"I doubt I would ever bring you back. But, you forget, I am a medicine man, and my way in life is different from most. If I took you, then brought you back, you would be ruined. I cannot do this to you."

"But, my debt would be repaid."

"At your sacrifice. Consider this, even if we were of the same race and well known to each other, I still would not be able take you for a wife without you first throwing this coward of a man away."

"What does it mean, to 'throw him away'? A divorce? But, I am not yet married to him."

"It means you must tell him you do not wish to marry him. Get some object—a stick perhaps—and say the stick is he and then throw it away. Only then would you be free of him, and free to marry another or no one… whatever it is you wish."

"Oh," was all she replied. Then, after a moment, she asked, "Did you say you love me?"

He sighed, yet signed, "I did." He looked at her strangely, however, as though he were confessing a sin. "I see now my mistake in thinking to use this game in a way where only you can win. I was wrong to think I could play the game where the result is already set. Of course you would object because, as you see it, you would not be 'saving my life.' My thoughts have been only to free you from me.

"But, I now understand it the way you see it," he continued. "This being so, the game of *Cos-soó* will not aid us. Perhaps we should speak our thoughts to one another until we are certain we understand each other. Perhaps this might free you. Can you agree to this?"

"I'm not certain. What do you mean by 'agree to this'? That we talk until I realize I don't owe you my life? If so, what you ask will not happen."

"No, this is not what I intend," he signed. "We will speak of the ideals we hold that cause us to believe as we do, and we will try to understand each other, knowing our differences are held deeply within our hearts. Perhaps our cultures are so far apart, we can never be together peaceably. And then, since we cannot agree, we would be free of each other."

"Oh?" she asked softly, then signed, "So now we must *talk* because you will not play a game with me unless we *cheat*? Are you really so confident? Or is it worse? Are you afraid you might lose the game to a girl...and without cheating?"

He shook his head. "I know what you are doing. You are trying to cause me to become angry so I will fight with you and play this game without good rules...rules that should favor you. You, who have never played this game, seem to think you might win against *me*." He emphasized the last word as he pointed to himself. Then, he gave her a haughty smile. "It will not happen."

She shrugged and said in English, "Oh?" then continued in sign, "Personally, I think you are a little too smug about this," saying the word "smug" aloud.

"'Smug'?" he repeated. Then, in sign, asked, "What does this word mean?"

"It means overly sure of yourself…and perhaps when you shouldn't be."

He laughed. "Do not mistake me. If you play against me, I will win."

Suddenly, Laylah saw red. She raised her chin a little and signed, "Indeed, this is what you really think?"

"It is."

"Well, I have this to say: I think you are in need of a good lesson." Again, she spoke these last two words in English.

"What is the 'good lesson' you speak of?"

"It is this. You are arrogant and conceited about this, and I would like the chance to put you in your place."

"Put me in my place? I do not understand."

"It means that I wish to show you the error in your thinking. Just because you are a man does not mean you can easily best me, a woman." She nodded. "While I welcome speaking with you of our deep-seated beliefs as long as you desire, I will agree to this only after we play the game of *Cos-soó*. And, it is to be played without cheating." Then she said in English, "You need, Mr. Eagle Heart, to learn a little humility, and I intend to be your teacher."

"What did you say?"

"I said," she signed, "I think you are greatly conceited and arrogant about this, and since I believe you shouldn't be this way, I intend to bring you to realize you have been too proud. So, I will take your challenge to use this game to free me from you. But, this will be a fair game, and I will insist you promise me you will play with all your cunning and strength of reasoning. And, after I win—which I hope I will—I will give your 'life' back to you by returning all of my winnings to you. Then, I will be free of my obligation to you, and we shall see if we still like each other at the end of the game. Only then will I agree to speak to you of our 'deeply held beliefs.'"

"And, what if you lose?" he asked in sign. "Do not think you will win if I play fairly and without the rules I have spoken of. I am good at this game and have never lost it…not once."

"Never? You have played this before and have utterly ruined another? You, a medicine man—a healer—have done this?"

"Several men have I played," he admitted. "I remind you, this is a man's game, and I am a warrior, too. This is a good way to best an enemy without killing him. And, these are the rules of *Cos-soó*."

"You have never lost? You have won even a man's wife?"

"I have." He raised his chin. "I have always given her back, however, for I do not wish to hear a woman cry."

Cry at the thought of marrying this man? It didn't seem possible.

"Huh! I think you are overly confident, Mr. Eagle Heart," she said aloud, then continued in sign, "If you win, you get it all...even me. Now, shall we play? After all, what have you to lose but everything you own? And, look at what you might gain by your cunning...everything I have and a wife you claim you want, but who will be a burden to you."

He frowned at her, then shook his head as he looked her straight in the eye as though she were an adversary. And, after a short pause, he declared in sign, "Are you seeking to tell me that I would be more of a woman than a man if you should win against me?"

"Never," she signed. "Simply being male, however, does not make you smarter than I am." Her smile at him was deliberately sassy.

He frowned, looked hard at her and signed, "We play."

CHAPTER SEVEN

"*M*r. Eagle Heart," Laylah said, putting her words into sign at the same time. "You have not taken the points for the two claws that are red side up. They count five each, yet you have not counted them by giving me ten sticks. Are you cheating so as to influence the game to favor me?"

He grinned at her. "I do not cheat. There were only two red claws turned up against three black claws on the throw. There are more black claws turned up than red, therefore it counts as nothing."

"Oh? You have to throw a majority of the red turned up in order for it to count?"

"It is so."

"Is it counted this way for the plum stones, the china, the buttons and even the brass tacks?"

"*Áa.*"

"Well, this makes the game interesting, doesn't it?"

His answer was merely a smile. He signed, "Do you not wish to play *Cos-soó* with me, then? Do you desire to talk instead? Perhaps you might tell me why your people insist on owning other people."

She frowned at him. "Behave yourself," she said and signed the meaning of her words. "I have already told you that, if you still wish it, we will talk when we finish the game. Not until then. I am intending to play this game with you, whether you like it or not."

He laughed, causing Laylah to look long at him. He was so very handsome, yet seemed unaware of his masculine beauty. Though they were

---

both clothed for warmth in deerskin robes, his obvious physical strength was in evidence in his wide shoulders tapering to a small waist, thoroughly outlined by the robe. His face shape was more round than oval, his eyes black as night and his cheekbones were high. Full lips and a nose shape that was only slightly aquiline complemented his virile attraction.

His black hair, loose from its braids, fell down his back in waves put there only because his hair had been set in braids for so long. Silver earrings hung from his earlobes, yet no feathers adorned his hair, even though he had worn them in his hair at the fort. Probably their being alone in this tiny shelter accounted for his lack of hair ornamentation. A portion of his hair—similar to bangs—hung down over the center of his forehead, although he often used his fingers to press those bangs upward.

She sighed. This man was the stuff of heroes, the most obvious heroism being his rescue of her. Oddly, he did not wish to have this status, and this fact was why they were playing the desperate game of *Cos-soó*.

"It's your turn," he signed.

"So it is," she responded and picked up the round bowl. She hit the bowl on the ground several times, letting the pieces rise up a few inches and fall down before finally settling it into what could be called her "throw."

She grinned. "Well, what have we here? The large claw is standing up and counts twenty-five, and I have a majority of the smaller crow's claws in red, three in fact, giving me twenty-five more. Four of the plum stones are turned black side up for twenty points. Three of the blue china which count for twelve, three buttons turned up for two each and four brass tacks turned concave for one point each. I win the hand and win your knife. What will you put up next?" She laughed and gave him the equivalent of ninety-six sticks which represented her throw, for, according to the rules, he kept track of her score and she, his.

"Do not be too confident," he signed. "I have never lost to anyone when I play this game."

"So you tell me. Be quiet now and give me your knife," she said, then signed the meaning of the words.

"My knife stays in front of me according to the rules, although it is yours."

"Fair enough. It's your turn."

"I will take my turn, but first I would like to tell you how it is that I have never lost this game. Are you interested?"

"*Áa*," she said in the Blackfoot language.

He grinned. "Then, I will tell you," he signed. "I decide first what throw I want and then determine my next throw will be exactly what I want."

"Hmmm," she murmured. Then, in sign, she said, "That's very interesting. Does it happen as you want every time?"

"*Saa*, not always. But, it occurs often enough that I have never lost a game, and this game is strictly known as a game of chance."

"I will have to think about this. Meanwhile, it is your turn."

****

"I believe we need to call a break."

Laylah glanced up at him, smiled, and, in reaction to her, he felt his heart take wing even while he strove to appear serious and intent. And, he must appear so. After all, she—a woman—was challenging him.

"Certainly we can have a break," she said and signed the words as she spoke. "But, don't forget that your knife, all your robes and your two horses are now mine."

"I do not forget."

She grinned at him again, and Eagle Heart thought he had never seen a more beautiful woman. Indeed, her hair was a mess, being tossed and tangled, and she wore nothing more than an unflattering robe of his own making. Yet, when she smiled, it was as though Sun shone through her eyes. However, there was a drawback to her lure: he had never played the game with anyone who was not only as good as he was, but was, perhaps, a little better.

She had taken to the game as though she had been born to play it. Quickly—and sometimes even before him—she knew the exact amount of the points in a throw with little more than a simple look. Often, she memorized the points. She kept excellent totals, even without the required sticks to keep track of it all, and she laughed while she played as though she were a carefree child. And, with every smile, every giggle, every delightful glance she gave him, he was falling much too deeply in love with her.

And yet, if she won as he wished her to do, he would have to let her leave him, for he did not fool himself into believing she would choose his lifestyle over the one she had been born to. Yes, if she won, it might possibly be the hardest task he would ever have to do to take her back to the fort.

Yet, as the afternoon wore on, and, as they reclined within their small enclosure, they laughed and joked about one thing or another as though they were fast acquaintances and well known to each other. But— and this was hard for him to believe—she was winning most every time she took her turn. It was getting to the point where he had little left to put up against her for betting.

Of course, she often accused him of cheating and trying to throw the game in her favor, but the fact was, he wasn't. He was playing with as much knowledge and cleverness as he possessed.

Perhaps it was male pride as she had suggested, but the idea of being completely bested by a woman was not a moment of pleasure for him. When he threw a game to give her favor, he still knew he was throwing the game.

In this, he was not.

Perhaps he should never have confided to her how he managed to win these games of chance, for she seemed to have perfected the method without any further assistance from him.

"I think you're right," she said in English as well as sign. "It is much darker outside now, and I believe it will soon be time to have our supper."

"Áa," he signed, "and I also have several chores to do, the care of our horses being one of those. I must also ensure this little hut is built well enough to withstand more of the storm, for I believe there are yet many days of the blizzard ahead of us. I would like to see to these tasks before we begin the game again."

"Very well," she said. "I will try to rest while you are gone, especially if we are to be up through the night."

"Do you need to visit and use the outside before I leave?"

She looked away from him and sighed, "I do." But she'd said it without signing the words. He, however, understood what she said anyway.

"Then, let us do this before I leave," he signed and spoke his words in Blackfeet. "But, I have a gift for you. It is one I think you might like very much."

"Really? You have a gift for me?"

"I do," he signed. "Stay where you are," he commanded, as though it had skipped his notice she could not get up and leave. But, he hoped she would like his gift and that it would help her attend to private matters with a little more ease.

Scooting toward the entrance of their shelter, he reached a hand outside and brought in the gift. As he brushed the snow off of it, he realized its purpose would soon alert her to a possibility of more freedom. It was truly a gift from him, for he had whittled this for her the last time he had gone outside.

"Is it a weapon?" she asked with sign. But then, as he watched her glance more carefully at it, he heard her exclaim, "It's a cane! Oh, let me see it and let me try to walk with it!"

Scooting toward her, for the shelter was not tall enough to stand upright, he presented her with the handcrafted object.

"Can I try it?" she asked in sign.

"Áa, please do," he answered.

"I can't stand up, but let me attempt to crawl to the entrance and then see if I can." She tried, but wasn't able to scoot all the way to the shelter's opening, since she was handicapped by an injured leg and a broken arm.

Seeing she had given up, he asked, "Shall I pick you up and bring you outside where you might see if this helps you to walk?"

She nodded.

He scooped her up in his arms then and, ducking through the small entrance, set her on her feet in the snow, allowing her to use the cane to hobble and hop toward the place set aside for the purpose so necessary to every living being.

Snow was falling around them silently as she admonished, "Don't you look!"

She didn't translate her words, but he didn't need the gestures of sign to understand her, and he turned his back to give her a little privacy. Luckily, she was finished quickly.

"I'm done," she said. "Shall I try to walk on my own back to the shelter?"

He turned around and nodded at her, following along behind her. He was happy to see she was, indeed, able to walk, even though her movements were slow and she hobbled on her left foot. But, before she began the ordeal of kneeling down in order to enter the shelter, she turned around and threw herself against him. His arms came around her instinctively. Snow was still falling, the wind whirling the flakes around them, and he closed his eyes, pulling her in closely toward him. And, for a moment, he imagined she was truly his by her own will and that he had the right to hold her.

When she said "Thank you, thank you, Eagle Heart. What am I to do? For I am falling too much in love with you, and I dare not do it," he didn't confess to her how quickly he was learning English and that he was beginning to be able to piece together what she said.

But, when she reached up toward his face and placed a kiss upon his cheek, he couldn't resist turning his head such a small, little distance to turn what was meant as a "thank-you-peck-on-the-cheek" into a kiss, lips to lips.

He was surprised when she kissed him back, placing her good arm around his neck and opening her mouth to his demand. And, he kissed her hungrily, as one lover might do with his sweetheart, as though he had every right to take her gift. However, his body was responding with all the fervor of a man in love. And worse, he could do nothing about it.

Yet, the kiss went on and on until he gathered enough of his wits about him to end the caress. But, he didn't let her go. Instead, he drew her closer into his arms, and, placing his chin on the top of her head, tried in vain to smother the passion he could little control.

At last, with the snow sticking to and wetting her hair, her robe and also his, he said, "*Kitsii ká komimmo,* I love you," secure in the knowledge that she had not yet mastered his language.

****

The night had come early this day and he had found that the darkness lent a disturbing edge to the storm, as though he should fear the Cold Maker. But, he was not alarmed by this being and so had continued his work on his last chore—the shelter—until he was satisfied it would hold up for several more days. Their survival depended on it.

Entering the small hut on his hands and knees, he was greeted with darkness, and he crawled toward the center of their abode where the fire was still lit, though it was low. Throwing a few branches on the embers of the fire, it kicked up and lent a soft light to their tiny space.

Glancing toward the woman he was beginning to know as *Ikamo'si-niistówa-siitámssin* – Steals-my-breath – he was comforted to see this beautiful woman sleeping soundly. It was good, for he recognized her resting as being one of recovery, not one fraught with pain.

It was warm in their shelter, for the embers of the fire, along with the deep snow blanketing the many robes thrown over several large pine boughs (which composed the walls of their tiny lodge), kept the heat within. As she slept, he picked up the stick he had whittled into a cane for her, which had earned him a kiss.

At the top of the cane, he had fashioned a handle in the shape of a rose. A rose: it reminded him of her, so beautiful in its innocence.

Taking out his knife, he began to correct his errors in creating the shape of the flower. And, as he worked over it, his thoughts went back to their talk earlier in the day.

She had courageously told him she loved him, and his heart had rejoiced. But, then she'd gone on to say she wasn't certain her love for him was the kind of affection a woman would hold toward her husband. Yet, only a few moments ago, she had confessed she was falling in love with him, although she didn't know he'd been able to understand her.

And, she had returned his kiss...and had done so with passion. Could this mean she might favor him as a husband?

Perhaps. But, it didn't matter. He was still who he was, which included all his responsibilities to his tribe. Plus, he must free her somehow – without cheating – from her misguided opinion that, because she owed him so greatly, she would marry him whether she wanted to or not.

Her viewpoint about this was one he didn't understand. To him, to all honorable men, it was a duty to assist any woman in trouble. Still, would he have put his life in danger to find her and keep her safe if he hadn't already felt affection for her? Probably. But, the truth was he *was* fascinated with her and the idea of getting to know her better had been, and

111

still was, irresistible. Plus, he cared about what happened to her…and perhaps this is what had motivated him.

Did she care for him in return? Apparently so, but not necessarily as a man who could be her husband.

And he? Of course he loved her. He'd told her the truth when he'd said he had loved her from almost the first moment he'd seen her. But, the love of a man when sincerely felt should not intrude upon her plan for her life. Thus, he had not stepped into her life until he'd had to.

Did this mean he would take her for his wife if she desired it? He would, since he had asked her the question and was honor-bound to take her if she wished it. Plus, he desired her. However, a union between them might possibly become known to his people as the shortest marriage in living memory, for he did not fool himself that she would like or fit into his life, nor he into hers.

Gazing at her over the coals of the fire, he felt like a starving man as he looked upon her beauty. Yet, if not for the storm and her man's inattention to her, he would have already left Fort Union, never to see her again. Though he was here with her now, he had not forgotten his only purpose in traveling to this trading post, and this was to search for and find his beloved brother.

His brother, Chief Chases-the-enemy, had led the thirty-man Blackfoot party to Fort Union, but had not returned home with them. He had disappeared, and even sending scouts out to find him had not produced a single track to be followed. Nor had the reason for his disappearance been known…until now.

Even knowing what he did, Eagle Heart still had no clue as to what was wrong. He felt his brother was still alive, for their mind-to-mind communication continued, but it was now irregular. This meant something was wrong. But, what?

Was it the Crow girl he had stolen? Had her family caught up with him? Had they captured him or wounded him?

Whatever had happened to him, he was deeply missed by many people in his tribe as well as his family, which included a child and a sweet, devoted wife. How would she take the truth of her husband's stealing a young Crow woman and disappearing with her?

Maybe he, Eagle Heart, might never tell her.

As Eagle Heart scooted toward his own sleeping robes—which were set across the fire from Steals-my-breath—he was careful to make as little noise as possible, thus allowing *Ikamo'si-niistówa-siitámssin* to rest.

But, it was not to be. He saw that soon she turned onto her back and stretched, opening her eyes. She looked at him from across the fire, smiled at him, and, in reaction, his heart flipped-flopped within his chest.

He waited a moment before speaking, afraid his hands and fingers might shake as he spoke in the gesture language.

After a moment, she asked, "How are our ponies?"

"They do well," he answered, using sign. "But come, it is dark outside now, and you might be hungry. Would you like to eat a supper with me before we again wage this war called *Cos-soó*?"

She laughed a little, and, as joy filled his heart, he thought there was not a more beautiful sound in all the world than her soft giggles.

"Do you need me to help you to sit up?" he asked in sign, speaking Blackfeet, also.

"*Saa*." She said the Blackfoot word aloud, causing him to smile. She switched to sign and continued, "I would like to try to sit up on my own. I might need your help, but I'd like to try to do it myself, first."

He nodded and watched as she struggled to do the task while clutching the robe around her at the same time.

"Should I look the other way?" he asked.

"*Áa*." Again she spoke the Blackfoot word. Then in sign, "I fear this blanket will fall from me, and then I will be mortified that you shall see me unclothed."

He nodded once more and turned his entire body around to give her privacy. However, he couldn't resist saying, even though he spoke in Blackfeet, "I have already seen you unclothed, and I was greatly taken by your beauty."

"What?" she asked. "What was it you said?"

"Nothing…is…it," he answered in English.

"You have learned those English words?"

"Yes," he spoke again in English.

"You are acquiring more of my language than I am of yours. I will have to take more notice of your words."

113

He shrugged, not knowing what exactly she'd said, but determined he would understand it all, and soon. He wanted to know what she was saying when she spoke without translating her words into sign.

She didn't comment further, causing him to become silent as he listened to the howling wind outside and the crackling of the fire inside. He breathed in deeply and recognized the smoky scent of the fire, but also the sweet aroma of her body which delicately filled the air. He felt almost mesmerized by it and thought he might never forget her fragrant feminine scent.

At last, she said, "I am ready to eat my supper with you. You may turn around now."

Because he was recognizing more and more of her words, he understood what she'd said and changed his position without asking for a translation. As he came to sit before her, he watched her closely, for she held on to the robe covering her body with one hand while she ran the fingers of her other hand through her hair.

He signed, "Shall I comb and braid your hair for you?"

"Comb my hair?" she signed. "Have you brought a comb, then?"

"Yes," he said in English.

"I…I would be pleased if you might do this task for me," she signed, then added in English, "I am certain my hair is a tangled mess."

He grabbed hold of one of his bags and, from within it, withdrew a wooden comb. It was one he'd made himself. Securing it in his hand, he scooted toward her.

"Do not move," he signed. "I will sit behind you and comb your hair from where you are right now."

"Yes," she said. "All right."

As he settled onto his knees behind her, placing his knees and thighs around hers, he realized too late this was not the optimum position for him if he wished her to remain unknowing of his desires. He changed position until he was sitting with his legs crisscrossed, his left leg under his right, as a man should. Then, bringing up his comb, he began the task of carefully taking the knots out of her hair, strand by strand.

"Hmmmm," she murmured. "This feels so good." Using one hand, she signed the words.

He didn't respond since his position didn't allow him to speak in the gesture language and, thus, allow her to understand him. However, bending forward, he couldn't resist pressing a kiss against the back of her neck.

She responded with a shiver, but he wasn't certain if this were a good sign or a bad one. Slowly, and with great pains taken, she turned around until she faced him and said, "Mr. Eagle Heart, I fear your embrace, and I'm sorry I threw myself into your arms earlier this afternoon. I'm sorry, too, that I wanted your kiss and enjoyed it so much that I would like more of your kisses. But, what would come of it if I asked you for more, and if you gave in to me? I can't go with you to your home. You can't return to my home with me as your wife, for I am still engaged to another man. Then, there is my father who would never recognize a marriage between us. And yet, I want you to kiss me again."

This was torture. Utter torture, for he had basically understood what she'd said, only he couldn't give in to her or even let her know he understood. Or could he?

Taking his comb in hand, he turned her gently around so her back was to him again and said in English, "Say...what...you...I...understand."

"What? You spoke in English again?" She looked over her shoulder at him. "Are you telling me you understood what I said?"

He nodded, then said, "Little."

She turned her back on him. "Well," she said, "you already know I love you like I might a brother. No, that's not right. I would never kiss a brother like I kissed you. How is it I love you, I wonder? If not like a brother, then ...?"

"Kiss...want...you. Kisses...many?"

"No, I don't want many kisses. We are alone, and I think further kissing between us might lead to my being unable to return to the fort with my maidenhood still being untouched."

"Kisses...no?"

She nodded. "Kisses. No. How do you say 'kiss' in your language?"

"*Sonai'sskip.*"

"That means 'to kiss'?"

He leaned forward and pressed a kiss against her cheek, saying, "*Sonai'sskip*. Kiss…means. *Sonai'sskip aká*. Kisses many…means."

She turned her face so her lips were only a fraction of an inch away from his and whispered, "One should say it this way: it means 'kiss' or 'many kisses.'"

He was unable to help himself as he pressed his lips to hers. Suddenly, desire flamed to life within him, the spark causing a very physical and male reaction.

But, it couldn't be; he could not act on it. And so, he backed up quickly away from her, and, putting an arm's distance between him and her backside, he repeated, "It means 'kiss' or 'many kisses.'"

"That's right," she said as she looked forward once again.

Using the comb as an object separating them, he stroked the comb through her hair, but her locks were so tangled he eventually set the comb aside and used his fingers to loosen the knots. Working from its length upward, he gradually succeeded in freeing her hair of its tangles.

"Hmmm, that feels good."

He didn't respond back to her, afraid to say anything lest his tongue lead him toward more sensuality between them. It might also cause him to take her in his arms and make love to her. He certainly wanted to. And, then what?

He could take her; he knew he could. She was willing…at least she was right now.

Yet, even knowing this, he couldn't do it. She was still weak from her injuries and of a mindset where she was obligated to do as he insisted. To make love to her now would be taking advantage of his situation over her.

And, he couldn't forget he must not do it without also marrying her. In fact, he couldn't make love to her at all, marriage or not. He had given his word of honor to her to not take her virginity. What he hadn't known then was that she might come to want him, too.

He shut his eyes, as if this action might cleanse his mind of lust. But, it was not to be. Her curvy figure, her delicate scent and even the silky feel of her hair, which he held in his fingers, urged him to take her in his arms and make urgent, wild love to her.

.

At last, he knew he had to put some distance between them. As soon as the tangles were out of her hair, he scooted around her and crawled back to his own place within their tiny abode.

"You are done so soon?" she asked. "How does my hair look? Is it still tangled? How I must look to you, with messy hair and nothing but a robe to put around me."

He shut his eyes, cautioning himself to remain silent.

"Well, please tell me, for I have no one but you for a mirror," she said in English. Then, in sign, she asked, "Do I look all right?"

"I have never known a woman to look more beautiful than you do at this moment. Had I not given you my word of honor, I would now be holding you in my arms."

"I don't understand you."

He smiled at her. "You look beautiful," he signed.

She grinned back at him. "Truly?" she asked with sign. "You're not simply saying this to keep from making an argument with me?"

He shook his head. "You are very beautiful." He'd said this in Blackfeet, but he didn't need to translate it. His admiration for her was almost a physical fascination, and he knew she understood.

He shut his eyes again, attempting to rein in his desire. He didn't speak. He was incapable of it at present.

"You are very quiet," she observed by making the proper signs. "Have I upset you?"

"*Saa*, there is nothing wrong, and I am not upset with you. I am simply lost in my thoughts."

Bringing forward a buckskin bag full of dried meat, he opened it up and took out a piece. Reaching out, he offered her the best of the meat after he had taken some for himself, of course, as Blackfoot etiquette demanded of him. As she took hold of the dried meat from him, her fingers touched his, and he thought he might explode without even having to make love to her.

"Here," he signed, "take the bag from me. I suddenly remember a chore I have forgotten." And, without awaiting her response, he came up onto his knees, crawled to the entrance and, throwing an extra robe around his shoulders, stepped out into the cold air which turned out to be a welcome relief.

With gusto, he threw himself into the chore of cutting up wood, utilizing no more than his knife. Still, it wasn't enough to cool his passion, and he plowed through the snow to where he had made their latrine. There, he spent some time digging into the ground below the snow with his sharp buffalo shoulder blade and dug up enough dirt to throw into the trench-like ditch he'd made.

The night was thick and dark now despite the white fury around him, yet he dared not seek their shelter. And so, he next waded through the deep snow toward where the horses were standing next to the cottonwood trees. There, he brushed them down, preparing them for the night. As he cared for them and petted them, he wondered how he was to get through the night without making love to this woman. But, somehow he had to do it. On this thought, he decided to construct a lean-to structure as a temporary shelter for the horses.

This ended up requiring more work than he had supposed it might, and, feeling a little cooler now that it was done, he took a deep breath. He thought he now might be a little more in control over his body and considered he might be able to keep his hands off of her.

He reminded himself that her feminine gift to a man was not his to take. And, with his passion cooled, he was certain he would be able to keep away from her. Perhaps, he thought, when he entered their shelter again, he might concentrate all his thoughts and efforts on their game of chance.

He was, after all, losing.

CHAPTER EIGHT

"*Ipii vai,* enter," called Gray Falcon to the scratch a visitor was making upon his lodge. He was surprised when his friend, Comes Running, was followed into the tepee by a young, pretty white girl. He recognized this girl, for he had seen her often within the fort; he knew she was the younger sister of Laylah, the beautiful white woman who so fascinated his friend, Eagle Heart.

Gray Falcon had not, however, expected a girl to come visiting—especially a white girl—and he didn't know what to do. How did one act toward such a one, especially since he had never entertained a girl within his lodge, let alone a white girl.

What was she doing here?

But, Comes Running was preparing to leave, and Gray Falcon called out to him, "Are you not staying?"

"I cannot," said Comes Running. "The girl found me and asked me to bring her to you. I have done this. Now, I must go and fortify my own lodge against the storm." And, this said, he left.

Not knowing what to do or how to respond to the girl, Gray Falcon came up onto his knees and gestured toward the opposite side of the lodge, inviting the girl to sit. She sat.

She was a pretty girl, with long, brown hair and eyes that seemed to change color with the clothing she wore. Several days ago, he had seen her wearing blue, and her eyes had appeared to be blue. Now, however, their color was not blue; instead, her eyes were a deep green, like those of a mountain lion's in the dark depths of the night. But, unlike a mountain lion's stare, her look was not that of a predator. Rather, it was fearful. Was she afraid of him?

It seemed unlikely, since it was she who had sought him out, not the opposite. He continued his study of her, though his gaze at her was fast and sharp, pretending he had no interest in why she was here before him — and in the middle of a blizzard.

Her face was shaped like a heart, as though it might mirror the emotions of compassion and love. But, lovely and pretty though she might be, she was much too young for a man's admiration. And, she was white.

At present, she was gazing around the inside of the lodge, and Gray Falcon was well aware when she eventually came to include him in her perusal, but she looked quickly away. At last, however, she said to him using sign language, "I have been asking about you."

He nodded, then gazed at her quickly. He signed, "Me? You have been asking about me? Why?"

"You are the friend of a man called Eagle Heart, are you not?" She had pronounced the name "Eagle Heart" aloud.

"I am," he signed.

"My...my sister is missing. And, according to my sister's fiancé, it is possible Mr. Eagle Heart left the fort to go out into the storm to find her and keep her safe."

He nodded.

"My father can't find her. Her fiancé can't find her. Her fiancé tells the story that she was thrown from her horse and was hurt bad and was in so much pain, Mr. Thomas, who is her fiancé, could not move her. He returned to the fort then and tried to secure a party of men to go back to her, but he could not raise one because the blizzard came upon us so suddenly. It is true he has looked for her since then. But, because of this frightful storm, no one can leave the fort for longer than several minutes at a time, for, as you know, there is danger of a man getting lost in the storm's wrath. Still, my father found he could not sit at home and do nothing. So, he and Thomas left the fort in the middle of this blizzard to try to find her, but they could not do so, and they barely managed to make their way back to the fort again.

120

"Please, I am here because you are Mr. Eagle Heart's friend, and I was wondering if you might know if he went to rescue my sister. Mr. Thomas has said he believes this is so. Please, do you know if this be true? Did your friend go to her? Is he with her?"

Gray Falcon didn't answer at once. After all, didn't the elders teach the boys that a real man must first think through his thoughts before speaking? Yet, he was impressed with the girl. Young though she might be, she had yet mastered the language of sign well enough to make herself understood by him. Still, what could his reply be to her?

No man was under any obligation to tell others what he planned or what he might do, and this included his friend, Eagle Heart. A man made his way in life without needing the assurance of another. It was what made a boy into a man. Still, it seemed only logical that if Eagle Heart had known the woman, Laylah, was in trouble, he would have gone to her.

But, how was he to tell this girl these truths in a way that might set her mind at ease, and without further questioning? At length, and after more thought on the matter, he signed, "I do not know this with certainty, but I suspect my friend might be with her. If he knew she were in trouble, it is to be assumed he went to find her and keep her safe." He didn't add that he believed this because his friend was captivated with the beautiful woman, Laylah; it wasn't necessary to make this known to the girl. One had only to observe the manner in which Eagle Heart glanced at the woman, Laylah, to know he was besotted with her.

"Mr. Falcon, do you really think he might have gone to her?"

"I do. He is not here with me, though this is his lodge. Have no fear. He would not become lost if he went to find her. And, finding her, he would take care of her."

"But, what if he found her too late? What if…what if… What if she needs a doctor to attend to her?"

"What is a 'doctor'?"

"You call them 'medicine men,'" she signed.

"My friend is such a man. If anyone can save her and keep her warm through the storm, it will be my friend. Do not worry."

Gray Falcon meant what he said. He doubted Eagle Heart would have found the woman too late. If his friend intended to find her and save her, so it would be. Further, he knew Eagle Heart would do everything within his power to keep her alive. And, his friend did have this kind of power.

"Please, sir, I thank you for what you have said, but I am very worried about my sister, and I have come here to ask if you might please take me out of here and into the blizzard to look for my sister in case he didn't find her…." She sighed. "I am sorry to bother you, but I must do something. I cannot sleep for worry over her. I cannot eat. I would leave on my own to find her, but I cannot go into the blizzard alone. I know this. I would become lost and most likely would die. But, sir, I have not known what to do to help my sister or who to turn to. Neither my father nor my mother understands how devastated I am at my sister's disappearance.

"And, then I remembered you and Mr. Eagle Heart are friends." She paused and looked once more around the lodge. "Will you help me to find her?"

Gray Falcon was impressed with the girl's compassion for her sister, as well as her courage in seeking him out to gain his assistance. However, he could not give her what she wanted, and so he signed, "I…I have no way of finding him. There will be no tracks for me to follow, and, without tracks that show me where he has gone, I can be of no help to you."

When the young girl began to weep, Gray Falcon despaired. He had no knowledge of what to do for a girl like this. And, not knowing, he remained silent.

"Sir, please. I must try to find her. I know where she last was, for Mr. Thomas could tell us that much. Perhaps you could take me there?"

He didn't answer at once. How did a man speak to a girl like this and bring her to understand the dangers of this kind of storm? How did he tell her they might likely die if they were to leave here and traipse through the storm, not knowing where they were going? How did he answer her pleas without causing her more grief?

He couldn't. And, even though his heart was touched by the girl's love for her sister, he knew he would not be able to help her. At length, he signed, "I dare not take you away from here. Storms like this are best used to settle down in one's lodge and endure through them. If I were to go with you into the blizzard, we might get lost. Death could be the result."

She glanced away from him and asked, "May I stay here, then? I can't go home."

"You are too young to be alone with me. Do your parents know you are here?"

She didn't answer.

"I am sorry, but you cannot stay here," he signed. "Come, I will walk you to the gate of the fort."

"Sir, please don't send me away." She glanced down. But, soon, lifting her glance to his, she signed, "It took me most of the day to summon my courage to come here to speak to you. Please do not make me leave."

He frowned at her. "I cannot keep you here. We are alone, and you are too young to be here with me while no one else is in the lodge with us. Also, you will be missed, and when they look for you and find you here with me, there will be trouble for me, for my people and for you, too, I think. But, I will tell you what I will do. There is perhaps a way I might be able to reach my friend. But, I must be alone to accomplish this, and I must do this in the ancient and proper way. You cannot be here while I reach out to him, for you would distract me. I will take you back to the fort, and you may come here tomorrow to see what I have discovered. Come, I will walk you to the fort's gate so you do not lose your way in the storm."

"No, please don't send me away. Please."

He didn't speak. In truth, he didn't know what to say to this girl or what to do with her, and he had been honest: he was afraid there would be trouble because she was here with him…and alone with him.

"Couldn't I sit in the back of your lodge? I would turn my back on you."

"No," he signed. "It is not right that you should be here with me when no one else is present. I cannot state this too greatly. And, if you wish me to try to contact my friend, I must be alone."

She didn't answer. She simply sat before him and stared down at the buffalo robe she sat upon. At last, she signed, "I am afraid I won't be able to return here tomorrow because I am gone now, and they will be strict with me tomorrow. Please, I won't be any trouble to you."

Gray Falcon sighed. "What you do not understand is that you are already in trouble," he signed. "After a certain age, no young girl may be alone with a boy of my age. What is your age?"

"I am fourteen."

"No, you cannot stay here. You are old enough that you could be thought of in an ill manner if you stay here with me. I do not wish this for you. I do not wish this for me."

She sat still for a moment, then began to cry.

He sighed. What was he to do? Eventually, he gained her attention and signed, "Stay here. I will see if one of the women in our band will allow you to stay with her in her lodge."

"You would do this for me?"

"I will try. I may not be successful." He didn't look at her to see what her response might be. Instead, he rose and trod toward the entryway; leaning over, he prepared to crawl out of his lodge. But, he didn't.

Looking back at the girl, he signed, "Did you bring any of your things with you? Extra clothing? Food?"

She shook her head. "I had to run away quickly."

He didn't answer. Instead, he pulled back the flap to his tepee and stepped out into the snowy blizzard.

****

To say Gray Falcon was bewildered was an understatement. How had the girl come to know he was Eagle Heart's friend? He had noticed the girl when he had come into the fort, it's true, for she was pretty. But, he hadn't paused to gaze at her with any interest. She was simply a young white girl.

And, she was much too young for him to be interested in as a man might be with a woman, although he realized this might not always be so. He was older than she, but not too much older. He was nineteen winters, and, though their ages separated them now, there might yet come a time when they could meet as adults. But, that time was not now.

As he stepped toward his uncle's tepee, he hoped his uncle's wife would be in residence there. He wished to send the young girl there, into his auntie's care.

If he could accomplish this, he would be able to return to his own lodge, there to pray and to meditate. If he were lucky, he might be able to reach out and speak to his friend. So far in his young life, Gray Falcon did not possess this skill, although he knew his friend could talk to and understand all kinds of animals and plants, as well as people.

Truth was, he doubted his skill. Perhaps because he was still considered a young man, he had not yet gained the ability to speak mind-to-mind with another at a distance. But, he would try to contact his friend.

Because of the wind and the whirling circles of white fury, it was not easy to locate his uncle's home. Still, he knew his uncle's lodge was near, so he plodded onward and was pleasantly surprised when the lodge loomed up before him.

He scratched on the tepee's entrance flap and was summoned to enter, which he did at once.

As he straightened up, he called out, "*Oki,* greetings, hello."

"*Oki, isahkímao,* Hello, nephew. *Tsá anistápssíwaatsiksi?* What is it? Please, sit. Are you hungry?"

"*Saa,* I am not hungry, but I would enjoy smoking with you, for I must ask your advice on a matter."

At once, his uncle brought out his pipe and tobacco. He asked, "Do you wish to counsel with me?"

"*Saa,* I do not. At least, not at present. I have come to ask for your wife's assistance with a problem I am presented with."

"My wife?"

"*Áa,* I have need of her aid and your advice, *Aaáhs,* Uncle. There is a white girl in my lodge."

"A white girl?"

"*Áa,* yes. Her sister has gone missing, and she wants me to take her out into the storm to find her sister. As you know, I cannot. Her sister is the pretty woman who sometimes works at the trading counter."

"The same woman who has so enchanted your friend, Eagle Heart?"

"*Áa.* It is said by a white man that perhaps my friend left the fort to go and assist this woman, for he became aware she was lost in the storm."

"If he knew, it is to be assumed he is with her now."

"I have told the white girl this, but she is so upset, it does not help to calm her. She tells me she cannot sleep, nor eat, and she has snuck away from her home to come here and find me because she remembers that I am friend to Eagle Heart. I have asked her to return to her home, but she is afraid that if she leaves now she will not be able to come back here tomorrow to seek me out and discover if I have been able to communicate to my friend."

125

"There will be trouble if she does not go home."

"I know this," said Gray Falcon. "But, she will not go. I have come here to see if this girl can stay with you, for I cannot convince her to return to her home. And, I will not force her to go there."

"She may stay with us for as long as she wishes," spoke Gray Falcon's *iksísst,* his auntie. "Poor girl. Do not hesitate to bring her. Is she hungry?"

"She might be. She brought no food with her, nor clothing."

"We will help her. Bring her to us, and we will do what we can to welcome her."

"I am thankful to you for your help. I will go to my own lodge and bring her here."

Gray Falcon sat for several more moments with his uncle and auntie, enjoying a smoke. But, soon he knew he had to return to his own lodge, and, rising up, he again braved the storm as he trudged toward his lodge. He would try to help the white girl, but, even ensuring she spent the night with his auntie, he was afraid the stir she might cause would be great.

****

Laylah laughed. She should be tired; she knew she should be. But, despite the temporary disability of her right leg and arm, she was not weary at all. She was enjoying herself too much in this game of *Cos-soó*...and in teasing Eagle Heart.

She signed, "I believe, sir, that you have lost this game."

"I have not lost. Not yet. I still have my moccasins in my possession."

"And your breechcloth."

He frowned at her. "The breechcloth remains upon me. It is not an item a man will make part of his bet."

Laylah smiled, quickly fluttering her eyelashes at him as though in innocence. "But, sir," she signed, "I thought you said the game isn't over until you lose everything. Does this not include your breechcloth? It is, after all, a piece of clothing." She giggled a little.

"Do not speak of this as though you are a babe." He signed the words and added another frown at her, which made her smile. He continued and signed, "Like a child, you play with fire."

"I don't know what you mean by 'playing with fire,'" she returned, using her hands to sign the words.

He shook his head. "Do not do this. I am a man full grown with manly desires. Know this: I will not stand naked in front of you and remove my breechcloth."

"I did not ask you to do that."

"Yes, you did," he signed. "We are talking all around the matter, and you are testing my endurance. Do not taunt me with the vow I have made to return you to your home with your womanly innocence untouched. I will not break my pledge to you."

"I am not asking you to break it. It is simply your turn, sir. What do you bet now?"

"My moccasins."

"And your breechcloth?"

He shook his head and laughed a little. "Do not think I am too embarrassed to do it," he signed. "I am not. What you do not understand is I want to make love to you. Do you think I do not know what lies beneath the robe you wear? And, if I become naked, what do you think might happen?"

"I'm sure I don't know."

"I am sure you do. Let me say this to you in a way you cannot fail to understand: if we ever marry, then I will stand before you naked. It will not occur before then, if it ever does happen. Now, stop this. Your words keep me from concentrating on the game."

"Do you think I do not know this?"

He laughed and shook his head once more. Bending over, he took his moccasins off his feet and held them up for her to inspect. Then, he signed, "I bet these moccasins, even though they mean very much to me, for they were made for me by my sister's hand."

"No wonder they are so prettily beaded."

"I have two sisters, and the one who makes these is the youngest. She is the best in our tribe at sewing footwear. Many people have asked her to make moccasins for them, and they give her many gifts for her work. Now, be still while I take my turn."

"Yes, sir." She smiled.

He took hold of the bowl and struck it on the ground several times, the pieces jumping up and scooting around the bowl. At last, he let it come to rest.

Laylah counted up his points quickly and easily. "This is a good roll, sir," she signed. "It will be a difficult one for me to beat, for the big crow's claw is standing up. In all, I count seventy-five points. Do you agree?"

He nodded. "And, now it is your turn. If you win this roll, you will take the game and will have in your possession all that I own...even my best buffalo pony and the robe that is around my shoulders."

"But, not your breechcloth?"

He shook his head. "We have already talked about this. Do you take your turn now?"

"But, I did not agree that I can win while you retain your breechcloth."

"It matters not. The breechcloth remains where it is."

"Oh, very well." She grabbed hold of the bowl with perhaps too much vigor.

He grinned at her. "You are not a very good loser."

"I am, too, a good loser. I'm letting you retain your breechcloth, am I not? Now, hush. I'm taking my turn for the win."

He smiled at her, but remained silent. And, Laylah, deciding what she wished her throw to be, struck the bowl on the ground several times, watching as the pieces jumped up and danced within its round surface. With a few more thumps on the ground, she let the bowl lie still and looked within it to count up the points of her throw.

"Oh, my. Do you see what I do?"

"Áa, I do." He glanced up and smiled at her. "The large claw is up, counting twenty-five. All four small claws are red-side up, making sixteen. Three of the plum stones are black-side up, giving you twelve. None of the china are lying blue-side up, so this counts as nothing. But all five trade buttons are up, giving you ten. You only need three points to win."

"And ...?"

"Three of the brass tacks are curved inward, which counts for three. You win, but by only one."

He laughed at the same time she did.

128

"I now have nothing," he signed. "It is as though I have lost my life, for I must now start my life over if you will have no pity on me and return my possessions to me. I will have to go to all my relatives and beg them to clothe me and feed me."

"Oh, that is true. I forgot. I won all the food, too, did I not?"

"So, you have."

"Well, hand me all of your things."

"You have only to reach out and take it all from me."

"But, you know I will not," she signed, then said aloud in English, "I have come to love you, Mr. Eagle Heart. Gladly, I will give it all back to you."

"What did you say?"

She grinned at him and signed, "I give all this back to you, Mr. Eagle Heart. And now, I believe we are even, are we not? You saved my life and now I have saved yours."

"Áa, it is so. We are, as you say, even. Do you feel joyous in your win?"

"No," she signed. "I still think you should have given me your breechcloth."

"Then, marry me and it shall be yours."

Was he teasing her? She glanced up into his dark, dark eyes. No, he wasn't bantering with her. He looked to be completely serious.

At last she answered, signing, "You know I cannot marry you. I am still engaged to another and you…" She sighed before she continued and signed, "Why should you have to decide between me or your people? Or worse, losing your power because you married me? If this were to happen to you, I do not know if I could ever forgive myself."

"It is possible none of these things will happen. I know I have said this to you, but I have been thinking much about this, and it is now my belief that my people might come to love you, and, also, if we marry, I do not believe I will lose my power, for I will not have used you in a bad way."

"I…" She glanced away from him.

"Think of what you have to win." He paused, and, when she looked back at him, he signed, "My breechcloth would be the beginning of our life together." His eyes twinkled as he smiled yet again. But, she did not return the gesture.

"Mr. Eagle Heart, if I were Blackfeet or even a member of any other Indian tribe, it would be different. I would, indeed, marry you. But, I am not, and so I cannot. I have been raised differently than you. I could not easily leave my society, nor my family. Please try to understand."

He didn't answer, and his attention seemed to shift suddenly inward. At last, he signed, "I do understand. Now, I think the sun is rising in the east. I must investigate if the snowstorm blew itself out in the night and we, who have been playing this game all night, did not notice. You need to sleep. I must determine how many more days of the blizzard are left. There will be signs to tell this. Perhaps, if you wish it, we can talk more after we have both rested. For now, I must ensure all is well with our ponies and with this little shelter. You...sleep."

She nodded and watched him wistfully as he crawled toward the tiny entrance to their shelter. Quickly, he pulled on his leggings and shirt, donned his extra buffalo robe, grabbed hold of his buffalo hat, and, without even looking back at her, he left.

She sat still for several minutes. Was she doing right? It seemed she was. After all, she couldn't live in his world, and he couldn't betray his people by leaving them to live with her at the fort.

Yet, if this were really the way the future must unfold, why did the mere thought of it make her so sad? Shouldn't she be elated to be going home soon? Seeing her family again? Thomas?

Thomas... She had forgotten about Thomas. What was she going to do about him? Could she still marry him?

Perhaps. After all, she had once loved him. Couldn't she do so again?

Yes, she could. Indeed, if she were to fulfill her duty to her family and unite their family fortunes, she must. After all, it wasn't so bad. When looked upon in a logical manner, what had happened between her and Eagle Heart was little more than several days set outside the normal passage of time. They had been enchanting days, and, with the prejudice of the rest of the world at bay, she had fallen in love with him. But, would such a love last for a lifetime? Especially when they shared very little else in common?

No, it would not. She reminded herself that she'd had an astonishing and beautiful experience with Eagle Heart, and she'd been treated to a world she hadn't known existed.

But, it was not *her* world. And her world was not *his*. Indeed, there was no friendly place where Eagle Heart and she might live. At least there was not one she knew of.

Her people, who considered the Indian people only slightly better than wild animals, would never accept him. And, his people might not like, and might even despise, her.

But, these thoughts were not pleasant, and she did not wish to present a sad countenance to Eagle Heart. Forever, she would remember him and her love for him. And so, naturally, she wished he might have good memories of her, also.

She tried to make herself smile.

Yet, strangely, no amount of happy thoughts brought her a sense of joy. What was it she had once told Eagle Heart? That she had changed? That, regardless of what she decided, happiness would never be hers?

Was she destined, then, to live a life much like that of her grandmother, to never be able to grasp true happiness? Sadly, this might possibly be so.

CHAPTER NINE

The warm Snow Eater, a chinook, blew in a few days after they had finished their game of *Cos-soó*. It had melted the snow so quickly, it had appeared as though the shallow creek at the bottom of the coulee might easily become a river that would flood this valley.

But, Eagle Heart would not let the rising river harm them, although the water from the melting snow might sweep away their tiny home some time during the day. However, by then they would be gone; today was the day when he would take Steals-my-breath back to the fort.

Although it was true the Windmaker had given them another few days of fast winds and heavy snowfall, today was different. The warm winds of the Snow Eater would ensure the snow would soon be gone. And, he wished to find the party of white men—who would surely be riding about looking for her—before they found him.

As he felt the warmth of the wind caressing his cheeks, he thought back to the early morning when he had awakened to hear the cold, northerly winds being silenced by the calmer, warmer gales from the south. Reluctantly, he had realized today was to be the day he would return Steals-my-breath to her home.

He had awakened her then, and had told her he would be escorting her back to the fort today. He had said no more than this before he had left their shelter to sing his praises to Sun, the Creator. He had bathed then and had dressed appropriately for the day, donning his white leggings, his white moccasins and his white shirt.

But, though he might like to spend more moments here, praying, the time had come at last to retrace his steps to their tiny shelter. Turning away from the sight of the sun arising in the eastern sky, he paced silently back to their little hut. Seeing it, he was reminded of his joy in being with Steals-my-breath and recalled watching her hobble into and out of their shelter. Always, she had used the cane he'd made for her, it seeming to have become a symbol of her independence from him. And, he was glad of it in many ways, but not in others.

The cane had allowed her to make discreet and "necessary" visits to the outside without his help. And, although he had always stood watch over her when she was at her bath, he did not mention this to her, hoping she would thoroughly enjoy her freedom. Indeed, this kind of individuality was very important for her so she could make the wisest decisions about her future, even if this meant she might decide to leave him.

Over these last few days, they had spoken only a little of their separately held beliefs. Instead, they had played different and simpler games with one another — ones that did not cause a person to become utterly ruined. And, when evening had come, they had related stories to one another of the legends they each remembered from their youth. He had also learned her language a little better when she had told her stories, and, although he couldn't speak English well, he could now understand most of what she said.

He had not told her this, and there was a reason for it: he had wanted her to speak what was on her mind without realizing he knew what she was saying. In this way, he had come to know she loved him, but not enough to cause her to want to leave her people and marry him.

And, he had not, and would not, press her. He would let her go. He had promised her this. But, he doubted he would ever forget her. Indeed, he might love her forever.

Did this mean he would never marry another? No, Blackfoot men were expected to marry, to have children and raise a family. He would marry, and possibly might even come to love another. But, he would never forget She-steals-my-breath. Always, she would have a place of honor within his heart.

At present, it was still early in the morning. As he crawled into their tiny shelter and inched inside it, he looked upon this beautiful woman whom he had come to love with all his heart. Gone were his considerations about the society he belonged to— the medicine men—and whether or not they might accept her as his wife. In truth, he didn't care whether they approved or not. He loved her. This was all that mattered to him.

Gone, also, was his fear he might lose his power. This would not happen for the good reason that he had not coerced this woman into lying with him. Instead, he had loved her while keeping his distance.

As he settled into their abode, he asked, "Did you bathe while I was gone?"

"I did," she answered with sign. "Will you help me to put on my dress? I am sorry to have to ask this of you, but I cannot do it on my own because my arm is still broken, and I cannot put it through the dress's armhole."

He nodded, knowing this would be a form of torture for him, because, though he had kept his distance from her for these several days, the truth was he wanted to take her in his arms and make her his woman. For him, it was a physical problem as well as a spiritual one.

Yet, he helped her to dress, since her arm was still wrapped up tightly and he was well aware this made it difficult for her to clothe herself without someone else's aid. At least he had finished it without giving reign to his lust.

After she was fully dressed and sat before him, beautiful in her green and fancy white-man's dress, he wished he didn't know there was little beneath her dress, since many of her underthings had become useful rags these last few days. He thought back to that first night, when he'd had to cut her underclothes away from her to save her. But, now he wished she wore the delicate attire, for they added another layer of protection against what he wished to experience with her.

As he gazed at her now, he saw her sitting up straight, for, although he knew her right leg was still not fully healed, it had mended well enough to allow her to sit with her legs to the side. He was glad to see it.

And, though he was pleased to know she was healing well, even this—simply gazing at her—was torturous, since he wished to marry her and take her to his home. Yet, he would not force her to go with him. She would come with him willingly or not at all.

At last, he knew they were prepared to leave, and he asked in sign, "Are you ready to go?"

She nodded, and, as she came up onto her knees, he watched her closely, seeing the wetness in her eyes as she looked around their little abode. Then, speaking in her own tongue, she said, "You may not understand this, Mr. Eagle Heart, but I am going to miss this place. And, I am going to miss you most terribly, I think. Indeed, I don't know how I am going to live my life without you. But, I must try to do it, for I cannot live in your world. And, you cannot come to live in mine."

He swallowed. "Me...marry you...then you no...leave," he said in English.

"You know I can't do that," she signed. "I might ruin your life, and I cannot do this to you. Besides, where would we live? We would be welcome nowhere, and a woman needs a place to live. You know this. I know this." Then, in English, she continued, "But, don't think I won't miss you, because I will." She didn't look at him. And, he didn't say a word in response, at least not at first.

After a moment, she looked up at him, and he signed, "You do not have to go. You can stay with me. I will say this once more, and then, if your answer is still 'no', I will not again ask you this before we go to meet your people. So I repeat my question to you now. Will you be my wife?"

"Oh, Eagle Heart, please don't ask this of me. You know I cannot. I am still engaged to another man. You know this. You have even told me you cannot marry me unless I end it by throwing him away. I have not done this."

"If you come with me, he will understand it is ended. It is as good as throwing him away."

He watched her closely as she bit her lip. And, as he looked at her lips, he recalled again the sweetness of her breath and how soft her lips had felt against his own. The desire to touch her was almost more than he could tolerate.

Yet, he would endure the physical pain and ignore the urge to take her in his arms and hold her. He had given his word to her to keep her innocent. He would not cross that line unless she agreed to cross it.

"And, what would we do about my family?" she was signing. "My mother? My father? My sister? I would never see them again. And, what if your people do not accept me? Would you then have to divorce me and bring me back? Or would we have to live in the wilderness, away from everybody? And, if we had to live away from others and if we had children, who would our children's companions be?"

He didn't speak at once. He tried to find his tongue. He couldn't, for the loss he was experiencing, even while she stood before him, was almost more than he could bear. Indeed, when he might have answered her back, he did not speak at all. She had taken his breath away again, but this time in a different way.

He signed, "I do not know the answers to your questions. But, I understand you cannot marry me." He paused. Then, in sign, asked, "And now, are you ready to go?"

She hesitated until, at last, she responded in the same language of gestures, "I am." She looked away from him.

"Follow me," he said simply with his hands as he turned away and, bending, scooted out of their shelter. Soon, she joined him in front of their little abode, and he watched her as she gazed outward and toward the creek which was now overflowing its banks. There was still snow on the ground, making the world appear white, but here and there the green grass surrounding the creek peeked through the ice that covered it. Soon, their tiny shelter would give way to the flooding waters.

He had already brought their ponies to stand in front of the tiny lodging, and he watched as she reached out toward her gray quarter horse, petting its neck. He asked in English, "You...mount pony...wish it?"

"Thank you for asking, Eagle Heart," she answered in English. "But, I do not want to ride. It might be hard for me to do, considering my arm. But, I have my cane, and I think I can manage to walk all the way to the fort. Besides, I believe I need the exercise."

He nodded and handed the reins of her mount to her as he asked, again in sign, "Do you want to lead her?"

"Áa, I do. Mr. Eagle Heart, I see you have tied the robe I was wearing to my pony. But, it is yours, not mine. Are you meaning to give it to me?"

"I am," he signed. "It is no longer mine. It is yours to keep. Perhaps when you look at it, you might think of me."

He watched her carefully as a tear came to her eye. She bit her lip.

He didn't mention that his blanket now contained her scent, also, and he would not be able to wear it without thinking of her and perhaps experiencing again the feeling of his loss.

He signed, "I cannot keep it because every time I would see it, I would think of you."

"*Iniiyi'taki,* I am grateful for this gift."

He smiled as he listened to her speaking a little of his language. Then, he signed, "It is good you should have it. We will now leave and will set our path out of the coulee by the north entrance, because it will be an easier climb for us. It is a little farther from the fort, but it will be less difficult for you."

And, with little more to be said, he set a slow pace toward the northern section of the coulee.

Soon, they stood upon the broad prairie, and, turning, he set their pace to the south toward the fort. They didn't speak to one another. There was little to say that hadn't already been said. And, for days now, they had known the moment would come when they would have to part. It wouldn't be easy for him, and he suspected it might be the same for her. But, it had to be done.

Soon, he saw a party of riders in the distance. They were coming toward them. Although they were still a good distance away, Eagle Heart's eyesight was good enough to pick out her father from the rest; he was in the lead. Curly Mustache, the man she was to marry, was probably with them, also. At present, they all looked like tiny dots on the horizon, but soon, he would have to confront them.

What would be his welcome? Would they greet him heartily for saving this woman's life? Or would they wonder what he had done with her and to her in all these days? Would they want to kill him for what they believed might have happened between them?

Astutely, he realized it would be the latter, and he steeled himself to face what might be the white man's anger, instead of his gratitude.

Looking over his shoulder, he signed to Steals-my-breath, "They come."

"Where? I don't see anyone."

He pointed.

"I still don't see them."

137

He shrugged. "Let us continue our path toward them. You will come to behold them soon enough."

It took little time for the two parties to meet, for the white traders had set their horses to running toward them. Soon, Eagle Heart was able to distinguish more faces, and he was glad to notice Gray Falcon was riding amongst the white men. If there were to be a fight this day, Gray Falcon would help to even up the odds.

Though it was unnecessary, the white men rode furiously toward them, and, when only a short distance away from himself and Steals-my-breath, they reined in, their sudden stop kicking up dust and rocks and creating a dusty cloud around them. They then formed a line of defense against him.

But, he did not flinch back from them. It was, after all, what he had expected, and he stood straight, facing forward. If he were to meet his death here today, he realized he would do so bravely and with no regret, for he had not done wrong by this woman.

He was glad, however, to see she didn't rush forward to meet her people. Instead, she stood by him, looking outward, her countenance sad and the tears still upon her cheeks.

But, because she had already made her choice, there was only one action for him to take, and he gestured her forward, saying in Blackfeet, "*Itapoo!* Go!" Then, he continued in his own language, saying, "We have spoken of this time when you would have to leave me, and we knew it would be hard for us to do. But, as you go, do not think I love you less. From now until the sun no longer shines, I will love you. Now, go. *Itapoo.*"

She signed, "I wish I had learned your language as well as you have come to know mine. What did you say?"

He simply shook his head.

"Goodbye, Mr. Eagle Heart. Always, I will remember you. Always, you will be in my heart."

At her words, he almost wept. But, now was not the place to show weakness. Big tough men were watching them.

He saw when Gray Falcon separated himself from their throng and set his pony to walking toward them. He was followed by a young girl who was also pacing toward them and leading her mount behind her. In addition, there was an older woman following along behind her. The more mature woman—perhaps Steals-my-breath's mother—rode a small mustang. The younger girl Eagle Heart recognized as Steals-my-breath's sister.

He nodded to Gray Falcon, including the young girl and the older woman in his perusal. Quick though his glance was at the other woman, he realized she, indeed, had to be Steals-my-breath's mother, for the woman was still pretty and looked very much like her daughter.

The sister seemed to be the only person capable of movement as well as speech, and, as she dropped the reins of her pony, she ran forward to hug Steals-my-breath, crying out, "I have been so worried about you, Laylah. Do not ever do this again. Mr. Gray Falcon convinced the others to let me and our mother accompany the men here, and it is he who tried to find out what had happened to you, but he was unable to reach Mr. Eagle Heart with silent words. I have cried until I am almost sick because of my tears."

"I am sorry, Millie. But, I was well taken care of, as you can see. Hello, Mother."

"Hello, Laylah. I have cried very much, too, and I am very happy to see you." Steals-my-breath's mother was still sitting atop her mount when she glanced down upon *him* and said, "Thank you, Mr. Eagle Heart, for saving my daughter. I will be forever in your debt because of what you have done for her."

Eagle Heart nodded briefly, quickly, glad that Steals-my-breath had explained to him—and he understood now—what it meant to be in a person's debt.

Amelia McIntosh glanced up at Eagle Heart, also, and, catching his eye, said, "Thank you," before she gently placed her arm around Steals-my-breath's waist and stepped toward the waiting line of men, escorting her sister with her. Her mother followed, still astride the mustang.

As Eagle Heart watched Steals-my-breath walk away from him, he felt his pulse beating hard against his chest and neck. It wasn't, however, from fear. It was grief. He would miss She-steals-my-breath, perhaps more than he had ever reckoned.

He watched as the trader, Robert McIntosh, dismounted and took his daughter in his arms. The older man hugged his daughter heartily and placed kisses against her head and her cheek. Eagle Heart heard him ask Steals-my-breath, "Was he kind to you?"

"Yes, Father. He saved my life. Without him coming to me, I would not be standing here with you. I tell this to you, truly. I would have died there but for him."

"But, did he take your…"

"He did nothing to me, Father. He saved me, fed me and helped me to heal. That is all. He is an honorable man, and we owe him much."

Only then did the elder McIntosh, her father, glance over toward *him.*

Eagle Heart met the unspoken question and the threat without flinching. But, it was understood between them: if his daughter was not as pure as she had been before her accident, McIntosh would seek him out and kill him.

Eagle Heart didn't acknowledge the man in any way. But, he did meet the trader's stare without cowering away from him.

Steals-my-breath's sister looked over her shoulder toward Gray Falcon and signed, "Thank you for assisting me."

Gray Falcon answered her by a single nod. The younger sister stepped up to the waiting line of men, with her own and her sister's ponies in tow behind her. Within little time, Steals-my-breath, her sister and their mother passed into and through the several lines of the white men.

"Do you think we have a fight ahead of us?" asked Eagle Heart of Gray Falcon, using signs.

Gray Falcon answered by a quick shake of his head. "They are happy she is alive. But, they have great distrust of you, my friend. I fear they do not know what to do about you. Do they harm you for being alone with her for these many days? Or do they stand back and do nothing because they know she would not be here were it not for you?"

"Áa, I can see their doubt, as well as their displeasure, for both of their mindsets appear to me as though they are as solid as the earth beneath my feet. I suggest we do not move, we do not go forward. We do not retreat from them, either."

"Whatever happens, I will stand here with you, my brother."

"I know. There may yet come a time when I will do the same for you, for we have many trails ahead of us."

Gray Falcon answered by a quick nod.

Eagle Heart watched as Curly Mustache, the coward and weakling who was the man Steals-my-breath was to marry, dismounted and stepped toward Steals-my-breath and her father. As Eagle Heart looked on, he felt sick to his stomach, seeing the yellow-bellied man give this fine, beautiful woman a hug and a kiss.

It was at this moment the desire to leave this place blossomed big within his heart. But, he would not back down; he would stand his ground until the white men left.

Steals-my-breath's father separated himself out from the others and trod toward Eagle Heart, the sound of his boots loud over the solid ground. Briefly, he stopped directly in front of him. His eyes, as he squinted, were a green color, much like his daughter's. But, there the resemblance ended. The man's hair was brown, without Steals-my-breath's characteristic golden color; it was also long and slightly unkempt. He gazed slightly upward, for Eagle Heart was the taller of the two.

His voice was hard and angry as he spit out, "If I find you have done harm to her, I will hunt you down and kill you. You know what I mean by harm, Injun?"

Eagle Heart did. Yet, he said nothing and did nothing but meet McIntosh's angry stare with as little emotion as possible. He didn't nod to McIntosh. He didn't acknowledge the man in any way. Nor did he back away from him. Confronting the man and his threat face-to-face and eye-to-eye was enough.

"Damned Injun ya are, I say." And, being the first to look away, McIntosh spit over the ground. Bending over, he stomped on the place where he had spit and said, "This is what I'll do to you if you have harmed her."

Eagle Heart didn't speak nor did he withdraw his stare at the man. He met the threat issued to him with a man-to-man glare, doing nothing, saying nothing. At last, Steals-my-breath's father turned on one foot and stomped back to the others.

The entire party left then. Eagle Heart watched Steals-my-breath go. Once, before they had all moved too far away, she looked over her shoulder and glanced back at him. It was easy for him to recognize the conflicting emotions reflected in her eyes: happiness to be amongst her own people, yes. But, also, there within her gaze was a great sadness which he well understood. They might never see each other again.

And, yet, they loved one another. Indeed, he could see now their separate futures might be filled with loss and grief, unless some happening caused them to reach out for one another again.

His eyes teared, yet he didn't look away; he would face his grief as a man. He was still young, he had a future ahead of him, but he also knew the time yet to come would never be as bright as it might have been were he to have been able to call Steals-my-breath "*nit-o-ké-man,* my woman."

But, he was not without understanding her or why she had made this choice. In many ways, it had to be.

CHAPTER TEN

"*Why* does *he* never come to the trading room anymore?"

Laylah's sister, Amelia, gave her a look of great sympathy as Amelia said, "I have seen the tortured looks you give the door of this room, Laylah, whenever Mr. Eagle Heart's friend, Gray Falcon, comes here to trade. So, I asked Gray Falcon about Mr. Eagle Heart and why he never appears here to visit with you. He told me his friend, Mr. Eagle Heart, is not currently in residence at the fort. He left this part of the country on the same day when you returned here. He has gone away to try to locate his brother and rescue him, if needed. This appears to be the only reason Mr. Eagle Heart came to our post originally: to find his brother and escort him home.

"Gray Falcon has also told me," Amelia continued, "that both he and Mr. Eagle Heart will work together to find Chief Chases-the-enemy. As soon as Gray Falcon concludes his business with Fort Union, he says he will leave here to meet up with Mr. Eagle Heart, for his friend will be blazing a trail Gray Falcon can follow."

"Mr. Gray Falcon said all that?"

"Yes, he did."

"Well, I am glad to see you have become a friend of Mr. Gray Falcon, for I believe he is a good and honorable man. But, what does it mean to blaze a trail?"

"I am sure I don't know."

"I suppose it might be a way of finding a trail in the wilderness."

Amelia shrugged. "You miss him, don't you?"

Laylah shut her eyes against the tears that too quickly sprang into her eyes. It had been a week since she and Eagle Heart had parted. And, in all this time, she had missed him. In truth, so greatly did she miss him, she was beginning to wonder if she had made a terrible mistake.

Was her life to be one of heartache without Eagle Heart? Surely not, and yet, she couldn't stop thinking of him and wishing she could be with him again, talk to him again.

She squared back her shoulders, realizing she had best ignore this brief glimpse into what the future might hold if she had, indeed, made an error in judgment. Surely, she had done the right thing. Hadn't she?

After all, she was acting as she was expected to do and as she was honor-bound to do. Truly, how could she have done anything else but leave Eagle Heart?

She couldn't have and still kept hold of her principles.

Yet, she was finding herself once again making excuses as to why she couldn't marry Thomas right away. And, every day her father reminded her of her duty to the family to marry him, as though she had forgotten it.

What her father didn't know was this: if she hadn't realized her responsibility to him, to her family and to Thomas, and, if she hadn't observed Eagle Heart's good example by keeping his word, she might not have returned at all. She had been that close to running away.

Yet, her father had taken to speaking harsh words to her, as though only his anger might ensure the marriage between Thomas and her.

"Blast you, girl! 'Tis your duty to me and your family to unite our two families. Since your engagement, it has always been you dragging your feet, not Thomas. Well, it is going to stop, and it's going to stop now!"

Laylah drew in a deep breath. In truth, she understood what was expected of her and her obligation to her family. What was hard for her to come to grips with, however, was the gradual realization that she would never experience with Thomas the full expression of love she felt for Eagle Heart.

Indeed, when she went to sleep at night, she brought to mind Eagle Heart's image, for it helped to calm her. Often, in thought she heard again his quiet humor; she even listened for his laughter on the wind. And, sometimes, she recalled the feel of his kiss.

So much did she miss him, she had even tried to make contact with him via the mind-to-mind talk. But, it was not to be. If he heard her, he never answered.

Meanwhile, Gray Falcon had come into the trading room, and, as he stepped up to the counter, he glanced quickly at Amelia before looking away from her. He signed, "I have news."

"You do?" answered Millie with sign.

"My friend has sent word to me that he has found a clue about where his brother has gone. Soon, he will leave here to mark a trail that I will follow as soon as I am finished with the trading I must do."

"Then, he hasn't left yet?" asked Laylah with sign.

"He has gone from here, yes, for this fort is a dangerous place for him, as it is for all our people. Not only are we surrounded by our enemies, the Crow and the Assiniboine, but now the white man has become an enemy, too. But, my friend is not yet far away."

"Oh?" asked Laylah. "Do you know where he is, then?"

"I do not," answered Gray Falcon.

"Can you contact him using the mind-to-mind speak?" asked Laylah with signs.

"I cannot. I do not have this power. Not yet. How do you know of the mind talk?" he asked.

"It is how Mr. Eagle Heart found me in the snowstorm. I heard his voice and answered him. We talked, then. But, we have not been able to do it again." Looking down, she noticed her hands were shaking.

"He has blocked his mind from this post," signed Gray Falcon.

"What do you mean?"

"This post holds some good memories for him, yes, but some bad ones, also. And, if he thinks you are to marry another, he will impede having communication with you. It would be in his mind to not cause more hurt. And so, unless he wishes to speak to you, it will not happen."

"Oh." She glanced down toward the counter.

"Well, here you are, Laylah." Thomas' voice was low, but there was an edge of annoyance in his tone as he spoke to her. "I have been looking for you."

Laylah reached up to dry her tears and turned to welcome her fiancé. She sniffed a little before smiling up into his handsome face, but instead of enjoying his company, as she knew she ought, she recalled another face and other words coming from a man she respected and apparently still loved. She couldn't help herself, and she recalled again Eagle Heart's words about Thomas:

"He is a coward. A real man does not leave his woman on the prairie alone. If you were to perish there, I would perish with you. Remember this."

Laylah did remember, and she cried again. Turning away from Thomas, she grabbed hold of a handkerchief. She blew her nose, then said, "I seem to have caught a cold."

"Perhaps it is because of this work you have been doing all week long," suggested Thomas. "Would you like to come for a ride with me? Feel the wind against your face?"

Laylah shook her head. "It sounds wonderful, and I...I thank you, Thomas. But, I have too much to do here."

"Do not do this to me, Laylah. What happened out there was not my fault," Thomas said, reasserting himself. "But, I promise you, it will not be the same as it was before. I have now learned to be cautious. And, you will be happy to know there is no prediction of a storm coming here today. I have asked the Indians." He laughed.

She smiled a little. "This is, indeed, good. But, please, Thomas, I...I cannot go out for a ride. I don't feel well. Please excuse me." And, with these parting words, she turned from him to flee quickly away, heading directly to her room.

Thomas Sutter frowned, watching her sudden departure. He set his lips into a thin line and shook his head as a deep voice spoke up from the goods-and-supply area which was situated in the rear of the trading room. The man said, "I heard your exchange with my daughter, but do not give up on her. She will become herself again soon, I know." With these words, Robert McIntosh stepped forward and came to stand on Thomas' left.

"It had better be soon," warned Thomas to the man who could very well be his future father-in-law. "Indeed, pretty though she is, I will not wait for her forever."

"You will not have to, Thomas. You will not have to."

****

The suggestion of riding out onto the prairie was an idea Laylah could little resist. But, she would not go with Thomas. Rather, she would make this trip alone. Perhaps the wide spaces would serve to ease the affliction within her heart.

Also, if she were to be truthful, she would have to admit it was impossible to resist leaving the fort to go in search of Eagle Heart. If he were still somewhere in the fort's vicinity, could she find him? Would he have set up camp close to where they had once sat out the blizzard?

Feeling a little happier, she left the trading room to rush to her quarters in the proprietor's part of the house. There, she dressed as quickly as she could for an excursion out-of-doors and, using her cane, hobbled toward the livery. There, she was able to attain help in saddling her pony, Honey Sugar, for, with her right arm broken, it was a task she could not do alone. She was glad to see the gate was open, and she fled out of it, wistfully hoping no one in the fort took note of her flight.

Interestingly, Honey Sugar appeared to know where to go. Laylah didn't even need to steer the animal. Hoping she might catch Eagle Heart still in residence at their shelter, Laylah found she could barely breathe. She had so much to tell him.

Keeping to a fast pace, she came quickly upon the coulee. But, rather than ride her pony down a hard pass, she dismounted—though with some difficulty because her ankle wasn't fully healed—and walked her mount down into the ravine. At last, she beheld the place where she and Eagle Heart had once encamped. It looked to be still there.

She smiled. Was he within?

Throwing her pony's reins to the ground, she limped as quickly as possible to the place where she and Eagle Heart had so recently resided. But, she saw at once that where their shelter had once stood, nothing remained to indicate the adventure she had once shared with Eagle Heart. Nor was Eagle Heart anywhere to be seen.

147

Was it really such a short time ago when she'd had Eagle Heart's attention all to herself? Though only a week had passed since they had sat out the storm together, it seemed like a lifetime ago.

As she stood looking at where the hut had once been, she realized she might never be the same again. She had thought she would be able to start her life over, as was expected of her by her family. But, more and more she was coming to realize this might be impossible.

She shouldn't feel this way. After all, she had made her choice and had refused Eagle Heart's proposal. And now, having done so, she should try to live with it and marry Thomas, as was expected of her. But, could she marry Thomas when, to the depths of her heart, she felt she belonged with Eagle Heart?

Perhaps another question she might ask herself was this: was she ready to throw away the lessons her grandmother had taught her? Hadn't her grandmother married a man she didn't love? Hadn't it ended in a bad way?

Truly, it was beginning to seem to Laylah as if she were plunging headlong into as heartbreaking an experience as her grandmother's.

When she had left Eagle Heart, she hadn't fully realized the extent to which she had changed. Had it taken losing Eagle Heart to pound some sense into her, to see him more clearly? Because of the differences in their cultures, she had been unwilling to break with her former ideas of love and marriage.

But, it was a mistake. In her heart now, she knew it was a mistake. Was she, however, too late to tell Eagle Heart she had changed her mind?

Gray Falcon had said his friend had blocked his thoughts from her. She knew he had done this because he did not wish to interfere in her life. Would it follow, then, that he might leave, never to know she was experiencing a change of heart?

He might do exactly this if she couldn't get a message to him either through her own efforts or via Gray Falcon. Perhaps when she rode home tonight, she would seek out Gray Falcon, ask him to find Eagle Heart and beg him to relay a message for her.

She worried, because one aspect about this was becoming very clear to her now: she would never forget Eagle Heart, even if she married another and never saw him again. Nor would she ever stop loving him.

Oddly, along with acknowledging what was truly in her heart, came a sense of responsibility and an awareness of greater self-confidence. At least she knew now that what had been between Eagle Heart and herself was more important than others' ideas—as well as her own mistaken belief—of how she should live her life.

The idea was freeing somehow, and this spurred her on toward another realization: she had to throw Thomas away. Really, she had no other option.

Besides, she was fast becoming aware that Thomas possessed an injurious trait she had chosen to ignore; one that had almost claimed her life: he did not wish to give up any part of his privileged life to be of service to another. Indeed, he had valued his own comfort over hers and had left her for dead, apparently after engaging in a show of trying to find her. He had only left the fort twice in search of her, and, according to Millie and her mother, hadn't tried again.

At last, it was clear to her. He did not love her.

Yet, he at least deserved that she should speak to him and inform him of her change of heart and her wish to not marry him. And so, she would seek him out, and possibly would do so tonight. She would not criticize him; she would simply let him know she wouldn't marry him. And, perhaps this, once done, would allow her to come to Eagle Heart with an open and clean heart.

She could only hope Eagle Heart might still wish to make her his woman. If, however, she were to discover he didn't, what would she do? Return to Fort Union?

No. She couldn't. Perhaps, were this to be a reality, an alternate plan might be to return to St. Louis, for she would always be welcome at her grandmother's house. Yes, this was a good plan. But, if she left this country and didn't marry Eagle Heart, would she become, then, an old maid?

Perhaps.

Oddly, the idea of leaving behind the security of her own world did not cause her to turn away from what she felt she must do. Truly, it would be hard to live Eagle Heart's lifestyle when she was not accustomed to it and didn't know its rules and mores. But, it was worse thinking she might have to live her life without him.

Yes, as soon as she returned to the fort, she would find Thomas and speak to him; she would break off their engagement, and then she would try to contact Eagle Heart once again with the mind speak. If this didn't work, she would try to find a way to convince Gray Falcon to take her to Eagle Heart or at least relay a message for her.

And so, it was on this thought that she turned to leave, and that's when she beheld the gray wolf watching her. At first she was afraid of the creature, but then a memory returned: it was the recollection of the wolves lying next to her freezing body, keeping her warmer than she would have been without them.

She owed them her thanks.

Hesitantly, she watched as the wolf slowly paced toward her. Using her cane for balance, Laylah came down onto her knees to show the wolf she wasn't a threat.

Her voice was almost a whisper when she asked, "Were you one of the wolves who, many days ago, came to help me? If you were, let me tell you how much I appreciate what you did that day."

The wolf bent down to rest its paws in front of it, its back legs sitting upon the ground as though it were ready to spring up and retreat in an instant.

"I wish I had something to give you, wolf, but I don't. I came here without food. I don't know really how I can properly thank you. I wish I could speak to you in the mind-to-mind talk like Eagle Heart can, but I can't."

The wolf looked her directly in the eyes before it came up onto its feet and turned around, trotting back in the direction it had come. However, before it went too far, the animal turned around and asked in distinct mind speak, "Where is the human boy?"

"The human boy?" Laylah asked uncertainly, also using the mind-to-mind form of talking. Was she really speaking with a wolf?

"Your mate," answered the wolf.

"My mate? Oh, you mean Eagle Heart?"

"Yes."

"I don't know where he is. He is gone from here. I was hoping he would be here, but he is not."

The wolf didn't answer. Instead, it turned away and trotted off again. In the distance, Laylah could see another wolf waiting for the one who had approached her. The first wolf had been a female, she realized, because the one she had talked to was smaller than the bigger wolf lingering in the shadows.

Laylah watched them both as they trotted away, though the female paused once and turned her head to take another look. Briefly, Laylah brought her good hand up in the sign of a goodbye, and it was some minutes before she realized she had spoken to a wolf as though this were an everyday occurrence and as easy to do as speaking with another human being.

What else was she going to learn in this wild land?

No wonder she now understood she could no longer marry Thomas. She had forever changed.

***

You were with *him*, weren't you?"

"No, Father, I was not with Eagle Heart, if that is who you mean. I simply went out for a ride."

"After declining to ride with your fiancé! Do you think he didn't notice?"

Laylah did not answer. Instead, she tried to take a step around her father, who stood in the way of her exit from the livery. He reached out to stop her.

"You do realize," he accused, "you have created more gossip about you than is good for our family. Because you were lost with that Injun for well over a week, it is now said he had his way with you."

"That's ridiculous, Father. Nothing like that happened. He did nothing to me. He promised me he wouldn't, and he didn't."

"Hush your mouth, now. How you defend him, as though he is your husband-to-be instead of Thomas."

"I am not defending him. I am telling you the truth. You do realize I would have died if he hadn't found me, don't you? I almost died, Father. Eagle Heart sat up with me through the night, caring for me. I am here now only because he found me and came to my aid. But, if I am defending him, then so be it. You have noticed, haven't you, that Thomas would have let me die?"

"That's enough of your sass, girl. I won't hear any more from you. Better you would have died than to be with the Injun for a week."

She gasped. "Father, you can't mean that!"

He didn't answer. "Now, you listen here, young lady. You are going to marry Thomas, and you are going to marry him tonight. I want no more backtalk from you about this. There is a priest here, a man of the cloth we know as Father Pierre, who is making his way west. He has come to stay with us for a while. I have already spoken to him about marrying you and Thomas."

"No, Father, I don't want to—"

"So, that Injun did have his way with you, did he?"

"He did not, Father. I am telling you the truth about this."

"I will make up my own mind about that. Now you listen up, ya hear? There *will* be a marriage between you and Thomas…and tonight. I am tired of you wavering back and forth about this marriage. I am stopping these rumors about you, and I'm stopping them now. I will not have my daughter talked about as though she has lain with every dirty Injun within the fort. Now, go to your room, where your mother and your sister await you. They will prepare you for your wedding. Do not think to go elsewhere. If you leave, I will follow you and will bring you back here. Do you realize the task I've had convincing Thomas to still marry you? He was ready to wash his hands of you."

"He left me there to die, Father! And, I would have done so if not for Eagle Heart."

"Why, you little tramp. Defending the Injun yet again. You, girl, disappoint me. All I can say is you *better still be a virgin.* If you are not, I will seek out that Injun, and I will have my revenge. Do ya hear? Now, go!"

Laylah wanted to speak out again, but realized it was pointless. Her father rarely worked himself up into such a rage. But, when he did, it was best not to cross him.

She bit her lip and, stepping with a limp around her father, paced as fast as she could from the livery, heading straight toward the gate. But, it appeared her father had issued orders about her, for the gate closed before she could even come close to it.

Realizing she didn't have a choice in the matter, she turned around and headed in the direction of the main house. Her room was in the southern part of the house, and, as she stepped toward it now, she wondered if she were destined to live the same kind of life as her grandmother, after all.

Karen Kay

CHAPTER ELEVEN

"*You* look so pretty," complimented Molly McIntosh, Laylah's mother, who stood off to Laylah's right and slightly behind her. "Are you happy now?"

Laylah didn't answer. Instead, she looked away from her mother as well as the reflection of her image in the mirror. She was seated in front of the vanity in her own and Amelia's room; her sister was standing in back of her and Amelia's hand stopped mid-brushstroke as she admonished, "Mother!"

"What?" asked Mrs. McIntosh. "What did I say that is wrong?"

"Please, how can you ask Laylah a question like this? Can't you see she is very unhappy?"

"I...I..."

"Personally," Amelia interrupted, "I think she should run away and marry Mr. Eagle Heart. After all, he saved her. No one else did. You do love him, don't you, Laylah?"

"I...yes, I mean, I..." What did she say to her sister's question? Of course she loved him. Worse, she missed him. Indeed, she was now convinced she'd made a terrible mistake by not going with him. "I do love him," she admitted simply. "Indeed, who would not? I have never known anyone like him. He is a man of honor; he is a man who entertained me with games and a glimpse of his gentle humor as we awaited the end of the blizzard. He made a shelter for us so we would be warm; he took care of the horses as well as me. He kept the fire burning in our little hut, and he kept me warm and well fed. I am alive now only because he possesses more

154

courage than any other man in this fort. I have told you all the truth when I tell you that, had he not come to find me, I would have died there. I do not exaggerate. I am telling you the truth."

"Do you see now, Mother? She loves *him*. Not Thomas. She loves Eagle Heart, and, personally, instead of helping her into these wedding clothes so she might marry Thomas, I think our efforts would be better spent if we were to help her escape all of this. She should not have to marry someone she doesn't love."

Their mother cleared her throat, as though in disapproval.

"Do not say anything in the negative against my words, Mother. You know I speak the truth. I think we should try to help Laylah leave here. You know Father has given the order that she is not to be able to go out of the fort."

"I know this," said Mrs. McIntosh. "I was there when he issued the order. Now, before you accuse me of anything else unsatisfactory, Millie, let me say that I think we should help her to leave, too."

Both girls turned toward their mother. Both girls gasped.

"Do you think I didn't see the way Laylah looked at *him*? I saw the way he looked at her, too. And, I knew then what I was trying hard not to see, and what I now know is true: they are in love. You realize, Laylah, that if you do go to him and marry him, your way, as well as his, may be filled with hardship and prejudice. We don't even know what all their beliefs are. You might come to hate the Indian life."

"I know this. I have thought of little else since I realized I made a mistake in leaving him. He wanted me to stay. He asked me to marry him, to be his woman, as he says it. But, I couldn't. After all, I knew nothing of his life or his tribe, and I was also engaged to marry Thomas. In truth, I still know very little of his life or his tribe or what my role would be as his wife. There is something else you should both know: if I leave to go to him, I might never see either of you again, for Father has threatened to seek revenge on him."

"You could visit us now and again, couldn't you?" Amelia asked.

"I…I would think I might. But, I don't know this with certainty, and I am thinking my reception here would not be very welcoming were I to return after marrying him. Perhaps, if I do go with him and we came back here to visit, Eagle Heart might be harmed because he dared to take me—a

155

white woman—as his wife. Do not think I have not considered these possibilities."

"Yet, you still want to go to him?"

"I do, even though I don't know where he is. But, yes, I do want to be with him. Others may condemn and gossip about me and Eagle Heart, but I am speaking the truth when I say he did not violate me. He saved my life, told me stories, played games with me and was a gentle companion. And, always he treated me with respect...and perhaps with affection. At least I like to think so."

"I daresay he felt a great deal of affection for you if he asked you to stay with him," observed Mrs. McIntosh.

"Yes."

Molly McIntosh sighed deeply before admitting, "Now, Laylah, my beautiful daughter, please let me tell you this: I do not think you would be very happy here, married to Thomas. Personally, I was not pleased to observe he did not do more to try to find you. Your father accomplished a great deal more, mustering together some men and leaving the fort in an effort to find you every day. Thomas helped, yes, but he was never an organizer of these groups. And then, Amelia left the fort to seek out an Indian to help her try to find you."

"Mother! You knew about that?"

"Of course I knew about it. Your father does not think I am sensible enough to see what is going on beneath my own nose. But, I am aware of what happens here. I witness many things. And, I was disappointed in Thomas, and now I am disenchanted with your father, also. Mark my words, Laylah, I think it would be a mistake for you to marry Thomas."

Laylah blinked back a tear, for she had expected her mother's admonishment instead of her support. Laylah said simply, "Thank you, Mother."

"But, what are we to do? The men seem to believe they are in control of you, Laylah, and perhaps this also includes me, as well as your sister," said Mrs. McIntosh. "Well, I disagree with these men who are acting as tyrants. I'll tell you what we're to do: we are going to help you leave this fort. I do not know where Mr. Eagle Heart has gone; I overheard what Mr. Gray Falcon said today in the trading room, that Mr. Eagle Heart has left here and is not close to the fort. I think this is good for his own safety, but, you may think because of this, you might not be able to reunite with him. I don't believe this is so. If you leave, Laylah, he will find you. I saw the love he feels for you, my daughter. There was no mistaking it. The noble Indian might be said to be a stoic man, and he might be trained to meet adversity without emotion, but Mr. Eagle Heart could not hide his admiration of you, Laylah. Yes, if he comes to discover you are free, I am certain he will find you.

"Now, Millie," continued Mrs. McIntosh, "go at once to the livery and saddle Laylah's pony, since she can't do this with her arm still in a sling. Make up any excuse you like about why you're doing it. Tie some supplies to the pony: food, blankets, extra clothes." She smiled. "I just happened to have left these very things in the stable—by the far right wall."

"Mother!"

"You did?"

"Laylah, if you love this man—"

"I do."

"Then you must try to find your happiness with him. I do not wish you to live the same kind of life as my mother, your grandmother, did. She was never happy. Oh, she was sometimes content with me and my brother and sister. But, it was not the same sort of happiness I saw in your eyes when you looked at Mr. Eagle Heart. I am right, aren't I? You love this man with all your heart, don't you?"

"Yes, Mother."

"Then, we are going to help you escape. Now, my children, let me tell you about my plan."

****

As Eagle Heart gazed out over the brown prairie that stretched below him to the horizon, he expanded his vision to encompass not only the plains, but also the ledge where he sat atop one of the highest bluffs in this part of the country. He could see the prairie below him, the brown grasses now awash in the reflection of the reds and oranges, the pinks and blues of the sunset. In the sky, the sun was no longer visible as it had fallen down below a mountain range, however, its rays of red, orange and even pink beamed out from behind the hills.

He had been here seven days. He hadn't gone too far away from the fort. Not yet. The reason he had not done so was because he was feeling

Karen Kay

so disheartened he knew a safe passage across the prairie would not be possible. Alas, in his current emotional state, he could make deadly mistakes.

He also realized he should try to cleanse himself within the healing heat of a sweat lodge. This might help to mend the emotional damage to his heart.

But, he couldn't make a sweat lodge. Not here, within the territory of the enemy. Plus, he required another medicine man from within his own society to sweat with him, for it was not an activity a man did alone. Besides, the needed fire for the sweat lodge would signal his location to his enemies, whose keen sense of smell would lead them here.

There was yet another activity he could take in an effort to heal his soul: he could fast. But, no, he ruled this out, as well. The very nature of fasting would make his body weak, which was often needed for a man's spiritual well-being. However, it was not a choice he could take while he still remained in the country of the Crow and the Assiniboine.

And so, he was left with memories of *her* crowding his mind, and these thoughts were heavy. Was she now already married to the other man? She might be. And, if she were married to that man, he wished her well. He would always wish her well.

This was not a problem for him. His problem was simple: he desired to be the man who would live the rest of his life with her.

But, she had not wished to become his woman. Even now, he recalled her words telling him she didn't want to be the cause of taking away his power, or perhaps being the cause of the wrath of his people. He realized now he had been foolish during their first few days together. He should have kept his doubts about this to himself.

After all, only a short time alone with her had brought about an awareness that he did not need to explain himself or his actions to others. Indeed, a real man makes his own decisions and either reaps their benefits or flounders in their wake.

He had been a fool, yes. For, what had come to flourish between him and Steals-my-breath was a love that had burned so deeply within, it had radiated a kind of luminous beauty. It would never die. He knew it. Perhaps she did, too.

158

Yet, he had to move on with his life, as did she. But, he would never forget her. Never.

He stood up to face the setting sun and say a prayer to Sun, the Creator. As he brought his lance up toward the sky, he sang:

"Sun, the Creator of all, You who have made everything in this world, You who know who I am and know what is in my heart; You know, also, that as I am going away from here, my heart is staying behind. To You, I will I admit the sadness within me overwhelms me. But, it matters not. I know I must release She-steals-my-breath from my life and from my thoughts. I told her she is free to live her life as she wishes. And, I meant it when I said it. What I didn't know was how hard it might be to live my life without her.

"I know now that it shall be impossible for me to forget her. I ask You only to have pity on me as I leave the white man's fort behind. I must not shed a tear, and yet, I know I will cry, for I might never see her again in this life. Help me to keep my heart strong as I leave. To show I am sincere and to give thanks to You, I leave You this piece of smoked meat. It is Yours."

Bringing his lance down to his side, he stepped toward the simple shelter he had made of pine boughs. It sat toward the wall of the cliff, beneath an overhanging rock. The ledge was large, and he did not fear turning over in his sleep to find himself falling from this high cliff.

Perhaps he would start on his journey away from here this very night. With the evenings coming earlier and earlier in these last days of autumn, the darkness would lend him the possibility of more time spent on the trail. Perhaps he might make better progress.

Yes, it was a good plan. He had to get on with his life, and, because the night was the only safe time to travel when in enemy territory, he would make his trail away from here this night.

At least he could throw himself into another grand purpose: to follow the trail of his brother, to find him and bring him home. This he would now dedicate himself to.

With this thought in mind, he made his bed, determining it best to rest a little before setting out upon the trail. In truth, he had only lain down when he became aware of the two wolves in his peripheral vision.

In the mind speak he said to them, "Hello, my brother and my sister. You are always welcome in my camp. Stay as long as you wish."

And, as he turned his back on the cliff wall behind him, he shut his eyes and was soon asleep.

****

Laylah wore a white dress to signify her innocence. While it was not truly a wedding dress, the gown was yet beautiful and lacy, and therefore was the dress of choice to suit this occasion.

Its material was made of a silky blend of satinet and muslin, with off-the-shoulder lace sleeves and a soft half-dress pelerine that doubled as a short feminine cloak. Because the dress was made of satinet, it created a swishing sound as she paced toward the parlor, where the wedding was to take place. The sound of her dress over the wooden floor helped to calm her nerves, and she was glad of a temporary reprieve.

Would her mother's plan work? It would have been easier, of course, if she could have escaped the fort without the additional trauma of attending a wedding she prayed would not take place.

But, apparently her father had feared she might try to run away from what he thought was her "duty" and had set a sentry at her door to escort her to the parlor and the intended wedding. Although she would have preferred to be open and frank about what was in her heart, it was not possible now. Her father had his reputation to protect, and this included dictating to his daughter what she must do to appease him.

Laylah sighed. She would rather not *have* to pretend she was properly submissive. But, she was glad her mother had predicted this very scenario and had devised her plans to accommodate this adverse turn of events.

With her hand holding on to her mother's arm, Laylah paused before the entrance to the parlor.

"Do not forget my advice," whispered her mother. "You must not stop or turn back once you start running. Rather, you must rush straight to the gate. Millie will be there to ensure the common door within the gate is opened for you, and, once you are outside the gate, Mr. Gray Falcon has consented to help you up to your seat on your mount. Do not be frightened of him, because, until your arm fully heals, you will require assistance with this."

Laylah nodded, the motion so small, it could barely be seen. She watched as her father stepped down the aisle and approached her. Her mother waited a moment only, then turned and paced toward the right side of the room.

Robert McIntosh offered his arm to her, and Laylah placed her hand upon the sleeve of his jacket. She didn't look at him, nor did she speak to him.

It was perhaps a turn of kindness that one of the fort's engagèes had produced a guitar and was strumming the beginning measures of the favored Wedding March. To the beat of the rhythm, her father pulled her down the aisle beside him.

The parlor was a small room, and, as she stepped forward, she took note of several clerks whom she knew personally and by name; these were standing on her left and were the majority of the guests. No Indians were present. On the opposite and right side of the room, she beheld her mother, who held a handkerchief up to her eyes.

There was a definite rhythm to the song, and she found her footsteps were keeping time to the beat, the sound of her low-heeled slippers acting much like the throbbing of a drum.

The veil over her face kept her expression hidden, and she was glad of it, for her emotions were a mix of anxiety, dread and fear.

Looking forward, Laylah beheld the priest, Father Pierre, who was dressed in the traditional black and white. He stood ahead of her, watching her. Then, she took notice of Thomas, who was standing on the priest's right. Amelia was present and had taken her position on the priest's left. Amelia, however, looked worried, and a frown pulled her brows together.

Perhaps there was good reason for Amelia's nervous countenance, since Laylah's escape depended upon the common door in the gate being open. Once Laylah and her father had paced all the way forward, her father patted her hand and stepped away from her, taking his place next to Thomas.

This was a signal for Thomas to come to her side. He did so and, presenting his elbow to her, invited her to put her hand on the sleeve of his coat. She did so.

Was her mother's plan going to work? The only element in the strategy's favor was one of surprise and perhaps the disbelief that the

McIntosh women had conspired to allow Laylah to follow the wishes of her heart. Would it work?

Father Pierre opened his book and began to speak, when, without a word, Laylah turned swiftly around and ran as fast as she could from the parlor. Her low-heeled shoes gave her a slight advantage, though it might not be enough, for she could not outrun a man. And, she was limping.

However, the element of surprise seemed to have swept over the small assemblage and no one reacted quickly enough to follow except her mother, who, once the two of them had exited the room, placed two chairs against the parlor's door, effectively locking it for a short time.

"Hurry, Laylah. And, may you and your young man give me many grand babies. Remember, I love you."

"I love you, too," Laylah said between deep breaths. "Goodbye, Mother."

"Goodbye," whispered Molly McIntosh, and then Laylah was gone.

She didn't look back but concentrated instead on reaching the door in the gate, hoping her sister had charmed the men in charge of it into opening it. Any minute now, she felt as if someone might overtake her, and, because of it, her steps became faster and faster as the gate loomed up tall in front of her.

"Hurry, Laylah. Gray Falcon will help to seat you on your pony. May you find happiness with Eagle Heart. You know you take my love with you as you go."

"I know," returned Laylah. "I love you very much, also."

Soon, the door swung inward, allowing a small opening in the gate, and Laylah hurriedly fled through it. As planned, Gray Falcon held the reins of her pony, and, placing them in her free hand, he lifted her up onto her seat on the pony.

With his left hand, he whipped the pony's rear end, setting the animal into motion, and, as she and Honey Sugar rushed away from the fort, Laylah's dress trailed behind her, over the rear end of the pony. Looking back briefly, Laylah thought her trailing dress looked alive, as though it were a kindly spirit come to help her.

Bending toward her pony's ear, Laylah said, "You know where to go, don't you, girl?"

Briefly, her pony shook her head, as though to say, "Do you need to ask?"

Laylah smiled.

CHAPTER TWELVE

*E*agle Heart awoke with a start. Some unknown sound had awakened him. He didn't move. He dared not breathe.

Had the enemy found him, after all?

Here came the sound again: a rustling echo made by some being, something alive. Slowly, with stealth, he inched his hand toward the knife at his waist.

"At last you are awake, my brother."

At once, he recognized the mind speak of his sister wolf. He answered, "I had thought you and your mate would have moved away from me by now."

"We cannot," came the reply.

"Why can you not?"

"Because we have news for you: *she* is back."

"She?"

"Your mate. She has returned to the place where you saved her."

"Steals-my-breath? She is back?"

"I saw her. My mate did, also."

"Steals-my-breath…" He whispered her name. A flood of joy, of surprise and even shock swept over him, and, for a moment, he was incapable of movement.

His sister wolf said in the mind-to-mind talk, "We stayed here while you slept. How could we leave when she is there and you are here? You cannot make babies when you are not together."

Eagle Heart laughed. He said silently, "It would, indeed, be hard to do."

"We leave now unless you have need of us."

"I believe I can find my way back to the coulee," he said silently. "Do you need food?"

"We would be happy to have whatever you can share."

"Here, what I have in my pouch is now yours." He reached into a medium-sized buckskin bag on his hip and emptied the contents of the dried meat on the slab of the rock which had been his bed. His sister wolf took a slice of the meat and brought it to her mate, who was keeping his distance from Eagle Heart, the human being.

Eagle Heart came up onto his feet and stepped toward his two horses. While he quickly placed his blanket onto the back of his Appaloosa, he glanced toward the sky, observing the star constellation of the Seven Brothers. From this constellation, he estimated the remaining evening hours, realizing the night was only half over, and, if he were lucky and pressed his ponies—changing mounts often—he could probably make the coulee before daybreak.

But, he must ride as fast as the wind. Making his buffalo rope into reins, he placed the grip into his pony's mouth and then jumped onto the Appaloosa, having picked up the rope of his packhorse. Without thinking too greatly about direction, he set his path south and east. Before he left, however, he spoke to the wolves, saying, "Thank you, my friends."

"You are my brother," said the she-wolf. "You are human, but you are also one of us. We are tied."

"Yes," he replied in the mind speak. "We are tied."

****

Laylah had little knowledge of what to do in the wilderness when no one else was with her, helping her. She didn't possess the skill of creating a shelter from nature, nor did she know if she were safe from any predator—both animal or human—who might venture into this coulee. And, this was not her only problem: she was frightened.

However, she took in a deep breath for courage as she stood firm against succumbing to her fears. She had seen there was no choice but to escape from the fort; she would not change her mind now simply because she was afraid. Besides, there were some matters so important and so dear

165

to the heart they were worth the risk of harm: one of those was liberty and the right to live her life unencumbered. Obviously, her father thought she had no rights — not even the right to change her mind about whom she truly loved and whom she would marry.

No, she would not back down. She would not go back there. Somehow, she would make the best of it.

This decided, she couldn't help wondering where it might be safe to sleep. It was becoming obvious to her that she would be here all night...and alone.

It was worrisome, for she had no means of protection against discovery. After all, her father could easily ride here and, discovering her, could drag her back to the fort. And, then what?

Surely Thomas would not look favorably on another attempt at matrimony. No, Thomas was not the problem in this matter. It was her father.

Of course, she could hide, but, if her father did find the coulee, he would see her pony even if she weren't immediately visible. Laylah sighed deeply. It was pointless to hide, and she wouldn't do it.

Still, there was danger from other predators, and she feared her small pocket pistol might not be enough protection. But, at least her mother had packed the pistol for her.

She had never been alone on the prairie at night. For as long as she could remember, she had been protected against the troubles that often accompany adult life. Indeed, she had rarely been allowed to venture very far from the fort and, until now, this had not been a problem. But, though it was frightening to be here with no one else, a new feeling was beginning to take root within her: she felt empowered by simply coming here and being here on her own decision.

Looking outward and toward the horizon, she found she could appreciate the beauty of the night. It was cool, yes, but it was not raining nor snowing. There was also a half-moon rising up over the distant horizon, its bright beams blocking out the light of perhaps a million stars which were close by to it. Yet, as she looked up, she saw the Big Dipper well enough and wondered if Eagle Heart might ever come to learn she had escaped the fort and had returned to the place where she felt close to him.

Where was he? Was there still an invisible wall between their mind communications? And, if he continued to refuse to "hear" her, what would she do?

If he did not open himself up to her soon, it was possible she might never see him again. Because of her insistence to return to her old way of life, he probably thought she had already married Thomas. And, his own code of ethics would not permit him to interfere.

This, however, was going to make it difficult to find the man; no one knew where he was, not even his friend, Gray Falcon. Even this evening, as soon as she had settled herself into a seat on the grassy soil beneath a willow tree, she had reached out with her mind again to try to contact Eagle Heart. But, again, there was no answer.

She understood why there was no answer, for Eagle Heart was an honorable man. What he didn't know was how a week without him would change her; nor could he be aware of her acknowledgment of how dismal her life was without him. If nothing else, this past week had proved to her that her love for him was more powerful than the draw of her own culture.

She missed him. Indeed, she yearned for him more than she could ever have envisioned she would. They had touched one another spirit to spirit, soul to soul...and more. Passion had also stirred between them, and in a most elemental way, although neither of them had acted upon it, nor had either even mentioned it to the other. But, truth be told, she desired to be with this man physically. Their one kiss had proved this to her, and she ached with the need for more of the same.

As she sat beneath one of the willow trees lined up with the other trees close to the creek, she despaired. What was she to do?

She couldn't go back to the fort. But, what if Eagle Heart continued to prevent any communication between them? How could she ever let him know she'd changed her mind?

Looking forward, her vision caught onto the rushing water of the creek, which seemed to be in a hurry to go somewhere. It was a lovely stream, looking as though it were hiding secrets, because, as it dashed over the rocks and sand, it shimmered and shone like sparkling jewels beneath the starlight.

It was not a quiet stream, either. Indeed not. It gurgled and splattered as it hurried on its way. However, its babbling sound brought her a little peace of mind, and, looking outward at it, she felt the tranquility of nature seep into her soul. It was as though Nature were urging her to let go of her fears, which, in turn, allowed her to think of the future...at least for a little while.

Winter was around the corner, and she knew she couldn't stay here. She was bright enough to realize her lack of skills might cause her ruin or even her death. After all, she didn't know how to hunt in order to feed herself nor how to create a fire from friction. The only skill that might aid her was the knowledge of how to build up a fire once it was started.

She moaned. Her father had ensured she knew sign language so she could communicate with the natives on these plains, but he hadn't taught her how to survive in the wilderness if suddenly left on her own. Perhaps he had never envisioned this might ever occur in her life.

Instead, most of her education had been composed of the three R's: reading, writing and arithmetic. But, beyond that, she'd learned little else except how to become a perfect ornament on her husband's arm and, also, how to manage his household so well he would barely notice her accomplishments.

These skills—while they were definitely skills—would not do her any good on the open prairies of the Montana territory, especially with winter coming on. What would she do in the midst of a hard winter if she didn't find Eagle Heart, and soon?

She would return to St. Louis where she would stay with her grandmother. She had already determined this. It would be the only choice available to her. But, perhaps she could remain here a few days before heading out to Fort William and then on to St. Louis by way of the last steamer going south. Thank the good Lord that Fort William was not far away.

Yes, she could remain here for a little while, if only because her mother had ensured there were food and supplies aplenty, enough to allow her the leisure of staying hidden away for a few days. When her supplies ran out, however, she would leave here and trek to Fort William.

Rising up to her feet, she stepped toward the grassy spot where she had hobbled her pony. When she had arrived here earlier, she had ensured Honey Sugar was secured next to a cottonwood tree, remembering that Eagle Heart had told her the bark of this tree was a good source of winter food for a horse.

Reaching up, she untied her packets of supplies and set them on the ground. Then, she took hold of the blanket still lying upon Honey Sugar's back. When she placed it over her arm, her pony neighed, then nickered slightly.

Laylah smiled and reached up to pet her horse. "You are such a good friend," she whispered. "We will stay here tonight and tomorrow, perhaps longer. I shall, however, seek another and better shelter for us both tomorrow."

Honey Sugar sighed, as though to say she understood.

Laylah turned away and had once again taken her seat under the willow tree when she heard the thought, "Is it true? Are you back? There in our coulee?"

Laylah laughed and somehow cried at the same time. "I am here," she answered. "I have been trying to reach out to you. How did you discover I am here?"

"The wolves found me and told me I should come to you. My wolf sister told me it is hard to make babies when we are apart."

Laylah cried. "They came to you?"

"Yes. My sister, the she-wolf, was concerned about you and did not understand why I was not there with you."

"Are you coming here?"

"I am. You did not marry him?"

"I did not. I have run away from the fort. It is no longer a home for me."

"Then you will be my woman?"

"I will. I missed you. I missed you so very, very much. I didn't know it was possible to long to be with someone with so much passion. I ache with the need to be with you."

There was no reply and a lengthy silence ensued.

"Eagle Heart? Are you there?"

"I am. I am coming to you. Not only do you take my breath from me when I am with you, but sometimes you steal my ability to communicate with you in our mind speak, also."

"Is this good or bad?"

"It is good. I should be there with you before daylight. It is in my mind to make you my wife, my Sits-beside-him wife. Do you agree?"

She cried again. "I do. I have never loved anyone like I love you, Eagle Heart. I want to spend my life with you, even though I am afraid."

"Why are you afraid?"

"Because I know nothing about the Blackfeet and nothing about your camp, and I know almost nothing about how to survive in the wilderness. It is frightening to think of all the skills I don't have in order to survive in this part of the country."

"I will be with you to help you learn these talents and also to help ease you into my tribe and tribal life. My people will come to love you."

"And, I wish to be with you, but I don't know if what you say about your people is true. Yet, I can promise you this: I will try to make our life together a good one."

"I know you will. Where are you in the coulee? Are you in a safe place?"

"I have made my seat under a willow tree close to the creek."

"I see it."

"You see it?"

"I do. I think you will be safe there. I will look at the prairie around you to try to determine if there is an enemy nearby."

"You will look around this place? From where you are now?"

"Yes."

"I...I don't understand."

"I am a man of mysterious ways."

"I still don't understand."

"Since I was very young," he said in their mind-to-mind talk, "I have been trained to take on the duty of being a healer for my people. There are many ways to help people to become well. But, only our medicine men are able to use the gifts sent from Sun, the Creator, to aid a man or a woman to become healthy again. Some of these ways include being aware of what is taking place in the environment, even at great distances."

There was another pause in their communication, and then he said, "I do not sense any danger to you for now. I must set my mind to get to you quickly, and so I will end our talk here. You have only to reach out to me if you need me."

"I will," she said with her mind. "And, Eagle Heart, I love you!"

"And I, you."

Their communication ended.

He is coming to me! Oh, how I wish I had a mirror, for I would look my best.

Laylah sat up away from the tree, wondering for the first time what clothing her mother had packed for her; she didn't wish to meet Eagle Heart wearing a dress that she had donned for a different wedding. She had better discover quickly what other clothes were packed.

****

Eagle Heart rushed over the short, brown grasses of the plains as though there were a prairie fire at his back. His attention was outward and all around him, but it was mostly fixed on the horizon, which he could see clearly because the light from the half-moon outlined the prairie, with all its flaws and bumps. As he hurried over the plains, he was not afraid his pony might step into a prairie-dog hole. He had decided it would not be so; therefore, he knew it would not happen.

He had already planned to ride through the night, if needed, to get to her. And, once he was with her, he intended to make love to this woman; at least he would do so as soon as he found and erected a safe shelter for them. Perhaps then, if she were willing, they could make love for several days, spending their time doing little more than admiring one another, both physically and spiritually.

He inhaled deeply, then sighed. The coulee would not be safe for them. They could be too easily discovered, and at a time when her father would be angry, perhaps to the point of committing murder.

As he watched his path along the moon-bathed prairie, he felt confident enough in his pony's sure-footedness so he might let his thoughts drift a little, and he found himself reaching out to her.

"I love you," he said in the mind-to-mind discourse.

"And, I love you," she returned. "As I am sitting here on my blanket, I am hoping you have an extra breechcloth with you, for I intend to keep the one you'll be giving me."

He laughed. "I am afraid you will have to keep more about me than my breechcloth."

"Oh?"

"It is merely the symbol of the start of our lives together. I fear you will have to keep me, also…and any children we make together."

"I am pleasured to hear you say it."

He smiled. "Is there a man who has ever been as happy as I am? I did not know it is possible to be filled with so much joy…and lust."

"Lust?"

"Even when we were together, I was barely able to keep myself from sweet-talking you into lying with me. Do you not remember the many times I had to leave our shelter suddenly?"

"Is that what those visits outside were all about? Of course, I remember."

"Do not mistake me. I wanted to make love to you many times when we were together. And now, knowing you are also wanting to be my woman, it is almost all I can think about. I warn you, it might be several moons before I am fulfilled. Perhaps I never will be. I hope you will be happy with this."

"Mr. Eagle Heart, I am certain I will be delighted with whatever it is you feel needs to be. You do know I will be pleasured, indeed, to hold you in my arms. It is not you, alone, who is joyful—and perhaps lustful, also—about our coming marriage. It is possible I will treasure our closeness even more than you, simply because I am a woman and desire to have you in my arms continuously…if it were only possible. Speaking of being close, how far away are you now?"

"I should be in our coulee before daybreak."

"I shall await you. I am so excited you are coming here to our coulee, I don't think I will be able to sleep. Of course, I now owe my gratitude to the she-wolf. Did you know I was able to talk to her in the mind-to-mind speak? She asked me where you were."

"What did you tell her?"

"I told her I didn't know."

"Áa, this is why she came to find me and tell me of you. She is a babe from one of the litters of the mother wolf who found me and nurtured me when I was a baby. She is my sister."

"Your sister… What a beautiful thing to say about a wolf…about all life, actually. I didn't know my life could feel this full, and I don't think I

172

will ever be the same again, and it is all because of you and my love for you."

He didn't answer right away.

"Eagle Heart? Are you all right?"

"I am well. I wonder if my thoughts and my tongue might always feel as though they are tied when I am with you. I must concentrate on my passage over the prairie now. Again, you have only to reach out to me if you need me."

"I will."

The communication between them dropped again then, as it had to. A man might be able to take his attention away from his path now and again, but, in order to remain safe, a man did have to pay attention to the environment around him. He was, after all, in enemy territory.

****

Laylah had exchanged her white gown for a clear, navy-hued day dress with large gigot sleeves and a tiny waist that fell into a "V" in front. The skirt of the dress was full and was not embellished, yet the material was elegant, made of blue satin, and it felt like silk beneath her fingertips. Her shawl was an off-white color, and, although it looked flimsy, it was made of cashmere and so was warm. Black boots completed the outfit. Hopefully, the boots would allow her more ease in walking.

She had no hat, even though a proper young lady should, but it couldn't be helped; the hats this season were large and so could not be easily packed. Perhaps, if she tied a ribbon through her long hair, it might suffice for the head gear she lacked. Reaching into the bag she had placed next to her, she found a blue ribbon and proceeded to thread it through her locks.

She was happy with her choice in the navy dress; she no longer felt like a sitting target for any predator, having been dressed all in white, and here within the darkened night. She smiled. Indeed, the navy dress gave her more of a feeling of security. It was then she realized she had nothing to give Eagle Heart as a wedding gift. He wouldn't expect one, of course, and he wouldn't ask for one. But, she intended to give him one anyway.

Perhaps the blanket she was knitting could be completed as she awaited Eagle Heart's arrival here. Had her mother included this particular coverlet and several different spools of yarn?

Coming up to her knees, she bent over to search through her bag and found what she was looking for underneath many articles of clothing. Her mother had often commented on the beauty of the colors she had chosen for the quilt; perhaps this was why she had included it.

Bringing out the knitting needles, the yarn and the unfinished blanket, she set the covering on her lap and the yarn at her side. Even though she was encumbered with a broken arm, she happily set to work. The colors in the blanket were a deep blue and white, for these were the pigments of the sky, which, for her, represented the tranquility of nature. They also signified her feeling of gradual independence from the tight confines of her society.

As she set to work, she took a deep breath, enjoying the sweet aroma of the oxygen-filled, dry prairie air. She smiled.

She couldn't remember ever feeling so happy.

Hurry, Eagle Heart!

She had said the words to herself, forgetting her thoughts might be heard by him.

"I am," he responded.

She sighed and set to work over the blanket, intent on finishing it before he arrived.

CHAPTER THIRTEEN

The intense, deep black of night covered the land in these early morning hours. Dawn would follow shortly, though there were currently no gray or silver shades of color in the sky to announce the coming sunrise. Not yet.

Because Eagle Heart was in a hurry to get to her, he rode his Appaloosa pony into the coulee instead of walking him down the ravine's northern entrance. Behind him, and on a rope, trotted the Nokota, his packhorse.

He knew where Steals-my-breath was. Hadn't he seen her beneath the willow tree? As he trotted his pony along the creek, he kept his path within the tree line as he expanded his sight out toward the horizons on each side of him.

Although he could not detect any current hostile presence, he realized again the unfriendly environment that surrounded this place. Her father, as well as others from Fort Union, could discover them here all too easily. And, besides this, there could be a fight if a Crow or an Assiniboine war party came upon him unawares. No, he and Steals-my-breath would not be able to linger here.

Quickly, before approaching Steals-my-breath, he slipped off his pony and dipped into the water, washing himself with clean sand from the bottom of the creek. He washed his mouth and hair, also, remembering how important cleanliness was in tribal life...and perhaps to one's new wife, as well.

He intended to make love to this woman and soon, although the right place for this was not here. He knew a location only a few days' ride from the coulee; it was one where they could be hidden and secure. Hidden away in a valley between two mountain peaks in the Big Horn Mountains, the vale was known by the Crow as No Man's Trail.

There could be other problems from the locals there, but the populace in that part of the country was rarely hostile. At least he and Steals-my-breath would be out of reach of his enemies. Plus, her father and his search party would then have to conduct a grand search for them, since they would expect him to make a wedding shelter closer to the fort.

Being secure was important. They should enjoy their first days together as a married couple without fear from some unknown hostile source. Reaching down, he untied his breechcloth and pulled it off, replacing it with a different tan-colored one. This white breechcloth—the one he usually wore—would be his first gift to her.

****

She jumped. What was this? She'd been so intent on finishing the blanket, she had lost track of what was happening around her.

But, something had fallen into her lap. Fearfully, she picked up the object and stared at it. It was a long piece of white buckskin. It was wet, as though it had only recently been washed, and was sewn with porcupine quills and beads, and...

Why, this was... With pure joy, she burst out laughing.

"Eagle Heart!" she blurted out. "You are here."

"I...am," he voiced in English, though she still didn't see him.

"I am glad you remembered to give me this. It is my first gift from you, although perhaps not so much of a gift, as you do owe this to me."

"I...do," he agreed, using the English language again, though he was still not visible to her.

She shook her head. "I have heard, of course, that an Indian man's stride can be so silent, he can sneak right up on a person. But, until now I have not experienced it. Where are you?"

"I cannot...show...self...no breechcloth," he explained in English. "Naked, am I...without it."

She giggled, and, as though her laughter were a kind of magic, he dropped down to the ground, having been seated upon a strong branch of

176

the willow tree. He came to stand in front of her. And, as the soft light from a few stars bathed him in a gentle luminescent glow, she thought he had never looked more handsome. But...

"Why," she signed, "you are fully dressed."

"I am not," he responded with the sign language. "I have given you my best breechcloth."

"But, you are wearing your leggings, your moccasins and your shirt, which hangs down all the way to your knees, and I suspect you have replaced this breechcloth with another." She smiled as she threw the blanket to the side and, jumping to her feet, quickly hobbled toward him. He opened his arms to her, and she went into them quickly, as though they both were magnetically attracted. "How glad I am to see you," she murmured. "Now, my world is right again."

Without warning, he picked her up and began twirling her round and round. When she laughed, he did, too.

"My woman." Again he spoke in English. "Woman...mine...now... you." He kissed her then, a long, hot kiss. Even when he set her feet on the ground, he didn't stop kissing her. Instead, his lips caressed her face, her lips, her eyes, her nose, her cheeks...even her ears. As he came up for air, he drew away from her slightly and signed, "I desire to do more than share kisses. I am bursting with the need to love you as a man and his woman should. But, I fear we are not safe here. We must go to another location where no one can find us. I do not wish anyone to come upon us, which might cause me to take my attention away from the beauty of you."

"I am glad to hear it, since I, too, believe we should leave here." She giggled a little. "But, can't we linger in this gully, even a little? I have fond memories of this place."

As he gazed down at her, she recognized the fire lit from within him, and he signed, "I would like to stay here, also, but we cannot. Dawn will soon be on the horizon. It will be bad if someone from your fort finds us, or worse, a band of my enemies comes to make war with me. We are finally together. Let us not allow someone to force us apart. But"—he hesitated—"we could ride one horse together to a place I know is safe from the eyes of others." He grinned at her. "That way you will be in my arms."

"Hmm. I like your idea. But, I fear I cannot do this because I rode my own pony here. I cannot leave her here and with no one to care for her."

"You will not have to," he signed. "She is with my own ponies. She will be happy to follow along behind us."

Laylah reached up and, placing her arms around his neck, came to stand up on her toes, then showered him with so many kisses on his neck, she had to pause to catch her breath. He set her a little away from him as he signed, "I cannot make love to you now. There is too much danger here. And, yet, when you kiss me like this, I am ready to make love to you."

"You are?" She watched as he shut his eyes and drew in a deep breath. "Show me," she said in English.

"I cannot." He whispered the two words in English, then continued in sign, saying, "You have not known a man yet, and I am in no hurry to rush into our lovemaking when there is not the time to do it right. Come here." He drew her in close to him, so close, the evidence of his need could not be mistaken.

"Oh," she breathed out against the softness of his velvety buckskin shirt. It was true she'd never known a man, so the evidence of his manhood could have scared her a little, but it didn't. Instead, it excited her.

And this, accompanied by his promise to make love with her, almost caused her to swoon. However, she didn't. Instead, she took a step backward. "Let me gather up my things, and let us go," she said, coming down flat-footed on the ground. "The sooner we get to this place you speak of, the sooner we might come to know a little bit of heaven."

"What...'heaven'?" he asked in English.

"It is where God lives," she answered in sign, speaking in English at the same time. "It is a place of peace and beauty, and I think you and I together will find a bit of it in each other's arms. I must hurry now to gather my things together."

"You must, but do not think I will let you go so easily...and without another kiss," he said in Blackfeet as he lifted her up off her feet once again.

Laylah didn't know what he'd said, but she suspected it had something to do with lovemaking, for he kissed her deeply, his lips over hers, his tongue tracing the inside of her mouth and her teeth, his tongue playing with hers. She sighed and he groaned.

"More love...I want," he said in English. He set her down on the ground and signed, "But, we must do no more here. Already, I see the silver rays in the eastern sky. Soon, the sun will rise, and we must be gone from here. Quickly, get your things."

Laylah turned away as though to go, but before she left she came to stand on tiptoes again and placed a kiss on his cheek. Then, she giggled and spun away.

But, he caught her around the waist before she had gone too far, and, bringing his head down to hers, ran his lips over hers yet again; he found her cheeks with his lips, then her eyes and even her nose. He stopped, inhaling deeply. "Go…now!" he said in English, releasing her slightly as he signed, "We have only a little more darkness left of the night, and then we rest."

"Why will we rest? I thought we were going to a place where we can be alone."

"We are," he signed, "but only a tribe with many warriors dares to be on the move during the day, and, even then, only when within one's own territory. When alone on the prairie, one travels by night, and a man must be careful to cross his trail often if he is in enemy territory. Where we go is a few days' travel."

"Oh. I will hurry, then."

He nodded, but didn't release her until he had run his hands over her back, up and down, then farther down, bringing her hips in close to his. It was as though with his hands he were laying claim to her, and she thrilled to the idea of becoming his woman. His words were slightly blurred when he said in Blackfeet, "Do hurry. My need is great. And, I would be on the trail."

****

A beautiful, cloudless day threatened the blackness of night as the rising sun loomed on the eastern horizon. So inspiring was it to see the faint light in the sky, it seemed to Laylah as if the environment around her were paying tribute to both her and Eagle Heart. Although her new husband had sped the ponies over the prairie in the hours of the early morning—seeming to take as much advantage of the blackness and shadows as possible—Laylah was not at all tired. Indeed, she felt energized.

She could tell their direction was headed mostly south, since the colors of the sun were on her left. In the distance loomed several buttes and cliffs with purple and snow-capped mountains rising up behind them. As she looked ahead, it was in Laylah's thoughts that Eagle Heart was pushing onward toward those buttes.

The sun was already beginning its journey into the sky by the time they reached the first butte. As the beginning rays of the sun painted the sky in a luminous silver hue, Laylah knew daylight would soon follow.

It seemed to her they were blessed with a bit of luck because they reached the nearest butte before the sun began to color the sky with pinks, reds, oranges, blues and even purples. According to Eagle Heart, their path would be to keep close to the river he called the *Otahkoika,* the Yellowstone, though she hadn't even caught a glimpse of it yet.

True to his word, Eagle Heart had shared his seat with her on his pony. At first, she had sat side-saddle in front of him, his arms around her. But, soon they had changed positions, and she was now situated in back of him, her arms around his waist and her legs spread apart. His quiver full of arrows lay against his hips, within his easy reach, and his bow hung over his shoulder. His gun was sheathed in a rifle-shaped buckskin object made specifically for this. His shield and a great deal of buckskin rope hung from a loop on his pony's side and in his right hand was his lance.

It did make her wonder who had made all these beautiful clothes and objects for him. He'd said he had two sisters. Had they created these things for him? Even his weapons? Or had he made these himself?

When he had changed positions with her and had placed her in back of him, he'd explained it was necessary for him to be in front in case they encountered trouble. In this position, with her sitting in back of him, he could more easily face an enemy and muster a defense against him.

"Soon…we…stop. Must…good place…find." He spoke in English.

"What is a good place?"

"Humph!" he grumbled in his throat. "Be…easy…hide. Coulee, no. High. Go…high…up. See…plains…all around." As their ponies stood on the floor of the prairie, he pointed up, meaning they were about to climb the butte. "High…safe…more."

"Oh," she responded in English, against the softly tanned hide of his shirt. "I must learn your language. You know mine better than I know yours. Maybe you can teach me."

"*Áa!*" The sound of the word was more of a rumble coming from his throat. "*Áa*…but…trouble."

"Oh! It will not be any trouble."

He looked at her from over his shoulder and grinned.

"Oh, you! You're teasing me."

"What...mean...'teasing'?"

"It means," she explained in English, "joking with me...perhaps even flirting with me."

"'Flirting'?"

"Flirting means to talk to another in an arousing, sexual manner," she signed. "Like a man and his woman might do when they are trying to cause the other to want to make love."

"I?" He actually pointed to himself. "Try...make you...want love...from me?"

"Yes, this is what it means."

He laughed. "I like...word. You...want?"

"Yes, I do. So, you needn't tease me."

"Woman...should know...me, husband...tease heap...much. So...love...make...often."

She laughed.

"We...walk...up high...now. Find...good place...camp. You off...get...now."

"What? You're not going to dismount first and help me down?"

"Man...not help. Keep...ready...fight much. You...walk ponies. Walk...behind man."

"Why?"

"Man...defend...first one...look at...enemy."

"Oh, I understand now," she said, drawing her left leg over her right and sliding down from the pony on the right side, imitating Eagle Heart. She had taken note earlier that he mounted and dismounted on the right side of the pony, not the left.

She switched to the gesture talk and signed, "You are walking in front of me so you will be the first to confront any danger."

He nodded and dismounted, handing the buckskin reins of all three ponies to her. His hand lingered over hers in the exchange before he signed, "We climb now. The sun is almost all the way up in the east, and we must be hidden by the time it rises fully into the sky."

She nodded, but her entire body was responding sensually to his touch. It stimulated her, however, in a good and pleasant way. "Very well," she said simply as she followed him up the steep butte, glad that she had been wise enough to wear boots and that her mother had been good enough to pack them for her.

She didn't mention the feeling of desire which had swept over her only a moment ago. Nor did she tell him of the ache within her and the physical yearning to be close to him, the wanting to feel him next to her. Somehow, it seemed out of place at a time when they needed to get to safety, but after that...

She smiled.

****

They were already well within the sheltered region of the deep forest of evergreen trees when the sun began to color the sky with the pinks and reds, blues and purples of a rainbow. The colors were mirrored on the dry brown grasses below her, and their beauty seemed without measure. Although she wished she might stare at the surrounding splendor of nature and admire it more, she, instead, turned her back on the eastern horizon and looked forward and up. It was still relatively dark within this forest of pine and cedar trees, and, as they wound their way up the steep cliff, the scent of the pines as well as the raw smell of the earth accompanied her steps and caused her a good feeling, as though she were at peace at last.

The horses she led gave her no trouble as they each found their footing over the sometimes grassy and pine-needle-covered ground. It seemed to her that the sound of their hooves over the solid terrain was comforting, and she found its clatter relaxing. At times, the horses snorted as though in protest of the high climb, but, for the most part, they simply followed her.

Having now entered into the darkened forest, she was feeling sleepy and wondered why they weren't stopping to make their camp beneath the boughs of these trees. But, tired though she was, she was not inclined to ask Eagle Heart about it. This man had already proven he knew more about this wild land than she might ever realize. She would be wise to simply follow him.

There was a small clearing in these woods, but he didn't lead them into it. However, there were flowers inside the glade that also grew out beyond its edges. Suddenly, he stopped and came to squat next to a grouping of these flowers. In his own tongue, he began to speak lowly and softly, and it appeared to her as if he were talking to the flowers.

This was soon done, and she watched as he reached for his knife, which was sheathed at his side. Without pause, he began to dig down deeply into the soil, turning up several of the flowers, including their roots. These he placed on the ground before him.

He was still squatting next to the plants when he once again spoke to them quietly in his own tongue. He indicated with his hand both those flowers that now lay at his feet, as well as the ones still standing and firmly attached to the ground. With this done, he sprinkled a yellow powder over the flowers he had dug up by their roots, and these he placed into one of the bags he wore around his shoulders.

Next, he brushed the ground with his hands and feet until it looked as though no one had paused there. When he looked back at her, he grinned and said in English, "These...for you."

When she smiled at him, he stepped toward her, reaching out to take her hand in his and bring it up to his lips, where he proceeded to place a kiss upon her wrist. The pleasure from a mere kiss was so unexpected, she groaned and looked away. And, when she at last looked forward and at him, he grinned at her and said in English, "Soon...you be my woman."

To which she replied, "I already am."

"Know this," he said, again in English. "Soon...also...be mine...in body."

She grinned at him. "It will be my pleasure."

"Áa," he said. Then signed, "I intend to make it so."

****

At last, they came to a place where a bluff jutted out from the butte. It was level and large in size and backed up to several pine trees which clung to the rock-solid side of the butte.

Eagle Heart pointed to the trees. "We will make our camp there," he signed. "The trees will hide our fire and the smoke from it, and their branches can be used to make a hasty shelter, one that is hard to see even by an enemy scout, if anyone should be following us. Once I have made the shelter, I must go back and cut across our tracks so anyone following us will be led in a wrong direction. Some of our passage over the earth, however, I

183

will need to erase completely from the earth. Only in this way will we be safe for a little while."

She nodded. "Should I come with you?"

"*Saa.* It will be easier for me if I, alone, go to confuse our trail. If you are with me, my attention will be on your safety and not on the impressions made in our mother, the earth."

"I understand," she signed, but she felt uneasy. He was doing most of the work, while she had little to do except be at her ease and watch him. "What would you like me to do?"

"Gather some dry wood. Enough to build a fire."

"I can do this."

He turned around and smiled at her. "I know."

She found a small, wooded area nearby and soon had collected enough of the varied small and large branches to make a fire. When she returned, the lean-to was already set up, and a small fire had already been lit. With a quick look inside the shelter, she was surprised to discover Eagle Heart was not within.

Looking outward, she saw him stepping toward her, and soon they were both sitting within their new abode. With the open end of the refuge facing the cliff and the more natural-looking logs and pines branches looking toward the only approach to this ledge, Laylah supposed it was as secure a temporary dwelling as could be constructed.

"Where did you go?" she asked.

"I scouted the environment around this butte to see if any enemy is about. A man does not rest until he has ensured there is no danger from man or animal close to his home."

"Did you find any?"

"I found nothing," he replied in sign, "except a beehive. Sometimes bees can become an enemy. But, not today. There were no bees in the hive."

"Oh," was all she said. "Where are the horses?"

"I hobbled them within the small woods below this ledge. There, the grass is still green and the little stream running through those woods will keep our ponies happy. And now, these things done, it is time for you."

"Me?"

"*Áa,*" he said aloud, then in sign continued, "I notice you are still limping and your ankle is swollen. The roots of the flowers I picked today should aid you in healing." He took off one of the bags he wore around his shoulders and took from it a bowl that looked as though it were made from a buffalo's horn. Next, he set up a tripod over the fire, and, from a string attached to it, he hung the bowl.

He signed, "One of our water pouches is hanging behind me. Would you hand it to me?"

She rose up and stretched a little to get it, offered it to him and then watched as he emptied the water into the bowl. Perhaps as long as a half hour passed as they waited for the water to boil, but at last it began to steam.

Oddly, they didn't speak to one another during this time. Instead, he looked at her so directly and with so much passion within his gaze, she began to feel as though with a look, alone, he made love to her.

In response to him, a sensation of desire rose up within her, and, at the core of her body, a sensation of raw need clamored for her attention.

What was happening to her? To them?

"Come here," he whispered in English, and she found herself scooting around the fire until she sat beside him. "Give me your ankle," he signed.

She didn't even think to refuse.

He spoke to her in English and said, "These"—he indicated the flowers—"*ek-siso-kit*...bear-grass.   I   cut   up...when   you   gone. Roots...for...sprains. Here, put leg...in hand."

She nodded and complied, raising her skirt a little. With his knee, he held her injured ankle over the boiling water containing the bear-grass roots. With his hands, he massaged her leg upward until his fingers found her core.

"Come closer," he encouraged. "While hold...ankle over fire...make love...to you."

"But—"

Then he touched her there between her legs, and any protest she might have made died. Indeed, she thought she might explode with the pleasure of his hand against her. And, with his every touch, she felt herself surrender to him a little more and found her hips and his fingers were keeping time together. He said, "It...good."

But, she was beyond speaking. Her world was on fire.

"Spread legs," he coaxed.

She didn't even think to disobey. And, as she twisted and turned against his touch, she felt as though she burst with sensation, as one erotic pleasure after another filled her senses. She had never before experienced a gratification this intense, this sweet. Was this what being married was all about? If so, she wanted more of it.

He lifted her skirt, and she watched him as he looked at her there. He said, "Must...keep ankle...over steam. We do again...maybe ankle better then."

And, they did, indeed, do it again while he supported her ankle over the steam...and again, and again, on and on, until all the water eventually evaporated from the bowl.

"Water gone," he said, as he used his knee to guide her leg to the buffalo robe she used for sleeping.

"So it is," she said.

"Don't want...leave. Want...do more. But...must go. How ankle feel?"

"Much better," she signed. And I think, my husband, this is a very good way to cause the swelling in my ankle to go down. But, I am concerned, Eagle Heart, for you have not yet sought the same kind of pleasure. Shouldn't you? Isn't that part of love? If it is, there is time to do it."

"*Saa*, it is true what you say, but must not do yet."

"Why must you not?"

"Danger. Fight...maybe. Forbidden make love...before war. Take strength away."

"But, we are not at war."

"We at war...until we...at safe place. Want to love...bad. Cannot."

"Well, my husband, if this is the way it is, the sooner we get to the 'safe place' you speak of, the better."

He sighed, saying in English, "It...so. Must go now. Do not...wish to go. Will leave...food...for you, but we...no stay...here. Must go to...*Miistáksoomahkihki nan,* Big Horn Mountains. There we stay. Safe there."

"How long will you be away, then, cutting our trail?"

"Much time," he continued, speaking in English. "Go back over trail. You eat… drink water. Sleep."

"And, what about you? When will you sleep?"

"Soon. This one…not sleep…until no…harm from enemies. We go…valley, *Miistáksoomahkihki nan*. It safe. No trail…there. People there… sometimes tricky…but friendly. Will work through… day. Return…nighttime. Then we leave. You know…we fleeing?"

"I suppose I have noticed that we are on the run," she signed. "But, why is it necessary to flee? No one will find us here."

"Not true. Easy…to find…for scout. If scout come, we not safe from my enemies…and…yours."

"I have no enemies in this country."

"Now…do." As he drew her skirt back down around her legs and settled his own clothing, he continued to speak, but now in sign, and said, "As soon as you came to me and became my woman, you have made enemies. Your father is one. Curly Mustache is another. And, when they cannot find us, they might hire Crow scouts to come after us. I fear they may already be on our trail. Therefore, we must hurry, but we must also be careful. This is why I go to confuse the path we have made. Stay within this lodge and rest. If you must leave, there is a place on the side of this shelter where there is good drainage. I will be back here when it is dark. This one" — he pointed to himself — "loves you."

And, with this said, he came up to his feet, then ducked under the entrance to their shelter and was gone.

****

On the second evening, it began to rain, and it was not a simple torrent. The rain came flooding down cold and heavy. Nor did it pause for even a moment, so continuous was the downpour. Because they were riding as fast as their ponies could travel, it sometimes seemed to Laylah as though the water droplets slapped her face. But, since it didn't let up, she had become accustomed to it.

She had also grown to be used to her hair hanging wet around her neck and down her back. At present, she wore the buckskin robe Eagle Heart had given her, the one that had been her only clothing during the height of the blizzard. This robe she had placed over her dress, and it did, indeed, do much to keep her warm.

Now and again, she heard a peal of thunder behind them, and she shivered, remembering the result of another lightning storm. As though it might protect her against the thunder and lightning, she had long ago drawn the robe over her head and shoulders, letting the length of it drape down over her pony.

They made a procession of five—two human beings and three ponies—as they hurried over the prairie, skirting the hills and bluffs. It was she who kept hold of his pack pony, for it pulled up their rear. She was next forward in their line, and she was following Eagle Heart, who, despite the rain, kept them all going at a fast pace. Now and again, she looked up to ensure he was still visible, for the rain was so unremitting and hard. And, it was comforting to see he never ran his pony so fast as to be out of her sight.

Sometime in the night, they reached the Tongue River, their path now taking them south and west. Long ago, she had stopped riding the same horse as Eagle Heart; apparently, they were so deeply within Crow country, it was not now safe for the two of them to share the same mount.

It was in the middle of the third night when they began their ascent into the mountains. Their path was now an unmarked trail beneath the great pine and cedar trees of the forest. The rain was less here, if only because the trees acted much as an umbrella, keeping the full force of the storm away from them. Yet, their pace continued to be quick, even though they were now riding within the mountains and their way tended ever upward. Now and again, they would come to an open and natural clearing within the forest; however, Eagle Heart never led them into or through these open places. Instead, he guided their horses around the dells, keeping themselves well-hidden and within the forest.

It was with some relief when they at last came to look upon a narrow and long stretch of a valley, situated as it was between two mountain peaks. Here they paused, looking out upon the land that seemed to go on without end. The early morning gray skies were slowly giving way to a little sunlight; here and there could be seen a glistening light shining down from the sky and touching upon one living creature after another, both animal and plant.

The vegetation in this part of the valley seemed to be mostly sunflowers, blue and pink lupines and others; in truth, the vision before her was as colorful as a rainbow. And, the profusion of their multicolored flowers and their green stems, their leaves and the sweetness of their blooms combined to fragrance the air with a pleasant, natural perfume.

Perhaps even more unusual than the bright colors, however, was the height of these blooms. Truly, some of the flowers stood as tall as her pony's back.

Perhaps it was the lack of oxygen in this high place, but the flowers seemed to be scented more intensely here. It was a strong, yet a pleasingly sweet aroma. And, it caused her to imagine these plants were welcoming her and Eagle Heart to this sweet, expansive valley.

There was, however, no clear path through the wild growth. Cedar and pine trees predominated here, and they covered the smaller foothills which nestled in close to the mountains. The air felt clean and fresh in her lungs, but perhaps there was not as much of it up here, being so highly situated within these Big Horn Mountains.

To say this part of the valley was picturesque would not have done the scenery justice, because, with the snow-covered mountains sheltering the foothills, and the colorful green-and-brown-yet-flat land going on and on as though without end, it appeared as if this scene belonged to heaven, not to this earth. And, the day had only begun. Imagine the beauty of this place when under a full midday sun.

Eagle Heart motioned to her, asking her to bring her horse up level to his. When she did as instructed, he motioned outward, saying, "Be...this...No Man's Trail."

"It's stunning," she whispered. "But, you say few people ever come here?"

He nodded. "It is so."

"I wonder why. I would think this would be the perfect place to camp."

"Now...maybe," uttered Eagle Heart in English, then he switched to sign. "Too few buffalo, though elk, deer and mountain goats are numerous. Winters are hard and long. Residents can be difficult to understand for most."

"Residents? Are you talking about the animals? Antelope, deer?"

"Áa, but...more."

"More?"

"You will meet them," he signed. "They are curious to greet strangers. But, they will come to you. Do not fear them, for they have never hurt any one of us. Come, let us set up a good shelter, for I would like to pause here and rest. This is the safest corner in this part of the world, and it is here, I think, where we might come to know one another as a man and his woman." He then said in English, "Good...place...start our...life. Maybe you...make...breechcloth...give...me...then we play *Cos-soó*...again...you take... cause you...wife and...smart."

She laughed.

He continued in sign, "After we erect a hut for ourselves and secure our ponies away from all eyes, let us eat as much of our food supplies as we like. Later today, I will hunt and scout the land here, for, although I have been here before, to be a successful hunter I will need to make a good memory of the land, for there can be changes to it, even if a man has hunted here many times in the past."

"Yes, I understand. But, while you do this, what are my duties to be in this wild life?" She asked the question with both words and gestures.

He shrugged, then signed, "Perhaps your only duty is to enjoy your time here. When we reach my people, then you might learn to skin an animal and make it ready to cook its meat. Perhaps you might discover the art of making hides for clothing. But, this last can wait until you meet the women of my village, for they keep these secrets within their societies. While we are here, I am hoping you might come to love your life with me. It is our time to be with each other without others coming between us and without the responsibilities of tribal life."

She smiled. "Well, this I can promise you," she said in English and also with signs, "I will give you all my love and for all my life."

His gaze at her was hot and passionate as he signed, "May I always do that which will cause you to love me. Come, it is time for me to set up our lodge in this beautiful valley. When done, I think we might retire to the lake where we can wash and pray."

CHAPTER FOURTEEN

$\mathcal{T}$he temporary shelter took little time for her husband to erect. Eagle Heart called it a "wiki-up," but to Laylah it looked much the same as their other temporary shelters. This one was slightly wider and taller than the others; several poles were stuck in the ground and were made to bend inward, where they were securely tied together. Evergreen boughs became their walls and roof. And, so well did the structure fit into the environment, it might have gone unnoticed if one didn't know it was there.

Pulling the woolen blankets and the buffalo robes off the ponies, Eagle Heart paced toward their shelter and placed them on the ground within, leaving a space in the middle for a fire. Exiting their wiki-up for a few moments, he soon returned, carrying many large stones in his arms, which he set in a circle in the middle of their hut.

Again, he left their lodging, returning with pieces of dry wood; he set these down next to the stones. In one of his bags, he pulled out what looked to be dried grass, some twigs and what looked like dried punk. These he made into a circle. Reaching back into the same bag, he pulled out a piece of flint and set it down on one of the stones. Carefully, he took off the buckskin bags he usually wore around his shoulders, placing them on his blanket. Then, he looked up at her.

Meanwhile, Laylah had taken a position to the right of the entryway of the little hut and had sat down. She wasn't certain which side of their quarters was hers and which was his, but when she saw him position his blanket on the left side of the shelter, she set up her position directly across from his.

He grinned at her and, when she returned the gesture, he arose and came around to her side of the lodge, squatting down in front of her. He said in sign, "Come, there is a lake nearby where we can wash. We can also pray there. I believe we should go before *Naató'si*, Sun, the Creator, as a man and his wife and invite Him into our marriage."

"Yes," she said, smiling at him.

He offered her a hand to help her up and said in English, "When leave...take...hand and we... go to....lake together."

As it turned out, the water was within a short walk from their wiki-up. Plus, it seemed to Laylah as though "the lake" had more in common with a stream than a lake. Its color was fascinating, however, being a deep, muddy blue, which made it a good reflecting pool. Also, this body of water seemed in no hurry to go anywhere, and perhaps this was why Eagle Heart called it a lake.

The sun was high, the day was mild, and the clouds overhead—as well as the mountains on each side of the valley—were reflected in the water, causing the stream to look as if it were hiding the clouds and mountains within its depth. Narrow in width, the stream yet flowed slowly away into the distance until she could see it no more.

Listening to the lonely call of a loon and the music of the thrushes, as well as the sounds of the tree branches rubbing together as they swayed in the wind, caused Laylah to wish to sing aloud with them. But, she didn't, for soon Eagle Heart, who retained hold of her hand, lifted both their arms up toward the sky and began, himself, to sing:

"*Naató'si, amo náápiáakii itstsíí nitohkiimaam (Sun, Creator, this woman is my wife).*

"*Oostóyi omimmo (I love her).*

"*Kitsikák omimm ohpinnaana (We love you).*

"*Nitohkiimi annohk (I have a wife now).*

"*Naató'si, amo náápiáakii itstsíí nitohkiimaam (Sun, Creator, this woman is my wife).*

"*Nit inaanssat Kiistó okamaino anno (I ask you to witness this)."*

As soon as Eagle Heart dropped their arms back at their sides, Laylah murmured and signed, "I don't speak the Blackfoot language as well as you speak English. I know you said something about love, but I didn't understand the rest. Please, will you tell me what you said?"

In sign language, Eagle Heart answered, "I asked the Creator to behold us as a man and his wife. I also told Him we love one another and wish to spend our lives together. We love Him, too. I told this to Him, as well."

Looking up at Eagle Heart, she felt as though she had never been more in love with this man. Indeed, her admiration of him felt instinctive, as though her blood carried his impression within her. It was strange, also; for, although she should have thought to bring God into His rightful place within their marriage, it wasn't she who had conceived of it and had done it.

But, she was not left long to ponder about this, for Eagle Heart had turned to her and said, "Come, we…wash off…dust from…trail. Last…in water…must kiss…other." And, with nothing more said, Eagle Heart stripped down to his breechcloth and ran into the water so quickly, he seemed to practically streak by her.

"Not fair," she protested with a laugh. "I have on many more clothes than you do."

"Then you…must kiss…me. Come…hurry."

"Why hurry?" she asked.

"This one"—he pointed at himself—"needs kiss."

She giggled, yet stripped off her dress and dropped it down over his clothing. She didn't take off her undergarments, however, since she was still a little shy of him.

"You have not fully undressed," he complained, using signs.

She smiled. "I have, too. A proper woman does not take off her undergarments in front of a man. I will go no further. Not now."

"I am…more than man…to you. I am…husband."

"Prove it," she signed.

He laughed even as he waded to the shoreline. Standing over her, he swept her up into his arms, then turned to run back into the water.

Laylah was surprised to discover the stream was deeper than she had assumed. As he waded with her into the middle of the water—thoroughly wetting her clothing—she saw that, in the river's deepest part, it rose up to his mid-chest. As he put her down onto her feet next to him, he bent down to steal a kiss from her, his lips capturing hers in a graze that expanded almost at once into an erotic dance of lips and tongues.

However, he pulled away from her suddenly, tapped her on the shoulder and said in English, "I touch...you must...touch me. If cannot do...I get...more kiss."

"No! You didn't tell me we were going to play tag."

He danced around her, bobbing up and down, tempting her to reach out to try to touch him. But, instead of even trying to do it, she splashed him.

He laughed, then dipped down under the water, where he swam around her as though he were a freshwater shark. Of course, it was bound to happen sooner or later: taking hold of her feet, he pulled her off balance, dragging her underwater, too.

But, she hadn't had a chance to take a breath and so she soon surfaced, gasping for air. She didn't, however, hesitate a second before she took a good breath and plunged back under the water. He grabbed her, and, as they swam together through the water, he pulled her body fully against his.

They twisted and turned together, their legs and feet seeming to dance as though they each one knew the steps needed to propel them through the water. First, he was on top of her as they glided under the water, then twisting, he set her on top of him.

But, it seemed he could stay underwater longer than she. Quickly she rose up to the lake's surface, again gasping for breath. He materialized in front of her, and, without a thought, she tapped him on the shoulder, exclaiming, "You're it."

At once, she submerged and swam away from him as fast as her paddling allowed. But, as he was swifter than she, he quickly caught up to her and, taking hold of her under the water, brought her up and over him, placing her legs around his waist.

He surfaced, keeping her legs in place around him and her arms secured around his neck. He kissed her again, only this time, his caress included her eyes, her cheeks, and even her ears.

Oh, my, her ears seemed to be ultrasensitive, and she longed for him to never stop. But, it wasn't to be. His lips again sought hers, his tongue working magic on her lips, and then, with his hand, he began to rub her all over, from her back to her breasts and lower still. Slowly, gradually, his touch came down to rest once again on that ultrasensitive place between her legs.

At once, she was swept up in the instant passion of this moment and this man. It felt so good, so right, to be here with him like this, and she moved her hips against his hand, urging her body toward the all-consuming apex she now knew existed. All else around her faded except him, his hand, his kiss and his love. It was as though the environment had been in competition with him for her attention and had lost utterly.

She whispered against his lips, "What are you doing to me? It feels so good."

"I...loving you."

"Is this how it's supposed to be always?"

"*Áa,* always."

She couldn't help the way she was moving in reaction to his touch, and, as he continued to stroke her, the rhythm of their sensual dance took on a life of its own. And, when he took her underwater where they danced and stroked and strained together, a deep pleasure, much like the one she had already experienced with him, grabbed hold of her and wouldn't let go. Quickly, he surfaced with her, and she at once took in many deep breaths, all the while relishing in the deep pleasure that shook her body. It went on and on and, as the passion of satisfaction swept through her, the stormy waves in the water were its sole witness. So caught up was she in the moment, she reached out for this man in spirit and joined with him soul to soul, already being attuned to him physically.

Suddenly, his thoughts were as clear to her as if they were her own. Had one human being ever been so closely entwined with another? Even her heart was responding to him, for it beat excitedly.

Her breathing became a quick pant, and she asked the question uppermost in her mind, "Have I become you? And have you become me? I feel as if we are one and the same."

"We...close. We like one, but not...this way all time. I still me...you still you. Sometimes, get so close, we...be each...other. Our love...good. It much good. It much rare...too. Two spirits...join like this."

195

She said, "Yes, I feel this way, too." She paused only a moment before asking, "You seem so wise, though you appear to me to be too young to know so much about a husband and a wife."

"Not...very young. Tepee...small place...for...big family. Good place...for...learning. All...life loves. Learn...much. Many...widows in camp...too."

"I don't think I understand."

He smiled at her, but said no more.

Suddenly, she did grasp his meaning, and she blurted out, "Oh." She paused. "But, my husband, I don't think I satisfied you. I know there is more."

"You...very...wise, too. I good ...for now. This not...right time...do more. Too many...duties I have. But...right time...for you. Tonight we...finish what we start."

"Do you promise?"

He nodded.

Yet, whether this was a right time or not, his hand still rested on her core, and his touch seemed to connect them physically, spiritually and emotionally to one another. She whispered, "Eagle Heart, you are a part of me. And, you have been so for many weeks now. But, having found such pleasure with you, I feel even closer to you now."

"I, too," he said in English, and then he kissed her again, his tongue dancing with hers while his free hand massaged her everywhere. "Wish," he said, "duties...be done. But, they...not done. I water...ponies...shelter them. They...must not be...easy for...others to see. Must hunt...look at...land...also."

"Must you?"

"Ponies...sick if not...cared for. Must...hide ponies...for their...safety...ours, too. Must hunt...food. Are you...able...walk?"

When she nodded, he let go of her legs, allowing her feet to touch the bottom of the stream, although he seemed to change his mind and took her up into his arms again before he waded to shore. He said, "I...take you to...wiki-up. You...safe...there."

Still carrying her in his arms, he negotiated a path through the valley's bountiful undergrowth, taking her to their shelter and, bending, entered their wiki-up. With a few steps, he brought her to the right side of their home, and, as he gently let her feet touch the ground, he kissed her and said, "*Kitsikaká komimmo,* I love you."

"I like that word, *kitsikaká komimmo.* It means, 'I love you', right?'"

He nodded. "If you...want, I...teach you...Blackfoot tongue. You...teach me...speak English."

"My husband, you already speak English."

"But, speak bad."

"It's not bad, but, yes, it is a good idea for us to be able to be fluent in both our languages. Will you be gone a long time?"

"Until...night."

"It seems so long."

"Not too...long," he said aloud before switching his words to the language of sign, saying, "If any of our neighbors come visiting while I am away, it is customary to offer them tobacco, which they love. Please understand, I do not wish to leave you on our marriage day. It is that I must."

"Yes, all right."

He nodded and turned away from her to step toward his own place within their lodge, and, picking up his bags, which he'd set out upon his sleeping robes, he placed all but one of them around his shoulders. Still speaking with sign, he said, "I give this bag to you. There is plenty of tobacco in this pouch for those who might come here to meet you. If a grizzly bear should come visiting, give him as much food as you can. He should not bother you. Mostly our neighbors will be curious about who you are. Animals tend to treat you as you treat them. If you speak to them kindly, use soft words toward them and treat them well, you should have no trouble. I will try to finish my duties as quickly as I can."

"I understand," she said and signed, "but what am I to do while you are gone? I am unaware of what the women must do when their husbands are away."

"Perhaps you could sleep," he suggested, again using signs. "Both of us need more sleep. Or, if you prefer, you could always rearrange our shelter so it suits you better. If you feel you can do so without harm coming to you, you could try to find a spot where you might be able to roast meat and cook. It is best to construct this place out of doors. But, do not start a fire until I return."

She nodded, and he came around to her side of the lodge, taking her in his arms where they remained for some time. At length, he set her away from him and signed, "I wish my duties weren't so important, for I desire to be close to you always. But, a man does not rest his head until he has made a mental map of his surroundings. I love you with all my heart. Look for me in the early evening." Bending, he kissed her, but it was a simple kiss.

She whispered, "*Kitsikaká komimmo.*"

Turning around, he stepped toward the lodge's entry and, bending over at the waist, exited their shelter.

CHAPTER FIFTEEN

*L*aylah looked toward the evening with great anticipation. She had so much to tell Eagle Heart.

Why hadn't he given her more details about the "residents" of this valley? She'd been visited today by a baby deer and its mother, by a raccoon and her offspring. Even an elk had come calling. And, then there were the others….

Somewhere during the afternoon, she'd lost her fear and had dragged out a blanket in front of their wiki-up so she could work on finishing the quilt she was making for Eagle Heart. With the quiet mountains defining the valley and the sun warming the top of her head, it had felt to her as if she worked in paradise.

"What you…making?" asked Eagle Heart in English.

Laylah jumped almost an inch off the ground. "Eagle Heart! Let me know when you are near me. You quite startled me."

"These…pretty colors. Blackfoot colors. Blue…white. What making?" He asked this in sign, but also spoke in English.

"It is my wedding gift to you, my husband," she answered, coming to her feet and extending the blue and white blanket toward him. "I do not know yet how to make things for you with animal skins, but I know how to knit and this is a blanket I've now finished, and it is for you. I give it to you with all the love in my heart."

"And, I take it from you, with all the love in my heart," he said, as he held the blanket out in front of him, his gaze upon it one of admiration. "It is beautiful, like its maker. I love it, and I love you. Always, I will love it.

199

Come, sit with me in front of our home." He smiled at her. "Here, I have a blanket you may sit on."

She laughed and took her seat beside him. After a short while, she signed, "I am glad you are back. Why didn't you tell me about those who live in this valley?"

He grinned. "Want it...be surprise," he said, then switched to sign and continued, "I thought you would like to make the discovery about this tribe on your own."

"But, you could have warned me. My husband, they are little people. Little people. I didn't even know people so small still existed at this time and on this planet."

"I do not know about the rest of the 'planet,' as you say," he signed, "but the Crow have long lived with the Little People. Some say the reason Crow warriors are often successful in battle is because the Little People possess magic and, with this magic, help the Crow warriors to win many of their wars. Did you give the people tobacco?"

"I did."

"*Soka'pii*," he said in Blackfeet, then changed to sign, saying, "That should have made them friendly toward you. I am glad. Now, come, I found a buffalo calf in my travels and have brought home this food, but I know you have not been taught yet how to remove the skin and fur from the animal and then cut up the meat so we might roast it. I will help you and teach you how it is done. Have you set up a place yet to roast meat?"

She shook her head.

"Let us roast the meat inside our lodge, then, where we can have more privacy. It will add a delightful smell to the interior of our lodge."

It was so agreed, and Laylah soon discovered he was right. Before long the roasting meat added a delicious scent to their newly constructed home. Even the fat, sizzling over the fire, added to the feeling of comfort.

As Eagle Heart sat opposite her, and, with the fire crackling between them, he smiled at her, and she returned his grin. But, she looked quickly away. For reasons she could not readily state, she still felt unusually shy with him.

Perhaps aware of this, Eagle Heart rose up and scooted toward her. Sitting next to her, he took her hand in his and began to massage it, bringing it up to his lips, where he placed sensuous, wet kisses over each one of her fingers.

She shivered.

"Do you…like?"

"I like it very much."

He signed, "We have been several days on the move and riding our ponies as fast and as far as they can travel without overly tiring them. Except for today in the water, there has not been time to love one another as a man and his woman should. In truth, had there not been so much of a threat to us, I would have made love to you before today. Then, perhaps you might not feel shy with me."

"I do not feel this way. I am not nervous with you."

Looking down at her, he merely smiled. "If I turn you onto your stomach, I could rub your back. Do you think you might like this?"

She moaned. "I believe I would like it very much."

"Then, let us do it. Will you help me remove your clothing?" he signed. "If I am to massage you, you should be naked."

She gasped, and he grinned down at her. She returned his smile, although she looked away from him quickly.

"But," he continued in sign, "your clothing frustrates me. I don't understand how you get into your dresses or how you get out of them. Can you help me?"

"Of course," she responded, although she still found it difficult to look him in the eye without remembering their passion from this afternoon. However, she came up onto her knees and removed her dress at once, leaving her body still clothed in a knee-length chemise, a demi corset and petticoats; then, she removed these, also. But, she was still feeling timid with him and placed her arms over her breasts when she said, "Well, here I am at last, sitting naked before you, while you, my husband, are still fully dressed, even though you have promised me that you will stand before me naked once we have married."

With no more said, he arose and threw off his clothing in a haphazard fashion, adding his clothing on top of hers. At last he stood before her in no more than a breechcloth.

"My husband, you are still dressed."

The breechcloth came off in a fraction of a second and was added to the pile of clothing, and Laylah was nothing if not properly respectful of the evidence of his manhood. He was that beautiful…and rather large.

She sighed, then signed, "I know a little about the love to be shared between a man and a woman and how it is done, but I don't have any idea what to expect. I am hoping you will take a moment to enlighten me."

He signed, "I intend to dedicate my life to doing this."

"Is it so complex, then?"

He laughed a little before signing, "Not complex. But, a man and a woman should come to know what pleases each other, and sometimes this might take a little time and effort. Come, let us love one another, then we can have a meal, and afterward we will do it again. Right now I would like nothing more than to massage you, and perhaps, if I am lucky, to create a desire within you for loving me tonight. Turn onto your stomach."

She nodded and turned over at once.

He touched her everywhere, from the top of her shoulders, down to her buttocks, then lower to her thighs, calves and feet. And, everywhere he stroked, he also kissed. Gradually, a burning passion filled her being. While she was still lying on her stomach, he parted her legs slightly, his fingers finding her erotic core. Oh, my! Pure pleasure raced through her.

Laylah was well informed of the facts of life; what she hadn't known was the obsession to be so close to him. And, now she knew why: making love was not purely physical, though of course that was part of it. No, a man and wife's lovemaking was more. It was being one with him in spirit; it was loving him so much, she almost burst with it. Perhaps this was why it was so pleasurable. By the act of love, they were becoming closer and closer and closer.

The power of such a spiritual and sexual appeal, she had not expected. Kisses, yes, she understood wishing for his kisses. But, to hunger for him, to yearn to be closer to him than was physically possible, none of this had been known to her.

"Eagle Heart," she whispered, "why do I want to do nothing more than make love to you? Why am I wishing for you to be a part of me, always?"

He groaned, even while his fingers found her most sensitive core, causing her to feel as if she might burst with the same kind of pleasure she had experienced both on the trail and today in the water. It was as though he were creating magic there at her core.

Perhaps it was magic, for, all at once, that ultimate gratification, so familiar to her now, surged within her, sweeping through her entire system. Again, she couldn't control the urge to move, and she twisted her hips against his touch.

"Oh, my," she whispered. "Not only are you the man of my heart, you are also the man who stirs my very soul."

"Áa," he murmured softly. "It same…I feel. Hope you…not just… sweet-talk…me."

"My husband, I am not trying to flatter you. I am simply telling you I love you more than my language permits, for there are no words to describe how I feel. I want to do this again, and I want you to experience this, too. Can we do this again tonight?"

He laughed and turned her over so she was lying before him face up, and, without pausing overly long, he said in sign, "It is in my thoughts that we should do this a great deal more than once tonight. Perhaps we might love each other every morning and every evening… or as many chances as we get. We should love often. But, perhaps you should know this: we are not quite finished with what we have started here…now."

"Of course. I am sorry I am talking instead of urging you to make love to me."

He simply grinned at her and said in English, "No need…urging. I…already there. But, I…lie with you. Let you…feel my…body…against you." Then, in sign, he continued, "Do not be afraid of seeing me ready to love you, for I am bursting with the need of you. It will hurt you the first time, I fear. But, if we do this often, it should hurt you no longer. Your body is meant for this."

"I know. I thank you for your warning, but you do not frighten me," she signed. She squirmed under him and became aware that, for her, there was nothing so potent as this man. If this were what love was about, perhaps she and Eagle Heart might have many children, for she desired to have this man close to her and in her arms as often as possible and making love to her every hour of every day. She smiled up at him and said, "I think I am ready for you to love me."

"Perhaps," he quickly signed. "But, please let me determine if the time is right, for I would not hurt you too much in this, your first time in learning of a man's desire. I am going to spread your legs and let you feel my love first with my touch, alone, like we did this afternoon at the lake. There is time for more than this later."

"What do you mean by this 'more' and 'later'?" Laylah spoke in English and without making signs. "Perhaps I should tell you I intend to know all about love now, tonight. Don't you know, I am so in love with you, I want everything about you to become a part of me? We have already touched one another spirit to spirit and become close even without the act of love. And, now, I know the feeling of love. But, we have not experienced our passion together at the same time, and I want to know this. Tell me, do you think there might come a time where I cannot tell where I end and you begin?" She sighed before continuing, "I want you in my arms, in my life, in my dreams and in my prayers. If it has anything to do with you, my husband, I want it in my life."

Because she had spoken swiftly and hadn't translated her words into the gesture language, she was stunned to look up and see tears in his eyes. She whispered, "I knew you would understand some of what I said, but you understood it all, didn't you?"

He nodded. "Long...have I...understood your...words. Speak...your tongue very...bad. But, we...teach each other."

"Yes, yes. I want you, Eagle Heart. I want your children, I want a home with you, but, most of all, I want you in my life."

He collapsed against her, although he moved the majority of his weight to the side. She was aware it took him a moment or two to compose himself, for he tried to speak several times. At last he said in English, "Always...I want...do...things that...make you love me."

She grinned at him. "Well, you'd better get to work on it, sir, because I am set to make love to you all night."

His laughter was like a heavenly sort of music, and he wasted no time using his touch alone to pleasure her. But, it seemed to her as though he were merely frustrating her. As pleasurable as it had been before, she now wanted more. And, she whispered, "I am ready for you, my husband. Thank you for your consideration, but I want you...all of you. I am ready for you to love me. Are you ready for me?"

He grinned down at her as he came up onto his knees before her. "Long...I...ready." Taking hold of her legs, he placed first one of her legs and then the other over his shoulders and said in English, "This way of loving...I see you. I make...love...look into...eyes...same time."

And, then he joined himself with her. "So...long," he said, "have I wished...for this, I... hard time...holding back."

"No, please, don't hold back," she whispered, even while she met his movements with those of her own.

"Don't...understand. I...wait too long. Hard to...stop."

"Please don't stop."

But, it appeared he wasn't taking orders from her, and he moved against her in a way that brought on the same kind of exquisite pleasure she now understood was a part of lovemaking. She twisted her body along with him, complementing him. And then, looking up into his eyes, she felt again the ultimate sensation of loving this man. Casually, she wondered which was more pleasurable, watching him as he stared down at her or experiencing the feel of him as a part of her.

But, at last it appeared he could hold back no longer, and, moving against her, he took control of their lovemaking and bore into her with all the pent-up energy of a young man long desiring his woman. He was not long meeting his own plateau of sensuality and pleasure, however, and, with the final push against her, he gifted her with his seed.

For many moments, neither of them moved, both of them breathing heavily. At last, however, he fell to her side and brought her up, placing her over him.

She lay upon him, stomach to stomach, breast to breast, her legs straddling him around his waist and hips. She was aware her hair had spread out over his chest and noticed its color seemed in conflict with the hue of his darker skin. Idly, she watched as he brought up a hand to play with one of the locks of her hair, and that's when she saw the two scars, one on the right side of his upper chest, the other on his left.

"What are these?" She traced the scars gently. "Does it hurt when I touch them?"

"No, it does not hurt," he spoke, both in sign and in Blackfeet. "Those scars are from my prayers to the Creator, Sun."

"Scars from prayers?"

"We call it the Sun Dance, a time when a man hopes to communicate with Sun, the Creator."

"Perhaps someday you might tell me more about this, for I am not certain I understand what a prayer and a dance for the Creator have to do with scarring. But, perhaps not now," she whispered against his shoulder. She paused for a moment before asking, "Are we going to do it again?"

He smiled up at her as his black eyes met hers. "Indeed we will do it again,'" he signed, "but let us rest for a moment. If you will look up"—he pointed—"you will see a full moon through the smoke hole at the top of our shelter. Would you like to take a walk with me to the lake and watch the moon as it shines down upon the water? We do not need to get dressed; I will take my robe and perhaps, wrapped together, we can admire the moon and the stars."

"Yes, I like this idea."

He smiled at her as he stood up naked and offered his hand to her, helping her to arise and bringing her nude body in close beside him. He said in English, "You...feel...good. So good, might ...try keep you...always naked."

She giggled a little and said, "Well, two can do this. If you are to keep me naked, then I wish you to be always naked with me, also."

He laughed. "Little...happen then...except love. Make babies...many. Not good...for...you...space between...babies important. But tonight, it good...we be naked...first night...together as man and...his woman."

"I like the sound of that: a man and his woman. Or perhaps, a woman and her man?"

He made no comment on this as they stepped away from their shelter and slowly walked toward the lake's shoreline. His robe covered them both, and he kept his arm fastened securely around her waist. Standing together, first he and then she looked up into the wide blackened sky littered with millions, perhaps billions, of tiny dots of light.

She had never seen the stars shine so brightly, and she wondered why. Was it due to where they were, being located so high up in the mountains? Or was their brightness caused by the position of the full moon, which hung low in the eastern sky? Or maybe it was both.

Nevertheless, it was, indeed, a moment of unparalleled beauty. As a feeling of utter joy swept over her, she sighed, realizing she had never felt as though she, too, were a part of the exquisiteness of nature. And, all this was hers because of the love shared between her and Eagle Heart.

"See you...path in sky?" Eagle Heart pointed toward the Milky Way. "This path...we call...Sparkling Wolf Trail. It on this...trail, *Poia*, Scarface, returned...after visiting Sun."

"I remember this legend," she said, "for you told it to me when we were stranded in the blizzard. It is the legend of the man who journeyed to the Sun so he might marry the girl he loved. Didn't they return to the land of the Sun after they married?"

"*Áa*, they did, but...before they go...they taught...my people ...sacred sweat...lodge...songs...we sing...still."

"Yes, I remember you telling me about this. And, is it the Sparkling Wolf Trail that Scarface and his wife used to travel between the earth and the land of the Sun and stars?"

"It is so."

"How beautiful a legend it is—perhaps as beautiful as this valley, with snow-capped mountains rising up on both sides of us. As I look at their peaks now under the light of the stars, it seems to me as though the only reason for them being there is to protect this valley. Yet," she continued, "it is strange those mountains should be so deeply entrenched with snow, while here in the valley the grass is still green and beautiful flowers grow abundantly. Also, although it is cool here, it is warm enough for us to sit next to this lake. It is as though we have the best of both worlds."

"It is so," said Eagle Heart in English as he stretched out his arm to pull her in even closer to him. She responded by snuggling in toward him as intimately as she was able.

Even still, it seemed to Laylah that she was not as close to Eagle Heart as she might like to be. It seemed funny to her how the idea of crawling beneath his skin—if it could be done—appealed to her. Only then might she feel she were close enough.

She spoke her thoughts aloud, saying, "I wish I could make love to you throughout each and every day. Or, if we couldn't do this, perhaps we could never be apart from one another. What am I to do? I desire to be in your arms always."

He sighed before he said in English, "I...lucky man."

"I feel in a similar way as you," she said. "Lucky."

As she looked outward and toward the lake, she became aware of another strangeness: she was not cold. Indeed, with Eagle Heart's buffalo robe wrapped securely about them both, and, with their arms hugging one another, neither one of them shivered, though the air in this place was cool.

Eagle Heart drew his arm away from her for a moment and signed, "Because this valley is so high up from the prairie floor, and because it is nestled between two of the tallest mountains in this part of the country, it gives a man protection against invaders. It is why so few people have knowledge of this place or come here."

"Truly? How is it you know this valley well enough to bring me here?"

"My father has often brought me hunting here," he said in sign.

She frowned. "But, didn't you say this is Crow country? Couldn't you have attracted a Crow war party by coming here to hunt?"

"We could have, it is true, but we never did. And, I think the reason is because the Little People who live here under the earth protect us. My father learned of this place through a family of Little People."

"Oh my, a family of Little People? But, I thought you said the Little People help only the Crow tribe."

"This is usually true. But, my father's story is a little different," he signed, speaking in Blackfeet, also. "When my father was very young and unmarried, he became part of a war party going into Crow country. It was his first time being on the war path. It was a small party, for he and his friends were still quite young and were only trying to raid the Crow for horses, not take lives. However, a Crow war party of many warriors found them and killed them almost to a man. My father was left for dead. It was told to me by my father that the Little People found him and were ready to kill him, too, for they have always favored the Crow. But, there was a young girl in one of the families of these Little People who looked upon my father with love and would let no one near him. Only she would attend to my father's wounds.

"My father grew well again, and, as he became stronger, he began to hunt for her and her entire family, sharing only the choicest meats with them. She is the one who showed this land to him, and he walked it with her often. They talked very much, for he taught her the Blackfoot language. I was told they often held hands. They even sang together. The snows came twice and still he walked this land with her. You see, he loved her, too. But, their love could never be. You have seen that these people are only as tall as a man's knees and sometimes smaller. Even she knew it could not be.

"After a few years, she told him she had no choice but to let him go back to his own people, he to marry another and she to do so, too. But, she asked him before he left if, once a year, he might come back to this valley to visit with her and to hunt for her people."

"And, he has?"

"Áa," Eagle Heart said in gestures and in the Blackfoot tongue. "My father has never failed to return here at least once a year. As I grew older, he began to bring me to this place, because if anything ever happened to him, he wished me to carry on in the same way as he so as to ensure her family was always well cared for. He loved her very much. He still loves her."

"What a beautiful love story," Laylah murmured. "Did you ever meet her when you came here with your father?"

"I have. The Little People do not age as quickly as we do, and it is said they possess an energy which can produce magic. Her name is Auk-a'pii; her hair is dark brown and curly, and she is beautiful. But, she has her own family now, as does my father. Yet, always, they have loved one another. Never has it mattered that he and she were from different races of people. I have seen them together, and there is happiness all about them when they are together. My father says it causes Sun and even the stars to smile.

"Neither her husband nor my mother, nor any of their children," Eagle Heart continued, "care that the two of them are in love. Her family loves him. And, so I love her, too. My father rarely brought my older brother here because my brother walks a different path than I—his spirit living more in the physical realm than in the spiritual world. He could not see the Little People. Perhaps you should know that if ever my father is unable to come here to hunt, I am bound take his place."

"Of course you will." Laylah was disconcerted to discover she was on the verge of crying, for the story touched some deep place within her. And, she wondered what else was she going to learn in this wild and unchartered land?

"You would not object to this?" he asked in sign. "It would be my duty to carry on as my father had done."

"No, of course I would not object. Although perhaps," she added, "you might allow me to join you on these trips? You must be aware I love it here, too. It is, after all, my first home with you since you have become my husband."

He nodded. "Your heart is generous," he signed. "And, these people will come to love you. But come, your compassion reminds me that I wish to make love to you again this night." He reached out to take hold of her hand. "However, we should not make love here with all the many little eyes to watch us. It might make you nervous." He stood up, bringing her with him.

"And you? Would this not make you uneasy, also?"

He signed. "No. It matters not to me. Still, I would like our love to be private. Come. I find I am anxious to love you again. Be warned. I may never tire of making love to you."

"Oh, I hope you won't, my husband. I really hope you won't tire of me."

"What you speak of is impossible. Perhaps, in old age, the fire between us might require us to relight it from time to time," he said in sign. "But, the flame go out? It will not happen." He shook his head. "*Saa,* it not happen."

CHAPTER SIXTEEN

One day turned into another. In the mornings, Eagle Heart left their simple home to hunt, and, when she asked him why he always traveled so far away on his quest for game, he told her a man never looks for or kills animals for food close to where he lives. To do so could make a man's home very dangerous, indeed.

During the afternoons, Laylah made it a point to help Eagle Heart skin the animals he brought home. She also aided him in preparing their meat for roasting, learning this skill gradually. But, Laylah noticed a few aspects about skinning an animal she had never witnessed before, and it made her curious.

Always, Eagle Heart said prayers over the beast he had killed, and Laylah, under his influence, had begun doing much the same. Laylah noticed, also, that Eagle Heart gave away much of their food to the Little People and to any of their other animal friends who came to visit.

Once, she had questioned him about this practice of giving away a good deal of their food, and she'd asked, "Do you think it wise to share so much of the meat we have?"

"We have plenty, more than we need, and the hunting here is good because so few predators come to this valley."

"Of course," she said. "Still, wouldn't it be wise to preserve some of it? I remember during the snowstorm you had a good supply of dried meat. Could you show me how to prepare meat this way?"

211

"Áa," he signed. "I will show you how to smoke the meat, and your suggestion is a good one. We should make meat for hard times. But, an honorable man gives away as much food as he consumes. It is his duty to ensure his friends are as well fed as he is. If he has to hunt more often, so be it."

"No wonder the animals love you so much."

His simple smile at her gave her much pleasure, as though he bestowed a little bit of heaven on her.

The evenings were all she could have ever wanted, for she had this man entirely to herself, and, after their supper, they made love throughout most the night, both of them catching up on their sleep between lovemaking.

Sometimes Eagle Heart even slept in late, delaying his hunting until the afternoon. Indeed, the days and evenings were romantic in so many different ways, and Laylah couldn't remember ever being so happy.

One afternoon, as she was assisting Eagle Heart in skinning the deer he had brought into their camp, she asked, "What is the yellow powder you sprinkle over the animal you have killed? I hear your prayers, and I understand why you pray over the animals, but what is the yellow dust for?"

"I will show you," he signed.

She nodded.

"Hunting is and should always be a prayer," signed Eagle Heart, "for a man must take the life of another in order to ensure his own family does not starve. Being so close to the animals one needs to kill in order to survive, a man becomes aware of the creation of life all around him. It is why we pray over the animals we have killed. But, we do more.

"It is possible I might be able to show you how we try to help the animal we have killed. I think I could do this with this deer, because the living spirit of this animal has not yet left its body. If you watch closely, you might be able to see the spirit of the animal as it departs its body."

Laylah frowned. "I thought animals didn't possess a spirit."

"There are white trappers who have told me they believe this, also, and they are welcome to think this if they choose. But, my tribe and all the tribes around us, even our enemies, know that all of creation is alive; all things are made up of the same rocks, stones and dirt of the earth and all are alive. But, you must decide this matter for yourself. Watch."

Eagle Heart began to sing and pray over the animal as he usually did, and, taking some of the powder from the small bag he always wore around his neck, he sprinkled the yellow dust over the animal, the color of the dust catching hold of and reflecting the rays of the afternoon sun.

"Do you see it?" he asked in sign. "Look for the aliveness of the animal rising up out of its body. It is not physical, but if you pay close attention, you might see it because you, too, are spiritual. Here comes the spirit as it rises out of its dead body. Do you perceive that it follows the path of the dust I have sprinkled, its path guiding it up toward the sky and the Creator of all, Sun?"

Laylah had looked on and at first had seen nothing. But then, glancing all around the animal, she became aware of something rising up and departing from the body of the animal.

Not really sure what she was looking at, she yet watched as an invisible something left this animal's body—she even watched it as it followed the yellow path upward toward the sky. With what must have been large eyes, she turned her head to stare at Eagle Heart.

She whispered, "I didn't know animals had a soul."

He signed, "Have you not now seen one leave the body of this poor deer?"

"I did see it."

"We are all connected," he told her in sign, bringing his two hands together, linking them as though in brotherhood. "We all live and enjoy the thrill of life, and we all die. All life must depend upon animal or plant life, or sometimes both, to become food so all may live. Plants do the same, taking what they need from our Mother, the Earth. All life must do the same as we do. Simply because we must eat does not mean we must divorce ourselves from the life that is all around us and pretend it is not also alive and lives much the same as we do."

Still feeling as if her eyes were mirroring her incredulity, she remarked, "Should I not eat meat, then? Perhaps I should change my diet so I am eating no meat at all?"

"Do you ask this question because you think plants do not have a spirit that, like us, desires to live?"

213

"Of course a plant doesn't have a spirit. It is only a plant, after all."

He smiled at her and reached out to take her hand in his, bringing it to his lips. Then, releasing her hand, he signed, "Come, let us finish skinning this deer and putting its meat over the fire, and I will introduce you to the plants, for all things are connected and all things on this earth are alive. And, if it is alive and if it is on this earth, it is, like us, spiritual. When the body dies, that which makes the plant or animal aware it lives, is released. We of the Blackfoot Nation at least try to guide its spirit up to the sky and to Sun, the Creator."

Laylah frowned. Even though she had "seen" the spiritual entity leave its body and float upward, this was too new and too different a viewpoint for her to readily accept as true. But, it did cause her to wonder if she had really been truly living before she'd met this man. Wolves who, when asked, came to her aid; a deer as a spiritual being; the love of the Little People and now plants, too? They, like human beings, were alive and possessed a spiritual quality about them? She swallowed hard before asking, "What is the yellow dust you sprinkle over the animal?"

"Pollen."

She nodded.

"Come," he signed, "let us finish this task and then, if you will follow me, we should go and talk to the plants."

And, Laylah did, indeed, help him finish the task, knowing they would do exactly as he said they might do. And, before they sat down to enjoy their supper, she found herself silently conversing with the flowers that graced a beautiful and colorful meadow….

****

"I…love you…always."

"And, I will always love you, my husband. How do you say those words exactly in Blackfeet? As you know, I am trying to learn your language."

"And, you are learning it faster than I have acquired your language," he signed.

"I don't think so. You are already talking to me in English, and I can barely string together a thought in Blackfeet."

"You are kind," he signed, then said in English, "What…you wish?" He grinned at her. "You want…me…tell you I…always love you?"

"Yes, of course, but no! I want you to tell me how I say that to you, not how you say it to me."

"*Soka'pii.* You...say...'always, husband...will I...love you.'"

She laughed. "I know how to say it in English. I want to know how to say it Blackfeet."

He grinned at her. "*Ha'ayaa.* You say '*Inaapiim, kitsiiká komimmo.*'"

"Say it slowly."

"*In-aapiim, kits-iiká ko-mimmo.*"

"*In-aapiim, kits-iiká ko-mimmo,*" she repeated. "I think your idea of us learning to speak each other's language—and to speak it well—is a good idea. Perhaps we might devote a little more time to doing this in the evening."

He nodded. "*Soka'pii*, good. I would speak English...good. Here...come close."

She laughed. "I don't know how I could get any closer to you. We are both of us naked, I am lying on my side right next to you and my leg and my arm are all over you, trapping you against me, while my head is resting on your shoulder."

"Trapped...am I?"

She giggled.

"Know...I how...get we...closer."

"Oh?"

"Here, lie...under...me. I...show you."

Again, she laughed. "You need to move, then. You are too heavy for me to get you into position over me."

"I...? Heavy?"

She smiled. "Oh, please..."

But, in this he was compliant, and within a short time he maneuvered her neatly under him while he came up onto his forearms over her, his lips teasing first one and then the other of her breasts. "Promise...when...have first...child...share you its...milk with me."

She chuckled. "But, I will need the milk for our baby."

"*Ha'ayaa!*" His look at her seemed suddenly sad. "None...for...me?"

"Oh, all right. You can have a little. Perhaps when we make love."

He sighed. "*Soka'pii.* Then I...not starve."

"My husband, you are such a good hunter, I do not think we would starve."

"Flatter...me...you do," he said, as he came up onto his knees between her legs, positioning each of her legs over his shoulders. He whispered in Blackfeet, "Without your love, I would starve. I may never tire of making love to you...many times...every day."

"Oh," she murmured, smiling up at him. "How glad I am to be learning your language, for I understood what you said. And, I wish you to know that I, too, want this. Do you promise?"

"Try...I will. You...learning Blackfeet...fast."

"But, not as quickly as you have learned English. And, I do not speak it well enough yet. Now, come here, and let us make beautiful love together."

He did not hesitate to give her what she desired and soon became one with her, uniting their bodies, and, as she met his movements in the age-old dance of love, she looked up into his deep, black eyes and felt as though she were becoming more and more a part of him. Yes, she was still who she was, but...she was now him, too.

It was a strange concept and an odd feeling, yet it was pleasing. And, as they met on love's high plateau together, she knew that forever this man would be in her heart. Always...

****

Eagle Heart awoke with a start. He was sweating profusely and, sitting up, realized his sleeping robes were wet. His arm was still around the beautiful woman curled up beside him, and he experienced again the happiness that had become so much a part of his life since he had married this exquisite, yet spiritual woman.

Nevertheless , though he was happy beyond what he had ever imagined possible, he had dreamed of his brother this night. It was not a "medicine" dream, foretelling the future. Nor was it a bad dream. Perhaps it was simply a dream to remind him about his original purpose in leaving his home to make the long journey to Fort Union.

And, it seemed he did need reminding, for his attention was where, perhaps, it should be for a newly married man. But, he must not lose his way; he had traveled far across the prairie and mountains—and even hostile country—so he might find his brother and bring him home.

True, he'd had little to help him along the path of discovery, for the mostly silent and distant communication between him and his brother—which had at first flourished—had stopped almost entirely. Indeed, he had no clues as to what had happened to cause this. Worse, he had no means to determine where his brother was at present.

Of one fact, however, he was certain: his brother was still alive. But, where was he? And, why was his brother not responding to Eagle Heart's attempts to communicate in the age-old manner of the ancient scouts and medicine men?

Leaning down toward his wife, who was securely nestled within his arms, he kissed her gently on the forehead and began the slow process of disentangling their limbs. He needed a moment to think, and this required him to be alone.

He wouldn't go far away, for a man must always guard his wife against any possible danger. But, he could sit outside their little abode and let the familiar sounds and sights of nature calm him enough to perhaps reach out toward his brother again.

Rising up to his feet, he grabbed hold of his breechcloth and leggings and tied them on. Next, he drew on his shirt before stepping into his moccasins. Quickly, he reached out to grab his quiver full of arrows and his bow, which were always positioned within easy reach. He placed them over his shoulder, then bent to set his sleeping robe next to his wife; perhaps she could snuggle against it. This done, he grabbed another of his buffalo robes and threw it around his shoulders. Bending at the waist, he crawled out of their shelter and stepped into the night.

He stretched before sitting down in front of his lodge, keeping his senses alert to any possible danger to him or to his wife. But, he saw no outright danger; plus, his perception of his environment did not show any enemy in the vicinity.

"I am glad to see you are happy, my son." The voice was speaking in the Blackfoot tongue, was high-pitched, soft and was one he recognized. It was Auk-a'pii, the little woman whom his father had loved...still loved.

"My heart is happy to see you have come visiting, Auntie. My wife is still asleep, but won't you sit with me? Might I offer you a fine piece of meat to eat, or perhaps some water to drink?"

"Thank you, but my supper was filled with good meat from your hunt, and I am no longer hungry nor thirsty. But, I would be honored to sit with you." She came to his side and sat next to him. As she looked up at him, she asked, "How is your father?"

"He is well," answered Eagle Heart. "One of his sons is a chief of a different band of our tribe, and his other son is, as you know, a medicine man. My father is happy, but I think his heart longs for the moon of flowers when he can visit here again and be reunited with you and your family."

"Perhaps he might bring his wife here to meet us. He loves his wife well, does he not?"

"He does. And, she loves him. Perhaps he might bring her here. I will tell him what you have said, and, since she no longer has small children to care for, she might come for a visit, also."

"I am glad to hear it," replied Auk-a'pii. "And, I am pleased to see you with a beautiful bride. I sense she loves you very much, as you love her, too."

He nodded.

"But…"

Eagle Heart waited.

"Something troubles you. I know you well, and, although I am aware you are happy with your wife, I have to come to realize you are troubled."

"Áa."

"What is it, Ohkó. I will listen. Perhaps I and my people might be able to help."

He sighed. "You bring me great honor, Auntie. But, a man does not unburden himself or speak of his troubles to a woman." He smiled. "Even a small woman."

"Of course you would feel this way. It is part of your Blackfoot heritage," said Auk-a'pii. "But, there is no one else here who knows you as well as I do. And, years and years ago, I used to listen to your father when he was worried. I have a good ear for this and like to think I helped him. Perhaps, instead of calling me 'Auntie,' you might think of me as a medicine woman. After all, my people are sometimes able to capture and use the energy and enlightenment of good magic."

"I am certain you helped my father greatly, Auntie—the medicine woman. And, I know your people are able to sometimes use magic to help others."

She sighed, then, in a small voice, asked, "Is it about your brother?"

Eagle Heart groaned deep in his throat. But, at last, he said, "It is. But, how did you come into this knowledge?"

"I am a medicine woman to my people."

Eagle Heart didn't respond.

"You look for him, do you not?"

Her question was met with silence. At length, however, Eagle Heart confessed, "I cannot speak of this to you. You may be a medicine woman, but you are still female, and a true man does not place his burdens upon the shoulders of a such a one."

"But, you do not know where he is. Is this true?"

Eagle Heart smiled down at the very small, but lovely woman. "It seems you are bound to have this conversation with me, whether it is manly to do so or not."

"*Soka'pii*. I am glad you realize this."

His laugh was spontaneous and of good humor.

"I have always loved your father, and I extend my love to you, also," said Auk-a'pii. "But, you know this. Please, do not fear that you will be less a man because you speak to me. Please, tell me, what is the trouble?"

Again, Eagle Heart sighed. At last he replied, "I do not know. He disappeared at Fort Union. Discovering this, I went to the fort to find him. It was at this same trading post where I met my wife. And, so much happiness do I find with her, I forgot the sadness within my heart because of my brother's disappearance. When I was at the fort, I was able to discover he stole a Crow woman, and they disappeared together. After this, I tried to reach him with the silent communication we both can speak. At first, we were able to connect in this way. No longer can I do this with him, and I do not understand why because I know he is still alive."

Auk-a'pii nodded. "I understand now. It is good you have told me this, for I may be able to help you locate him. Let me speak with the elders of my people and suggest that we try to find your brother in spirit. Sometimes my people are able to do this. I cannot promise we will discover where he is. But, I think we could try."

"I would be honored and grateful if you and your elders could do this, since it would help me to determine where I should go. He is much loved by all his family."

"I know he is because I also know and love your father."

As Eagle Heart smiled down at the little woman, he said, "And, he loves you, as I do, also. If we were from the same tribe of people, we would be family."

She laughed a little. "It does not matter, this tribe you speak of. Forever, your father, your mother, your brother and your sisters are my family, as my family is yours. I will try to discover more about your brother's disappearance." She arose then, and, even though he was used to witnessing how small she was, even he was surprised to see the top of her head barely reached up to his shoulders. But, it seemed she had more to say, for she said, "Perhaps I should tell you this, also: your wife's father and a Crow warrior are tracking you. They mean you harm. You, personally."

"I know. I have become aware of them. I believe they are yet three, perhaps four days behind me. They come on, day after day, despite my cutting our trail and erasing our camps."

"They will not find you, for we will never let them discover you while you are here."

"Auntie, you bring me great honor, but I would not be the cause of bringing evil into this valley. I do not know how my father-in-law and his scout found my trail, except if perhaps this Crow warrior can see over great distances, and this is how he has discovered me. If so, he could come here. This means I must go."

"I do not agree, for we would never let them find you. Yet, I understand. You are so like your father."

Eagle Heart smiled. "Many of my people have also told me this."

Gently, she touched his arm. "I will come to you tomorrow and tell you what our elders have said about your problem. Sleep well, *Ohkó*, because, since you are determined to leave here, I fear your next several days might be without sleep."

He nodded, and, in an instant, she was gone. If one did not know these people well, one might think she had disappeared as though swallowed up by the air. But, Eagle Heart knew differently; he was aware there were entrances scattered here and there within this valley that allowed the Little People to appear above or below the ground.

Indeed, he was honored she had sought him out to speak with him. He would ensure he left many presents for her, for her family and for the others in her clan before he left this valley.

Feeling a little calmer, he crept back into the wiki-up he shared with this beautiful woman whom he loved with all his heart.

****

"He comes."

Laylah peeped open one eye to glance up at Eagle Heart. He was awake, was moving about their lodge and looked to be concentrating on the particular, yet difficult, task of attaching an arrowhead to an arrow. Over the last several weeks since they had been in residence here, he had hung many of his weapons, his buckskin bags and different assortments of beaded regalia on the walls of their shelter—always within his reach. She could see he had taken these possessions from the walls and was setting them into a neat pile next to the entrance.

She stretched, placing her arms over her head. What a wonderful dream she'd been having—a dream which included her, Eagle Heart and their five children. But, as she came more fully awake and looked up searchingly at Eagle Heart, she realized he was in no mind to come back to bed: he was fully dressed in leggings, breechcloth, moccasins and his knee-length shirt. Even his hair was braided, instead of being left long and falling down his back. He looked much too handsome for a young girl's heart, but there was an air about him that made him look dangerous this morning, as though he were expecting a fight...and soon.

Perhaps this was because his dress today included his shotgun and several knives, as well as his usual quiver full of arrows and his bow. Beside him, and leaning against their shelter, stood his lance, and still hung upon the wall was his shield. Also, tucked within the belt at his waist were two more guns, and placed diagonally across his breast was a leather sash containing a great deal of ammunition.

"Who comes?" asked Laylah as she sat up and fluffed her hair.

He didn't answer right away, but instead stepped toward her and squatted next to her. In response, she came up onto her knees and placed her arms around this man, gifting him with many kisses upon his face and his lips. Because she was still nude, she could easily feel the butter-like texture of his softly tanned shirt, as well as the hard leather and cold metal of his ammunition sash.

In response to her, he pulled her into his embrace and, reaching forward, caressed first one of her breasts, then the other. She listened as his breath became strained and faster. Yet, he was soon setting her away from him.

She sighed. It appeared she was not going to coerce him back into passion this morning.

He bent down a little, however, and placed his forehead against hers. Then, in English, he answered her question and said, "Father...yours. Comes."

"My father?"

"And...Crow scout."

"I guess this means we will be leaving?"

He nodded. "*Áa, Ikimopii aakíi*, I fear...this...true."

"*Ikimopii aakíi*? What does this mean? I've not heard you say these words before now."

"Woman," he signed quickly, "who sits in place of honor. Sits-beside-him-woman." After signing this concept, he looked away from her, his attention seemingly fixed on the knife sheath at his side.

"Oh. I remember you calling me this once before, but in sign language. What is a sits-beside-him-woman? A wife?"

"*Áa*," he agreed, his concentration still elsewhere. But, he nevertheless explained, "A sits-beside-him-woman...is...first wife, honored wife of...man's heart."

Laylah went suddenly still. *First wife?* What did this mean? She coughed, then sat back, out of his reach.

Thinking perhaps she hadn't heard him correctly, she asked, "Did you say it means a 'first wife,' as in the idea of a man having a second wife?"

Glancing back at her, he answered in sign, "Or a third or fourth wife. As you probably are aware, a man might have even more wives if he is a chief and if there is too much work for the women in his family. It would be his duty to take more wives, because a man must not overly burden the women he loves." He looked away from her as he continued to sort through his things.

But, it didn't matter if she had his attention or not. She was momentarily stunned and found she could do little more than stare at him. At length, however, she asked, "Does this mean you could take another or several wives besides me, while still being married to me?"

"*Áa*, I could," he said in English, though he did not look at her. "But...man must have many horses or must be...chief or heap good hunter...have more...than one wife. Man must...be able...feed his family. This...man's duty."

She murmured, "Are you a chief?'"

"*Saa*, not chief. Am only...medicine man. Not...rich. Not many...horses... could give for...wife."

"Maybe you are not rich in horses, but you are a heap good hunter."

He gazed up at her and grinned, but said nothing, which she had come to learn was his usual response when he agreed with her.

"So," she continued, "since you are a good hunter, then you could marry another woman, or maybe two?"

"You not worry," he said in English. "If...you need help, I can do."

"You can do what? Marry another woman?"

"*Áa*."

Indeed, it appeared he could. Why hadn't he mentioned this before they had married? Surely, he must know her society did not allow a man more than one wife.

Or did he? He seemed to be rather lacking in knowledge about her culture.

Her breath caught, and for several moments she couldn't move. Then, contradictorily, it felt as if she were in motion, for she was trembling.

She opened her mouth to say something, anything, but found to her dismay she couldn't utter a word. Only one fact screamed at her: she was married to this man, yet he could very well take another woman as a second wife.

Suddenly, her nudity bothered her, and she reached down to bring the blanket up to cover her upper body.

Eagle Heart, however, appear to not notice her withdrawal, although he did, at last, look up at her. Scooting forward, he drew the blanket down to her hips and reached out to trace one of her breasts with his fingers. She backed away from him, and her action at last brought his attention more fully upon her.

He frowned before asking in English, "Wrong? Something...wrong?"

She nodded. It was all she was capable of doing at the moment. Words failed her.

"Much...we must...do...today. But...this important. I listen. You...speak."

She gulped, opened her mouth to try to talk, but accomplished no more than swallowing...hard.

He backed away from her and came to sit down upon their sleeping robes, his legs crossed in the traditional Blackfoot Indian–style. He repeated, "I listen."

Meanwhile, Laylah was beyond being able to think coherently. *First and second wives?* How could he casually mention a first wife and perhaps many other wives, and do this as though he were speaking of a custom as common as the sharing of a meal?

Have I made a mistake in marrying this man? Although I love him with all my heart, I could never live with him if he took another wife.

He didn't say a word; nor did he look at her. Instead, he seemed to have found an abundance of patience within him, for he did nothing more than wait and stare at the ground.

At last, she was able to murmur softly, "I...I don't know what to say."

He signed, "I...not hear this."

She swallowed again, the lump in her throat refusing to budge. Several times she attempted to speak, but her voice failed her. Instead, a tear streaked down her cheek.

"What...wrong?" he asked again.

She shook her head from side to side. Reaching out, he traced the tear as it ran down her cheek, but she looked away from him, causing his hand to fall away.

"Wife? Wives? Or...lack of ponies...no wealth?" he asked. "This...what last said. Makes...you cry?"

She bit her lip. She didn't really wish to speak to him about this—at least not right now. She felt...odd, as though she were spinning. And, at the moment she wasn't certain she could piece together an entire sentence.

Truly, what she really needed him to do was leave and allow her to dress and perhaps grant her a moment to think. But, it didn't appear as if he were in a mood to go anywhere. And, she felt alone as she attempted to sort through the jumble of her thoughts:

My husband could take another wife. If he did, I would have to leave him. But, I love him. How could I leave him?

Suddenly, she couldn't tolerate the conflicts spinning around in her mind, and, clutching her robe closely around her, she jumped up, ran to the lodge's entrance, bent over quickly and stepped through the entrance flap. At present, she required time alone, and, as quickly as possible, she fled toward the lake.

Once at its shore, she threw off her robe, ran furiously into the water and quickly submerged herself into its cold depths. It was not merely cold, it was freezing this morning, and she shivered. Yet, she didn't care. Perhaps the frigid temperature might allow her more clarity of thought. At least, she hoped it would.

CHAPTER SEVENTEEN

What was wrong?

Why had his wife suddenly become incapable of speech? And, what had he said to cause her to cry?

Wife? Wives? This had been one of their topics of conversation.

It didn't make sense. Why would this ancient and common custom—one meant only to unburden and comfort one's first wife—cause her to cry? He went backward in time within his mind, recalling his words: he had told her casually of the tremendous workload placed upon the women of his tribe. At the same time he had informed her of his lack of wealth in horses.

His wife was not stupid. Had she pieced together the realization that he, as a medicine man, would not be able to present a girl's father with enough horses to obtain a second wife?

Did she fear this might cause her to become overburdened? That, by marrying him, she had lost the life of leisure she'd known at the fort? It could be this last, since he had observed her existence there had been one of ease.

Was this his woman's worry? And, if this were what was wrong, could he relieve her mind?

As he followed her out of the wiki-up and paced toward the lake, he began to recite inwardly what he might say to her. He set his destination toward a stubby willow tree—one that sat close to the lake, yet was out of her view. And, as he sat down beneath it, he thought of the best way to approach this matter with her.

226

"I am glad to see you are awake and moving about early this morning, *Ohkó*, though I understand what sometimes keeps you in your lodge until late in the morning." These gentle words were followed by high-pitched, yet soft, laughter.

Eagle Heart grinned down at the tiny woman who was standing beside him. "And, I am happy to see you, also, Auntie."

Auk-a'pii sat down at his side, and, as soon as she did so, she almost became lost in the luxurious grasses and flowers that grew beneath the short willow tree. Looking up at him, she asked, "Was the rest of your night restful and free of dreams?"

"It was. And, I thank you for our conversation."

"You are welcome. I am glad to know you slept well after our talk."

He nodded.

"I have come to tell you what the elders have decided, for I was able to speak with them this morning. They have reached a decision, and we have all agreed we should help you. Many of us tried to reach out to your brother, but there was only one amongst us who was able to see into the far-off places of this land. He now believes he has located your brother and those who are with him."

Although Eagle Heart rejoiced inwardly, he did no more than simply nod outwardly.

"You have been right in believing he is still alive," continued Auk-a'pii. "A Crow woman and her baby are with him, as well as a Big Person. The Big People are the reason he is gone, of course."

Of course? Eagle Heart, however, did not speak these words aloud. Patiently, he waited.

"Your brother and the Crow woman are in the Apsáalooke, Beartooth Mountains, not far from here. If you leave to go there, please remember this is Crow country, and we advise you to use great caution once you set foot out of this valley. This same particular elder who located your brother has also observed your brother and the Crow woman are moving camp often, but he believes they have stopped at Lone Elk Lake, and he feels they may be there for several days. Another of our elders believes your brother is using the Lone Elk Lake area to hunt, for he became aware of their food supply, and it is low. As you know, the region abounds in bighorn sheep and mountain goats. Why the Crow woman and her baby are with

227

your brother or what they might mean to him, we do not know. But, another of our elders thinks the trouble began with a Big Person and the Crow woman's baby. He believes, also, that your brother has saved the Crow woman's life, as well as her baby's life, twice. There may be others of an unknown origin involved in the trouble. But, we do not know more than this. Again, we believe your brother is camped within the Lone Elk Lake region."

"*Iniiyi'taki,* I am grateful to you and your elders. You have discovered much more than I would have been able to do. I will always remember your kindness toward me and my brother. Will you relate my gratitude to your people and tell them I will leave you most of our food stores, as well as all of my tobacco? We will take with us only what we might need for the journey into the Beartooth Mountains."

"You are generous and kind. But, you might need all of your food on your journey."

"I can see what you are thinking, but we have plenty. I will take no more than what we will require. The rest will be yours. I only wish I could give you and your people more."

"It is enough. We are very happy to help you, *Ohkó* . And now, having delivered our knowledge to you, please excuse me. I must leave to go home. Because I still have young children in my home, I fear without me there to watch over them, they are bound to have found some sort of mischief to pursue."

He nodded and smiled at her. "*Áa.* Go to them. Here…" Eagle Heart drew off his silver earrings and handed them to Auk-a'pii. "These are a gift to you and to your family. If your family likes them, perhaps I might make more of them for you in the future."

"*Iniiyi'taki, Ohkó.*"

"We will be leaving here today. Please extend my love to the rest of your family. I will return here as soon as I can."

Auk-a'pii nodded, and, turning, she was gone, disappearing as though she had vanished into the air. But, because her coming and going was not unusual to him, he barely noticed.

Instead, he turned his attention to his wife.

Gazing toward the lake, Eagle Heart realized his wife had emerged from the water and was sitting alone on the lake's tiny shoreline; her robe was wrapped tightly around her. Even from where he sat, he could see she was shivering, and, now and again, he watched her shoulders shake from what must be grief, not cold.

Because he knew he needed to try to alleviate her concerns, he was anxious to talk to her; there had been many ideas he could have said to her earlier and hadn't done so. At the time, he had been distracted.

But, because he rarely acted on impulse, he sat for a moment so that he might recite simple words he could say to give her comfort. It shouldn't be difficult to relieve her fears. After all, he loved her more than life, itself. And, he knew she loved him. Therefore, it shouldn't be too difficult a task to bring happiness back to her eyes.

****

Something touched her left shoulder, and, looking up, Laylah saw that *he* stood beside her. He came down onto one knee and reached around her robes to pull her into his embrace.

She sighed. Whether for good or for bad, it felt good to be back in his arms. Pulling her in toward his chest, he placed his chin on top of her head.

Several moments passed while they sat thusly, until, at last, he murmured in English, "I love you more…than…ever loved another. Cry, do not. Heart…mine…is…yours. You part of me now, part…of my spirit and…body. Tell me, would you…talk…to me what…happened?"

She sniffled and nodded. But, what could she say? *You are a bigamist?* No, those words sounded so bare and accusative. She couldn't say them to him.

Perhaps she might simply ask him about the Blackfoot custom of marriage. Yes, this was a good place to start.

Taking a deep breath for courage, she asked, "Please tell me, is it your intention to marry more women?"

"*Áa*, I understand…your concern, for there…much work…in my…camp. Know…I will do this so I…not…burden you. As medicine man…I not rich in horses, but am…good hunter. So you no cry. Will take…other wives as…can afford…so you not…work too hard."

In response, she sat up out of his arms and, backing away, looked him directly in the eye. What she was hoping to find there within his glance, she didn't know. But, suddenly, his words created a fury of shock waves shooting through her mind, and she began to shake. Taking a moment, she looked inwardly to find solace so she might remain calm. But, it was not to be. The deed was done: she had married a man who believed polygamy was good and a common way of life.

It would seem she had made a substantial mistake. But, now what?

She couldn't blame him for his beliefs. This was the way he had been raised. Yet, she did not share this custom—could never share it. After all, she was Christian, and her God forbid polygamy.

What was she to do?

She tried to contain herself, but in the end she couldn't help it: she cried again, and her tears caused her to hiccup uncontrollably. Quickly, she jumped up out of his arms and ran toward the wiki-up with all the speed she could muster.

Once inside, she dressed quickly, as though her life depended on it. And, maybe it did, because sitting naked with this man on the beach while he calmly discussed his other—and future—wives, was a little like dying.

With no thought to the beauty of her attire, she threw a dress over no more than a simple chemise, pressing the wrinkles out of her skirt as it fell to the ground. She did even less grooming with her hair, merely running her hands through her long locks. Carefully, she stepped into her boots, then took a deep breath for courage, for she must confront this man, and she didn't know really how to do it.

She couldn't remain married to him under these circumstances— indeed, not. Not only was polygamy *not* her custom, her Faith *forbid* it. Yet, she loved this man with all her heart. His kindness, his care of her during her convalescence, his quiet humor and his spiritual insights caused her to yearn to be as close to him as possible.

But, contrarily, this—his desire to take more than one wife— spurred her on to take some sort of action. She would have to leave him...and quickly. But, first, shouldn't she ensure they were speaking about the same thing? After all, there were language barriers between them.

What if she had been so upset at the mere mention of a second wife, she'd misunderstood him? Or what if he had misunderstood her?

Perhaps if she talked to him as calmly as possible, she might discover his true intentions. Or perhaps he might decide he didn't really wish to marry another woman. Maybe, just maybe, she might be able to change his mind if he insisted polygamy was in their future.

But, if this were so much a custom with his people, and, if he had his heart set on marrying other wives, maybe she should ask him to take her back to her own people, even though going back to Fort Union was unthinkable.

Might she be able to convince him to escort her to the nearest trading post in this part of the country? Although another fort might not be as comfortable as Fort Union, she could still spend the winter months there. And, in the spring, when the steamboats operated again, she would return to St. Louis.

Yes. She really had no option but to speak to him and determine if her fears were real. She would be as calm as possible when she approached him and she would ask for his help. She was, after all, alone with him and in a location where she could not easily find her way back to Fort Union, nor did she know how to get to the nearest trading post, if this were what she decided was her best course of action.

Plus, and this was important: she was utterly dependent upon him for her survival. She had no means by which to hunt, nor did she know how to clean game without his help, nor how to make a fire without flint. She didn't even have the skills to construct a shelter that would protect her from rain or snow. Indeed, she would require his cooperation.

But, there was an even larger problem than any of these: they had both invited God into their marriage. This meant her God, the Creator, or Sun—as he called his God—were part of their union. Yet, his God allowed a man to commit polygamy, whereas her God forbid it.

Should she tell him this? Would it make a difference?

Realizing she had no choice but to conquer her inability to speak with him, she threw her hair back behind her shoulders, stood up and, bending to exit the wiki-up, stared at the ground as she took a step forward. But, that one step took her straight into his arms: he had been standing within a few feet of the entrance.

Looking up into his dark, dark eyes, she murmured, "I must talk to you."

He nodded. She turned around and, looking over her shoulder, noted he was following her back into their temporary—yet what had been and still was—their honeymoon lodge.

Quietly, she sought her side of the wiki-up and hoped he would step toward his place within the lodge, also. She did not wish him to sit next to her, at least not at present.

Luckily, he did as she'd hoped and sat across from her. He did not look at her, and she'd expected this, for she had come to realize this was a form of etiquette he followed—not looking directly at a person—to show respect and courtesy. She had also come to learn that it was only within the privacy of their own lodge that a married couple joked with and enjoyed longing looks at one another.

She breathed in deeply, let her breath out quickly and said in English, "Let us talk about the marriage custom of taking more than one wife, if you please."

He nodded.

"Is it true? Might an Indian man have as many wives as he can afford?"

"*Áa*," he said, then switched to sign language, saying, "A man is often required to take another wife."

"Required?" she asked in English.

"*Áa*, it is so. A man must be ready to go to war, for there are times when his family and his tribe need his strength. He might lose his life. If this man is killed and he has a wife and children, his brother is expected to take care of his widow and her children. Since my people have no slaves or servants as some of the white traders do, it is best that a man marry his brother's widow."

The lump in her throat became pronounced, but she swallowed it, knowing that, difficult though it was, she had to know more, even if the telling of it, in all its painful details, was heartbreaking.

While she was struggling to speak, he said in English, "Camp life...also give much work to woman. Man expected...take other wives so all work not fall...on...one woman. I...not want you...work too hard. Will take as...many wives as can, so...you not work hard."

She opened her mouth to speak, then closed it. Once again, she felt out of her depth. Her head spun suddenly, and she found it impossible to think, let alone to envision what to say in response to him. But, she realized she had to put her feelings aside. And so, she switched to communicating in the language of gestures instead of English. At least, in this way, there would be no mistake about what she was asking.

She signed, "If you find your brother is no longer alive, will it be your duty to marry his widow?"

"*Áa*."

She started to tremble again, and her hands shook as she signed, "Is a woman in your tribe also allowed more than one husband?"

"I fear…not," he answered in English. "You…must be happy…with one. No need…woman marry more. Too much work." He added a smile to his words.

But, she was beyond looking upon this with any attempt at good humor. She stared at the ground, placing her arms around her midsection, as if in defense. Then, to be certain there was no mistake and she truly understood him, she asked again in sign, "You, the man I have married, could take another woman as your wife?"

"*Áa*," he said. Quickly, however, he switched to using sign language and said, "It is allowed and sometimes is expected. But, if I have to marry another, like my brother's widow, know I will still love only you."

"You would not make love to her?"

"*Áa*, I would for it is expected, but—"

"You would?"

"She would be…wife." It was all he said, but his silence about his "duties" to this other wife communicated what his lips did not.

Laylah let out a squeal, high-pitched and painful.

He heard it and signed, "I would think only of you, though, when I was with her. I do this because I love you."

She gasped and gazed down at the buffalo robe she sat on, then looked up and stared at the entrance to their lodge. She couldn't do this any longer. She couldn't talk to him about this. It was simply too heart-wrenching.

She bit her lip, jumped up and, without any further words or looks, fled from their lodge. Where she was to go, she didn't know. All she was certain of at the moment was that she needed to put as much distance between herself and Eagle Heart as possible.

****

This had not gone well, and he could little understand why. Didn't she know he was committing himself to do all he could to make her life as good and as leisurely as possible? He had tried to explain: he was a medicine man. He didn't go to war or excursions for horses unless his insights were needed to see the possible outcome of a war party's foray into enemy territory.

In other words, he was not a rich man, and it wasn't always easy to hunt for and feed more than one wife. Yet, he would do it...for her.

Or was her upset due to something else? She had not liked the idea that a man carried a duty to marry his brother's widow, which included the physical part of marriage.

But, no. This could not be what was wrong. Hadn't he witnessed the white man adhering to the same marital rules as the Indian? How many times had he observed the white traders and trappers—those who had married into his tribe—taking responsibility for more than one wife?

Surely, those men wouldn't marry other women if their society disallowed the practice. Could her upset, then, be due to discovering he was not a wealthy man? Had this come as a shock to her, realizing she would have to work harder than others? Perhaps he should have told her about his life as a medicine man and what exactly were his duties before they had married.

But, he had thought only of their love for one another and their happiness in being together. As he continued to make guesses about their trouble and how to bring peace between them, his gut clenched, for he wished to have no trouble between himself and his woman.

He arose more slowly than she had done. It wasn't that he wished to leave this shelter and look for her, it was that he must. He knew what his duty was toward his wife, and it was to protect her. Thus, he had best discover where she had gone.

But, there was time. This valley was safe, and she would leave tracks he could follow. Heaving a deep sigh, he stepped slowly out of the lodge.

****

Within moments, he discovered his wife hadn't gone far away, and this was good. He could turn his attention to breaking camp. Keeping a part of his awareness on her and the environment around them, he began to dissemble the wiki-up, returning its branches, its mud and its stones to the earth. So, too, did he bury the evidence of their fire by brushing the hearth where it had been. He did the same with the ground on which the lodge had been built.

Earlier, he had arranged their possessions onto his pack pony and had placed their riding blankets onto their own mounts. At present, with the buckskin bits positioned into each one of their pony's mouths, there was little left to do. He was ready to leave.

Was she?

He sighed, for, if he were to approach her now, he anticipated another argument. Stepping toward the lake—she had positioned herself upon the water's narrow shoreline—he approached her, keeping himself clearly visible to her.

Coming up next to her, he squatted at her side and murmured, "Have discovered where…brother is. He not…far. We go now."

"I am not going anywhere with you," she said, "unless you will agree to take me to the nearest trading post, where you will leave me."

He inhaled deeply. Indeed, he had been right: there was a kindled fire within her, and he could easily see another, and perhaps worse, argument brewing.

He utilized both sign and Blackfeet to say, "I cannot take you to the nearest trading post. Not only is this post in enemy territory, it is farther away from here than where I will find my brother. He is in trouble. I must go to him."

"Very well. Earlier this morning, I believe you told me my father is approaching?"

"Áa, he and his Crow scout are on our trail, and they must not come into this valley, for I will not bring danger to our friends who live here."

"You go to your brother, then. I will stay here and await my father. It shouldn't be too long."

He signed, "Your father and his scout will not come to this valley if I am gone from here. They are tracking me, not you. Where I go, they will go."

"I don't care. I'm not leaving with you. I will remain here."

235

KeyKaren Kay

"And, what will you do?" he asked with signs. "How will you survive? Do you know how to construct a good shelter? Do you know how to hunt, to skin the game and cook it over an open fire? Do you have the skills to make a fire without flint?"

"You could leave me your flint and perhaps a knife."

He drew in a deep breath and continued, "Even if I let you have my flint and one of my knives, if I left you here alone, I fear you would die from hunger, the elements or both."

She looked away from him, and he was left with little to do except admire her profile. She said, "Then, so be it."

In English he said, "Will not...leave you alone. If I go...you die here. You...must come...with me."

"I will not. If you are so concerned about me, then stay here or take me to the nearest trading post."

He was afraid his sigh communicated his frustration. He said in English, "I cannot. Reason...came to...fort...to find...brother. He close. Must go."

"*Soka'pii,* good," she shouted. "*Kakó,* go!"

"You come, too."

"I will not. Even if my father is tracking you, when he discovers I am not with you, he will come for me. I will wait here for him."

"Too much time...you be alone. How he know...where...you are? If your...father find me...will kill. He not find out...where you are...if I...dead."

She shrugged.

In response to her seeming indifference to his demise, a spark of annoyance flamed to life within him, and he asked, "You wish...he kill?"

"Of course not. And, I don't believe he would try to do this to you. He might intimidate you, but I don't believe he would ever carry out his threats. So, there would be time for you to tell him where I am."

Infuriated, he sighed. "There be...no time. This why he...after me: to kill me."

Although she knew her father had, indeed, threatened to kill Eagle Heart, she couldn't help saying, "That is a lie! He would not do this! It had to be no more than a warning."

236

"I not lie. He gave word…he kill me…if do deed that…cause us…to marry. He knows we…married."

Her only response to this disclosure was to come up onto her feet and step away from him.

"Where…going?"

She didn't answer. All at once, however, she stopped as though she had run into a wall. She cried out, "Where is our wiki-up?"

"I take…down."

"No! How could you do this to me?"

"I not…do to you. You come…with me."

"I will not!" Suddenly, she turned and fled into the woods which surrounded the lake, leaving him no option but to follow. He caught up with her easily enough, and, while dodging her attempts to hit him, stopped her long enough to pick her up in his arms.

"You coming…with me."

She kicked out at him, but it was to no avail. He was stronger than she, and it was easy enough to keep hold of her and prevent her jerks and jolts from doing him any serious damage.

His direction was toward the horses, and, once he reached them, he forced her into her seat on the back of her mare. But, she quickly dismounted from the other side of the animal and ran back through the woods.

He shook his head, knowing what he had to do. Yet, upset though he was with her, he was reluctant to put into practice what he had to do. Sighing, he set off after her.

Again, he caught her easily enough and with the same result: he had to block her kicks. This time, however, before depositing her onto the back of her pony, he took hold of a buckskin rope hanging upon his own mount and, forcing her again onto the back of her mare, tied her hands together in front of her.

But, this wasn't enough. She would still try to escape, and, being perhaps a little stubborn, she might accomplish it.

Heaving in a deep breath, he paced toward his pony once more and grabbed hold of another rope. As though seeking advice, he glanced upward and tried to envision another way to bring her with him. But, he could think of none, and, approaching the mare, he did the deed: he tied his wife's feet together under the belly of her quarter horse.

Standing next to her, he said, "You coming…with me."

Fire blazed from her eyes, and he was expecting her to vent her anger in another way, to perhaps yell or spit at him. But, she didn't. Instead, she said only one word, and not even in a loud voice—"Bigamist."

"What word mean?" he asked.

"You know what it means."

"Do not…know."

She didn't answer. Instead, clenching her jaw, she stared away from him.

"You would…die here. Not let you die. Now…must erase tracks. You…stay here," he said unnecessarily, since she could do little else.

She didn't utter another word to him, however, and soon, with both human and pony footprints dusted from the face of the earth, he trod back in the direction of the horses. She didn't even glance at him.

He easily jumped up onto his own pony, straddling it, and, reaching out, took hold of the rope tied to her horse's reins. His only words to her were, "We go to…Beartooth Mountains. Not far."

****

The sun was high overhead and felt warm on the top of her head as they slowly forged through the wild, unmarked paths of this beautiful valley, leaving behind their honeymoon spot and, seemingly, their happiness. Only a few weeks ago, they had ridden hard and fast to get to this valley, yet Eagle Heart was keeping the pace slow in leaving it. Was this because there was no path through the grasses, the weeds and the flowers? Or was it because they were still in Crow Country and were traveling during the day? Perhaps it was both.

But, though the different kinds of grasses and the flowers grew to a man's height, and, though the flower stalks often caught on her skirt, it was not a great inconvenience. Indeed, their lack of speed gave her occasion to let her thoughts drift.

On one hand, she was glad Eagle Heart was insisting she accompany him, because without him she would die here. On the other hand, the mere thought that he might desire or be required to take another wife made her wish to be away from him, or perhaps to hit out at him.

She hadn't done that, and the reason had most likely been because she had been so shocked she'd barely been able to talk to him, let alone acquire the energy to declare war against him. But, the biggest problem about his attitude of taking more wives was that she understood him. She didn't like it, and she couldn't live with it, but she did understand.

This was the way he had been raised. These were his mores. She wasn't going to change them by arguing with him.

Indeed, if his ideas about acquiring multiple wives were so deeply entrenched within his mind, she might never be able to change it. And, if she couldn't change his considerations, it was better that she cut her ties to him now.

She inhaled deeply, and the sweet perfume of the flowers acted like a balm for her scarred heart. Yet, there was another smell here, and it was not so sweet. Along with the fragrance of the flowers was the pungent scent of the mud and the tall grasses. And, as it stung her nostrils, it reminded her again of the smack of his betrayal.

But, was that fair? He hadn't really betrayed her, at least not yet. What he didn't know is she did not intend to stay around and wait for his eventual unfaithfulness. He had warned her of his intentions…good. Now it was her duty to leave him.

She had heard him say they were traveling toward the Beartooth Mountains, and she wondered where the mountain range was. Its name brought on visions of stark, sharp cliffs and little vegetation, and, if the place were named correctly, it was bound to be a hard, rough journey, especially because both her feet and hands were tied.

Still, despite this, she might have tried to turn her mare around and leave this man. But, he was keeping hold of the rope tied to the reins of her pony, and this alone caused her to have to follow along behind him. Indeed, it seemed there was no escape for her, and, because his strength was naturally stronger than hers, she could not physically fight her way out of this…except perhaps by the use of her tongue.

Oh, how she wished she didn't love him so much. But, she did, and she knew, despite all the reasons why she shouldn't, she would love him until the day she died.

Still, as soon as she could, she would break free from him. Love him, she did, but living with him...and other women...would be impossible, not to mention demoralizing.

For now, she was doomed to follow him...or was she? What if she...? Unexpectedly, an idea formed within her mind, and, finding her voice, she called out, "I'm thirsty."

He didn't answer. Nor did he turn around.

"Excuse me, but did you hear me? I'm thirsty."

"Not breaking," he answered. "Water...in pouch on horse. You...drink it."

"I can't reach it. Surely you remember my hands are tied."

He didn't answer.

"Mr. Eagle Heart, look to our left," she cried. "We seem to be following this river. Surely, it wouldn't be too hard to lead our horses down to it where we might all have a good drink."

"Not enough...cover. Later."

"But—"

"Later."

Looking forward, she frowned at him as he led their mounts through what was clearly no trail. Interestingly, she had never seen him so well armed. Indeed, he looked like a human arsenal. What must have been a long rifle, covered in a beautifully beaded and long sheath, hung from a rope on his horse. His lance was similarly secured. There were two flintlock guns casually stuffed into his belt, and upon his back was his quiver full of arrows, his bow slung over his arm.

Every so often, she would catch sight of the sash that contained his ammunition, for he was no longer carrying it upon his person. Instead, he had secured it on his horse in front of him.

Obviously, he expected trouble from an enemy. What he hadn't prepared for, she hoped, and what he was going to get, was trouble from her. She was not about to meekly follow him.

Negotiating her pony through the tall undergrowth, she came up beside him and said, "I need you to stop, for I have needs to attend to."

The look he gave her might have sent an enemy scampering. However, she endured it.

He said, "We not stopping here. Unsafe. Not enough cover. You...must wait."

"I cannot. You did not give me enough time to attend to requirements and other needs before we left."

She heard him growl as he stared away from her. He said, "Ahead...little more cover. Not long time...to...reach."

Once again, he took the lead, and she dropped back behind him. She glared at him as he rode ahead of her, silently admitting her needling him wasn't much of a weapon. Still, it was all she had, and she was going to use it.

CHAPTER EIGHTEEN

"*I* need you to untie my hands and feet."

At last, they had stopped so she could attend to all things necessary. Eagle Heart had found a seemingly perfect location in which to call a halt. As she had brought to his attention, their trail was following the water, keeping them close to it, and, eventually he had discovered a location where they could break and recoup yet would not cause them to be openly visible to an enemy.

After all that had happened this day, this little spot seemed perfect. As she sat atop her gray mare, she looked up toward the sky, recognizing the tall stands of the ponderosa pine, the red cedar, the balsam and the Rocky Mountain juniper trees. The trees looked to be old and had grown up together in a manner which sheltered a pathway to the water. Indeed, as she gazed farther outward toward the water, she became aware that the same kind of trees grew along the shoreline, some shooting up straight out of the water.

She sighed. It was good because their horses could drink from the stream without gaining the attention of an enemy, if any were about.

As Eagle Heart had led her into this clearing, he had told her the name of the lake was Red Lake. However, to Laylah, as she looked outward through the trees, it appeared to her again that the body of the water looked more like a river than a lake. For one thing, the distance across the water from one shoreline to the other appeared to be so short, one might easily swim it. For another, the waterway flowed and curved around several hills. It did not simply sit in one place.

But, none of this mattered. For the moment, she felt safe and protected, especially when she breathed in the aroma of the pines, particularly the butterscotch-like fragrance of the bark of the ponderosa pine. This, mixed up as it was with the chest-of-drawers aroma from the red cedar, helped her to think more clearly. Ignoring for the moment that her hands and feet were still tied, she grabbed the reins Eagle Heart had dropped as he had dismounted. She pulled these toward her and, using these, guided her mare, Honey Sugar, down to the water. The path from the small clearing to the lake was awash in shadows due to the trail being covered from above by the tall pines. Lingering under these as she made her way to the water, she and her pony eventually reached the beach, and, while her pony bent from her neck to enjoy a refreshing drink, Laylah looked out upon the loveliness of nature's beauty.

At the edge of this small hub of trees was a rocky beach; though a little farther away, Laylah beheld a beautiful white sandy beach. She smiled, for its shoreline looked like a perfect place to leisurely enjoy the rays of the sun—were it not so cool and were her hands and feet not still tied.

Eagle Heart led his own spotted Appaloosa, as well as the Nokota packhorse, to the water. And, as he stood beside her, he said, "Before I...untie. You...must promise you not run away."

"Where would I go?" she asked without vowing to do or not do anything.

"This is...question you ask...not promise. You must...promise you not run away." Nevertheless, he untied the buckskin that held her feet together; her hands he left tied.

She sighed. "Are we still within the valley you call No Man's Trail?" Holding onto her gray mare's mane to steady herself, she brought up one of her legs over the pony's back and, with her legs together, slid down to the ground.

"We are," he answered in English. "But we...leave...few days. For now we safe. This little people land...they guard."

She glanced outward at the stunning scenery of greens, browns and the pure blue of the water. The same kinds of trees lined the mountains on each side of them, and, in this spot, those trees also trailed all the way to the beach.

Once she was safely back in St. Louis, she would miss all this. She knew she would. Always, would the memories of No Man's Trail remind her of the happiness and love she had found with Eagle Heart...even though she'd had no choice but to leave him.

If only... Again, she sighed and held out her hands toward him. "I still need you to untie my hands so I might attend to...private matters."

"Yet, you ask this...without making...promise."

"It's just that it seems so unnecessary. Where would I go without you? I don't know my way back to the place where we had stayed, and I don't know where we are going."

"You know...way back. We not...go far yet. And, you smart...could get there."

She looked away from him. It was true. She was aware they had followed the river here. It would be easy enough to retrace their path.

Still without looking at him, she said, "Oh, all right. It's silly, but I promise I will not try to run away while we are here. There, are you happy?"

"Not happy. You say, no try run away...while we here. Must promise not run away...ever."

"Ever? I will not promise you to not run away ever. There must be some limit to the promise. For instance, while we are traveling to the Beartooth Mountains, I might promise you not to run away while we are on the trail. Or I might tell you I won't try to run away from here or after we find your brother. But, I will not promise to never leave you."

Her short tirade earned her his laughter, and he signed, "You plan to get away from me in any way you can, don't you?"

"Of course. You're holding me hostage," she said.

"You not...hostage," he responded in English. "You wife."

"Barely."

"What word mean?"

"It means as soon as possible I will...I will..." She shut her eyes and breathed in deeply. "I can't say it."

"It good...you cannot say it."

She glanced away from him. "Are you going to untie my hands?"

"*Saa.*"

"Then, how am I to attend to my needs?"

"I will...help."

"You will not!" For goodness sake, the man certainly had his gall.

He said in English, "Then, you...promise."

Frowning, she shook her head and glanced back at him. "This is blackmail."

"What...'blackmail'?"

"It's...it's...knowing something a person has done that's bad, and the one person, having found out about it, threatens the other person to make their bad deeds known to everyone unless the person does some deed this one person wants."

He merely shrugged and brought his arms up, crossing them and placing them over his chest. "This not blackmail. You not do...bad. What I want...simple. Want...your promise not run away."

"Oh, very well," she answered. "I promise I will not run away tonight."

He grinned at her. "It not...for tonight," he said. "It forever."

"I will not say it. Either untie my hands on my promise to not run away tonight, or I'll figure out how to do what I must on my own." She held her hands out in front of her again.

But, instead of untying the knots—as she'd expected he would—he reached out and brought up her hands, still tied, to his lips and kissed every one of her fingers, first with his lips and then added his tongue to the caress. But he didn't stop there. He spread his sweet kisses to encompass her palms, also.

"Don't," she said, but she let out a tiny cry of joy, silently moaning.

As though her cry were an encouragement, he trailed his kisses up one of her arms to her neck, then down to her chest, where he paid tribute to each of her breasts through the cloth of her dress, and, were he not holding onto her around the waist, she might have collapsed, for she had bent backward, had thrown back her head and closed her eyes. But, he wasn't through with her, and, kissing his way to her other arm, he caressed and grazed it, too, showering her with his touch all the way to her palm and her fingers.

He said, "Want make love to you, my woman."

She groaned, and he brought her hands, still tied, up over his head, placing them around his neck. Pulling her in closely, he murmured, "Love me."

"I cannot," she murmured. "I am too upset with you to make love to you. Besides, you are wearing much too much armor. And, I thought you couldn't make love when you are at war."

"I not at war. Not yet. We still safe...in valley."

"You look like you are going to war. There are so many weapons on your person, how do you expect me to even hug you?"

"Like this." Picking her up, he left the horses to their grazing and stepped back into a denser part of the woods. Still holding her, he leaned her up against the smooth, yet stringy bark of an old, fragrant ponderosa. Next, he placed her legs around his waist, and from there it took him only a moment to slide both his and her clothing out of the way.

She gave him no resistance, even though she thought she ought to. But, she was beyond complaining. Instead, when he touched her privately, she melted against him, inviting him, despite herself, to love her there.

He whispered, "I ready for you.... You ready for me?"

"Yes. Please love me," she said before admitting, "I missed our lovemaking this morning."

"I, too. Love you, always," he whispered against her ear. "No one...else. Only you."

"But—" Even as they strained together, reaching and climbing toward that high plateau of utter sensual appeasement, she whispered, "What about the other women?"

"No other I ever love. Do not leave...me."

"But—"

"Do not want...another."

And, then it happened: together their exertions brought her to the ultimate in carnal pleasure, and she danced with him, tripping over the sensuous realm of pleasure. She was shuddering in the aftermath of desire when she uttered against his shoulder, "Then take no other wife."

And, although they had paused for a moment before resuming their passion, they were still entwined together when he began to laugh, softly at first, and then with more vigor, until his laughter seemed to be uncontrollable. Although he was still safely nestled within her warmth, and although they were both still breathing heavily, he yet brought her head and shoulders in toward him as he whispered, "You not wish...help with...much work? I thought...I thought—"

"No! Not if you mean by 'help' to add another wife to our family...."

He was still within her inner warmth when he said between low chuckles, "I not...very smart. Thought you upset I only medicine man...not rich...maybe not able...have...two wives. No second wife...more work for...you. I love only you. If...you not want...other wives, I not do."

"You won't?" He was beginning to move and push within her warmth again, and she met his gyrations with those of her own.

"I won't."

"Do you promise?"

"I promise."

As though they had become renewed with life, their love turned vigorous. It was as if silently they were renewing their commitment to one another, both physically and spiritually. And, as he led her again toward the ultimate thrill of marital pleasure, she suddenly asked, "But, what if your brother is no longer living, and his wife is then a widow; wouldn't you have to marry her?"

As he thrust within her inner warmth and bore against her, he whispered, "There other...ways...I...help...her without making her...wife."

"Really? You would find another way to help her? You wouldn't *have to* marry her?" she asked, even while he continued to lead her again to the peak of their exquisite pleasure.

He murmured, "I not lie. If you not want, I not do."

All at once, Laylah felt tears welling up in her eyes, even while her body was straining against him. And, as pleasure overwhelmed her once again, she cried out in relief, not only because of the pleasure of love, but also because her worries were suddenly leaving her.

He was not long in following her in the absolute pleasure of lovemaking. And, as he let loose his seed within her, he whispered, "I...glad you not want second wife. Not easy...for me. I not rich in ponies. But, you sad?"

"No, I'm not sad. My tears are because I love you so much. I don't ever wish you to marry another woman so long as we are married." She wiggled a little against him, causing him to gift her with a masculine groan. Only then did she murmur, "I forgot to tell you: my religion forbids a man to marry more than one woman."

"Your God...forbids?" He sighed against her shoulder.

She nodded.

"But, other white men...marry into tribe. Many wives, they have."

"They are wrong to do so."

She was still crying and he was laughing when he said, "We both...show emotion very...bad. Come, make love...to...me again, but maybe... not against tree. We...try...make love beautiful again."

"Yes, please."

As he began to disentangle his body from hers, he brought her hands up over his head and untied her bindings. And, as he released her legs from around him and her feet once again touched the ground, he began to laugh heartily, and, as one chuckle followed after another, it appeared he might never stop.

Still, he managed to say, "Love you...more now...after settle first fight. Feel...so close...because know who you are...better. Want make love...all time. Never stop."

She began to laugh, too, intermixed with her tears. But, she was able to whisper, "Sounds silly, but I agree with you and I want this, too. May our arguments always end with us in each other's arms."

"*Soka'pii*. Or...make love...when...quarrel."

This made her giggle, and she said, "If only we could. But, I fear it might be impossible."

"Not impossible. Remind us...we love...more and better...than say bad words."

She breathed in deeply and was immediately aware of where they were: of the clean, earthy scent of the pines, as well as the butterscotch-like scent of the ponderosa tree bark. Contented, she murmured, "I believe I might always think of you and our love whenever I smell butterscotch candies."

"What is?"

"Butterscotch candy?"

He nodded.

"It is a sweet, like maple sugar. But, my husband, let us make a place where we can love each other through the night, unless you think it best we push on toward the Beartooth Mountain range yet this night."

"It good. We stay here. Tomorrow...night...soon enough...we go back on trail."

She smiled. It was good. They had survived their first disagreement—and, in a way, it was symbolic of how they might settle any future clashes. For this, their first fight, had been fought over major principles, both hers and his.

Moreover, she had become aware that, by renewing their love, all things were possible. And, as the night closed in around them, they set out to show one another that lovemaking was, indeed, one of the most beautiful of God's creations.

****

Gray Falcon heard the scratch on the buckskin covering of his lodge's entrance. At once, he knew the identity of the caller without even looking.

He said, "*Ipii*, enter."

When Amelia McIntosh stepped into his lodge, he greeted her with a quick nod and a smile. Indeed, in these last few weeks, he had become used to her many visits; he even looked forward to them. At first, he had considered her a nuisance, but with her continued determination to speak with him, he had become used to her—and considered her to be a friend.

She was a pretty girl in her youthful demeanor. Her brown hair often shone with health, and her facial shape looked more heart-like than round or straight. Her cheeks most often were rosy, and her eyes were gray—the color of his namesake, the gray falcon. But, the color of her eyes was unusual, for it often changed depending on the shade of her clothing.

She was not flirtatious with him when she came to visit, nor was he with her. This made it easy to be friends. Usually, their conversations concerned his friend and her sister, and it was through Amelia that he had learned of Eagle Heart's marriage to the woman his friend called *Ikamo'si-niistówa-iitámssin*, Steals-my-breath.

"I've come to inform you of what my father is doing," Amelia told him using sign language, for they had neither one learned the other's language.

He nodded and gestured toward the place across the fire opposite to him. It was his way of asking her to be seated.

As she sat down upon the buffalo robe which he had long ago placed there especially for her, she continued, "My father has hired a Crow scout who brags he can track anyone or anything, and he and my father have left the fort to go in search of my sister and your friend. My father has told my mother he intends to catch your friend and my sister together, and he means to kill Eagle Heart and bring Laylah back home." She glanced away from him, and he saw so much sadness within her look he felt compelled to rush to her side and give her comfort. But, she was not his to touch nor to hug, not even as one friend might give aid to another.

"My mother begged him not to do this," continued Amelia, "but, my father is determined. 'No daughter of mine,' he'd said, 'is going to leave a perfectly good man at the altar to run off with a savage.' Even now, my mother is in her room, crying. I have come to you to ask if your business at the fort is done and, if it is, if you might be able to track behind my father and the Crow scout. It is in my mind to ask you to prevent my father from killing your friend. If my father really does find them and he murders Eagle Heart, I know my sister will never forgive him. And I would not ever see her again."

He nodded and, by way of gestures, said, "I will do as you ask. The trade I came here to do is finished, and I have been preparing to go on the trail of my friend and join him in his search of his brother. I have only delayed leaving because he is newly married and would not appreciate me interrupting his first days together with his bride. But, now is the right time to go, though only a few weeks have passed."

"You will do this for me, for my sister, too?"

"Áa," he said, then continued in sign, "If your father and a Crow scout are on his trail, I must leave at once. It is good that all my trading is now concluded."

"I want to come with you."

Gray Falcon was taken aback and signed, "You cannot. It is not safe for you to come with me."

"I would, too, be safe. My father would never hurt me."

"It matters not. Bullets can go astray as can arrows. And, there is another reason you cannot go: you must not be alone with me on the trail.

You are too young and others will think that we… No, if your father means to kill my friend, where I am going could be very dangerous."

"I know," she signed. "I still want to go with you. And, I disagree with you about being alone together. After all, I'm here with you now, and nothing has happened."

"*Saa*," he said. He then signed, "There are many others in this camp who can see our shadows on the tepee, and I have always ensured our silhouettes are never close together. You also come here frequently, and so many of my people are accustomed to seeing you with me. But, being on the trail with me is different. We would be entirely alone."

"I know."

"Instead," he continued, "please stay here and keep my friend's lodge with you until either he or I can return and claim it from you."

"My mother could do this, and I could then go with you."

"*Saa*." The word was more emphatic said the second time. "It is too dangerous. You are too young. People will think bad things about you if I allow you to travel with me and if I don't also marry you. And, you are too young for me to marry."

"I am not. My grandmother on my father's side married my grandfather when she was fourteen. I am fourteen, soon to be fifteen."

"You forget. I have not asked you to marry me."

She glanced up at him with a look of reserve in her eyes. It was an emotion he had not witnessed in her demeanor before now.

She asked, "Are you married to someone else?"

He sighed deeply, then signed, "I am not. But, you must not do this. It is the man's place to ask the woman."

"I am waiting…."

He laughed. He had often found her to be an amusing girl, but this… He was Indian, she was white and her father was tracking his friend, Eagle Heart because he had dared to marry his other daughter. This was trouble. She was trouble. And, it was drama he did not wish to court.

After a moment, she breathed in deeply and signed, "If you will not let me go with you, will you at least kiss me goodbye?"

"*Saa*," he said. He followed the word with sign and said, "We are not a married couple that we might kiss, and I say this again: you are too young for me to marry. You must be content to grow up and wait."

"And, then you'll ask me?"

He chuckled again. "If I were to marry you," he signed, "I would be as bad off as the hawk who must do the bidding of his mate. Always, you would be squawking at me like the female sparrow to do this or that. A man likes to have peace in his home."

"Well, I can see I will have to do it, then."

"Do what?"

She came up to her feet, paced toward him and, bending, kissed him on the lips. He was startled — not by her behavior, because he had come to expect these kinds of occurrences from her. No, he was shocked because it felt good. Too good.

He looked up at her with new eyes, but he did not kiss her back. Instead, he scooted as far away from her as his lodge would allow.

Nevertheless, she followed him, knelt in front of him and signed, "I will never forget your friendship with me at a time when I desperately needed a friend. And, I hope you will never forget me."

He nodded. He would not forget her, nor would he be able to put her kiss very far out of his mind. But, all he signed in response was, "Do not fear. I will always remember you. Will you come here tomorrow to see me off on my journey and take the tepee and other possessions from me?"

"I will."

"I will be leaving early in the morning, before the sun is up in the eastern sky."

"I know," she signed. Then she smiled at him as she came up to her feet and, turning away from him, strode toward the tepee's entrance flap. Before she stepped over the bottom fold, however, she looked over her shoulder and smiled at him again. She whispered, "Wait for me," in English, and then she was gone.

He didn't know what she'd said, yet he nodded all the same. And, as he watched her go, he prayed the time when she would grow into adulthood might pass quickly, for he did wish to see her again and experience her kiss once more. But, perhaps when they were both a little older.

CHAPTER NINETEEN

$\mathcal{L}$aylah had a bad feeling about this. It wasn't as if she feared for her own safety. Regardless of what happened, she knew Eagle Heart would protect her.

But, who was watching over him?

What were they going to find in those mountains besides his brother? She didn't doubt her husband for a moment; he would find his beloved brother, Chases-the-enemy. But, there was trouble, as well as mystery shrouding the truth of Chases-the-enemy's disappearance: why had the man stolen Little Dove, a Crow woman? According to Eagle Heart, his brother was happily married, with children. What was Little Dove to him? Was she so beautiful he'd had to marry her, too?

She shivered. There was turmoil brewing ahead of them. She could feel it spiritually and even physically, for she was shivering. But, what kind of danger was it?

Also—and perhaps worse—her father as well as an enemy Crow scout were on their trail. And, her father had already threatened to kill Eagle Heart. He had said so once to her. Apparently, he'd told this to Eagle Heart, also. She shook her head as though the action might dislodge the fear from her thoughts.

Meanwhile, the rhythm of her pony's stride had become a backdrop of sound against the occasional squawks of a nighthawk. Once, the hooting of an owl had unnerved her. But, soon the song of the wind, as it picked up its pace and blew through the pine and balsam trees, dispelled her fear.

The sky overhead was blacker than she was accustomed to seeing. Clouds filled the sky, and there wasn't a star or moon to be seen, although here and there she could discern a brief silhouette of the moon behind the clouds.

In the distance, a wolf's mournful howl sent shivers over her spine, but Eagle Heart seemed unaffected by it. However, the one wolf's sorrowful wail was soon joined by another similar yowl, then another and another until there was a chorus of howls.

Eagle Heart stopped his forward progress, turned around and guided his mount next to hers. Coming in close, he said, "Many wolves...howl like that...mean storm coming. We...must continue...stop when...storm comes. Only then...will build shelter."

She nodded, but when she gazed upward, she saw only a cloud-filled, blackened sky. Perhaps those clouds would be the beginning of another blizzard.

"Do you think the storm coming might be a blizzard?"

"It possible."

"Do you believe it might cause my father and the Crow scout to lag farther behind us?"

"*Saa.* Likely they go through...storm or...they lose...trail."

"I don't understand. Why should we stop if they do not?"

"Not good for you...go on."

"Do not think of me and my comfort. I do not wish for them to find us. Storm or not, if we must push on to remain ahead of them, I will bear it."

"Humph! We see how bad...storm is. Will decide then. Must always think of you. You...my woman now."

She nodded. But, she was disturbed by her premonitions and said, "I have a bad feeling about this. I don't understand it, but it seems to me as if...as if death lies ahead of us."

"I, too, feel this."

"Then, why must we find your brother if there is death to greet us when we, at last, discover him?"

He didn't answer right away. It was dark. She could barely see his features, but she did recognize that she had somehow caused him to sit up a little straighter in his seat. He threw his head back and lifted his chin as he uttered, "Does this one" — he pointed to himself — "look like...coward to you?"

"Of course not. There is nothing about you that is cowardly."

"If it be your sister...would you dare... madness ...so you find her?"

"Yes, I would. Oh, all right. I guess I can understand why you are doing this. But, I will warn you, my husband, so hear me: don't you dare die in trying to save your brother. Do you understand me? Be a hero if you must, but don't you dare die."

He relaxed a little, and she thought she saw him grin at her before he said, "All live. All die. But...maybe not die tonight."

"Make sure of it, my husband. Do not die. It is an order to you from me, your wife."

He grinned at her. "What is...'wife order'?"

"It is a strong — a very strong — way of saying you are entrusted with a responsibility. And, the duty I am trusting with you is this: you are not to die. Do what you must, but remember what I have said." When he nodded, she added, "I have a really bad feeling about this."

He said, "I know. I share...same feeling. But, have...responsibility to family, to brother. Am not coward. Will find him, help him...if possible."

She didn't answer. Instead, she stared away from him.

"*Oki*, come. Must push forward...and...hope storm weak. If strong, we...stop, make camp."

"Yes. All right."

He turned his Appaloosa around. But, before he left, he touched her hand and said, "You...not die...either. Order from...husband."

She smiled. "I will try my best not to."

He gave her a brief nod, then trotted away to take the lead once again.

****

As Eagle Heart looked up, he was glad to see he had, at last, reached the foothills of the Beartooth Mountains. Their climb upward had been difficult. Not only had the temperature dropped, but, because there was no trail through the forest, their way had been littered with large windfalls of dead branches, causing him to have to stop and hack through the wood with his buffalo-shoulder blade in order to blaze a trail.

At least the predicted storm had not been in the form of a blizzard. It had been difficult enough, but the snowflakes had been large enough to fall quietly, and the wind hadn't been overly strong. As a result, the land had come to look as though it belonged in the clouds rather than on the earth.

They hadn't stopped to make a shelter and rest. Indeed, his wife had insisted upon them pushing on.

But, he was well aware the Crow scout and his father-in-law were pressing in upon them. And, although he threw several large branches into the pathway behind them, those would not stop the two men from making better time than he and his wife, considering the obstacles in his and his wife's way.

Looking ahead, he forgot his woes momentarily as he admired the Creator's hand in the life around him. Pine trees rose up majestically on each side of him, and the snow on the ground here was not too deep. It was strange, and quite pretty, to behold the bright leaves of the bushes still wearing their fall colors and now sprinkled with snow.

It was good. Whatever his future woes might be, these sights and the frigid air wiped his mind clean of any fear he might have had about what lay ahead of him. Inhaling deeply, the pine-scented atmosphere imparted an even greater feeling of the magnificence of His work, and a calmness of purpose entered into Eagle Heart's spirit, despite the knowledge that his father-in-law and the Crow scout were less than a day away.

Was it only last night when he had finally located his brother's position within these mountains? Although there was still no communication between the two of them, he at least knew the broad area where he would find his brother.

He only hoped he would discover his brother's exact position and free him before his father-in-law and the Crow scout caught up with them. He was aware there would be a fight, and it would be a hard fight, for he did not wish to harm his father-in-law. And, if the Crow scout chose to be part of the struggle, it would be trickier still. Nevertheless, Eagle Heart was preparing himself for the coming battle both mentally and spiritually, as well as physically.

Although he, as a medicine man, did not seek to fight unless he had to, it didn't mean he couldn't. Certainly he was trained to go into battle. All

256

Indian men were expected to be able to repel an enemy and to hunt. Indeed, without the skills to hunt, a man's family would starve. And, without the ability to go into battle willingly, one's family and one's people might perish. A man was expected to do this and more without flinching or cowering.

As a boy, his first education had been as a hunter and a warrior. His next training had taken years, where he had learned the discipline and ethical choices necessary to become a scout. It was as a scout where he had mastered the skill to go into a fight if he had to, and to win it. However, it was a point of pride that a scout never started a fight. Instead, he tried to avoid it by using the emotional "war" tactics known only to the scout.

His instruction as a medicine man had required several more years of learning, of fasting and acquiring the secrets of his trade before he had been admitted into the ranks of these honored men. But, this education had come a little easier to him.

Glancing over his shoulder, he took a moment to admire his wife. This kind of life was new to her, and yet she never complained, even when she was greatly inconvenienced.

He smiled, thinking of this very morning when their bath had inevitably been icy-cold. Her lips had almost turned blue before he had rescued her and had wrapped her in a warm buffalo robe. But, she had smiled at him and had dressed, becoming ready to set out upon the trail within a short time.

She had also impressed him when, only a few days ago, she had spotted the leaves and flowers of the *Ek-siso-kit*, the bear grass plant, the root he had used to remedy her sprained ankle. She had only seen its flowers and leaves once, yet had been able to recognize it in its wild state.

She was intelligent and clever, as well as beautiful, and he considered himself to be a fortunate man. He would watch over her closely when they, at last, arrived at his village. She would need help and gentle coaching, for her ways were different from theirs in many respects. His sisters, especially his youngest sister, might be good teachers.

He returned his attention to the matter at hand. A few days ago, he had stopped doubling back and crossing over his own trail. The Crow scout was not fooled by these common Indian tactics of creating confusion. Besides, the Crow scout had located him spiritually and was leading his father-in-law by this kind of intuitive knowledge, ignoring the physical markings left over the earth. The result of his trouble in trying to confuse the Crow scout was that it had cost him valuable time.

Passing by a particular clump of trees, he all at once surprised a bear who had taken up residence over the trail Eagle Heart was blazing. But, the bear gave them no chase and quickly disappeared within the forest of pine trees and bushes.

"Was that a bear?" his wife asked.

"*Áa*, it was. But, he is gone."

"Why did he leave?"

"I...surprise him," he called back to her. "Bears not...bother us. Bear attack...rare to my people. We both...creatures of Sun. We not attack unless have to. He happy...leave trail to us. He in hurry...get to winter sleep."

"Yes, you are most likely right."

"Ahead is...good place...we stop."

"You know where you are?"

"*Áa*," he said over his shoulder. "When...arrive at...berry bushes and silver-grass clearing, we stop. Have first meal. I tell you...where...brother is. Also, where Crow scout is."

"You know where they both are?"

"*Áa*. Prepare for...fight. Both...are close."

"No! Please, no!"

"We talk...when we stop. I tell you."

"Shouldn't we hurry, instead?"

"We stop. I tell you. We eat. Then go."

He was happy to hear no response from her and no further argument. He would impart what was expected of her if there were to be a battle, and it consisted of mainly one rule: remain alive. He would tell her in the most calming way he could about why his life was not as important as hers. Flee if she had to, but, most importantly, she must stay alive.

He would try to make her promise this: even if he died today, she was not to fight. Her duty was to live, to stay alive.

True, he expected an argument from her, yet he intended to win this particular battle. After all, if she were with child, there would be two lives to be saved.

****

Their early morning meal was almost finished when he became aware that he was being watched. In his peripheral vision, he beheld a shadow. Turning his head, he was pleased to see the silhouette was his sister wolf, and alongside her was her lifelong mate.

Although he realized wolves never stayed in one place, he was still surprised to see her. Smiling at her, he said with the mind-to-mind speak, "Hello, my sister. You show me great honor to be here with me on this day. I have come to this place to rescue my brother."

"I know," said the she-wolf in mind speak. "My mate and I have been following you."

"You have? Why?"

"You are in danger, my brother. We wish to help. Finish here, then follow us. We will take you to your brother."

Not amazed, for he understood the intelligence of these creatures, he nodded. "You have seen him?"

"We have. He, his mate and child are caught in a trap. We cannot free them."

Eagle Heart nodded, then said aloud to his wife, "Look at...wolf. She...my sister. She your sister." He switched to speaking sign language and said, "My sister-wolf is here with her spouse to help us. She has seen my brother and tells me he is in a trap, and she cannot spring him from it. She and her mate are ready to take us to him."

"I know," said Steals-my-breath. "I heard the two of you speaking. I believe we should go with them at once. What is your opinion?"

"I think...same."

"Should we leave our things here?"

"No. Bring all...horses. You...take them. I...must have hands...free...to fight. Crow scout...your father...come soon."

"No! Then we should leave at once."

"We will," he signed, "but first, will you give the wolves what smoked meat we have while I pack our things? My weapons must be in ready use for me."

"Of course I will."

And, as Eagle Heart watched his wife, with her generous heart, give every bit of their food to the wolves, his spirit burst free with happiness and pride. What a woman!

CHAPTER TWENTY

"*Is* that your brother, there within the circle?" asked Laylah.

"*Áa*, it is."

"You are right to say your brother looks much as you do. Next to him must be Little Dove, the Crow woman. I did not know she had a baby with her. Did you?"

"Not until...few days ago."

She nodded. "But, what is wrong with them?" asked Laylah. "They don't seem to be moving. They are standing, obviously alive, yet are not stirring."

"They move. We not see it."

"Why?"

"I not...know."

"Where are we?"

"This...Mystery Lake. Elders tell...much secrets...around lake. Odd happenings...here. Blackfoot people...no come here."

The female wolf had placed herself beside Eagle Heart, while her partner stood to their left, alert, but seemingly unwilling to go too near the human beings. In this place were both tall as well as smaller evergreen trees and they surrounded a small clearing. But in one spot within the glade, there appeared to be a circle with nothing in it, where even the grass didn't grow. Dry dirt and rocks filled the space. All about them were a few inches of snow and ice, but not within that circle. Why was it so different from the surrounding countryside?

The she-wolf said in the mind-to-mind talk, "We tried to pull them out of trap. Something is wrong."

Laylah heard the wolf as well as Eagle Heart's reply. In the mind-to-mind talk, he said, "Do you see the light around them?"

"No," said the wolf.

"I don't see it either," said Laylah.

"There is a circle of light around them and a sunbeam shining down upon them within the circle," Eagle Heart said in mind speak. "Special place. A sacred place. I feel close to Sun here. I think our rules for life do not apply within the circle of light. But, why are they standing there as though there is no life in them? And yet, if you watch them closely, you might see them breathe. Also, do you see the Big Person?"

"Yes," said the wolf. "The Big Person has been here many days."

"I don't see it," said Laylah in mind speak, also.

"He or she is standing behind the trees over there." Eagle Heart pointed to their left.

"I still don't see it."

Suddenly, Eagle Heart pushed Laylah away from him and yelled, "Go! Run! Hide!" He did the same to the she-wolf.

Out of nowhere, the Crow scout emerged, and, drawing his knife, he crouched down and slowly circled Eagle Heart. Eagle Heart bent to meet the Crow scout's threat and he, too, brandished his knife. Adding to the confusion, the wolves growled and came forward; they hunkered down , their teeth bared at the Crow scout.

"This is my fight," Eagle Heart said aloud to the wolves and waved them away.

"No!" Laylah screamed. Her father was standing alongside the Crow man, and she watched as her father drew his pistol. She cried out, "Stop this, Father!"

"Stand aside. I will see him killed!"

"Father! No! He is my husband."

"No Injun will ever be my daughter's husband."

As the Crow scout and Eagle Heart circled each other, preparing for the fight, Robert McIntosh aimed his gun at Eagle Heart's head.

"Father! No! Don't do this! He is my husband and I love him!"

She hadn't seen the other Indian warrior until he was suddenly there, appearing as if from the air in back of her father. He was none too careful in placing his knife blade at her father's neck. Blood dripped.

"*Innaapiksist náámaa!*"

"He says to drop your gun or he will kill you." Laylah translated the words as she recognized this man. "Gray Falcon, where did you come from?"

McIntosh dropped his weapon.

"*Iitsska stam!*"

"He says the fight is to be fair." Again, Laylah translated the Blackfoot words.

Suddenly, the Crow scout took a swipe at Eagle Heart, forcing Eagle Heart to jump back, barely missing the death blow.

Laylah screamed, then realized her mistake. What if she distracted Eagle Heart? What if she caused him to take his eyes off his opponent?

She bit her lip. She couldn't simply stand here and watch her husband in a fight to the death. She also couldn't interfere; it could cause her own or Eagle Heart's death.

But, she had to do something.

Glancing toward the circle, she stared at Little Dove. All at once, she wondered if this Crow man held some relationship to Little Dove. After all, some man had fathered her child. Was this perhaps why the Crow scout had agreed to help her father in the search for Eagle Heart?

It was a wild chance, but if this Crow man held any kinship with Little Dove... Would it stop the fight?

It was certainly worth the gamble. Without thinking too greatly about what she was to do, she raced toward the circle and, with all of her might, broke through the light and the force surrounding the ring. With energy combining with her determination, her momentum was strong enough so she was able to push Little Dove and her baby out of the circle.

Still in motion, she tried to take a step forward, out of the trap. She couldn't. Worse, suddenly everything outside this small circle was moving as though with the momentum of angry bees. All at once her thoughts became heavy, also, until at last she couldn't even think. Why? What was wrong?

Although she could barely push through a thought, she could at least pray. Not able to close her eyes, she yet prayed until even simple thoughts were becoming impossible.

Still, she tried.

****

The sound of the explosion caused both the Crow scout and Eagle Heart to cast a hard look in the direction of the blast. Even Gray Falcon dropped his attention from the white man. The Crow woman and her baby had burst through the circle of light as though shot from a gun and were now lying on the ground. But, more importantly, they had somehow gotten outside the circle.

"*Saa!*" Eagle Heart screamed. His wife was now entrapped within the ring. The fight forgotten, he raced toward the sacred circle. How did this work? He had to think fast.

No, this did not call for thinking. Without another moment passing by, he backed up, and, taking a leap forward for luck, sprinted into the ray of light, grabbing hold of and pushing his wife through the barrier.

He had hoped to be in such a state of excited motion that he could get himself back out, but all he managed to do was to push the toes of a single foot through the barrier.

As quickly as he could, he tried to speed up his mind and struggled to force his hands through the wall of light and into the environment outside. He managed to get the fingers of one hand barely through the barrier. But, he couldn't move. He was caught. Truly caught.

****

Laylah's mind was still working in slow motion, and she didn't at first realize where she was or what had happened. At last, however, she began to think again and, looking around, realized she was lying outside the bright circle. But, how had she done it?

Gazing back within the ring of force, she realized she hadn't managed to get out of this by herself. Eagle Heart was now caught in its light along with his brother.

Looking around, she saw Little Dove and her baby lying on the ground, unmoving. The Crow man was by their side, the woman's hand in his, and he was crying, speaking to the woman in words Laylah didn't understand.

So, she had been right. There was a relationship between them.

Taking her attention away from them, she began to cry. What was she to do? Her husband had saved her, but now he was entrapped within the awful ring of light.

"No!" she cried out. "I love you, Eagle Heart. I told you not to die. Please don't leave me."

"Laylah?"

Through her tears, she looked up into her father's face which was devoid of all color. She cried out, "You! Father, what is wrong?"

Her father didn't answer. Indeed, he was shaking. He came down onto his knees beside her. Gray Falcon stood behind them both. He frowned, but it appeared even he knew not what to do.

"I…I…" began Robert McIntosh. "What is that thing?"

"I don't know. All I can see now is my husband is entrapped in it. It seems as if by saving the Crow woman, Little Dove, from the trap, I have, instead, ensnared my own husband inside it. But, you could get him out!"

"I…I can't." Suddenly, he was crying. "I can't move."

It appeared he wished to say more, but couldn't. Was it shock? Laylah didn't know quite what to say or do. She had never seen her father in this state. He literally shook from head to foot.

Without saying a word, she bent in toward her father and took him into her arms, placing a kiss against his forehead. After a moment, she said, "I must go. I love him, Father. Don't stand in the way."

Rising up to her feet, she stepped quickly toward the terrible sphere of light. Gray Falcon followed her.

Part of Eagle Heart's fingers were free of the orb entrapping him and she touched them. How was she to free him?

If she were to run back into the circle, would she have enough strength to get them both out? If she couldn't do it, he would never let her remain in there.

As Gray Falcon stepped forward and placed his hands, palms up, against the light, Laylah suddenly heard the words, "Get them out!" in mind speak.

She looked around. The words came from the woods to her left, and, gazing there, she was surprised to see Eagle Heart's sister, the she-wolf, addressing someone who stood within the shadows. Who was she talking to?

"This is your fault!" the she-wolf continued. "Get them out now! We know what you did. The babe is not yours to take. Now, get them out!" She growled at some unknown entity.

Suddenly, and without explanation, a large and hairy beast—an obviously female beast—burst out of the woods and ran into the bright circle. There, the large person picked up Eagle Heart in one arm and Chases-the-enemy in the other.

Then, without pausing a moment, the large and hairy female shot out of the circle, and Laylah was surprised to see the ring of light had not entrapped the beast within it.

Laylah ran forward, following the gigantic person. If she had to, she would fight the beast for her husband. And, she would win. She swore to herself she would win.

****

Still carrying himself and his brother, Chases-the-enemy, the huge beast flashed into the woods. Once within the sheltered environment, the she-beast carefully and delicately set him, Eagle Heart, on his feet and laid Chases-the-enemy on the ground.

Calmly, Eagle Heart stared up into the beast's eyes. Silent understanding passed between the big female and him and, when at last Eagle Heart smiled at the beast, he had a good idea of what had happened to his brother and why he had run away with Little Dove.

The large she-beast suddenly turned around and sped away and was gone so quickly, her disappearance reminded Eagle Heart of another kind of people who could appear or disappear seemingly at will.

"Go with the Creator, Big One, and thank you," said Eagle Heart in Blackfeet. As he bent down to pick up his brother, he was suddenly besieged by feminine arms coming around him from behind.

Turning, he found himself embracing Steals-my-breath, this precious and courageous woman. Tears filled his eyes as he thought of her heroism.

"Didn't I tell you to hide if there was trouble?" he asked in perfect English. Then, in Blackfeet and sign, he said, "And, before I knew what you were doing, you were saving Little Dove and her child. Oh, my precious, precious wife. Has anyone ever been so proud of his woman?"

She laughed. "And, who saved me?"

"There is a difference. It is my duty. What you did was because your heart is big. I am so proud of you."

"We must go to your sister, the she-wolf," said Laylah. "It is she who saved you. It was she who spoke to the Big Person and demanded she get you and your brother out. What a wild land this is, where wolves and humans live in love and peace, side by side. Let us help your brother to stand and then go to the wolves."

"Indeed, we will," he said, again in perfect English. "But, first…" Picking her up, he twirled her round and round, and, when at last he let her feet come to rest again on the ground, he kissed her once, then again and again.

He said, "I will never tire of loving you. I promise."

CHAPTER TWENTY-ONE

"*And*, what was I to do?" asked Chases-the-enemy, using sign language, so he was understood by all. "I saw the Giant Person take her baby, and Little Dove asked for my help. As a man and a human being, I was called to aid them. It was my duty to answer her plea regardless from what tribe she hails. But, the Giant took us on a long and dangerous journey through one mountain range after another. We have been many places over this land, and several times I have rescued the baby, only to have the Big Person steal him again.

"You ask how we came to be entrapped within the sacred circle. It happened in this way: Little Dove and I stumbled into the trap during a thunderstorm. We were wet and cold and were running to escape the Giant Person. And, suddenly we saw the light of the circle and beheld that all was dry within. Who would not have stepped inside?

"This is how we became trapped. I know not how long we were there, for the time passes so very differently within that circle. All outside the ring of light is in fast motion as you have seen. And, this, now, is the story of what happened to us."

Eagle Heart, his wife, Gray Falcon and Robert McIntosh sat on one side of the hastily constructed wiki-up, while the Crow scout, Strikes Fast, and his sister, Little Dove, plus her child, sat on the other side of the shelter. Between them was a fire.

Meanwhile, up on Granite Mountain, the trap remained unchanged by the trauma involving the human beings, the wolves and the Big People.

But, in a deep valley at the foothills of this mountain, the men had constructed this particular shelter so they might discuss all that had occurred without fear of being discovered.

Chases-the-enemy continued. "Now, my brother, I know you spoke to the Giant female. Can you tell us what this is all about? What did you learn? Why did she steal the baby?"

"I will answer your questions and here is what I have learned: The Giant female whom you speak of is a woman from the tribe of the Big People. She lost her husband and her son in a river, I know not where." Eagle Heart also spoke in the language of sign so all would understand. He continued, "Her son was killed, for she found his body, but not the remains of her husband. Since he never returned to her, however, she has assumed he is dead. She has grieved much, and her loss troubles her. When she saw the human baby on his cradleboard and hanging from a tree, she knew a moment of peace. She made the decision to take the baby and raise him as her own. She never meant the baby harm."

Eagle Heart looked toward his brother and continued in sign, "When you, my brother, followed her and stole the baby back, she, in turn, trailed after you. And, so began the dangerous game of taking the baby and running. She couldn't stop. When she did, her grief returned. Always, you found her, my brother, and many times she could have harmed you for, as you know, her strength is beyond ours. But, thinking you might be the baby's father, she couldn't do you or Little Dove harm.

"She now understands how the result of her grief has damaged others, and before she left she expressed regret for the danger and trouble she presented you."

Chases-the-enemy sat for a few moments before using the sign language to say, "It is a sad story. Yet, the baby was never hers to take."

"It is true. Still, she is troubled by her grief. If I could, I would try to make her heart whole again. Now, is there anyone else who has a question?" asked Eagle Heart in sign. When no one else spoke, Eagle Heart went on to sign, "I have a question of my own to ask the Crow scout, Strikes Fast. Am I right? Were you tracking me by finding me in the spiritual world?"

Strikes Fast nodded.

"You do it well," signed Eagle Heart.

Strikes Fast sat without visible movement. In time, however, he signed, "I am told I have a talent for this."

"Those who say this to you are right," signed Eagle Heart. "And, my friend, Gray Falcon, you are to be honored for coming here today. Your friendship and your strength are to be admired and you, my friend, are greatly thanked. And now, we must honor my wife, because, through her courage, we all came to our senses. And, somewhere out there is my sister, the wolf, who rescued us all. It is said by my people that a gun which shoots a wolf will never shoot straight again. This is a good saying. We should live with them as brothers and sisters. Do we all agree?"

They all agreed except one. Steals-my-breath's father, Robert McIntosh, sat within their council fire, yet he said not a word. Instead, he sat looking downward, his fists clenched.

"What say you, Father-in-law?" asked Eagle Heart.

"Damned Injuns, both Blackfeet and Crow," was all he said as he set his lips together so firmly, it looked as though there were a straight line where his lips should have been.

"Father!"

"And what kind of creature was that big thing?"

"Big People...what called," answered Eagle Heart. "Creator much loves them."

"Creator? As though you have any sense of religion. But, I'll give ya this, Injun, you win. I give up. You got her. Twice you saved my daughter, while I... But I don't like it, ya hear? Don't like it at all. And I don't like you!"

"Father!"

"I'm leavin'. I'm goin' back to where I belong. You comin', Crow?"

Strikes Fast shook his head.

"Stay...a while, Father-in-law," said Eagle Heart. "Long journey back. Stay. Help us smoke some meat. We give many horses. Other gifts."

"I don't want nothin' from you. Ya got my biggest asset—my daughter."

McIntosh came up to his feet and stared around the group. "I'm leavin'."

"Take horse...mine. Good buffalo horse. He...yours now." Eagle Heart stood up, too. "Come," he said. "Show horse to you. Give...you."

"All right. I'll take it. You owe me anyway."

As the two of them left the council circle, Eagle Heart said, "Take all horses...mine. I give you. Your daughter, I love."

"I'll take 'em. Now listen here, Injun. You better treat her right. If not, I'll kill ya."

"Her, I love. I treat...good."

McIntosh didn't respond.

"These now yours," said Eagle Heart as he led his Appaloosa and Nokota by their buckskin ropes and gave them to his father-in-law. "Spotted Pony is name...Appaloosa. Good buffalo horse. Goes Far is name...Nokota. Take...them. If must leave...go in peace."

It wasn't long before McIntosh had saddled his own horse, and, leading Eagle Heart's ponies by their ropes, made ready to leave.

But, before he left, She-steals-my-breath joined the two of them, and, taking one of Eagle Heart's parfleche bags from him, gave it to her father. She said, "It's full of dried meat. Please do not be angry with us. I love this man. I will always love him."

Her father sneered at her, which she ignored. Instead, she said, "Have a safe journey, Father."

Her father didn't reply. Indeed, he did nothing but scowl and, without a word, set out upon the trail.

Steals-my-breath's voice was almost a whisper, when she murmured, "He didn't even say good-bye."

"Do not...worry," Eagle Heart's voice was low and calming. "He losing you. Also, first time he see big people. Hard...sometimes...on a...man.

****

The Blackfeet Encampment
Northwestern Montana
Spring 1835

The winter had been a hard one this year with many snows and a few more blizzards, although Eagle Heart and Steals-my-breath had barely noticed. Pitching their own winter lodge within the Pikuni camp, they had

271

Karen Kay

spent many warm and cozy nights in each other's arms, and the difficult winter had passed them by almost without notice.

But, now it was spring. A warm "Snow Eater" had blown in weeks ago, and, as its name implied, it had eaten up all the snow. Their tribe, at present, had made the journey to Fort McKenzie on the Marias River.

"Come," said Eagle Heart to She-steals-my-breath. "Walk…with me into woods on shore…Marias River. Female big person there."

"Truly? She is in the forest? And, we are going there as though we are friends?"

"Áa. We…friends. News…I have…for her."

"News? You have news? This is the first time you have mentioned this to me."

"Áa," He nodded. "I know. Was not…sure before. Now… sure."

"Oh. Well, let us take a walk, then."

"Soka'pii."

They had done little more than step a few feet into the small forested area, when Eagle Heart said in the mind-to-mind talk, "Your husband lives. He is farther north in the mountains. It is almost straight north. Go to him. Make many more children. Live well."

"You found him?" asked Laylah.

"I did."

"Thank you," came the silent reply from the big person. And then, she was gone, disappearing so fast, it was almost as though she simply melted into space.

His wife turned to him and said, "You have been looking for her mate?"

"Áa. It took…long time. Now they be…together again."

"Oh, my husband. You have been very kind to her. I must admit, my love, sometimes you take my breath away."

"No, you one who stole breath from me."

She sighed. "Did you know sometimes I cry, because, until I met you, I didn't know it was possible to love someone so much."

"Yet," he said in perfect English. "I love you more."

She chuckled. "Impossible."

272

"Nothing impossible," he said as he took her in his arms and kissed her once, twice, then over and over as though to convince her that, after all, all things were possible.

In the distance, a wolf howled, its voice echoed by another wolf. In a seeming chorus, they howled again.

He said, "Sister wolf...and mate. She say they...well. They our family."

"Indeed, they are," agreed Steals-my-breath. "And I love them so very dearly. Come, my husband. I have need of a back rub...and more." She laughed up at him, and Eagle Heart smiled as he gazed at this woman who, still to this day, stole his breath.

Before he had met this woman, he would never have imagined such happiness could be his. "Come," he said. "Much love we share. I show you."

And, he proceeded to make his words come true, now and forever.

EPILOGUE

"*And*, so it came to pass what we have always known: that we are brothers to the wolf and to all life."

The old man looked around the circle of children. "Do any of you youngsters have a question you would like to ask me or something you would like to say?"

The same little girl who earlier had spoken to him in Blackfeet said, "I do, Grandfather."

"Yes?"

"Did Steals-my-breath come to live with the people and become one of us?"

"She did," answered the elder. "In time, she became a medicine woman for our people, working alongside her husband."

"And, did she and Eagle Heart really love each other all their lives?"

The old man smiled. "They did. They had five children, and some of their great-grandchildren live to this day. Always, they were looked to by our people because their love was so true, so strong and so beautiful, it gave strength to all the people. Always, they will be remembered as the man and his wife who brought joy and happiness to our people."

"I will remember, Grandfather. And, I will tell this story to my grandchildren so that we may all take heart."

The old man smiled. The people would go on. It wasn't really an ending. Indeed, it was a beginning.

THE END

About the Author

Multi-published author, Karen Kay, has been praised by reviewers and fans alike for bringing the Wild West alive for her readers.

Karen Kay, whose great grandmother was a Choctaw Indian, is honored to be able to write about a way of life so dear to her heart, the American Indian culture.

"With the power of romance, I hope to bring about an awareness of the American Indian's concept of honor, and what it meant to live as free men and free women. There are some things that should never be forgotten."

Stay in touch with Karen Kay by signing up for her newsletter;

https://signup.ymlp.com/xgbqjbebgmgj

Find Karen Kay online at www.novels-by-karenkay.com

Enjoy this excerpt from Book Two of the Medicine Man series, SHE CAPTURES MY HEART

PROLOGUE

The Trading Room at Fort Union, Montana Territory

May 1835

"Where can I find A'sitápi?" Gray Falcon asked in the language of gestures, though he spoke the last word in Blackfeet. "Have you seen her? I have come for my buffalo lodge and other possessions; they were left with her before I departed from here several months ago."

"*Pardón Monsieur,* only de Americanine or de French do I speaks."

Gray Falcon shook his head, one of the few physical gestures understood by all the tribes, as well as by the traders. In response, the trader, Larpenteur, shrugged his shoulders.

And, since Gray Falcon had brought no furs to trade, Larpenteur dismissed him by turning his back on him. And, without a word, Larpenteur stepped to the door of the trading room and was soon gone.

Gray Falcon sighed in response, clearly frustrated. Why had none of these traders learned the language so common to the people who lived on the prairie?

His asking this question brought to mind one of the reasons he had made the long journey to this Fort: A'sitápi, or Amelia McIntosh, as she was known to the whites. Were she here, he would be able to make himself understood.

But, where was she? Had she gone riding outside the gate? Perhaps. In truth, were she anywhere within the fort, she would have sought him out by now. The thought made him grimace.

She was more of a pest than a friend. And yet, friend she was. Indeed, she was probably his greatest ally within this fort, although he would have never sought out her company deliberately.

Saa, no, she had come to him last winter, invading his home in her quest to find her sister, who had been lost in the midst of a blizzard. But, even when she'd learned he couldn't help her, she had refused to leave.

He hadn't known what to do with her. Factually, he shouldn't have been alone with her. She was too young to be anywhere near him. She was also one of the daughters of the fort's Trader and was the younger sister of *Ikamóso-niistówas-siitámssin,* wife of his friend, Eagle Heart.

Hannia, the young girl could cause trouble for him and for herself, also. Luckily for him, his uncle and auntie had stepped in to act as a chaperone.

Yet, over time, he had become accustomed to her presence in his life, for she had made herself a frequent guest in his lodge—all too frequent. Perhaps he had become too used to her, causing him to forget she was also a favored daughter of the fort's Trader.

What to do now? He certainly couldn't ask his question of any of the Indians standing here within the trading room. All of them, with only a few exceptions, were enemies of the Blackfeet. He wondered again how any trading post could exist when the only people who could carry on a conversation in sign language were two sisters. But the eldest sister was now gone from this place, recently married to his friend, Eagle Heart. The youngest, *Isstsimm A'sitápi*, Annoying-young-person, the full name he had given her in Blackfeet, had taken her sister's place, since she, like her sister, could talk the gesture language.

Pushing himself away from the trading table, he turned and stepped to the back wall; settling in, he glanced around the room. The trading room was only moderately busy this day, which seemed unusual for the season of "when the geese come." Deliberately, he struck a leisurely pose, although he was ever alert and awake. And, as any scout must do, he glanced about the room quickly, reacquainting himself with this place, memorizing the differences between how it was now and how it had been several moons ago.

As he leaned back against the wall, he glanced casually at the long counter used for trading, or trading table as it was known to the Indian. At present, there was a large buffalo hide spread upon it. Off to the side of the table were several beaver pelts, mink, and even raccoon and skunk furs. As always, a large book with many of the white man's papers lay open on the counter.

Many wooden shelves stood against the back wall and at present, there were stacks of many furs, as well as neatly folded woolen blankets on those shelves. He had become used to the sight of the mounted moose horns which were placed on both sides of the counter. Today, these were displaying many different items of clothing, from belts and hats to moccasins and a few fur-lined jackets. There were even pots and pans, as well as kitchen tools, hung from those horns. Looking up, he saw that several kegs of whiskey stood upright on the highest shelves, out of easy reach of the Indians.

Robes, furs, moccasins, and buckskin clothing could be traded for guns, but no guns were on display today. Perhaps they had been put out-of-sight purposely.

Presently, four Blackfeet men—all of them friends and known to him—stepped into the room and trod toward the counter. Laying their stacks of furs on the counter, they waited patiently for Larpenteur to return.

With the addition of his four friends, himself included, there were now five Blackfeet men in this room. Glancing around, he counted eight men from the Crow tribe, four men from the Assiniboine tribe and two from the Gros Ventre. He reckoned these were pretty fair odds if there were to be a fight, for the Blackfeet counted as three for every man from another tribe.

But, there would likely be no fights, if only because all the Indians, himself included, had been divested of their weapons upon entering the fort; there were no quivers, no bows or arrows, no guns or rifles, no lances. Not even a knife could be seen upon the person of any Indian in this room.

The owner of this place, McKenzie, insisted upon stripping a man's weapons from him before entering the fort. The white traders stated this was a common practice within these trading centers, and was done for the Indians' and the company's safety. This rule was for Indians only, however, because the white men and trappers were always armed.

Realizing there would be nothing more to be learned here, he pushed himself away from the wall and tread silently out of the room. The solidly built entrance gate was open and was only a few steps away. But, before leaving, he took possession of his own weapons, pulling on his quiver full of arrows, picking up his bow and lance, tying on his knife sheath and grabbing hold of his muzzle-loading rifle.

He was about to step out of the fort, when suddenly, from behind, someone jerked him around and punched him in the stomach. The blow knocked him backward, and, as he rocked on his feet, he slumped to the ground. Immediately, before he had recovered from the first assault, strong arms jerked him upward and another strike followed, an upper cut to his jaw. A solid punch landed square in his face, and, as he spun around, his nose began to bleed.

Gray Falcon could barely stand, but was still aware enough and quick enough to pull an arrow from his quiver, set it against his bow and pull back the string, pointing it directly at his attacker, his intent clear. He accomplished this so speedily, his attacker stepped back, his face red with fury.

Alarm rocked Gray Falcon's world: this was A'sitápi's father. Still, his aim did not falter.

But, why was her father so angry with him? He was not left long to find out.

"Ya' dirty Injun," began McIntosh. "Yer the one's been sniffin' 'round my youngest daughter's skirts, ain't cha'? Well, no more. She's gone back ta her home, far away, do 'ya hear? Now, get out of here. Don't ever come back. Next time I see yer face, I'll kill ya. Ya got it? Ya' understand?" McIntosh waited barely a second before spitting out, "Ya filthy Injun. The likes of 'ya ain't welcome here. I'll kill 'ya next time I ever see 'ya. And, this ain't a simple threat. I promise 'ya. I'll kill 'ya. Now, get!"

Gray Falcon could feel his lips swelling, was aware blood gushed from his nose, and, though he could taste his own blood, he forced himself to stand up straight and scan in a three-hundred and sixty degree circle around him. Good. No one stood behind him.

Gradually, with bow and arrow still trained on the Trader, Gray Falcon backed out of the gate, stepping onto the brown, grassy terrain of the plains. He didn't say a word.

Several of his Blackfoot friends immediately surrounded him, their own bows and arrows drawn. Likewise, five of the fort's engageés formed a line against them, their pistols trained on them all. McIntosh spit forcefully at Gray Falcon, although the moisture fell short of its target.

"Don't ever come back 'ere!" shouted the Trader. "None of 'ya." And, this said, he pushed the gate closed.

That's when it happened: "Gray Falcon!"

At once, he recognized the "talk" so common to his tribe's medicine men—the mind-to-mind speak. Had he not been in a life and death situation, he might have rejoiced; such was its importance.

For most of his life, he had thought he might never acquire the ancient skill of communication commonly used by many scouts and by all medicine men. But, try though he might, he had not yet accomplished it—even though he came from a bloodline of medicine men.

Yet, he had "heard" the thought clearly. It came again, "What is wrong?" He now recognized the speaker. It was A'sitápi reaching out to him.

A'sitápi? The pesky white girl? The same girl and favored daughter of the trader who had this very moment beat him up, warning him against further association with the girl?

Though it was puzzling how a white girl was able to speak to him in the mind talk, he answered her in the same manner, saying in thought, "I have been looking for you at the fort. Where are you?"

"St. Louis. My father sent my mother and me away."

"Your father hates me."

"I know," she responded in the thought speech. "He has forbidden me to see you again."

"Did you tell him about our friendship?"

"No. I promise I didn't, although it has been out there in the open for anyone to see. Still, someone else must have whispered it to him. After Father came back from his trip out west, he was like a man possessed. He might not have been able to keep my sister from marrying Eagle Heart, but he was determined I would never marry an Indian."

"We are not involved in that way!"

"But, I'd like to be and he knows it."

"Did you tell your father this?"

"No. He was too angry at me…and at you."

"You are too young for me, and, even if I were inclined to like you in the way you suggest—which I am not—you would have to grow up first. You are only fourteen snows old."

"I will soon to be fifteen. I know some girls who have married at this age."

"Do not say this to me. You know you are too young for marriage, as I am, too. And, even if we were both older, you are too bold. It is a man's task to ask the woman, not the opposite. And, it is doubtful I would ever seek you to be my wife. You know this."

"Yes, I know. But, I can't help what's in my heart."

He didn't answer for a long while. At last, however, he said, using thought alone, "I am now forbidden from ever entering your father's trading post, and your father has threatened to kill me if he ever sees me again."

"I'm sorry," she said in the mind-to-mind talk. "Before I left, he told me he would kill you if he could and I didn't know what to do to prevent you from coming back to Fort Union. But, I've had no way to contact you except through the means of the mind-to-mind speak. I've been trying to do it, really I have. But, I have not accomplished it until now. I'm sorry my father has treated you this way."

"He will never let us continue to be allied with each other. Never again."

"I know."

"But," he added, "take heart; it is not so bad. We are even now "talking" to each other. He cannot stop what remains of our friendship if we continue to "speak" to one another as we are now. In this way, we can resist him and never have to be too far apart."

"Do you really mean what you've said? Do you, then, like me a little?"

"Of course I like you a little."

"Only a little?"

He didn't answer. At length, glancing around him, at his fellow Blackfoot allies, he said in mind-speak, "I must go."

"You are injured, aren't you?"

"I must go. Tonight, I will reach out to you again."

The communication ended.

Gradually, he, as well as his friends, withdrew to a safe distance from the fort, their weapons still drawn. He felt a gentle touch upon his arm and, looking down, saw his auntie beside him.

She said nothing. Instead, with a careful hand, she took him by the arm and guided him to her lodge, and, looking back, Gray Falcon saw the several Blackfoot warriors covering his retreat.

Sun, the Creator, had been with him today, ensuring he would come away from this confrontation with his scalp and his life still intact. This was without doubt. And, he had taken a giant step into becoming a medicine man. He had spoken the thought speech, and with a girl who wasn't even Indian.

Perhaps the day wasn't so bad, after all.

Made in the USA
Columbia, SC
29 July 2024